and then he was gone

Carol Gimbel

Prepared for publication by www.KrystineKercher.com

Cover design by www.KrystineKercher.com

Printed in the United States of America

Books by Carol Gimbel

Raven's Song
Ghost Horse
And Then He Was Gone

Shed no tears for fallen blooms.
They gloried in their season
Undeterred by death that loomed.
Just being was their reason.

~Woody Gimbel

When the almond tree blossoms
the grasshopper drags
himself along
and desire is no longer stirred,
then man goes to his eternal home
and mourners go about the streets.

~Ecclesiastes 12:5b

Dedication

And then He Was Gone is dedicated to the memory of my high school literary teacher, Homer Harmon who told me I would be an author someday. His piercing blue eyes and steely gaze kept the band and show choir in line for years. At our 20th high school reunion, I told him I used to think he could always tell what I was thinking.

He replied, “I could.”

Chapter One
Ridge

The convertible blasted through the guardrail. Like a giant dodo bird that wasn't supposed to be airborne but was, it sailed into the abyss. The driver of the white Pathfinder never hit his brakes. He sped around the curve and was gone. My heart leaped into my throat and lodged there. I couldn't swallow. Couldn't breathe. I jammed the gear shift into park, leaped from my still-running Forester, and raced to where the car left the road.

As I tried to find a way down, primal groans rose from somewhere deep within. Craggy granite walls echoed my terror, throwing back my screams. The ground plunged hundreds of feet just beyond what remained of the mangled guardrail. I knew that because I'm familiar with this road, not because I could see the bottom of the gorge.

Silence followed the crash. Complete. No more sounds of steel ripping through steel, then rock as the car somersaulted its way from boulder to boulder. The clatter of falling parts had stopped as the wreckage settled into the rocky bank near the river. I stopped screaming and listened. No cries from below, though my ears strained to hear something—anything. Forest animals, night birds, and tree frogs, the only spectators besides myself, were quiet as though fearing they, too, would be hurled into the ravine.

As swiftly as it came, the silence vanished, replaced by sirens winding their way along distant mountain roads. They drew closer. I had called 911 a few miles back. Help had been on the way. But too late. Behind me small rocks flew as cars skidded to a stop. Doors slammed. Voices, tense with trepidation, fought to be heard. People ran to where I stood beside a weathered Ponderosa pine, their feet crunching in loose gravel.

Dust from the wreckage swirled in a weak shaft of light far below. The lone headlight flickered and died. Any hope I'd had sputtered and died with it.

"No," I wailed, still peering into the abyss, although there was nothing to see now.

An old dude shuffled up beside me. "Didja see it happen?"

I gave him a brief glance. He wore baggy jeans tucked into barn-mucking boots. A stained plaid shirt hung loose in front. Probably a local.

"Nobody survived that," he said, shaking his head. He was right. "No way to get down there." Again, he was right. He peered over the edge. "Probably tourists. They take these roads too fast or get scared and clog traffic. Can't pass 'em." He spat a stream of tobacco which somehow missed my new white Adidas. "US 550 just claimed another life," he said, as though bringing news from on high.

I fought rage. His words ignited an urge to ram his John Deere cap down his throat. Already staggering beneath a load of guilt, I needed nothing more to regret. These people were statistics to him. He couldn't know they were my world.

Fortunately for both of us, he stopped talking.

A patrol car arrived, ending the wail of its siren. Doors slammed. Patrolmen, asking questions, made their way through the crowd looking for witnesses. Voices cracked through radio static. I heard bits and pieces of a trooper's monotone report. ". . . fatality accident...US 550...11:55 PM..."

Almost tomorrow, I thought, amazed that my brain had even grasped the words.

"I think the guy over there saw it happen," a woman said.

Someone added, "Three cars passed me like I was standing still. The one in front, a red convertible, went off that cliff. The green Subaru over there not far behind. Almost ran me off the road. It's a wonder he didn't go through 'at guardrail, too—or kill somebody." He said nothing about the Pathfinder.

Two uniformed officers came up beside me. The senior trooper peered into the ravine as the old guy had. "Not much to see, is there?" he asked.

Rhetorical question. The bottom isn't visible even in daylight. Tears blurred my vision. His face swam out of focus.

"Is that your Forester?" the trooper asked, writing on his pad. I nodded, hypnotized by red and blue flashing reflections on what was left of the guard rail. Voices cracked through the radio, blending with the murmur of the growing crowd and approaching sirens.

"Do you know how many occupants were in the car?" The trooper stopped writing and looked up, chewing the end of his pen as he waited. Bite marks on the pen indicated this wasn't a rare occurrence.

"Two," I said. It caught in my throat. I tried again. "Two."

"Glad I'm not on the search and rescue team," he said.

My eyes widened. I hadn't had time to wonder about that.

In response to my expression, he said, "They'll get down there. It won't be easy."

"When?" I asked. "I mean... when...?"

"They're on their way. If there was hope of this being a rescue mission, they'd try tonight. Since there isn't, I'm betting they'll wait for daylight. It's going to be a bear. Can't be hurried."

I swiped my hand across my eyes, embarrassed by the tears I couldn't stop.

"This isn't their first rodeo," he said, as if reading my mind. "They'll figure it out."

"You the guy who called 911?" the patrolman on my left asked. He was younger, not much older than me. The tag above his pocket said his name was Clayton Morley. He consulted his notes. "You're Richard Frazier?"

"Ridge," I corrected, surprised I remembered my name.

"Ridge? Oh. Like the tennis guy?"

"Yeah. Like the tennis guy." I almost laughed. I must be in shock.

"Do you know who was driving?"

I nodded but couldn't force words past the obstruction in my throat.

"Can you tell me who was driving that car?" he asked again.

I pushed hard to get the words out. My voice cracked. "My father. Grant Frazier."

"Senator Frazier?"

"Yeah."

"Your father?"

"Yeah."

"You saw the accident?"

"It was no accident," I said.

Trooper Morley stopped writing.

Chapter Two

April

Where is Grant? He'd asked what time I'd be speaking, so I assumed he'd slip in unnoticed. Like that ever happens. He tries to act modest and swears he doesn't want to "steal my thunder". He can't help it. It's who he is. He enjoys the stir he causes when he's recognized. Grant is always recognized. He's charismatic. Impossible to miss. When a politician's head emerges from the birth canal, it's already surveying the room for votes. Working the crowd. Don't let anyone tell you different.

Although he's fifty-two, he looks forty and is still head-turning handsome. He's deeply tanned year-round and easily stays fit because he's addicted to tennis. His decision to go into politics interrupted a successful pro tennis career. Between him and our son Ridge, who inherited his father's talent, our den is full of trophies. Our daughter, Riley Grace, has begun to add her own.

Grant's been a United States Senator for two years now and we've settled into a comfortable routine. It helps that Southwest Airlines has a direct flight from Oklahoma City to BWI. The kids and I visit DC often and he's home when the Senate isn't in session.

Several people complimented me as I left the stage. I smiled and thanked them. I snagged my purse, fished out my phone, and scrolled through messages and missed calls. Nothing from Grant. Strange. The uneasy feeling I'd ignored all morning burrowed its way back into my stomach.

Three texts from Riley Grace explained in great detail her dire need for new tennis shorts and a straightening iron. It appears her bottom is practically bare in her old shorts and her straightening iron is a "piece of crap, embarrassing beyond belief".

Her straightening iron is embarrassing beyond belief', but her bottom being practically bare isn't? The drama is so Riley Grace. I chuckled. That girl! This morning she tried to call eleven times during my half-hour presentation, which is a bit odd. When I'm on the speaking circuit, she doesn't call me at all and usually doesn't bother to answer when I call home. But if she wants something, she never just calls once and might call twenty times. Having eleven missed calls from her would be alarming, except she's Riley Grace. If she had been seriously injured, someone else would be calling. If she were in jail, she wouldn't get eleven calls.

A muffled cough pulled my attention from my phone. A man leaned against the concrete wall next to a red fire extinguisher. His stance appeared casual, but he was zoned in on me. A press pass hung from his neck.

"April Frazier?" he asked as I approached.

"Yes." I plastered on the polite smile I've perfected with just the right amount of benign interest and regret over not being able to respond to a yet unspoken request. "I'm sorry, I don't have time for an interview right now. Please make an appointment with my secretary."

He pushed himself away from the wall and stepped into my path. "I'm Fred Knight with the *Washington Post.*"

I'd been right, an enterprising stringer who hoped for a byline in the *Post*. I handed him my business card and repeated, "Please make an appointment with my secretary." I tried to move around him to the stairs. With a step to the side, he blocked me again. I finally looked at him. He was balding, wearing a black knit shirt dusted with dandruff. His baggy pants looked as though they belonged to someone else. His shoes were scuffed. He needed a shave.

"What do you want?" My polite mask cracked.

"Sorry to bother you at a time like this." He peered at me over his glasses.

"Well, then, don't," I snapped, trying to step around him again.

"Can you comment on your husband's accident last night?"

"Accident?" Suddenly, Grant not being here became a bigger deal. I focused on the tape holding Knight's glasses together and tried to swallow. I couldn't.

"You are April Frazier, right?" He thumbed up his glasses. They promptly slipped back down. "Mrs. Grant Frazier—the Senator's wife?"

"Yes." I backed away, looking around for security. "Leave me alone!"

"What can you tell me about Sable Amhurst?" He followed me.

"Who?" I stopped.

"Sable Amhurst." He referred to his notes. "The woman in your husband's car."

"Woman in Grant's car? That's ridiculous. Where...?"

"Durango. Colorado. Have you not heard?" Confusion flickered in his eyes.

I shook my head and backed away. "No." Did this idiot think I'd be on a stage speaking to 1,000 women if I knew something had happened to Grant? If there is something I don't know, and apparently there is, I do not want to hear it from a *Post* stringer.

I looked down at my phone. The unanswered calls from my daughter took on a whole new meaning. Panic took over. I turned and bolted.

The crowd making their way from the Leesburg Convention Center surged around me like sheep unable to find a gate. I plowed through them searching for a place where Fred Knight couldn't follow. I ducked into the women's restroom, darted into the nearest empty stall, locked the door, and leaned against it.

Riley Grace's best friend, Alise, says never go into the first bathroom stall. It gets the most use and therefore accumulates more germs. It's also more likely to be out of toilet paper. Alise thinks if people are too lazy to go farther down the line to find a cleaner toilet, they often don't flush. She's not wrong. Gagging, I flushed the toilet with my foot. I hit send on Riley Grace's number. Above the sound of water swirling around the bowl, I heard women shrieking. Knight had followed me into the restroom.

"Mrs. Frazier?" Knight yelled, his voice audible above the screams. "Are you in here? Mrs. Frazier?"

Riley Grace answered her phone, crying too hard to talk.

There are phone calls that bring you to your knees. Instantly. You get news that rips through your heart leaving gashes so deep that your yesterdays are forever separated from your tomorrows. Everything surrounding that moment is seared into your memory. Years later you can recite in detail what you smelled, tasted, and experienced. That call came in a bathroom stall. Beside an unflushed toilet.

"Riley Grace, stop crying! What are you trying to say?" I asked, terrified. "Talk to me."

"Mommy," she sobbed, sounding like she had when she was little and needed her mama. "Come home. Daddy is dead."

Chapter Three

Riley Grace

"There is one moment in childhood when the door opens and lets the future in." Graham Greene said that. Last week in Lit class we discussed what he meant. Nobody could define that one moment. Now I can. Your father dies, and you don't get to be a kid anymore. This morning the door opened and the future roared in. My daddy wasn't in it.

Mr. Greene thought embracing the future was a good thing. I have a different story.

When I was born, I slid out into the world and into my daddy's arms. I thought he'd always be around to catch me. He can't die now. I'm barely seventeen. I wasn't through needing him.

I've known my father is dead for eleven hours and thirty-two minutes. Thirty-three now. When the Highway Patrolman told me, I couldn't breathe. Like when I fell off the hay truck at Gramps' farm. All the air in my body whooshed out. I couldn't suck it back in. Time screeched to a halt. Like in a road runner cartoon when the road runner stops suddenly and the road piles up around him.

This tree used to be my hiding place. You can't hide from pain. It followed me up here. When I was little, this was my go-to place to hurt. It didn't help much back then either. I guess I forgot.

Back then being able to see forever from up here was a big deal. It seemed higher when I was shorter. Dad bought this house in Nichols Hills after we left the Governor's Mansion. The tree came with it. Actually, the tree was probably here a hundred years before the house was built. When Daddy realized how much time I spent up here, he built this tree house. It's actually three platforms spread out on different levels with no walls. Walls make a space feel small and would have destroyed everything I love about being up here. Dad understood that. He built a rail around the top level so I wouldn't fall off in case I wanted to sleep up here. He watched out for me like that.

One Fourth of July when I was three, we were at the home of friends for a cookout.

The pool was full of kids and the adults were sitting around talking and watching the kids.

But mostly talking. Except for Dad who hadn't arrived.

I couldn't swim, so I'd been wearing an inflatable vest. Mom removed my vest when I had to go to the bathroom. It was almost time to eat so she left the vest off and told me to stay out of the pool. But I had to tell Ridge something. He was playing with friends in the deep end and couldn't hear me, so I walked around to where he was. He still didn't hear me. I forgot the water was deep, so I jumped in. Nobody noticed.

Just then, Dad arrived, looked around and said, "Where's Riley Grace?" He heard me scream and jumped in. His new tailor-made suit, Italian shoes, and watch were ruined. I was screaming for my daddy. He hadn't even been there but I knew he would come. He was the one who came at night when I had nightmares and chased away the monsters. Who will chase away the monsters now?

Several years after he saved me, he saved the lives of people who weren't even his kid. On the way to Gramps and Penny's farm a wreck happened right in front of us. One of the cars was on fire. Dad stopped, jumped out, and pulled the people out of their car. He saved six lives that day. We have the newspaper pictures in a scrapbook.

People called him a hero and Superman. He was in the Governor's race at the time. Superman was featured in some of his campaign ads. He was always Superman to me. Saving those people was who he was. While others stood around not knowing what to do, my daddy jumped in and did it.

When he built my tree house, he'd never built one before. He worked on it all weekend and only stopped to eat and sleep.

My treehouse became my refuge and my favorite place to read. And spy on Ridge. I ate and slept up here. If it had plumbing, I probably never would have gone down. I haven't been up here for years. Today I needed its comfort and solace. It called to me.

Charlotte Bronte's *Evening Solace* was in a book of poetry Daddy gave me for my seventeenth birthday. It's a beautifully bound classic. A grownup gift. I couldn't relate to the line "the heart freshly bleeding" back then. Now I can. The part that spoke to me is the reason I didn't want a roof on my tree house. I love being up here at night when the sky gets all purply and moves in close. The stars twinkle on and look like I could reach up and touch them. It's like living in Miss Bronte's poem: "And it can dwell on moonlight glimmer, on evening shade and loneliness. And while the sky grows dim and dimmer, feel no untold and strange distress."

Solace is a new word in my vocabulary. I knew what it meant. I just never used it. I like the way it sounds when I say it, like I'm intellectual. Solace isn't just being alone. You choose solace. You're alone because you want to be, not because your father died, and friends don't call you back.

A good friend comes and sits with you like Job's friends in the Bible. Like Alise. We've been best friends since fifth grade. She was here last night and would be here now if she wasn't working a double shift at Giovanni's Italian Ristorante. It's actually just a pizza place. And Giovanni is actually just George.

But I have more important things to think about right now. Where is my mother?

She called me to say she finally got on a plane to come home. After that she fell off the radar. What if she was on the wrong plane? She has no sense of direction, I might be an orphan. Shouldn't a Mother be more careful when her children are on the verge of orphancy? Orphanage? Orphandom? Being orphans. What kind of woman doesn't think of that?

I don't know where Ridge is either. I've texted him a hundred times. I've sent him teary emojis and broken hearts and got nothing. My brother's not being here worries me more than Mom. Ridge, like Dad, is more reliable. My life is chaos. Mom is lost. Ridge is AWOL. I'm in a tree. And Dad is dead. We used to be just a normal family. If there is such a thing. Maybe we just think people are normal because we don't know them yet.

Chapter Four

April

Who is Sable Amhurst? Of all the questions swimming through my mind, that one most often comes up for air. Supposedly, she died in a car with my husband. This is all an atrocious mistake. Whoever Sable Amhurst is, Grant doesn't know her.

But then why does her picture appear beside Grant's on the front page of every national newspaper? Or so I've heard. I haven't seen the papers yet. The pictures are separate because AP and UPI were unable to find a shot of Sable and Grant together in their files. So far. I'm guessing people are digging through old files like their lives depend on finding a picture of Grant with Sable Amhurst. It took time to pick Monica Lewinski, in a blue tam, out of a Bill Clinton crowd all those years ago. Sable's and Grant's pictures were both studio portraits instead candid shots. Therefore, Sable hasn't been in the news. With or without Grant.

Sable Amhurst was beautiful. My cousin, Ali, who is at my house staying with Riley Grace, said so. But Ali's trying to downplay it. She said Sable looked young. Very young. Her picture might have been from a yearbook. This just keeps getting worse. But at least her name isn't Bippy, Bambi, or Boopy. Maybe she isn't a stripper.

I have no idea how I got back to my hotel. Obviously, I did. I've changed clothes. I don't remember packing or how I arrived at the airport. But I'm in the check-in line with a suitcase in hand, which I'm almost certain is mine, and contains most of my belongings. I overlooked a shoe, a diamond earring, and my phone charger when I slung things in the suitcase. The hotel called and said so. I really need my charger. I forgot to charge my phone last night. I blame that third glass of wine. I never drink when I know I'm the first speaker the next morning. But some college friends showed up that I hadn't seen—well, since college.

I couldn't get an earlier flight out, but the concierge ushered me to a private lounge to wait while she tried. I've learned that Grant died in a one-car accident in Colorado. Colorado? Why would Grant be in Colorado? He'd said nothing about Colorado when I talked to him Tuesday night. He planned to be here. With me. When he didn't show up, I figured he'd gone to Florida to Ridge's tennis tournament. But he would have called. None of this makes sense.

The state trooper I talked to in Durango had the total recall of Scott Peterson at his murder trial. His life goal seemed to be getting me off the phone. He said the accident happened near midnight. The car left the road at a high speed. The wreckage was at the bottom of a deep ravine. Just the facts, Ma'am. Good weather. The road had been clear. No traffic. No evidence the car had tried to stop. He said he'd have the trooper who'd "worked the scene" call me.

Nobody called. My father, Jackson Dale, had better luck. Maybe his name sounds impressive, or maybe it's the sound of authority in his voice. In any case, they'd given him more information. He learned Grant's body had been crushed beyond recognition The car's VIN and registration had been traced to Sable Amhurst. Very little of the car, a red convertible, remained. It took rescue workers hours to get down to it and even longer to find my husband and bring him up. Both occupants had been thrown from the wreckage. They told Dad if the accident hadn't been witnessed, the wreckage might never have been found. Horrible thought.

Dad said the trooper he spoke to suggested we have Grant cremated before the body was shipped back to Oklahoma. My vibrant husband has been reduced to "the body". Suddenly cold, I shivered.

I watched a Southwest Airlines jet taxi to the terminal while I wondered what had happened to my husband. The highway patrol said the posted speed limit on that curve was 25 mph. They said Grant had to be doing at least 70. But Grant didn't speed. Ever.

Too wired to sit still, I got up and paced past the large window. Tiny fingers had trailed through greasy smudges on the glass. Some mother had allowed her child to pick up a boat load of germs. I looked around for something to clean the window, which proved how far gone I was.

A dead fly lay on the windowsill. I didn't have to imagine its frantic fight for freedom against the cold uncaring glass. I, too, wanted to escape the nightmare of my life. How do I rewind and get back to when I had a husband instead of "the body".

My mind rebelled. This was all a terrible mistake. It wasn't Grant! Someone else was speeding in a red convertible with a strange woman Grant does *not* know. I was so deep in denial I almost refused to get on the plane when an airlines representative came to the door and ushered me to a seat.

The plane taxied across several runways and then stopped. An hour ago, the pilot announced there was a problem with the electrical system. He said technicians were working on it and would soon have us in the air. Right. They've turned off the engines. I wondered if anyone had ever gotten off a plane and hitchhiked. I looked out the window gauging the distance to the ground and felt like that fly.

The lady in the seat next to me fished a pack of kid's pictures from a gawdy red purse and looked as though she intended to start a conversation. I gave her my "don't even-think-about-it" look which had worked with the kids when they were little. Not so much now. Come to think of it, not so much then either. She snorted, did an eye roll Riley Grace would've envied, and turned her attention to the man in the aisle seat. I heard her tell him that the contractor she hired to do the renovations on her house told her she was "muy bonita". If I were speaking to her, which I'm not, I'd advise her to fire him immediately. Obviously, he's vision impaired. I kept my mouth shut, but good grief, does she never look in a mirror? Why would the man in the aisle seat care? I want out of here. I'm guessing he does, too

Grant would've been on my case about how I just lost him a potential vote. Guess I don't need to worry about that anymore. Ali says I need something like a tennis net to catch all the things that fly through my brain before they fly out my mouth. She would be proud of me.

If Grant was having an affair with this Sable person, I would've appreciated the luxury of discovering it in the usual way affairs are discovered like finding lipstick on a shirt collar, receipts for expensive jewelry I've never seen, or an unfamiliar phone number scribbled on a torn napkin. Although, the phone number doesn't always mean anything. If a guy is having an affair, he knows her number.

Grant's suspected affair was proclaimed on the front page of every major newspaper. Well, of course. Grant never does anything on a small scale. I'm not blind. I know women throw themselves at my husband. But there's been no hint of an affair. Grant is too smart to have an affair. And he loves me.

Every question spawned several more. If Grant wasn't having an affair, why was he on a mountain road in Colorado instead of in Virginia with me? And why am I sorting through all this now instead of being inconsolable over the death of my husband? I should not be able to form a complete thought. I should be drowning in a torrent of tears. I'm as dry-eyed as when I walked off the stage in Leesburg before Riley Grace's message. Why? I'm a very emotional person. I cry over TV commercials and Hallmark movies.

I must be in shock. Hopefully, the media will view my lack of emotion as being a strong woman overcoming her grief for the sake of her children. Like Jackie Kennedy standing tall and resolute. Although Ridge is 21 and won't be nearly as darling as a four-year-old John-John Kennedy saluting his father's casket.

Grant's funeral won't generate that kind of coverage. Or it wouldn't have if Grant's death hadn't produced a national scandal. Grant was a senator, not a president, but Riley Grace said our yard looks like a circus. News crews have sensed a Ted Kennedy Chappaquiddick story and are camped in our yard wrecking my phlox and hydrangeas.

What is wrong with me? My husband is dead. Why am I thinking about the Kennedys? Because if I stop, I'll panic about having to raise my daughter, who doesn't like me, and living the rest of my life Grantless. Dissolving into a screaming howling hysterical blob on an oven-like plane full of irate people would not benefit anyone.

We've been sitting here for 2 hours. If we took off this minute, I'd still miss my connecting flight. I'm going to be stuck in the Atlanta airport. I *hate* the Atlanta airport. I truly believe Jimmy Hoffa is alive and well somewhere in the Atlanta airport and doesn't know where to get off that train thingy. My brain is totally fried.

I kicked my seat back and tried to sleep. But every time I closed my eyes, I envisioned the wreck, wondering if Grant had time to know he was going to die. Praying he didn't.

Chapter Five

Riley Grace

The back door opened and Ali came out. She came straight to the tree and started climbing.

Ali is my mom's cousin. She's pretty like Mom without even trying. This morning she threw on a pair of cutoffs and a T-shirt, pulled her hair into a ponytail, and came out to play tennis with me. Before breakfast. Before the world spun out of control. Before the Highway Patrol came to tell me my daddy died last night.

She hasn't had time to change clothes or put on makeup. She isn't obsessed about how she looks. Mom is ten years older. That's not a lot in people years, but Ali seems a lifetime younger. Ali calls me Rye like Ridge does. Sometimes she calls me Gracie like my friends do. Only Mom calls me Riley Grace. Formal. As though she doesn't know me well. Because she doesn't. Evidently knowing someone has nothing to do with DNA.

Ali sat down cross-legged beside me and looked down into the tennis court. Dad had it installed before we even moved in. It's pretty cool. Mom hired a landscaper to design the yard around it. Ridge and I kept running through her flowers chasing tennis balls. She finally gave up. I used to watch Ridge's tennis lessons from up here. He's a big-deal tennis star now but even when I was little, I knew what he did wrong when he blew it.

"This is an awesome tree," Ali said. "Wish I'd had one when I was a kid."

Ali had been kidnapped when she was two by a crazy lady who often locked her in a closet. She only found her way back to us three years ago. But she has adjusted so well, you wouldn't know she'd missed out on all those years of a normal childhood. She's the reason I try not to complain about anything. Because of her, I know how fortunate I've been. She had nothing.

"Did you like being the Governor's daughter?" Ali asked. The question sounded random, but she does that a lot—picks up on my wavelength.

"Nobody has ever asked me that." I considered it "No. It was like living in a goldfish bowl. Ridge and I loved living with Gramps and Penny at the farm while Mom campaigned with Dad. We got to be normal kids. When we moved into the Governor's Mansion we were supposed to be perfect."

"I can see that would be a problem."

"Yeah. As it turns out, I'm not great at being perfect. Neither was Ridge. He was always in trouble. Like when he carved his initials in a door frame."

"He rebelled."

"Yeah. Maybe. But maybe he just wanted to carve his initials in something. You would have thought he'd committed a federal offense. He was convinced he was going to jail for vandalizing state property." I smiled. "I might have told him that."

Ali laughed. "You were eight. Why would he believe you?"

"I don't know. Do you think Mom hasn't called because she's mad? I said terrible things on the phone. Maybe I was mad at Dad for dying and took it out on her." I thought about it. "No. I was mad at her for not being here."

"At least you're honest."

"Yeah, but now I wish I hadn't been. I'll probably never see her again."

Ali laughed. "You're being a bit dramatic. Her phone might have died. But she isn't lost. Lane tracked her down. She missed her connecting flight. She's at the Atlanta airport."

"Same thing," I grumbled. "She always gets lost in the Atlanta Airport."

"What's really bothering you?" Ali asked.

"I've been trying to remember when Daddy left for DC last week. I can't."

I wiped a tear from my chin with the back of my hand. How much can you cry before your tear ducts dry up? Does someone somewhere count tears like the guy trapped inside your laptop who keeps track of how many words are in your documents? "What if I didn't tell him goodbye?"

Ali picked a leaf from a branch and examined it like she'd never seen a leaf before. "Grant wouldn't leave without telling you goodbye. You've talked to him almost every day."

A tear plopped on my knee. "Yeah. He called every night."

"Did he mention going to Colorado?"

"No."

Ali nodded and changed the subject. "How are things with Bronc? Does he know you're in love with him yet?"

She was trying to distract me. It worked. I am crazy in love with Bronc Snyder and need to talk about him.

"No. Dad heard Bronc's last name was Snyder and told me to stay away from him. Not a problem since he doesn't know I'm alive."

"I'm guessing he knows you're alive."

"Dad said Bronc's father was reckless in high school. Dad knew him. They got high together a couple of times. I don't think Dad should've told me that."

Ali laughed. A real laugh, not one of those laughs like when people say "that's so funny". If they really thought it was funny, they would have laughed instead of saying it was funny.

"Dad thought Bronc's father might be in prison."

"Why?"

"I guess because he's not around. There are other places he could be and I fail to see how our fathers' getting high is Bronc's fault."

A ladybug landed on my knee. We watched it detour around the tear.

"Good point," Ali said. "Do you have classes with Bronc?"

"Just homeroom. He's a senior. I can't stop staring at him."

Ali grinned.

"He's hot. I love the way he walks."

"One foot in front of the other?"

"He has swag. Alise says it's the cowboy boots. They're red. She thinks they're *gauche*, but they're really cool."

"*Gauche?* Alise is a fashion consultant?" Ali raised an eyebrow.

"We watched old movies last Friday. Liz Taylor used *gauche* in a sentence. Now Alise works it into every conversation, even when she shouldn't. Come on! How could green beans be *gauche?* They're an inanimate object."

"I get your point." Ali was trying not to laugh.

"Alise wears baggy ancient OSU shorts with an OU shirt so who is she to decide something is gauche? Faded red and used-to-be orange? Disgusting. Who does that?"

"Evidently, Alise." Ali was still grinning.

"Alise hasn't decided whether she wants to apply to Oklahoma State or Oklahoma University. So she isn't going to risk offending either one," I explained. "Seriously, it's so stupid! Like she's going to run into the dean of OU or OSU at the grocery store in the produce department sorting rutabagas or something."

"Alise hangs out in produce departments? Why are you even her friend?"

"I know! Right? Back to Bronc. He doesn't care what anyone thinks about his boots or his truck." It occurred to me that since Ali knows I've never spoken to him, I have no credibility here about what he thinks. "He isn't like anyone I've ever known."

"Your mom said almost the same thing about your dad once. What's the deal with Bronc's truck?" Ali shifted her weight to get more comfortable.

"It's an old Ford. Two-tone."

"Two-tone?" Ali's eyes widened. "That is old."

"I like it. Nobody else has a pickup like that."

"I would imagine."

"I used to think his license plate had a bucking horse on it because his name is Bronc. Alise says all Wyoming tags have bucking horses. She says liking him because of a horse on his license plate proves my elevator doesn't go all the way to the top. That's not the real reason I like him."

Ali stopped shredding the leaf and looked up at me. "What's the real reason?"

"He looks like James Dean."

"James Dean?" Ali almost swallowed her gum. "Good to know your reasons aren't all superficial. How do you even know who James Dean is? He died before your father was born."

"I know. Can you believe guys were that hot way back then? After Alise and I watched *Cat on a Hot Tin Roof* and *The Last Time I saw Paris,* we watched *East of Eden.*"

"James Dean was hotter in *Rebel Without a Cause,*" Ali said. "Well then there now."

"Huh?"

"James Dean's famous line. People used to go around saying that."

"Oh. Like Mathew McConaughey's "Alright, alright, alright."

"Yeah. Jackson called the airport to see if there's a flight from Atlanta coming in tonight. We're going to the airport to see if your mom is on it," Ali said. "Do you want to go?"

"I don't know. I want to see Mom, but if Ridge comes home and we aren't here, I'm afraid he'll leave. Is Penny staying?"

Ali slapped a mosquito on her knee. "Yeah. If you're through being a hermit, she could use your help. Taking phone messages has been a full-time job. She has a cake in the oven and-"

"Strawberry cake?" I interrupted. That was rude. But it was important. Penny's strawberry cake is to die for.

"Yeah. And she's making potato salad. She wants to be here in case Ridge calls or comes home. You haven't heard from him either?"

I shook my head. "Nope. And this is getting weird. Where is he?" It was a rhetorical question. She didn't know, but I was getting worried.

Without answering, Ali began the climb down.

I had forgotten how much I loved being in this tree. As I followed her down, I wondered what other once-important things I've forgotten.

Chapter Six
April

I retrieved my carry on from the overhead storage and waited for passengers to shove their way past. The layover in Atlanta had been exhausting. Then a low-pressure system over Oklahoma turned the Boeing into the runaway mine train ride at Frontier City. The whole day has been a nightmare.

After I missed my connecting flight, the airlines had pulled strings to get me on this already overbooked flight. My seat, right off the galley and beside the plane's only restroom, was designed for pygmy flight attendants.

Wishing my phone had held a charge long enough to let my father and Ali know the time of my arrival, I exited from the passenger bridge into the Will Rogers terminal and was blinded by a wall of flashing lights. An army of reporters and news crews from every newspaper, radio, and TV station in Oklahoma blocked my progress. Reporters shouted a chorus of questions at once. I froze. Passengers in my wake pushed and bumped their way around me muttering obscenities. I was trapped and so were they.

"Mrs. Frazier, when did you learn of your husband's affair?"

"Mrs. Frazier, what can you tell us about Sable Amhurst?" Each of them tried to outshout the others.

"How long had your husband been cheating on you?"

"How did he meet her?"

"Was Sable a friend of your daughter's? How old is she?"

"My daughter? What...?" I stammered.

And then there were those who pretended to know me.

"April! April! April! Over here!"

"April, why was Grant in Colorado?"

"April, have you made funeral arrangements yet?"

"What?" I mumbled, "Funeral arrangements? I haven't been home..."

Above the pandemonium, an authoritative voice commanded, "Leave her alone!"

I'd know that voice anywhere and have never been so glad to hear it.

My daddy, Jackson Dale, shoved his way through the throng and wrapped his arms around me. I collapsed into them. In the safety of my father's arms, the flood gates broke.

"I've got you, Baby Girl," he whispered in my ear. For a few minutes he just held me, shielding me from the crowd. I leaned into him, shuddering and sobbing.

"We need security over here," Dad yelled.

Uniformed officers pushed their way through to us then began moving people back.

"I have her bag," Ali shouted from somewhere. Amazingly, we heard her above the roar of voices and began pushing our way toward her.

We followed security through the crowd and suddenly we were free. The officers stayed around us as Daddy moved us toward the door. His Ford F-150 was parked right outside. Ali had tossed my bag in the back. She opened the back passenger door, slid me in, and hopped into the front seat. Dad walked around to the driver's side. Two officers stood beside the pickup holding the throng at bay as we escaped.

"Where's your car?" Dad asked.

"Let's leave it for now," I said, "and get out of here. Ridge can come get it later."

"Oh, good! You've heard from him," Ali said.

I blinked. "My phone is dead. Haven't you?"

"No." Dad checked his rearview before pulling out. "Your daughter is incensed. We've heard from neither of you since she talked to you this morning. She's convinced she's an orphan. And an only child."

"I'm sorry," I sniffed. "I went to dinner with college friends last night. I should never have had that third glass of wine. I was too buzzed when I got back to my room to put my phone on the charger. After I heard what happened this morning, I threw things in my suitcase so fast, I overlooked the charger. What a time to be without it."

Ali handed me her phone. "Here, call her."

While I talked to Riley Grace, I heard Dad say he needed gas as he pulled into a station.

"I'm going to Norman," I said. "I have to find my son." I handed Ali her phone. "At this point, we're not sure he knows of his father's death, right?"

Ali spaced her words carefully. "There is no way he could live on this planet and *not* know by now." I heard worry in her voice, but she was trying not to upset me further.

"This is so frustrating," I said. Through the window I watched Dad replace the gas nozzle.

"April and I are going to Norman," Ali said as Dad got back in the pickup. "Jackson, you could drop us at her car and meet us back at April's."

I didn't miss the look that passed between them. Ridge wasn't at his apartment. We all knew that. But they also knew how close I was to losing my tenuous grasp on sanity.

"Nope," Dad said, "April, I'm not letting you out of my sight. Let's go find my grandson." He looked at me in the rearview mirror and winked. It brought back childhood memories. Before Mom died, Dad used to tease her and wink at me in the back seat.

As Jackson left the airport parking area and eased into the line of traffic on the I-35 on ramp, I settled back into my seat, grateful again for family. There will be countless decisions to make. Alone. For now, I'm perfectly willing to let someone else make them. In the front seat Ali called Riley Grace to let her and Penny know of our change of plan. As I listened to Ali visiting so effortlessly with my daughter, telling her about the mob at the airport and how awesome Dad was, I smiled.

In Norman, Dad exited I-35 onto Robinson and we made our way to Ridge's apartment complex.

Ridge's Forester wasn't in front of his building. No lights were on. No surprise when he didn't answer our knock. We stood around not knowing what to do next. I wanted desperately to look inside. Ridge wasn't here but maybe there were clues about where he had gone.

Grant has a key, but I've never needed one. Anytime I've been in Ridge's apartment, we've been together.

A guy walking his dog stopped. "Looking for Ridge?" He looked at me. "You're his mom, Right?" he added.

"Yes," I said wondering how he knew. "Have you seen him?"

"Not for a few days. Like I was telling the guy who was just here."

"Someone was just here?" I interrupted.

"Yeah. Pretty insistent. He pounded on the door like he was escaping a fire. I considered calling the cops."

"What did this guy look like?" Dad asked.

"I'm Chase, by the way. I live next door." The guy extended his hand and Dad shook it. "Let's see," Chase went on. "He was an older dude." He paused, looked at Jackson, and reconsidered. "Not as old as you. Fifties maybe. Not tall, but muscular. He walked like a bodybuilder. I wouldn't want to mess with him. Even with Ivan here, on my side." He nodded toward his dog, an Irish Wolfhound.

Though huge, Ivan was less than menacing. He looked at me and wagged his tail.

"Short grey hair in a military cut," Chase added. "He drove a white SUV. I think it was a Pathfinder. He pealed out of here like he'd just stolen it."

"Wonder who he was," I mused.

"He had a Colorado tag," Chase said.

We all looked at each other.

"Do you have a key to Ridge's apartment?" I asked. "In case of emergencies."

Chase told the dog to sit and rubbed a palm on his faded blue running shorts. Ivan remained standing and yawned.

"No. But Ridge keeps a spare key under that flowerpot." Chase nodded toward the orange pot with a dead geranium. "Guess it's a good thing Pathfinder Guy didn't know that." He grinned.

I wondered how secure Ridge's apartment could be if neighbors knew he hid a key under a dead geranium. We thanked Chase, found the key and the three of us trooped inside.

Chase had been right about Ridge not being around for a few days. Cornflakes and spilled sugar were scattered across the bar. Two bowls in the sink, rinsed, but not washed. Empty sardine cans in the trash. The fridge was nearly bare. Mustard, catsup, mayo, a half-full carton of milk, an opened cola bottle, a six pack of Blue Moon with two bottles missing. There was a six-pack of Cerveza Atletica, Grant's favorite, also missing two bottles. The empties were in the trash along with a large Pizza Hut box.

I look around the room. A Yonex poster covered the wall over the sofa. *Seize the Power* was written in large red letters which leaned to the right as if they were racing off the page. A player, slightly out of focus, lunged to return the shot. The player was Ridge. His racquet, a Yonex EZONE 98, dominated the picture. He'd picked up Yonex as a sponsor after a Wimbledon win.

Ali and Dad hovered inside the front door while I checked out the rest of the apartment.

The beds were unmade in both bedrooms. Snapshots were scattered across the dresser in Ridge's room, which I found unusual. Pictures are usually kept, unprinted, on a phone. The pictures were of one of Ridge's matches, as well as photos of Ridge and Grant, both deeply tanned and smiling big at a doubles match. The last picture was of Grant appearing relaxed and happy with his arm draped across the shoulders of a girl. Dark eyes dominated her face and peered up at my husband. Orange sunflowers covered her summery dress. Wind teased the hem of her skirt. She was laughing as she brushed strands of long dark wind-blown hair from her face.

"Well, hello, Sable," I whispered, as I memorized every aspect of the picture. Sable Amhurst was an incredibly beautiful girl. Pictures of Grant and Sable did exist. UPI and AP hadn't thought to check Ridge's apartment. I ran my thumb across Grant's face. This was possibly the last picture taken of him. I turned the picture over. My breath caught in my throat. I couldn't swallow.

"Dad and Sable" was scribbled across the back in Ridge's lazy scrawl. I couldn't breathe. My son had stabbed me in the heart. The pain was excruciating. Ridge knew about his father's affair! Ridge had always been a mama's boy. My little buddy. But that was before Grant became his tennis coach and he began seriously competing. He hardly ever came home from college anymore and we rarely talked on the phone.

Ridge's betrayal hurt worse than Grant's. Something I was still grappling with.

Who else knew? Riley Grace? No. Although she thought her father could do no wrong and worshipped the ground he walked on, she couldn't keep a secret.

I was tempted to take the snapshot with me but instead, slammed it, face down on the bureau.

A framed 8 x 10 of Grant and Ridge playing doubles at the US Open hung on the wall. I saw no evidence anywhere that Ridge has a mother.

I staggered to the bathroom. My eyes went straight to the EPT pregnancy test wrapper in the trash can. The test, positive, was also in there. Who had discovered she was a mother in my son's apartment? It had to have been Sable. Was Grant the father? I suddenly couldn't breathe again. I need to talk to Ali about this as soon as possible. But not now. I tried to think but couldn't. I have just lived through the longest most horrendous day of my life. My brain turned to mush. I felt like I've been in a train wreck. I've not only lost my husband today, I've lost everything I believed to be true. For the second time today pain nearly knocked me to my knees.

I found two more long dark hairs on a bar of soap in the shower. The shower, soap and towels piled on the floor, were all dry. They hadn't been used recently A nearly empty aftershave bottle had been also been tossed in the trash. Grey by Dolce Gabbana. The only aftershave Grant ever wore. Had Grant been here? Or had the Grey belonged to Ridge? Possibly either, or none of the above. Grant wouldn't be the only one who wore Grey. Shouldn't I know what fragrance my son preferred? There seemed to be a lot I didn't know.

Grant hadn't mentioned being here lately, although he sometimes stayed here when Ridge played in a tournament. It's been two months since Grant has been home. Of course, the bathroom trash may not have been emptied for two months, although the bottle and pregnancy test were the only things in it.

I rejoined Ali and Dad. Ali saw my face. Her eyes widened, but she said nothing.

We replaced the key under the flowerpot. In a daze I somehow made my way back to Dad's pickup with more questions than answers, trying to hide the fact I'd just been blindsided.

Nobody talked on the way home. Dad and Ali picked up on my mood and made no effort at conversation. Back at the airport I directed Dad to my car. The media either hadn't found it or gave up on us coming back tonight. I tossed Ali the keys. She unlocked my doors, grabbed my bag and slung it into the trunk. Numb, I slid into the passenger's seat. Jackson followed us to my house.

I have to find my son.

Chapter Seven

April

The helicopter carrying us to the runway where Airforce One waited to take us back to Oklahoma, lifted off, rose, and circled the Capitol. I looked down at the dome wondering if I would ever see it again. With Grant's death, my days of visiting DC had come to an end.

The funeral had been stately, a beautiful tribute, but long. Everyone in the Senate, along with acquaintances from evidently everywhere in the western hemisphere, felt led to say a few words. By the end of the day, I was beyond exhausted. I was headed for comatose.

I had failed to resemble the strong-silent Jackie Kenedy standing beside her husband's casket. But, on the other hand, I hadn't collapsed into a sobbing soggy mass on the white marble seal of the Capitol the floor. Riley Grace had been a tower of strength, staying beside me squeezing my hand in silent support when needed.

Friends that Grant and I had made along the way stopped to sympathize with me, saying all the right things. Nobody asked about Sable Amhurst or mentioned Ridge's glaring absence.

The fear, anger, and hurt that had swirled through me all day, morphed into terror and settled in my stomach. It had been five days since Grant's death and Ridge had not called or come home. He had not returned calls or texts, even from Riley Grace. When I was thinking clearly, I knew my son would not have missed his father's national funeral. For any reason. Ridge idolized his father. So where was he? None of this made sense. I wouldn't allow myself to believe he was dead. If my son was no longer on this earth, my mother's heart would know it.

I had only closed my eyes for a few seconds before my father's hand on my shoulder shook me awake. I sat up and blinked. The rest of my family were already crossing the runway to Airforce One. Riley Grace and Ali were chattering away as they brought up the rear. Lane walked beside them, his phone to his ear.

Skylar Watkins had pulled some strings to get us this ride home. Grant's closest friend had stayed staunchly loyal even through this scandal. He stood at the door of Airforce One ushering Grant's mother, brothers, and their families inside. Once everyone had boarded and we were ready for takeoff, Sky slipped into the seat next to Riley Grace who had chosen to sit alone behind me. Everything I do irritates her. Her best friend Alise would say, "Gracie is in one of her snits," and counsel me on how to deal with my her. Like she knows Riley Grace so much better than I do. But, actually, she does. Everyone, it seems, knows her better than I do.

Susan eased into the empty seat beside me. She reached for my hand, gave it a squeeze, smiled and said nothing. She understood the last thing I wanted to do was talk. We've been friends long before we were college roommates. Grant and I introduced her to Skylar. The four of us became an item. Through the years we have both been too busy to stay in touch the way we would like, but we don't need to. She knows my heart. She's going to be a great First Lady. Behind us, Skylar and Riley Grace were chatting away like two old ladies at a sewing bee. She was asking him questions about the plane.

"Have Presidents always had their own plane?" I heard her say and listened to his reply. I wanted to know, too.

"No," he answered. Until 1959 Presidents traveled on whatever plane was at their disposal. But John Foster Dulles noticed that Khrushchev and the soviet leaders were traveling on jets while President Eisenhower was still in prop planes. He was embarrassed and was instrumental in making sure the U.S. President rode in style. The first presidential plane was called Queenie."

"Queenie? How Presidential," Riley Grace scoffed.

"Maybe it was already named and they thought it wouldn't recognize another name. It had 40 passenger seats and a conference room." Skylar continued. "This plane has a conference room, an office that resembles the Oval Office in the White House, a presidential lounge, sleeping quarters, several restrooms, two kitchens, and 60 seats, which are roomier and more comfortable. It was during George Bush's term that Airforce One was nicknamed the Flying Oval Office because he did so much work in the air. In fact, he was flying when 9/11 happened. For safety reasons, the plane stayed in the air for hours. Security wouldn't allow him to land in DC. Gordon Johnson who was on the plane at the time, described it as the safest most dangerous place to be at that exact time."

"I can't even imagine what that was like," Riley Grace said.

Skylar nodded. "That was a somber time in history."

"Who uses all these seats?"

"Staff that the President will need on this trip and representatives of the media."

"So some journalism major lands a job with the Post and goes jetting off with the president?"

"There's a bit more to it than that," Skylar said.

"So many famous people must have ridden in this plane, Riley Grace said. "And today we are. My grandma will never forget this. By the time the sun goes down tonight, everyone in Kansas City will know she rode on Airforce One."

Skylar chuckled. "You hungry? You haven't eaten much today."

I was surprised that he had noticed. He's had a busy day.

"A little," Riley Grace answered. "Now that you mention it..."

"Well, let's go to the kitchen and see what we can rustle up," Skylar suggested.

They got up, still talking. Conversation faded as they moved away.

I closed my eyes and tried to sleep. Thoughts of Ridge chased each other through my mind. None of them ended well.

When I opened my eyes again, Skylar and Riley Grace were back. Riley Grace leaned across Susan and handed me a sandwich. Ham and cheese on rye. Dill pickles and lettuce. No tomatoes. I'm allergic to tomatoes. The bread had been spread with mayo with a touch of mustard mixed in, exactly the way I like it. I hadn't thought I could eat a bite. I inhaled it.

I smiled. "Thank you Honey, that was delicious. You made it yourself, didn't you?"

Skylar laughed. "The chef wouldn't let her. But I bet he has never made a sandwich under such strict supervision."

"There's a chef back there?" Susan asked. Her surprise was evident. "Is it Jon Luc?"

Sky nodded. "The President sent his private chef along in case anyone was hungry. You should go back and take advantage of his generosity.

"What a gift. We should go," Susan said. "Jon Luc's lobster salad is the stuff dreams are made of."

"I can't believe all of this," I said. "The President has been so kind."

"He feels terrible about what has happened to Grant," Skylar explained."

"Go see the kitchen, Mom," Riley Grace sai, "it's unbelievable! And guess what! Uncle Sky has a key to this plane's Oval Office. I got to sit where the president sits."

"Not many people can say that," I said. "come to think of it, maybe you shouldn't either. We don't want to get Sky in trouble."

Skylar laughed. "I've been in trouble for worse."

"Our first lady has very good taste. A lot of taxpayer's money went into the upgrade on this kitchen," Susan said. "But it doesn't come close to what Jackie Kennedy spent remodeling Air Force One when JFK was president. She hired a French designer. Of all the planes that have served as Air Force One, that one is the most famous. Her husband's body was flown back from Dallas to DC. The only President to be sworn into office on a plane, President Johnson, was on that same flight. Nixon made a historic trip to Moscow on that plane, and President Kennedy flew to Berlin for his famous speech."

"It's at the Airforce museum outside of Dayton, Ohio now, right?" Riley Grace said.

"Right," Skylar said, beaming a smile at her as though she just answered the million-dollar question without a lifeline.

I wondered how she knew that, too, but she often surprises me with her random bits of knowledge.

"Uncle Sky took me on a tour of the plane, Mom. You should go check it out," Riley Grace said. "He'll take you, too."

"I appreciate the offer, but if it's okay with all of you, Susan, I think I'd like to see the kitchen," I said.

On our way down the aisle, Lane intercepted me. "April, I just got in touch with the Colorado Highway Patrol. We need someplace to talk." He'd slipped back into his DEA role, his tone serious.

My heart leaped into my throat and lodged. I couldn't breathe. Lane's impassive face told me nothing. And everything.

I was finally able to catch my breath. "Ridge?"

Lane shook his head.

Chapter Eight

Riley Grace

"Whomp. Whomp. Whomp." A sound can be so familiar, it's not even heard. Like when the air conditioner kicks in. I drifted up out of sleep with a sense of dread, not wanting to wake up. Something terrible had happened and I didn't want to remember what. Then something clicked. I remembered. I remembered at the time I recognized the sound.

Ridge! I sat up. Fully awake. I kicked my way out of tangled sheets, jumped up, and ran to the window overlooking the tennis court.. He was slamming balls against the backstop.

I'd slept in panties and a t-shirt. I dug through a pile of clothes until I found some shorts. Hopping across the room on one foot. I pulled them on. Terrified he'd leave, I galloped down the stairs and slipped through the still dark house, snagging a couple of cookies on my way through the kitchen.

Ridge had been watching for me. He stopped hitting balls. "Hi, Squirt," he said without looking at me.

"Where have you been?" It was more of an accusation than a question and he didn't feel a need to answer.

"Ridge, where were you? We've been worried." I planted a hand on one hip for emphasis. Wasted effort. He still wouldn't look at me. "Mom went to your apartment."

"Yeah?" He dropped a ball and bent to pick it up.

"Yeah, you weren't there," I added, although he might already know that.

He still hadn't made eye contact.

"Want a cookie?" I offered one, as I took a bite from the other.

He shook his head, then realized it was a snickerdoodle. His favorite. He tossed a ball into a bucket and reached for the cookie.

"Thanks," he mumbled. He glanced at me, then looked away. But not before I had a chance to see his face.

I gasped. Sunglasses couldn't hide his swollen eyes. His hair was a mess. He hadn't shaved in days. "Ridge, you look like you've been in an explosion."

He swallowed the cookie and wiped his hands on his shorts.

"When did you last shower?"

He shrugged.

"Do you want another cookie?" I asked. "Or you could go in and get it yourself. You live here, too, you know."

He glanced toward the house. "Is Mom up?"

"I don't think so. She was up pretty late last night.

He looked relieved.

"I could make you a sandwich. Fried egg?"

Ridge loves fried egg sandwiches, but he shook his head and offered me his blue racquet. The Yonex. His tournament racquet. He yells at me if I even look at it. I stared at him.

"Wanna play?" he asked.

"Yeah, but not with your racquet. I'll go grab mine and put on some shoes."

He looked down at my bare feet and nodded.

I ran up to my room, shoved my feet into my Adidas and grabbed my racquet. And two more cookies on the way out.

Ridge was bouncing a ball on his racquet. I handed him the cookies. He ate them as he walked to the far end of the court.

A huge cottonwood, the home of my tree house, shades most of our yard. The court's far end is sunny. Ridge and I usually argue about who has to play there. This morning he went without question.

His serve was wicked, but I managed to return it. His forehand whizzed past me at warp speed. He's famous for that forehand. I lunged for it, but missed, despite the fact I've practiced a defense against it all week.

"Hey," I yelped. "Little sister here, not your worst enemy. You trying to kill me? Lighten up."

"Okay," he said, but he didn't. He ran me all over the court. I paid him back when I returned a ball he thought I had no chance of reaching and laughed at his startled glance. I've worked hard.

After the second set which he won, but not by much, he walked off the court, mopping his forehead with a towel. The towel wasn't one of ours, which made Ridge, the brother I know so well, suddenly feel like a stranger. I went in the house, came out with bottles of cold water and handed him one.

"Thanks." He gave me a rueful grin. "Good game."

"You missed my Friday lesson," I accused, swatting at a persistent mosquito.

"Yeah. I'm here now." He swiped the cold wet bottle across his forehead.

"That wasn't a lesson! It was an annihilation. I worked all week on the serve you showed me."

"You used it a couple of times. Good work. You've got it down."

"You could've said so," I grumbled, as I tried to open my water. The bottle was flimsy plastic. Water leaked out, but the top wouldn't come off.

Ridge reached for my bottle, held his bottle between his knees, opened mine, and handed it back.

"I just did. Listen, Rye," Ridge finally looked at me, "you're good. Really good. You have a quarterback mentality. You know where the ball will be before your opponent hits it. Your instincts are mind-blowing."

I blinked. He never praises me. Ever.

"I worked hard to get where I am," he went on. "I had to be good. Dad expected it. There was no other option. I grew up knowing tennis would be my life." He tapped his racquet against the side of his shoe. "Dad was on my tail all the time."

A blue jay squawked above us. Ridge paused and looked up. "You're better than I was at your age. And Dad hasn't pushed you the way he has me." A tear escaped under his Oakleys and rolled down his cheek.

I stared. I hadn't seen my brother cry since coyotes killed his dog at the farm when he was nine.

"I gave you my best shot this morning. You hung in there with me," he said.

A breeze pushed through the overhead branches. Shadows swayed at our feet. "You're going to be better than me someday," he added.

"Already am," I teased.

He didn't bite. "It's going to be up to you to keep the Frazier name alive in tennis. Pass on the legacy." He mopped sweat from his brow with a terry wrist band and gulped down half a bottle of water.

"You're quitting tennis? You can't!"

He swiped the towel across his face and gazed into the distance.

"Ridge, you can't! It will kill Dad. . ." I realized what I had just said.

"I already have," he said, his tone indicating he'd just made up his mind about something. He turned and strode toward his Forester.

"Ridge, stop! You aren't coming in? Where are you going? Why did you say you killed Dad? Ridge, Stop!"

He kept walking. I ran to keep up.

"You didn't kill Dad. What do you mean?"

He didn't look back.

I raced past him and edged between him and the driver-side door. "Who are you and what have you done with my brother?" I demanded. "I love you. Ridge, talk to me!"

"C'mon, Rye, get out of the way." He wouldn't look at me.

"Why aren't you coming in?" I was in his face.

"Get out of the way," he said, avoiding eye contact. He placed a hand on each of my shoulders and moved me away.

"You didn't go to DC with us for Dad's memorial service," I accused.

"Couldn't—I had to do something."

"More important than your father's memorial service?" I demanded. "Ridge, it was on national TV. His son wasn't there! How do you suppose that looked?"

He stared into the distance. "That's the least of my worries."

"You're breaking Mom's heart. She just lost her husband. How can you do this to her? Think of someone beside yourself!"

"If you only knew." He inhaled deeply and exhaled a long-ragged breath.

"Knew what? Ridge. What? Talk to me!"

He stepped past me and opened the car door. "Gotta go." He stood in the open door of his Forester just looking at me.

I looked inside. His suit, a dress shirt, and shoes were in the back seat.

"You aren't getting dressed here? Why wouldn't you get ready in your room? Here. With us. Mom is going crazy. You're her favorite, you know."

He didn't bite. It was sort of our joke although it was true. Dad and Mom were partial to Ridge. We both knew it. I didn't blame them. I loved him, too.

He almost smiled.

"You walked right past my room without doing your stupid knock. You didn't wake me up? Ridge, what's going on?" I was full blown crying now. He was leaving and there was nothing I could do to keep him here. I wiped my nose on my sleeve.

"I waited for you." He got in the Forester. With his expression hidden by his Oakleys, he stared at my face as though memorizing it. He sighed and looked away. "Thanks, Rye." He put the car in gear. "Love ya, Brat." He backed out and drove away.

I watched until he was out of sight in case he waved. He didn't. I'd always assumed Ridge loved me, although most of the time he acted like he didn't. But I couldn't remember his ever saying so. What was going on?

Back at the tennis court I began to get a sick feeling. Why wouldn't Ridge come in? His despair seemed way beyond grief. My brother was in agony. That's not a word I've ever used—until now. His mind hadn't been in our game. He almost let me win. I stopped in my tracks and stared. He'd left racquet, his Yonex, on the bench. Dread twisted my stomach. He left it on purpose. I began to panic. Ridge wasn't coming back. Ever.

Chapter Nine

April

I met Grant in my junior year of college. I had just ended a relationship with the guy I thought I'd spend the rest of my life with. Heartbroken, I'd sworn off men. The event planner who'd employed me was catering the Young Republicans drive for new members. I'd walked into the room with a tray of *hors d'oeuvres*. Grant had been watching people, mostly me, milling around the room for the last hour. He left his post by the wall and made his way through the crowd toward me.

"I'll have one of those," he said with a slow-motion smile. His eyes never left my face as he picked a bacon-wrapped chicken liver from my tray and popped it in his mouth. He frowned. "I hate chicken liver."

"You should test things." I said edging past him.

"Couldn't see it," he grumbled. "It was bacon wrapped. Dirty trick. What's that?"

"Water chestnuts."

"If that's all you got, we're paying way too much for your catering service."

"Take it up with the owner." I stepped around him.

"Wait!" He looked over the tray. "What are those?"

"Quail eggs."

"You're wasting quail eggs on this crowd? Most of these guys are too buzzed to know what they're eating." He gestured toward the open bar as he popped a quail egg into his mouth. He was probably the only one in the room without a drink in his hand.

"That's why they're eating chicken livers and water chestnuts. Aren't you concerned that wall might fall over without you leaning against it?" I nodded toward the spot he'd vacated.

"Ah, you've noticed me." He picked through the items on my tray as though undecided about his next choice but glanced up at me with an impish grin. Busted. He knew I'd been watching him, too.

"Try one of those," I suggested, nodding toward a cheese triangle.

He picked one up, looked at it, turned it over and tasted it.

"This is delicious. What is it?"

"The reason my boss hired me. They're made with filo dough and lots of butter. I wouldn't give her my recipe."

" Will you marry me?" He picked up two more.

"Not tonight. I'm working."

"What's your name?"

"I'm working. I have to go." I took a step.

He raised his hand. "Wait! I might want more of these." He pretended to inspect my tray again. He selected a stuffed mushroom and took a small bite. "See, I tested it. I learn."

"Do you like it?"

"Yeah. They aren't as good as your cheesy things. What's your name?"

"I don't give my name to people I don't know."

"Well, how do you get to know anyone? I'm Rich."

"How nice for you." I stepped away.

"No, wait. That's my name. Richard Grant Frazier. Richard and Rich are a bit pretentious, aren't they? Stuffy, right? I don't want people calling me Dick." He shrugged. "They probably do anyway. I'm thinking about going by Grant. Trying it out. I should probably just go by Grant. What do you think?"

"Oh. You're Rich Frazier."

"You've heard of me." He was way too happy about that.

He's going to be a slick politician. Someone had invested a fortune in those dazzling teeth which looked even whiter because of his deep tan. Of course, I'd heard of him. Everyone had heard of him. I wasn't about to tell him that.

"Yeah. Somewhere." I'd already blown it, but that was a pretty good save.

"Okay. You know me now. So, what's your name."

"April." I tried to move past him again.

"April what?" He stepped in front of me. "Look, if you're going to marry me, I need a last name. You know, for the marriage license."

"Dale. April Dale. I'm working." I scowled. "Now, go away!"

"Ah. Now we are getting somewhere. Can I have your phone number, April Dale I'm Working?"

He fished a pen from his pocket prepared to write my number on his hand. He was used to getting his way. I was a bit put off by his certainty that I'd give him my number, but unfortunately also intrigued. I had noticed him when I first arrived. Tall and handsome, he would stand out in any crowd. Now I really looked at him. He was older than I originally thought. He had emerald-green eyes, dark straight eyebrows, and a Roman nose. Like Michelangelo's David. Only nobody notices David's nose. He reminded me of a marble statue with an Olympic garland on its head. I gave him my number.

He wrote it on his hand, then punched some numbers on his phone.

My phone vibrated in my pocket. "You called me?"

"I tested it. See, I do learn. I'll call you."

"Okay," I said.

"Hey, wait! Don't you want to check my hand for other numbers?"

"I'm the only female in the room. Which is the only reason you're hitting on me."

He laughed. This time he let me walk away.

Guys like him, cocky and entitled, had a new girlfriend every week. Except, I really had never met anyone quite like him.

I didn't expect him to call.

I was wrong. He woke me up the next morning.

"Hello?" I said, still groggy.

"Hey, this is Rich."

"Who?"

"Oh. Grant. I've decided to go by Grant. Did I wake you up?"

"Yeah. What time is it?" I left work last night at 1:00 AM. He was still going strong.

"Doesn't matter," he said. "The sun's up."

"Good to know."

"I found this great little place tucked away in a strip mall. The outside isn't much, but the inside is charming, and they have great eggs Benedict. You said you like eggs Benedict."

"No, I didn't."

"Oh. You didn't? But you do, don't you?"

"Yeah." I loved eggs Benedict. But that was kind of scary.

"Wear shorts. After breakfast, we're going bike riding."

"I don't have a bike."

"I do," he said. "Well, actually I don't. I borrowed two from my roomie. Well, I didn't really ask. He was asleep. He's pretty intense if I wake him up."

"Most people are. Still, you do."

"Yeah," he said. "I should probably work on that. Right?"

"Right."

"How soon can you be ready?"

"What time will you be here?" I just agreed to go with him. He's good.

"Now. I'm front of your building."

"You are not! You don't know where I live."

"Yes, I do," he said.

I got out of bed and went to the window. He was sitting in a white Explorer. Two bikes were tied to the rack on the roof. He looked up and waved. How did he find me? Okay, this is getting creepy.

"So, what are you, some kind of stalker?" I asked.

He laughed. "Apparently. Get dressed."

I hung up and got dressed. Our wedding was six months later.

Chapter Ten
April

Sunlight, slanting through the enormous stained-glass window to my left, puddled into mosaic patterns on the blue carpet. I idly watched shadows shift and shimmy at the whim of the breeze moving through cottonwood branches beyond the window.

Before Grant died, if his death ever crossed my mind, and of course it hadn't, I wouldn't have believed a life force as powerful as Grant's could be snuffed out. He'd been a light too brilliant to be imprisoned in the bronze casket almost close enough to touch. And he wasn't. His body still hadn't been released by the Colorado coroner.

Behind me Aunt Carla Faye snored. Beside me her sister Grace, Grant's mother, also nodded off. Obviously, Speaker of the House Rayford Rueford's impassioned plea for our family to "stand strong in the aftermath of loss" left them uninspired. Undaunted, his voice droned on.

Who names a child Rayford Ruefford? What was his mother thinking? Maybe she named him before the epidural wore off. I wondered about his middle name. What goes with Rayford? I should Google it. Whitford? Maybe. Clifford? Oxford? Probably not. I must really be bored. I have no idea what one should be thinking at her husband's funeral. I'm new at this. But I'm guessing what's been going through my mind isn't close.

At Grant's national memorial service in DC, Speaker Rueford had mentioned he intended to come to Oklahoma "to say a few words" at Grant's funeral. The man had never said "a few" words in his life. I should have thanked him politely, because I am nothing if not polite, and informed him that it was a private service. That option evaporated when Vice President Skylar Watkins, announced he would be here.

I'd been concerned Skylar would turn Grant's service into a campaign rally. He didn't. His remarks, although not brief, were about Grant. He told a few humorous stories about some of their college escapades, most were examples of Grant's leadership ability. Grant stood out in the crowd even then. Fortunately, he left out the story about Grant getting caught sneaking out of my dorm room. I owe him big time.

I elbowed Grant's mom, whose snores harmonized with her sister's. Riley Grace was sitting behind Aunt Carla Faye. I looked at Riley. She caught my eye and gave me a small wave. If Grant was here, his brothers would know their place. His daughter would be sitting on the first row of her father's funeral. Beside her mother.

I have no idea where Ridge is. A distant cousin said he's here. She bumped into him as she was coming in. But she hasn't seen him since he was four, would she even recognize him? Grant always knew where Ridge was or knew how to find him. Like he had on our trip to Disney World.

I'd been hugely pregnant with Riley Grace. So, Ridge must have been—four, I guess—almost five. Grant, who was having more fun than Ridge, had been on a ride that no sane person would even contemplate. That was the thing about Grant. Whatever the occasion, he would be having the most fun.

People joked that Grant could have a great time at a funeral. It was one of the reasons they were drawn to him. He didn't attend parties. He *was* the party.

Disney World had been hot. Ridge was bored, tired, and fussy, and I was pregnant, hot, and fussy. Not a good combination. This had not been a fun pregnancy. Riley Grace had been difficult even before she was born. I'm relatively sure she kicked holes in several vital organs. I gained weight and my back felt like I'd been hit from behind by a wayward German army tank. I shook out some pills for my back ache and grabbed a water bottle from the backpack.

"Where's Ridge?" Grant asked, coming up behind me.

"Right there," I said, motioning to where he'd been standing.

"No, he isn't."

I straightened and looked around. Ridge was gone. Every horror story I'd ever heard flashed through my mind. I began shrieking his name. That only alerted everyone in a six-mile area that I should probably be committed. They cleared an area around me in case I was dangerous. If Ridge's name had been Scotty or Bobby, people would at least know I was calling a child. Another thing I can blame Grant for.

"I'll go this direction," Grant said. "You go that way. Meet me back here so we don't lose each other. And stop screaming."

After twenty minutes of fruitless searching, I went back to the bench Grant had pointed out. Fortunately, it was empty. I sort of melted onto it. It sounds like I waited calmly. I didn't. But as I mentioned, I was enormously pregnant, hot, and exhausted, with feet that resembled pontoons. When Riley Grace is on her "you've always liked Ridge best" kick, she likes to point out she's never been to Disney World, although Ridge has. But she had been there. Wrecking my body.

I heard Ridge and Grant before I saw them. They were singing *We Will Rock You* at the top of their lungs. Ridge was riding on Grant's shoulders. In the crowd, I couldn't see Grant. It looked as though Ridge was a very tall person bobbing along with a fist full of balloons. People were laughing and singing along as they moved aside like the parting of the Red Sea. Ridge didn't know the words in the verses, but he came on strong on the "We will, we will ROCK YOU!"

Half-crazy with relief, I ran to meet them. Grant swung Ridge to the ground. I scooped him up and covered his chubby cheeks, which tasted like chocolate ice cream, with kisses.

"Where have you been?" I demanded. I was ready to launch into how scared I was and warn him to never do that again when Grant gave me 'the look' and shook his head.

"I went to help a little girl," Ridge explained. "She was losted. So, I helped her find her mommy, but then I was losted. I couldn't find you."

"What did you do?" I asked.

"Daddy showed me a fountain and told me if I got losted, go there and wait for him." "You did?" I asked Grant. "When?"

He grinned. "When we came through the gate."

"How did you find the fountain?" I asked Ridge.

"I found a man who had little kids. I told him I was losted and I didn't know where the fountain was. He took me there."

"You looked for someone with little kids?"

Ridge nodded. "Uh huh."

"Why?"

"Cause someone with little kids would be nice. Like you and Daddy."

"That was really smart." I looked at Grant. He winked.

"They bought him an ice cream cone and waited with him until I got there," Grant said, getting into the conversation. "Smart and brave. Remember?"

"Yes, he was," I agreed. Smart and brave."

I snapped back to the present. Behind me, Aunt Carla Faye woke up with a loud snort. I tuned in to hear Rueford say something about Grant being one of "the chosen few".

He was right. Grant always knew what to do. How am I supposed to raise kids without someone who always knew what to do? In the midst of a church full of people I felt, to quote Ridge, "losted" and alone. Self-pity leaked from my eyes and dripped from my chin.

Grant's picture suddenly appeared on a giant screen as a video of his life began. I'd heard one had been put together, but I'd had no input and no time to wonder who did. The pictures and short video clips were accompanied by Louie Armstrong singing "A Wonderful World". The video began with pictures of Grant as a baby in the arms of his mother, then included pictures of birthdays and Christmas scenes with Grant's brothers, Paul and Farris.

The first song ended. "When I die, I want to go out like Elijah" began. I looked around almost expecting to see Grant. Who had chosen that song? Grant was a Rich Mullins fan and loved it. But when would he have done this? The pictures began including me. They depicted college days, several were the four of us, Grant, Skylar, Susan, and me.

There were pictures of our wedding, the births of our children, tennis tournaments, early campaigns, Grant with the kids in various stages of growth. There were more recent pictures of Grant and Ridge in doubles matches. Nobody knew where those pictures were kept. Grant had to have put this together. But when? Why? Who knew it existed? How did it get here?

Rich Mullins' song ended.

The next one began. Pink Floyd's "Wish You Were Here".

I laughed out loud, which earned me a poke in the back from Aunt Carla Faye. "Seriously, Grant? *Wish You Were Here?*" Why am I even surprised? People used to say Grant could have a good time at a funeral. I just didn't think it would be his.

Chapter Eleven

Riley Grace

My fifth birthday party was at the farm. Ridge and I lived with Gramps and Penny during Dad's campaigns, which was most of my childhood. Because Mom was usually on the road with him, it was easier on everyone concerned if Ridge and I lived with our grandparents. But that was okay, we loved being in the country. This would have been Dad's first gubernatorial race, but not his first campaign. He'd been a state senator before running for governor.

Election day loomed big and close. The campaign, desperate for votes, was in the last throes of battle. But I knew none of that then. I only knew I was five, which was a big disappointment. Everyone seemed to think being five would be a life changing event. It wasn't. It was just like being four. And my daddy wasn't there. Mom had arrived the day before with the biggest birthday cake I'd ever seen. But then I was five. I hadn't seen that many yet. The cake was an elaborate castle because I'd wanted a princess party. Mom also brought a lavender princess dress complete with magic wand, sparkly slippers, and glittery tiara. She'd blown up balloons and done all the things Mommies do to make birthday parties a success including the *Frozen* soundtrack. All afternoon, me, the birthday girl drove everyone bonkers by twirling around in my princess dress singing “Let it go”.

The weather had been perfect, one of those gloriously golden days that make me glad my birthday is in October. The air was cool, but sunny. The sky was a brilliant shade of blue, and there was no wind, a rare occurrence in Oklahoma. I’d been playing hide and seek with friends and cousins when a big red van drove up.

Gramps disappeared into the van and came out with my birthday present, a white pony named Picasso. Picasso had a plume on his bridle and a sparkly blanket over his saddle—truly a pony for a princess. From the moment I looked in Picasso’s eye, the blue one, he became my best friend. He was a Welsh pony, bigger than a Shetland. Through the years Picasso and I explored every inch of the countryside. Dad could never remember if his name was Picasso or Pizarro. He called him Pickles.

The party was perfect. Except for one thing. My daddy wasn’t there. Gramps and Penny kept reminding me that my daddy was a busy man. They believed he wasn’t coming, but I knew he would.

“Look!” someone yelled, pointing up. A red and yellow hot-air balloon floated high in the sky. It grew larger as it came closer. Everyone clapped and cheered as it began descending. I had never seen a hot-air balloon and neither had most of the other kids. By the time it settled to the ground, I was jumping up and down. In the excitement I might have wet my royal panties.

My daddy did a low sweeping bow, leaned over the edge of the basket, held out his arms, and said, “Your Royal Highness Riley Grace Frazier, your chariot awaits.”

Mom lifted me into the basket and climbed in with Ridge. Daddy held me close as we ascended. When people talk about their first plane ride, I brag about my first ride in a hot-air balloon. A plane ride is not even close. I think about it every time I hear the song Julie Andrews sang in "Mary Poppins" about sending a kite soaring. I became famous. I wasn't Riley Grace, the governor's daughter. I was the girl who had a hot-air balloon at her party. And a pony. It was the best birthday ever. I'd been wrong. Being five was awesome!

People called him Governor Frazier and later Senator Frazier. To me he was Daddy, the man who knew how to arrive at a party. I was the luckiest little girl in the world.

People have always said my daddy was bigger than life. I thought it was because he was tall—and he was—but that wasn't the reason. His personality was over-the-top huge. There has never been anyone like him.

On an easel beside the coffin, there is a portrait of Dad in a large ornate gold frame on a table surrounded by flowers. He's wearing a blue suit and looks very handsome and seriously senatorial. An American flag hangs in the background. I wish Mom had used the picture hanging over the fireplace in the den. In that picture, Daddy's wearing white tennis shorts and holding his favorite racquet and a huge trophy. He's deeply tanned and grinning big.

This memorial service, at home in Oklahoma City in our church, is supposedly a *private* service for friends and family. Right. I heard someone say there are 4,000 people here. That's more than the population of some towns. The church is packed because Dad served as a state senator and two terms as governor before becoming a United States senator. A U S senator is a big deal. He gets to help make laws and talk to the president, and stuff. Still, I wish this was an ordinary funeral. Something private. Actually, just family and friends.

Mom said, “But Riley Grace, everyone who met your father became a friend.” While that’s true, I hate having to share my daddy with the world. Especially today.

I reined in my wandering thoughts and tuned in to the speaker long enough to hear “…the chosen few…” What on earth is he talking about? Why is he even here? Mom said it was an honor that he wanted to ‘bring the eulogy.’ Well, he’s been bringing it for over half an hour. Somebody needs to shut him up.

I yawned. Evidently too loudly. Dad’s aunt Carla Faye turned around and frowned. Woops. I hope her face doesn’t freeze like that.

I leaned forward to see if Ridge was still sitting at the end of my row. Even though he’s wearing his suit, he doesn’t look much better than he did this morning. Wearing his Oakleys inside makes him look like the hoard of secret service men circling the church. A disheveled secret service man. Who maybe fell under a combine. He didn’t come in with the family and I wondered if Mom knows he’s here. When had he slipped in?

He looks as bored as I am. He’s jiggling his left knee. He does that when he’s anxious or bored. He can’t sit still. Alise says it’s energy he doesn’t know what to do with. He has to let it out somehow like a release valve letting off pressure or he will explode like an over-inflated tire. None of us want to see that.

Ridge and I should both be on the front row with Mom. Grandma had followed Mom out of the family room along with Dad’s brothers, Uncle Paul and Uncle Farris, which left me surrounded by cousins I haven’t seen for years. Dad would have noticed, stopped the procession and made sure Ridge and I were beside him. Mom is in a coma.

Ridge eyed the door. He's sitting beside it on purpose. Five minutes ago he fished keys from his pocket. He's bouncing them in his hand ready to eighty-six it. I know him so well. While I was trying to figure out a way to get to him without causing a disturbance, he bolted.

Chapter Twelve

Riley Grace

It was a reflex. I jumped up and followed Ridge, tripping over feet and stepping on toes to get out. So much for not causing a disturbance. Running through the vestibule, I ignored startled stares from the funeral staff, Secret Service, and people unfortunate enough to wander into my path. I found an exit and raced outside. I didn't know how I was going to stop Ridge and talk him into coming back if I caught him. I just ran.

Ahead of me, Ridge jogged across the parking lot.

"Ridge!" I yelled. Everyone within five acres stopped and stared at me. Everyone but Ridge.

I kicked off my high heels—actually Mom's—scooped them up, and ran after him. I was so intent on catching Ridge, I ran into the side of a pickup. Bronc's pickup.

Bronc was as startled as, but he recovered first. Leaning across the seat, he opened the passenger door.

"Are you hurt?" he asked.

"Follow that green Forester," I gasped, climbing in. Which wasn't as easy as it sounds. His pickup was old. And high. Getting into it should be an Olympic event and never attempted by anyone wearing a short dress. Something I wish I'd thought of sooner. I deserved extra points for degree of difficulty.

Confusion puckered Bronc's brow as he looked where I pointed. Ridge's Forester blazed toward the nearest exit, narrowly missing the white SUV that had just turned in.

I closed the door. It didn't thunk like a door should. It jangled and rattled like there were a bunch of loose parts inside it.

"Are you okay?" Bronc asked.

I stared at him as though English was my second language.

"You probably dented my truck," he explained. "That had to hurt."

"How would you know if a dent was new?" I asked. His pickup looked as though it had survived World War II.

"The old dents are rusty."

"Why are you out here?" We both said at the same time.

I looked for the seat belt. There didn't seem to be one. I've never even talked to this guy and I'm ordering him around. I probably should've introduced myself, but it seemed a little late for that.

"Hi," I said.

"I was worried about you." He wrestled with the gearshift and the truck lurched forward.

Me? He was worried about me? Cool. I didn't think he knew I existed.

"Why didn't you come in?" I asked.

He raised an eyebrow in disbelief of my naivete. "Are you kidding me? You have to have an invitation issued two months ago."

"It's a funeral. My father only died last Friday." I spotted Ridge's SUV. He was trapped by cars trying to find an empty spot to park.

"You honestly think they'd let me in there? Have you seen the Secret Service? Skylar Watkins is here. You probably know that," he added.

"It's a funeral," I repeated. Anyone should be allowed in. After they're frisked, of course." I grinned. That was an example of my dry sense of humor.

"Your dad knew Skylar Watkins?" Bronc asked.

"They were fraternity brothers. Roommates in college."

"Guess that tops smoking weed with my dad in the gym." Bronc said. "My truck would've been towed. It sort of stands out."

I looked around at the BMW's, Lexus, Mercedes, and Limos packed into the church parking lot. "Yeah. I guess it would."

"The guards have already zoned in on me. They've assumed I'm circling the field, deciding where to plant a bomb."

Bronc slowed to ease past an armed security guard patrolling on foot. He was talking into a mic as he approached. My window was rolled down. I leaned out, smiled and waved. When he recognized me, the expression on the guard's face was priceless. I laughed out loud and leaned back into the seat. It was the first time I've laughed since my father died.

"Gosh, that felt good!"

"There goes my plan to kidnap you," Bronc quipped. "You've been spotted in my truck."

An example of his dry sense of humor. I hope. "Yeah. Well, there's that."

"What are we doing?"

"Trying to catch my idiot brother." I loved the way that 'we' sounded. I pointed to Ridge's Green Forester, trapped by a stream of latecomers turning in.

Bronc stomped on the brake as a white Pathfinder cut us off, tires squealing as it made a U in front of us and raced after Ridge.

A space opened in the line of traffic on Council as Ridge reached the exit. He darted into it, barely slowing to make a left turn. A traffic light must have changed somewhere. A sea of cars rushed toward him. His tires squealed as he slid around the turn and accelerated. I gasped as a black Dodge Charger flew toward him. Ridge changed Lanes and the Charger zoomed past, narrowly missing him.

Cut off by the traffic, a white Pathfinder was forced to wait for a break in the flow of cars. We watched from a distance.

"Dang." Bronc shook his head. "Does your brother always drive like that?"

"He drives too fast, but not that fast. That was weird."

"So, now what?" Bronc asked.

"I don't know." Watching Ridge weave through traffic, I exhaled a long rush of air and stress. I'd left my father's funeral hoping to catch Ridge. But this is so much better. It's not one of my wild fantasies. I'm actually with Bronc. I tried to force myself out of his pickup to go back inside. It didn't work. I had imagined this moment for too long to end it this soon. "Let's go somewhere."

Okay, cutting my father's funeral was terrible. But, if Daddy was here right now, He'd say, "Go have fun, Bino. This day is too beautiful to waste inside." He's said it hundreds of times.

A white Pathfinder found a break in traffic and squealed into a left turn as Ridge had done. Perplexed, I watched him weave through traffic as though escaping the devil.

"Uh, I need directions here." Bronc reminded me when it was finally our turn.

"Turn left. Let's go to Martin Park. It's off Memorial."

I dropped my shoes on the floor, reached into my purse and fished out Chap Stick. Tennis dries my lips. I don't usually carry a purse. I'm always leaving it somewhere. I haven't had my driver's license for a year yet and I've already had to replace it twice. Today I'd be needing tissues. And mascara. I don't usually think ahead like that.

Bronc saw the gum in my open purse, pulled it out, and held the pack in his teeth while he shifted gears. He shook out a stick, unwrapped it, and popped it into his mouth.

"Want a piece?" he asked.

I laughed. "You're offering me my gum?" I've been with Bronc less than five minutes and already laughed twice.

"Yeah. Want some?"

Applying Chap Stick, I shook my head.

He dropped it back into my purse. "Are we close?"

"Yeah. It's up here on the right. It's a wildlife park," I explained. "But the animals are usually scarce this time of day. You've never been there?"

"No," he said as he turned in.

He parked and I opened the door and slid out. Without a parachute.

Bronc stood beside his door waiting. When I carefully picked my way around his truck, he looked down at my bare feet. "Where are your shoes?"

"In your truck. I can't walk in them out here. Funeral shoes."

He looked at the stony path. "You can't walk barefooted either." He scooped me up like I weigh nothing and carried me down the trail. "Where are we going?"

Bronc Snyder has his arms around me like it's the most natural thing in the world. Speechless, I pointed to a bench beside a creek.

At this time of day the park was quiet.

"Why have you never talked to me?" I asked as he set me down..

"Do I look deranged? I knew you were out of my league even before I realized you were Senator Frazier's daughter. And to be honest, I thought you'd be a snob."

"It never occurred to you that I might like you?"

The look he gave me indicated I had possibly once been a brain donor.

"But you came today," I pointed out. "Sort of."

"I hoped I'd see you...to make sure you're okay."

"I don't think you can ascertain if someone is okay by how they look."

It's the first time I've used the word 'ascertain'. I enjoyed the way it made me feel—like someone who uses words like that all the time. But as I said it, what he had just said about needing to know I'm okay dropped into my heart. Word by word. You don't need to know someone is okay that you just casually pass in the hall. He'd been crushing me, too.

Bronc seemed unimpressed by my extensive vocabulary.

"I don't think I'll ever be okay," I added, "and if I'm honest, I'm scared to death."

"Why?" Bronc scratched his nose.

I could tell he really wanted to know by the way his eyebrows scrunched up.

I've never been close enough to Bronc to know what color his eyes are. They're green. Emerald green with tiny gold flecks in them. Like my dad's. He has thick black lashes and dark eyebrows in spite of his hair being so blond. He's obviously in the sun a lot. Maybe his hair is sun-bleached.

"Why what?"

"Why are you scared?"

"Oh. I pulled my gaze away from Bronc's eyes and peered up into the clouds. "Ridge is even more messed up than I am. I don't know my mother. Dad was the glue that held us all together. The north on our compass. He's gone."

That last part actually came first. My eyes filled with tears. Grateful for waterproof mascara, I used both palms to wipe them away. "Without my daddy, I don't know what will happen to me. I'm going crazy. If people knew half the things I've been thinking, I'd be in an institution. I want you to like me and I sound like a lunatic."

"You aren't crazy. I thought some weird stuff after my dad died, too."

"Your father died? When?" I wasn't too shocked to blurt out my dad thought his father was in prison.

"Three years ago. In Afghanistan. I talked to him the morning he died. We just talked about normal stuff—my football practice, what he had for breakfast. Not stuff I would have told him if I'd known I'd never talk to him again."

I could relate. "I'm going to need you," I said, thinking out loud. "I don't know anyone else who's lost a parent."

"I'm here." He squeezed my hand. I smiled at him. He smiled back. "Maybe we're more alike than I thought," he said.

"How do I live without my dad?"

"You don't. But you learn to live in the love he left behind."

Across the trail a doe picked her way through the scrub oaks. Her speckled fawn danced behind her, stopping to check out every hollow log. We watched in silence.

"Don't you love this park?" I tore my eyes away from the deer to ask.

Bronc was grinning. "I love that you're an outdoor girl."

"And not a snob?" I teased.

"And not a snob," he said seriously.

"I like to hike and swim," I said. "I don't like to fish. I might like to fish, I just don't."

"You play tennis. You're good, by the way."

"I have to be. Ridge threatens to un-sister me if I embarrass him." I should have acted all cute and modest, but I am good. At tennis. Not good at acting all cutesy. "Are you into sports?"

"Football. Track. Cross country." He grinned. "I'm hurt you don't know that."

I felt my face get hot. He knew I'd been watching him.

"You should run with us. To build endurance. My mom does sometimes."

"Your mom runs?"

"She's a marathoner. She does a lot of training."

"Maybe I will," I said.

My text tone chimed. It was Mom. Woops. "I need to go," I said. "We're having a family dinner after the funeral. Ridge is AWOL. One of her kids should make an appearance."

"Cut Ridge some slack," Bronc said. "He has a lot of balls in the air."

"Balls in the air? What does that mean?"

"He has a lot to deal with right now. It's a circus term. It's fairly easy to juggle one or two balls. Adding more makes it difficult to keep them all going."

I nodded as though I understood.

"Well, let's get you back." He stood to go.

"Come with me. There'll be an extra plate."

He raised his palms as he backed away shaking his head. "Nope."

"You said you'd be there for me. You're already sleazing out?"

"As a sounding board. Talking is a good first step."

"Ridge won't be there. I think there's a law against wasting prime rib."

"Wait! Prime rib? If there isn't a law against wasting it, there should be," he said. But no way am I going to a fancy restaurant dressed like this. " He winked. "I never know which knife to eat my peas with."

I looked him over. He had on Wranglers, a white Polo shirt, and his signature cowboy boots. He looked fine to me. Mighty fine.

"Well, you're gonna. Wait!" I grabbed my phone. "I gotta text Ridge." I punched in my message and hit send. "Okay, let's go."

Bronc laughed. "Are you always this bossy."

I looked up from my phone. "Yeah. Pretty much."

Immediately my text tone sounded. It wasn't Ridge. It was Alise. Oh, bugger! I forgot Alise!

Alise: *Where are you?!!?*

Me: *Where are you?*

Alise: *By your car. Waiting. Where are you?*

Me: *On my way.*

Alise: *Hurry. I have to pee.*

Me: *Go inside.*

Alise: *No WAY!!! That mob is suffocating. I was almost killed trying to get out!*

Me: *Be there in a sec.*

Alise: *WE? WHO IS WE?*

Me: *Bronc, of course. On the way!*

Alise: *Five shocked emojis. Whaaaaaat?*

Chapter Thirteen

Ridge

I checked the rear-view mirror. Nelson was gone. I've either lost him or my mind is messing with me again. It never occurred to me that he would follow me to Oklahoma. But it should have. My father's funeral was national news.

Had he planned to walk into the church and gun me down? With Skylar Watkins there, the place had been crawling with Secret Service, as well as local police. He's lost it.

I accelerated to merge with traffic on Hefner Parkway from habit, heading south to I-35. Hard to believe there could be this much traffic when everyone within a three-state area is at my father's funeral. I glanced at my gas gauge and pulled into the exit lane. I coasted into On Cue practically on fumes and eased up to the first pump.

I dug through a pile of clothes looking for my American Express card. Almost everything from my closet is in my back seat too dirty to wear. Should I go to a laundromat or get out of town first? My brain is like a Rubix cube. Every new thought screws up whatever I had just figured out.

I found the credit card and inserted it into the pump keeping my eyes open for Nelson The sound of gas filling my tank provided cadence for the words pounding in my head. My father is dead. My fault. My father is dead. My fault. My father is dead. My father is dead. My father is dead...

When the pump clicked off, I replaced the nozzle, parked the Forester and went inside. I ordered a cheeseburger. While I waited I went to the restroom and changed out of my funeral clothes. Then I wandered around gathering soft drinks, chips, nuts, beef jerky, and trail mix to munch on later. I have boxes of protein bars in the car but that's all I've eaten for days. I ordered another cheeseburger. I bought a bag of ice to cool down some soft drinks. I plan to be in my car for a while—if I manage to stay alive.

I paid the clerk and took my lunch to the picnic table outside. I sat on the table facing the street so I could keep an eye on the cars driving in. I ached to go home. I needed to organize my thoughts. I miss my mom. She understood me when nobody else did. Every time I had fallen from my father's grace, Mom smoothed things over. Then she would bake me some snickerdoodles and we would sit at the bar in the kitchen, wash the cookies down with a glass of cold milk, and talk. I could talk to her about anything back then. And suddenly, my need to see my mother slammed into me like a Mack truck. My stomach tied itself in a knot. I couldn't put her and Rye in jeopardy. Maybe I could never go home. I concentrated on organizing my thoughts again.

First and foremost, Nelson killed Dad and Sable. He thought I was with Sable. And I was supposed to be. Sable had screamed, "Ridge, your father has been shot!" It was her last words. They echo in my brain every time I close my eyes. The bullet that shattered his skull had my name on it. That hasn't changed. Nelson has to know I was on his tail when he shot Dad.

That leaves me with two choices. My gun is under the seat of my Forester. I could make it easy for Nelson and take myself out. Which would end my guilt and self-loathing.

Or I could go after Nelson and turn the hunter into the hunted. One of us would be dead, and at this point, I don't care which. Making him dead would feel good. Really good. But spending the rest of my life in prison for a murder rap doesn't have the appeal one might think. I had a vision of my mother, old and decrepit, hobbling into prison on a walker to visit me. And she would. Something every guy dreams of.

I finished my cheeseburgers, tossed the wrapper in the trash, and got in my car. I jammed the gearshift into reverse and backed out. But then I just sat there. Where am I going? I should go back to Durango for so many reasons. No use going to my apartment in Norman and I can't go home and lead Nelson to my family.

That thought brought Rye to mind. When she begged me to come home this morning, she had no idea how badly I wanted to do just that. Her red-rimmed eyes broke my heart. I could never say no to those big blue eyes even when we were kids but I knew what she was talking me into would get us in trouble. And it always did. Going by the house this morning was stupid, but I had to make sure she was okay. Old habits die hard.

My mind drifted back in time. Getting away from my sister sounded like a dream come true. R.J. and I were sixteen when his dad had taken us camping in Colorado. Gramps had decided to come with us so Mom wouldn't think he was shirking his responsibility, and Rye had begged to come along. I had been adamant. This was a man's trip. No females allowed. Especially not the one who always got me in trouble. But Grandpa promised to ride herd on her. "We wouldn't even notice she was there," he'd said. Famous last words. We'd camped beside Lake

Nighthorse, a pristine lake surrounded by San the Juan mountains. The brochure promised great fishing and promoted a three-mile hike on the yellow trail. Yellow meant the trail was basically safe but had a couple of areas that demanded caution.

RJ's dad had run to Durango for supplies. He made us promise to be careful. Gramps said he'd take Rye on a paddle boat ride. How she ended up stranded on a bridge in the middle of our hike is beyond me.

The single-file suspension bridge spanned a deep gorge, but from the trail it didn't look all that treacherous. Right! The farther out we walked, the more the bridge swayed and the deeper the gorge became. My hands refused to release my grip on the rails long enough to take another step. By the time we reached the center, we were convinced we wouldn't live to see tomorrow. I got across by focusing on a tree on the other side and refusing to look down. I might have bent down and kissed the solid ground beneath my feet. I saw my dominance of the bridge as the portal to my manhood. I had stared down certain death and prevailed. RJ and I were giddy with relief when we looked at the map. The path led around the lake to our camp site. We didn't have to cross the bridge to get back.

We had just entered the woods when I heard my sister scream.

"Ridge! Don't leave me!"

I heard panic in her voice but had been too angry to turn back around. I knew without looking that she was on the bridge.

"Come on, Ridge, we can't leave her," RJ had said.

I was so angry at her and Gramps for not watching her, I refused to go back and get her. She could stay on that bridge till she rotted for all I cared.

RJ, my life-long-best friend, stared at me as though he'd never seen me.

"Do I even know you?" he asked. "Go get your sister! Or I will!"

Not my finest hour.

When we reached the bridge, RJ pushed me out on it and kept his feet firmly planted on earth. I moved his name to the top of the list of people I can't stand. As I tottered out on the bridge, I imagined ways to pay RJ back for this. But to be fair, no way could he understand why I was so angry. His sister wouldn't have gone camping. His sister wasn't his constant shadow. His dorky sister's only concern was the seating arrangement for Barbie and Ken's wedding. Why couldn't I have a sister who stays home and plays with dolls. A normal sister who doesn't get stuck on roof tops. Or in trees, or on ledges, or bridges? God hates me.

Rye was closer to our side of the bridge than I'd imagined. In fact, I was shocked to see she was almost all the way across when she panicked. She was eleven years old and had been braver than I'd been. So much for the portal to my manhood.

I started across. The bridge began swaying hard. Rye, who was already paralyzed with fear, screamed for me to go back. I was only too happy to oblige.

"Don't look down," I ordered. "Keep your eyes on me and take one step."

"I can't!"

"Yes, you can. Just one step."

"Okay," she said, her voice as wobbly as the bridge. But she trusted me.

She took a step. And another. She kept her eyes on me. I told her she was doing fine.

She calmed down. Until she got across. Then she fell into my arms crying hysterically.

"Thank you, Ridge, I love you!" she babbled making me feel like a complete heel. "You're the best big brother ever."

She needed me then. With Dad gone, she needs me even more now. But I couldn't take a chance on Nelson coming after me at home.

My text tone chirped. I barely heard it above the echoes of Rye calling me in my brain. Without looking at the screen I knew the text was from her. She has flooded my phone with texts since I left the house this morning. I jammed my phone in my pocket unread. She would be either reaming me out for leaving Dad's funeral, or for not going to Bamboo Cru for Mom's after funeral dinner. For a moment I considered going back.

But that would be insanity. I had a vision of Nelson busting into Bamboo Cru, guns blazing, looking for me. Even if that didn't happen, I'm not good at small talk. Especially with people who idolized my dad. People I haven't seen in fifteen years but I'm supposed to remember.

I pulled my phone out of my pocket, clicked on her message, and read:

RG: *Ridge, this is important. Don't drop your balls.*

Well, that was weird even for Rye.

Me: *What?????*

RG: *I mean keep your balls in the air. Don't lose them.*

With all I've had on my mind, not once have I worried about losing my balls. I shook my head and sent Rye a thumbs up emoji.

Chapter Fourteen
April

Bamboo Cru, the favorite of my three restaurants, is a cocoon of tranquility. It's not just a place to eat, it's an experience. The seating areas ensure privacy. The combined effect of the sage walls, lush foliage, and gentle Asian music, along with the melody of the waterfall, immediately slows my breathing and lowers my blood pressure. Usually. Not today.

I'd parked in back and came in through the kitchen but stopped short. I couldn't dive into that crowd without Grant.

These were Grant's friends. Grant's family. A wave of panic swept over me so intense, I stepped back into the kitchen to keep my balance. Grant was the life force. Without him, I'm...what? A whisper? A sigh? An echo?

I plastered on a prom-queen smile and hesitated on the other side of the door.

Vice President Skylar Watkins intercepted me beside a large potted *pachira aquatica* where he'd been waiting. He grasped my elbow and steered me into a wall of bamboo.

"I was wondering if I might speak with you when you're through here," he said.

"Yes," I said. "I have questions I haven't had a chance to ask you."

"If it's about Sable Amhurst, I'm no help I'm afraid. I've never heard of her. I'm as baffled as you are as to who she is or why she was with Grant. But I know Grant. There's a logical explanation. We'll get to the bottom of all this." He patted my arm as if consoling a small child.

"By the way, did Grant tell you we'd decided to make a bid for the presidency?"

There seemed to be a lot Grant had forgotten to tell me. "Oh, by the way, Darling, I'll be driving a gorgeous woman in her fire engine red convertible....." Where? Where would they be going on a deserted Colorado road at midnight? With herculean effort I pulled my attention back to Skylar who was still talking. What had he just said? Oh yeah.

"We?"

He smiled. "Well, by "we", I meant Grant and me. He would have run as my vice president. We formulated a plan to unite this country and make it strong again. When my term ended, I would usher him into the presidency behind me. It would give us the time needed to strengthen the economy and rebuild the defense system. Evidently he hadn't had a chance to talk to you." He shook his head. "What a loss. We could have done it, April. Now, frankly, I don't know how I'm going to do this without him."

"That must have been what he was referring to when I spoke with him Tuesday evening," I said.. "I'll help with your campaign any way I can."

"I'm counting on that. You're a dynamic speaker, you have a sea of devoted supporters and a large following on social media."

I was surprised and flattered that he knew. But of course he would.

"You know, back in college," Skylar continued, "Grant and I didn't select you and Susan for wives with the idea of looking for someone who would make the perfect first lady," Skylar smiled. "But we couldn't have done better, if we'd tried. You both have grace, poise and a strong presence."

"Thank you," I mumbled. But I'm pretty sure Grant did select me for just that reason. After our wedding, he checked 'suitable wife' off his list and moved on to the next step. If I'd known he had POTUS in his crosshairs, would I have married him? I don't know. I'm not Hillary Clinton who pushed Bill into office. Lost in thought, I missed what Sky had just said.

"You might consider..." His attention drifted to the entrance and his eyes widened. His mouth dropped open. "My word! Who is that!"

I followed his line of vision. Riley Grace's best friend, Alise, had just breezed in, followed by Riley Grace in a short black sundress. With her long legs and deep tan, she looked simply stunning. Her feet were bare. Her long blond hair fell in a satin curtain around her shoulders. She raked it out of her eyes with her fingers. The fingers of her other hand were entwined in the fingers of some boy I've never seen. He was taller and blonder than Riley Grace. They made a striking couple.

Riley Grace rarely smiles big enough to show off the dimple high in her left cheek, but it was evident today. Her happiness was a vibrant thing visible from across the room. She looked nothing like a girl attending her father's funeral dinner. I guessed the reason for her joy was the guy holding her hand.

"What?" I muttered in confusion. Skylar had just seen her two days ago. "She's..."

He looked back at me, his brow knotted with impatience. "The boy! Who is he? What's his name?"

Caught off guard, I couldn't remember. "Uh, I think..." Good grief! The kid was holding my daughter's hand and I had no clue. I assumed this was the guy Riley Grace had been talking about for months. What was his name?

"Snyder? Is it Snyder?" Skylar asked, his annoyance growing.

"Uh, yeah, I think,"I stammered. "That sounds right."

Skylar had forgotten me. "That has to be Rick Snyder's son," he said, already turning toward them. "My word, he's the spitting image of his father. His dad died saving a squad in Afghanistan three years ago. My brother was in that squad. He had a picture of the two of them over his mantel. He owes his life to Rick Snyder This kid looks just like him."

Skylar rushed to greet the newcomers trailed by secret service. And me.

Ali had greeted Riley Grace at the door. "...like James Dean," she was saying.

Riley Grace laughed. Not a polite forced that's-so-funny laugh. This was real honest-to-goodness belt-it-out laughter. At her father's after funeral dinner. I haven't seen Riley Grace laugh like that in months. And why was she talking about James Dean?

The Vice President shook the young man's hand, then draped an arm across Riley Grace's shoulder and gave her a hug. He leaned down and whispered something only she could hear. She rewarded him with a dazzling smile.

I stood behind Ali watching the scene. Everyone—except for me—seemed relaxed and sure of their roles. I went from being the grieving widow, restaurant owner, and hostess, to an insecure fifth grader who had wandered naked into the wrong classroom.

"Hi, Mom," Riley Grace said, when she noticed me. "This is Bronc. I invited him to eat with us. Hope you don't mind. We'll have an extra plate."

I gave her a blank stare. "Why do we have an extra plate?"

"Ridge isn't coming." She smiled and tapped Bronc's shoulder. "Bronc..."

When Bronc turned to smile at me, I realized why they were talking about James Dean. He looked more like a young Brad Pitt in *Thelma and Louise* to me, but whatever.

"No, I don't mind," I said, dazed. "Hello Bronc. Welcome."

Bronc extended his hand. "Nice to meet you, Ma'am. I'm sorry for your loss."

Someone had raised this boy right. He meant it. I saw sympathy in his eyes. I understood why Riley Grace was attracted to him. But how did she go from a distant crush to waltzing in holding his hand looking like she had just wandered off the set of *The Bachelor* with the rose? She's more like her father than I thought.

I shook Bronc's extended hand, "Thank you."

Before I could say more, Skylar, with a hand on Bronc's shoulder, ushered him off to meet Susan and his son. Riley Grace followed Bronc.

Alise, purveyor of all knowledge, was more than willing to catch me up. She chatted with Ali, trying to include me in the conversation.

"Riley Grace, wait." I grabbed her arm and drew her a short distance away, instantly feeling guilty when the joy on her face morphed into dread.

"What, Mom?"

"Where are your shoes?" Why was that the first thing I said?

She looked at her feet as though she'd forgotten they were bare. "Bronc's truck."

"Where is Ridge?"

She watched Skylar and Bronc walk away, then turned back to me. "I don't know."

"What do you mean, you don't know? How do you know he isn't coming?"

She jerked her arm from my grasp. Her eyes narrowed. "I sensed it," she said icily, "when he bolted out of Dad's funeral and drove away as though the devil was chasing him. I tried to catch him but he escaped."

Anger flashed from her eyes. She didn't break eye contact or blink.

"If he wanted to see you, he'd be here! My guess is he can't deal with his own grief and doesn't want to get bogged down in all your drama.... April."

She only spits my name at me when she's furious.

"Ridge's absence and your grief are all you think about, Mother."

Only Riley Grace can make "Mother" sound like a dirty word. She inhaled a deep shuddering breath and continued. "My father died, too. But unlike Ridge, I have been here for you. Not that you've noticed."

I stared at her. She wasn't through.

"When the highway patrol came to notify Daddy's 'next of kin', they notified me. Me. A seventeen-year-old girl." Tears swam in her eyes. "It was a nightmare."

"You weren't alone. Ali was with you."

Wordlessly, she stared at me, her blue eyes filled with unspeakable pain. We both knew that Ali being there was beside the point. Her mother was not.

"You have not once asked how I am!" She blinked. The tears, perched on her lashes like an Olympic diver hesitating on the high board, broke and streamed down her face. She swiped at them with the back of her hand. "You've barely spoken to me since Daddy died!"

Shocked, I stepped back. She's wrong. I thought back through conversations we've had since Grant's death. I couldn't remember a full conversation anywhere. Just words in passing. 'Did Ridge call? You still up?' Where are the keys? Did Ridge call? What are you wearing to the funeral?' No, I didn't ask that last one. I had no idea what she was wearing until she walked in.

"Well, surely we talked on the trip to DC. On the plane..."

Her mouth dropped open. She stared at me. "We didn't sit together!"

I straightened, pulling myself up to my full height. It didn't help. She's 3 inches taller.

"Riley Grace, don't speak to me in that tone. I'm your mother."

"Oh good, you finally remembered. If you'll excuse me, I'll be with the people who care!" She whirled around, narrowly missing a waiter carrying a tray of drinks. She recovered nicely and returned to the Vice President of the United States who was beaming at her boyfriend.

Bronc turned, looking for Riley Grace. He smiled when he saw her and held out his hand. She took it and he led her back into the group. Ali and Alise smiled as she joined them. Noticing the tears dripping from Riley Grace's chin, Ali dabbed at them with a tissue and aimed an accusing glance in my direction.

I stood in the middle of a crowd never feeling more alone.

Chapter Fifteen

April

Crickets and tree frogs provided subtle evening background music. My stepmother, Penny, and Ali's mom, Aunt Abby, had made my favorite appetizers. They joined my dad, Ali, and me on the veranda with platters of fruit, *hors d'oeuvres,* and cheeses which looked delicious. I was too tired to eat although I had hardly swallowed two bites at Bamboo Cru. I selected some fruit and crackers. Penny smiled. She's constantly trying to get me to eat.

"I'd spend all my time out here." Abby sighed, watching the koi streak through the ever-changing lights of the koi pond.

"I would, too," I said. "If I could. There's never enough time. What did Lane find about Sable Amhurst?"

Ali's husband, Lane, is a federal agent. With his connections, he seems to be able to find out anything about anyone.

"Sable was 24. She lived in Durango, Colorado where she was a part-time college student. I think Lane said she was a flight attendant on some airline." Ali paused to sip her wine. "We'll ask Lane when he gets here."

“This is s not how it looks.” But as I said the words, I was remembering the picture of Grant with Sable and the positive pregnancy test I found in Ridge’s apartment.

“Dose Lane know anything else, Ali?” my father asked.

“Not a thing. And I really did some digging,” Lane, himself, said as he walked out of the house closely followed by Ron Lang.

“I thought...” I began but gasped when I saw Ron Lang and forgot what I was going to say. He gave me a nod and a brief smile, unsure of his welcome. As he should be. I fought the impulse to stand up and scream ‘Why is he here’?

Dad got up and found two more chairs. Ron helped him drag them over.

Lane bent to give Abby a hug. “I see you made me those appetizers I love,” he teased, looking at the enormous tray. “Did you make some for the others?”

Abby smiled. “How’s my favorite son-in law?”

Lane pulled up a chair between her and Ali. “Better. Now that I’m here.” He settled into the chair and began filling his plate. “I’m starving.” He picked up the bottle of Argiano and looked at Abby. “Ah, you knew I was coming.”

Abby smiled.

Ron squeezed in between Dad and Penny. Someone mentioned he’d been at the funeral. Now he’s sitting across the table from me acting as though his being here is no big deal.

“Miss Amhurst has never been in trouble,” Lane said. “Not even a speeding ticket.”

“She doesn’t hang out with the DC set?” I asked.

“Nope,” Lane said, around a mouthful of chicken salad. He reached for the crackers. He grabbed a bottle of water out of the ice bucket and tossed another one across the table to Ron.

“She lives in Durango, Colorado?” I asked.

Lane nodded.

"Do you have an address?"

Lane grinned. "Do bears sleep in the woods?"

"Who sleeps in the woods?" Riley Grace asked, as she joined us. "Sounds like fun!"

I haven't had a chance to talk to her since her blow up at Bamboo Cru. Her mood seemed better, which probably had something to do with Bronc. She came home long after we did, hung out with us in the kitchen for a bit, then went up to her room. I figured we'd seen the last of her. She'd traded her black dress for cutoff sweats and an over-sized sweatshirt. She was still barefooted. I wondered if she knew where she'd left my black heels. Most of her hair was pulled up into a messy bun.

"Bears," Ali said. "Bears sleep in the woods."

"Of course," Riley Grace quipped. "Why would you be discussing anything but carnivores after a funeral?" She leaned between Penny and Ron and scooped up a handful of Goldfish. "Oh, yay, Goldfish. Hi, Mr. Lang," she added breezily, seeing Ron. She came around the table, hugged Lane, and grabbed some grapes.

"I think bears are omnivores," Ron said.

"We were talking about Sable Amhurst," Jackson said.

Riley Grace idolized her dad. I don't want his image tarnished. I'm not stupid enough to think she hasn't read the paper or seen the news. Still, I dislike discussing Sable Amhurst in front of her. My father didn't pick up on that.

" Sable?" Riley Grace flopped into a chair. "What about her?"

"How she knew your father," Ali explained. "Why they were friends."

Riley Grace's brow wrinkled in confusion. "Through Ridge, of course.." Unaware of our sudden interest, she tossed a grape high in the air and caught it in her mouth. She finally noticed we were all staring at her. "What?"

"How did Ridge know her, Dear?" Penny asked.

"Good grief! Sable is Ridge's fiancé." She looked around the table, her gaze resting on me. "You don't know that? How do you not know that, Mom?"

Everyone started talking at once. They all stared at me.

"Ridge is engaged?" I stammered.

"Do you live on another planet?" Riley Grace swallowed another grape. "Sable is all Ridge has talked about for months."

She shifted her weight and sat cross-legged in the chair.

"Ridge is engaged?" Penny asked.

"I already said that." I felt like an idiot.

Riley Grace scrutinized the blue polish on her toes as though she'd never seen it before. She sighed dramatically. Nobody can get as much into a sigh as Riley Grace.

"I guess he is. It's been like a soap opera. Ridge bought her a honkin' huge diamond. But Dad thought Sable was a distraction and Ridge was losing focus. They had a huge blowup about it. Dad and Ridge, not Ridge and Sable." She paused. While she thought about it, she tossed a goldfish in her mouth and chewed. "But maybe Ridge and Sable, too," she added. "They broke up. She's older than he is. Sable had a problem with their age difference. Ironically Ridge didn't care. It's just two years. It's not like she's drawing Social Security. Anyway, Sable gave the ring back, but now she's wearing it again..."

"Blowup? Who had a blowup? Ridge and Sable?" I should have kept my mouth shut. I looked worse by the minute.

Riley Grace sighed and rolled her eyes. "Ridge and Dad. I told you, Mom."

Grant hadn't talked to me about any of this. And when did Riley Grace start using words like 'ironically' and 'carnivores' in sentences?

Riley Grace's expression indicated I should be institutionalized as soon as possible.

"Dad thought Ridge didn't play well when Sable was at his matches. Sable broke up with him. Ridge was crushed."

"But they made up?" Ali asked.

"Guess so." Riley Grace exhaled another of her overly dramatic sighs. "He hasn't starved to death yet and he wouldn't eat when they were estranged."

Estranged? Did she just say estranged? I reached for the wine bottle.

Riley Grace tossed another grape into the air and caught it in her mouth. I started to tell her to eat grapes like a normal person, but I was tempted to see if I could do it.

"What else should we know?" Lane pulled a notebook from his pocket and began taking notes. "I've been looking for info in the wrong place."

"Sable was scared of some guy she worked with." Riley Grace got up. "Ridge had been trying to help her," she added over her shoulder on her way back into the house.

I felt like Rip Van Winkle just waking up. Where've I been?

Riley Grace returned with a can of cola and a fat slice of chocolate cake. I was on the brink of saying something about too much sugar this close to bedtime, but did I really want to lose another skirmish? I let it go.

"Have you met her?" I asked when she sat back down.

"Met who?" Unaware we were hanging on her every word, she'd already forgotten the conversation. She bit into the cake. Crumbs fell on her shirt.

"Sable."

"Of course, Mom. She was at most of Ridge's matches, taking pictures." Riley Grace glanced at me. "You've never met Sable?"

The question hung in the air. Everyone looked at me. Ali raised an eyebrow. I hate when she does that, but I get it. What kind of mother doesn't know her son is engaged and even worse, has never met the girl of his dreams?

"Well, I, of course... surely I have," I said, desperately trying to remember when.

Riley Grace rearranged things on the small table beside her chair to make space for her cola can. She glanced up at me and bit into the cake, smearing frosting across her chin like when she was five.

"Sable is really into photography. She took the picture of Ridge on the Yonex poster."

"She did?" I asked weakly.

"Have you seen her work, Gracie?" Ali asked.

Riley Grace nodded, inspected her frosting-smeared fingers, and wiped at the frosting on her chin with the back of her hand. "Sable has a good eye. She sees things other people don't. Some of her photos are on her Facebook page."

We all stared at her, but she was back to tossing grapes into her mouth and oblivious. "If you wanted to know about Sable, why didn't you ask me? I can find out anything you want to know."

Good question. Everyone at the table was wondering the same thing. I had no idea she knew Sable. But I might have if I had ever sat down and had a conversation with her. Ali and Lane were both looking at me. This would have been so much simpler if I had known my son was engaged.

"Are you Facebook friends?" Ali asked.

"Of course."

"How did Ridge meet her?" Lane asked.

"I think on a plane," Riley said, licking frosting from her fingers.

"Do you know why your dad was in Colorado driving Sable's car?" Lane asked.

"No clue." Riley Grace shrugged.

She saw nothing unusual about Grant being in Colorado with Sable. Why had I bothered to shelter her from gossip?

"How are you, April?" Ron Lang asked, seeing a need to change the subject.

"What?" I stared at him. Did he just ask that? I wanted to say, 'Well, let's see.... My husband—the man I love more than my next breath, the father of my children—died in a car wreck with a woman whose identity, until now, was the world's best kept secret. The media is camped in my front yard and I can't go out in public. I seem to have misplaced my son who I didn't even know was engaged. And...you...the guy who swore he'd love me forever dumped me in the middle of college mid-term exams with no explanation, shattering my heart into a million pieces that I still haven't found, waltzed into my house, and is sitting across from me pretending to care how I am. I didn't say any of that, but I'm scared I still might.

I shrugged. "Oh, you know."

"I do," he said not breaking eye contact.

"No," I said more forcefully than I intended, "You don't. You have *no* idea."

Totally unaware of my anger, Penny said "Yes, he does, Dear. He lost his wife."

I wanted to scream, "No he doesn't! His wife wasn't Grant! Not the same thing!" I glanced at Abby. Watching me closely, she gave her head a small shake. Abby is the only one who knew what that breakup did to me. I was living with her. She took me to doctors, got me on medication, and went with me to counseling sessions. I wasn't the only one afraid of what I might say.

Chapter Sixteen
Riley Grace

What is going on with my mother? Even before she drank two glasses of wine, she made no sense. Now, she's sloshing the third glass all over everything. Am I the only one who noticed how bizarre this is? We're trying to have a normal conversation and she keeps asking stupid questions. Grownups are weird!. It's like they hit 40 and their brain turns to Jell-o. Why isn't Gramps getting her a straitjacket or something?

Alise would say I'm not extending grace to my mother. Another one of my shortcomings, evidently. But I don't know what that means and I'm pretty sure Alise doesn't either. She heard it in church.

Up to now, I've been so upset about Dad, I haven't thought much about Sable. In all the newspaper accounts Sable was just 'the other person in the car'. No wonder Ridge looked like Tyler Mane in "Halloween". He lost Dad *and* Sable. I don't know how he even ties his Adidas or remembers to brush his teeth. If this morning was any indication, he isn't.

I really liked Sable. She never treated me like I was Ridge's little sister the way his other girlfriends had. When I talked to her, she zeroed in on me with those big melty Hershey bar eyes.

I loved her laugh. I'll never hear it again. Just as a fat tear slid down my face, Ali turned around to look for me.

"Hey, you. Why are you so quiet back there?" she asked. "Oh, no! Your eyes are leaking again. What's going on?"

I brushed at the tear with the sleeve of my sweatshirt. "Just thinking about Sable. And Ridge. He lost two people."

"So, I'm the only one in the family who has never met Sable?" Mom demanded.

Oh great. She's back to that. She looked around the table, then looked back at me. I took a deep breath, knowing whatever I said would be wrong.

Like me, everyone waited for her to realize that it was seriously weird that she hadn't known Sable existed before the wreck. I was in no hurry to point that out. She needed someone to nail her anger to. Her gaze swept around the table and landed on me. I sighed.

"Okay," she demanded. "If Sable was so important to Ridge, why wasn't she here Christmas? With our family. Tell me that!"

Wow! She's really buzzed. I had been sitting here minding my own business almost feeling sorry for her. I'd cut her some slack for ignoring me since Dad died. Okay, not really. But I tried. I gulped.

"Ridge wasn't here, Mom," I said slowly and carefully because my words wanted to come out fast. And loud. I watched expressions chase across her face. She should have stopped the wine two glasses ago.

"Not here? At Christmas? Well, Of course, he was!" She stopped and stared at me, trying desperately to remember. She blinked and her expression changed. "Well, I know that!" She said, finally remembering. "He went skiing."

"Right. At Telluride. With Sable."

"Oh." Her eyes widened.

"You don't know that because *you* weren't here at Christmas either."

"Yes I was! I was busy. All three restaurants were jammed. If I'd been triplets, I couldn't have kept up with it all." She laughed nervously, licked her lips, and looked around the table for support. "Christmas parties..."

Everyone at the table watched the drama unfold, silently.

I stood up. "Exactly, Mom. You weren't here. Dad and I took in a couple of movies, played chess, ate take-out Chinese. Pretty much like the last three Christmases." I took a deep breath. I knew what I was going to say was mean. I tried to bite it back. "It was Dad's last Christmas, Mom. You missed it." Oh, darn. I'd be sorry tomorrow, but right now it felt good. "Goodnight, everyone," I said. I scooped up a handful of goldfish and made a dramatic departure.

Chapter Seventeen

April

The clock blinked 5:30 AM. Who would be playing tennis this early? Praying it was Ridge, I jumped out of bed and raced to the windows in time to see Lane slam a serve into Riley Grace's side of the court. She returned it easily.

Though I doubted coffee would stay down, I made my way to the kitchen. Mostly from habit I turned on the Keurig. While it heated, I rummaged in the cabinet for something, anything, to stop the jack-hammer attack on my head. I slumped into a chair at the breakfast table in an alcove off the kitchen. A bank of windows overlooks the tennis court. I watched the match.

Last night I'd been too tipsy to be affected by what Riley Grace said. But in the middle of the night I woke up thinking about it and what she'd said at Bamboo Cru. While I don't see things the way she does, she is obviously hurt. We need to talk. Soon.

Ali came into the kitchen, made herself a cup of coffee and brought me one, too. Unlike me, she was already dressed. She stood at the window for a few minutes before she sat down. "Lane has his hands full," she said. "Gracie is running him all over the court."

She sipped her coffee, then turned her attention to me. "Ooooh, you don't look so good."

"I feel even worse," I groaned. "I'm never touching wine again."

"You were going at it heavy last night. You're entitled. It's been a rough week."

"Why are you dressed?" I asked.

"Lane has an early flight. I'm taking him to the airport. Before I forget, you had a call from Barber Brothers Jewelry. You had already left for the church. Evidently Grant had ordered something. It's ready."

"That's strange," I said, thinking out loud. "I'll call them."

Ali went to the fridge for cream. She scooped some into her coffee and looked at me, her face a question.

I shook my head.

The back door opened. Riley Grace came in and snatched a couple of cookies off the bar with one hand. She waved in our direction with the other.

"I'm gonna shower," she announced on her way to the stairs.

"I need one, too," Lane said. But instead of following her through the kitchen, he got a bottle of water from the fridge and joined us. "That girl is tough," he said, as he lowered himself into a chair beside Ali. "Who's her coach?"

"Ridge."

Lane gulped down half the water and lowered the bottle. "April, this is taking nothing away from Ridge, but Riley Grace has as much raw talent as he does. I'd put her up against anyone. Is she competing?"

"Not really," I said. "The coach at her school was decent ..."

"If she was my daughter, I'd find someone who could get her into some matches."

Lane blotted the sweat on his forehead with the towel draped around his neck. "I know Ridge is the golden boy, but Grant might have pushed the wrong kid."

I blinked. "Seriously?"

Ali looked at Lane. "What time do you need to be at the airport?"

"I have a couple of hours. I probably smell like three-day roadkill, but before I hit the shower, April, there's something we need to discuss."

I set down my coffee mug and gave him my full attention.

"I didn't want to tell you last night. Too many people around."

My heart lurched and missed a beat. "Ridge?"

Lane shook his head.

"Grant's ashes?"

"Yeah. Grant's body, I know you've been upset about not having the ashes yet, so I checked into it. He hasn't been cremated."

"What? Why not? I could still see his body?"

"April, you don't want to see his body." Lane laid his hand over mine. "You met my friend, Larry, at our wedding. He's like 007. He can hack into anyone's computer system. Thank goodness he works for our government. I wanted to know why the coroner won't release Grant's body, so I got Larry on it." Lane tossed the empty water bottle in the trash, got up and went to the fridge for another.

"The coroner's report indicates he found a bullet in the body. Grant was dead before the car left the road."

Too shocked to even form a question, I just stared.

Ali didn't have that problem. "So, it's become a murder investigation?"

"Right." Lane drained that bottle, tossed the empty plastic in the trash, and got up to get another.

"Why don't you get two this time?" Ali asked.

"The highway patrol officer investigating the case, found bullet holes in Sable's car yesterday," Lane said from the kitchen. "He must be good. I've seen pictures. Not much left of that car."

"Murder?" I echoed, finally able to speak. "Who would want to kill Grant?"

"Any number of people. Senators make enemies, you know." Lane returned to the table with two bottles. "But I don't think the perp was after Grant."

"Sable?" Ali asked.

"She must have been the target. She called 911."

"What did she say?" I asked, finally finding my voice.

"She told the dispatcher someone was chasing them." Lane twisted the cap off a bottle and drained half of it. "It's a miracle she could get through. Cell coverage is iffy in those mountains. She identified herself, gave their location, but got cut off. She was frantic when she called back. The dispatcher heard enough to know someone was shooting."

"Could Sable see who it was?" Ali asked.

"She knew who it was. Said his name was Brett Nelson. He drove a white Pathfinder."

Ali and I looked at each other. "He's after Ridge!" Suddenly I couldn't breathe.

"Do you know who he is?" Lane asked me.

I shook my head, unable to speak.

"Ridge's neighbor told us someone had been at Ridge's apartment pounding on his door." Ali explained. "He was driving a white Pathfinder."

Lane leveled a look at me. "How much do you want to know?"

"Everything," I said. But did I really? My stomach felt like a bowling ball dropped into it. I thought I might throw up.

Lane gazed out the window, buying time as he thought. "Okay. Nelson is a pilot for the airlines Sable works for. Worked for. She filed a harassment complaint against him three months ago. His wife's family is rolling in dough. I don't know why he's even working. She's from old money. We make money. She has money. Big difference."

"How do you know all this?" I asked. "Larry again?"

Lane nodded. "He's an ace. He's been tracking Nelson's phone. It pinged off a tower in Norman. You already knew he'd been there. It pinged off a tower near the church the day of the funeral."

Lane watched a water droplet forge a track down the side of his bottle. He looked up at me, his gaze measuring my reaction. Waiting for me to catch up. I did.

"Nelson was at Grant's funeral? Why?" I couldn't think. "Oh, no! Looking for Ridge!" I wrapped both arms around myself and rocked back and forth.

"Do you want to hear more?" Lane asked.

I nodded.

"Nelson' cell pinged off a tower near the wreck site. At the reported time of the wreck. So did Ridge's."

"No!" I stopped rocking and looked at him. Ridge was playing tennis in Florida."

"Evidently not. Ridge was at the wreck site most of that night."

"Ohmygosh."

"Ridge's phone pinged off the same cell tower around the same time Nelson's did. Ridge knows Nelson is after him. He's trying to keep Nelson away from his family."

I looked at Ali. "Can you stay with Riley Grace another day?"

"As long as you need me. Where are you going?"

"Colorado."

"No you're not." Lane shook his head. "April, that's not a good idea."

"I have to find my son! I need to see where my husband died. The Highway Patrol has been giving me the run around."

"I know you too well to try to talk you out of going." Lane looked at me intently.

"I'll go with you tomorrow. I have to be in DC today."

"I have to find Ridge!"

Lane swiped a hand across his day-old beard and exhaled forcefully through splayed fingers. "Okay. I'll see if I can pull some strings and get you on a plane. Look for Ridge and go to the wreck site if you must, but do *not* talk to the Highway Patrol until I get there tomorrow. Got that?"

"I won't. Promise."

"I mean it, April. Do not talk to the CHP without me! You can't know anything I just told you. If you slip, they'll be on you like flies on dung. Larry would be serving a pesky prison sentence, which would make him cranky.

I nodded, hoping my expression was properly meek.

"I have enough on my plate without having to fix your messes. Do nothing until I get there. Got it?"

"I won't," I muttered. "I should be offended."

Lane gave me a long level look, as if sizing up a boxing opponent.

"I said I won't do anything. I won't. I swear."

"Ali, I wish you could go with her to make sure she stays out of trouble, but you really need to be here." Lane's fingers drummed out a beat on the table as he thought. "Right now, I need to get in the shower and get to the airport." Lane tossed his empty plastic bottles in the trash and grabbed another from the fridge on his way out.

"Thank you, Lane, You won't regret this."

"I already do," he said.

Chapter Eighteen

April

I stashed my carryon in the overhead. and settled in my aisle seat. A man seated by the window was reading a paper and didn't lower it as I settled in. Good. The stodgy silent type. I usually wear headphones on planes to discourage boring conversation. I might not need them today and, hopefully, the middle seat would stay vacant.

I pulled out my cell and called Riley Grace. I hadn't talked to her since she stomped off to her room last night. She'd already been asleep when I looked in on her. She'd seemed to be in a better mood this morning, but she's seventeen. I never know.

"Hi, Mom," she said. Sounding cheerful. "What's up?"

"Hi, just wanted to let you know I'm on a plane. They're still boarding."

"You're on a plane? Where are you going?"

"Colorado."

"When did you decide that?"

"This morning."

"Why are you going to Colorado?"

"To stage a one-woman sit-in at the Colorado Highway Patrol office. Until I get some answers. And I want to see the wreck site."

"You're looking for Ridge, aren't you?"

I hesitated, choosing my words carefully. "Well, yes." I took a deep breath. "But I have a good reason. Riley Grace, can we sit down and have a long talk when I get home?

There was a long silence. ""About what?"

"Just talk. You keep saying we never talk."

"I guess."

"You just rolled your eyes, didn't you?" I accused.

"I did not."

"Yes, you did. I heard it in your voice."

A man, possibly once a sumo wrestler, bulldozed his way down the aisle. As my eyes followed his progress, I prayed, "Please, Lord, don't let this be his seat." I looked around. There weren't many vacant seats.

He stopped beside me, looked at the seat number and checked his ticket. Satisfied the empty seat beside me was his, he began stowing his carryon in the storage bin. He knocked out an empty Yeti which bounced off my head and down the aisle. He lumbered after it, captured it and stashed it back into the compartment. No apology.

I gasped as he wedged his way past me to his seat.

"Mom?" Riley Grace said. "What's wrong? You aren't having a stroke are you?"

I'd almost forgotten I held a phone to my ear. "No. Someone just stomped on my foot," I said, into the Sumo's massive backside.

He forced his super-sized body into his under-sized seat, which required a great deal of maneuvering and grunting. He began shoving a bulging backpack under the seat in front of him. It didn't fit. He picked it up and pulled things out. We were too packed in for him to be so busy. He held up a long sleeve shirt and tried to pull it on over his head. He'd be getting on my nerves even if I wasn't stressed to the max, he hadn't stomped on my foot, dropped a Yeti on my head, and just elbowed my ear.

"Is your foot broken?" Riley Grace asked.

I looked down. "Maybe not. Where are you?"

"I had a match with the coach. Now I'm at Alise's house."

"Why don't you guys go to our house? Ali is there by herself."

"Okay. Can Bronc come?"

"Bronc is there?"

"Yeah. Can he? I want Ali to get to know him."

"He met Ali at Bamboo Cru." We both knew that was beside the point.

"Mom." How can she inject so much disdain and syllables into a one syllable word? The girl should be on Broadway. Maybe she will be someday. And make enough money so her poor mom can retire. From what? What would I retire from? How much money is enough?

"Mom!"

"Yes," I sighed. We'll talk about this when I get home."

"Talk about what?"

"I don't know. My head hurts, my foot hurts, and I'm too tired to think... "

"You're hungover," she snapped.

Bye, Riley Grace. Love you..."

She was already gone.

Grant died under very strange circumstances leaving me to deal with the press, a missing son, and a hormonal daughter. I felt lost, abandoned, out of control. Like I'm trapped in someone else's life. I glanced at sumo. If only I was in somebody else's seat.

My phone vibrated. The text was from Riley Grace.

Riley Grace: *Sorry Mom. (4 crying emojis) Love you (4 emoji hearts, a giraffe, and a penguin.)*

I texted a reply, a kissy face and three hearts. Sometimes emojis say it all.

The flight attendant stopped by to ask if I needed anything. Her smile didn't reach her eyes.

"May I have a glass of wine?" I asked. "A white Zin, maybe?"

"As soon as we're in the air and leveled out, I'll be around with the drink cart."

"Oh, not until then? I really need it now. I don't want to be a pain, but..."

"She can't help it." Mr. Newspaper in the window seat lowered his paper, folded it, leaned around Sumo Wrestler and grinned. Ron Lang. "She probably needs the wine in an IV," he added.

"What are you doing here?" I demanded.

"You might want to cut her off after one glass," Ron told the flight attendant. "She doesn't hold alcohol well and she's still hungover from last night." The second person to point that out.

"I am not!" Just saying it made my head hurt.

"I'm surprised someone didn't have to pour you onto the plane."

"Why are you here?" I repeated.

"I'm visiting my cousin in Durango."

"You don't have a cousin in Durango! This man doesn't have a cousin in Durango," I announced to the flight attendant who looked like she wanted to be anywhere but here.

"Throw him off the plane!" I demanded. I might have pointed toward the door.

She gave me a frazzled smile and leaned across me. "Fasten your seatbelt, Sir," she said to Mr. Sumo.

"Can't," he said. "It seems skimpy." He pulled it out to full length to show her.

"I'll get you an extension." She hurried away.

"You might consider bungy cords," I said to her back.

She soon returned with the extension and a glass of wine. She gave him the extension and slipped the wine to me. "I'm not supposed to do this until we're in the air," she whispered, "but it appears you are going to need it."

Ron began trying to help with the seat belt extension.

I leaned forward and glared at Ron. "Lane sent you to spy on me!"

"Not spy *per se*." Ron grinned. "You're lucky I could get away on such short notice."

"Just stay away from me," I huffed and flounced back in my seat.

The flight attendant reappeared. "You have an emergency call, Mr. Lang. You can take it on the phone by the cockpit." She led the way.

He was back in a few minutes, looking grim.

"Who was that?" I asked as he settled into his seat.

"Lane."

"What did he say? The attendant said it was an emergency. What emergency? Are your kids ok? Are my kids ok?"

"I'll tell you later."

"Who isn't ok?"

"April, drink your wine. And shut up!"

"Is she your wife?" The Sumo asked Ron.

"Hell, no," Ron said.

"I can see why you don't want to sit by her." The Sumo nodded knowingly. "I used to have one like that." He looked me over, sizing me up. "Kind of pretty if you go for the bitchy scrawny type. High maintenance. Not worth the drama."

"Tell me about it," Ron sighed.

Chapter Nineteen
Ridge

The days bled painfully into a week. And then another. Things that ruled my life before the wreck don't matter now. I should be in school but I'm not interested in studying for exams. Or tennis. Every idle thought used to be about improving my game. Now, I can't form a thought. Dad had been my anchor, keeping me grounded. He had been my rudder, keeping me moving in the right direction. Sable had been my guiding light. Without them, I'm moving in aimless circles. Nothing matters. Yonex threatened to withdraw sponsorship. I don't blame them. I don't care.

I made my way back to my car, opened the door, and stared at the teddy bear sprawled in the back seat. I reached in, picked it up, and held it against me. It was surprisingly soft and cushy. Perfect for a tiny baby. Sable had bought it after she discovered she was pregnant.

I glanced over at the two wooden crosses someone had erected beside the broken guardrail. Probably Sable's mother and sister. I laid the teddy bear gently against them. I should leave.

Back in the Forester, I stared through the bug-splattered windshield, keys in hand. Where would I go? This terrible place where Dad and Sable lost their lives had a hold on me, drawing me back every time I tried to leave. I feel Sable's presence here. So I keep returning to this spot.

I leaned back, closed my eyes, and thought about my showdown with Brett Nelson. I'd just walked into the BWI concourse when I noticed the heated argument in a corner between a man and a woman, both in airline uniforms. One of her hands, raised in the air, was balled into a fist. The grip he had on her wrist looked painful. I'd like to think I would've intervened if she hadn't been beautiful, but I know me. She glanced in my direction, I saw her fear and acted before thinking.

"Oh, there you are darling," I said, changing my direction. I plastered a big grin on my face.

Her expression changed from fear to surprise. She watched me approach.

"Who in the hell are you?" the guy growled.

Ignoring him, I winked at her. I draped my arm casually across her shoulders and pulled her close. From this angle, I could only see part of her name tag.

"I couldn't find you, Sybil. Your directions weren't clear, Darling."

"Her name isn't Sybil, you idiot," the dude snarled. "Get the hell out of here."

I dropped a kiss on the top of her head near the cute little airlines cap. "She's my little Sibbypoo. Let go of her arm." I looked down at her. "Darling, have you never mentioned me?"

She frowned and for a minute, I feared they both might kill me. Sanity rushed in and I realized she might not want me in the middle of whatever this was. But beneath my arm her shoulders shook.

"This doesn't concern you." The guy glared at me. "Beat it, Buddy."

"I'm pretty sure it does, *Buddy*," I said. "Your hands are on my girl. Back off!"

Still glaring at him, I kissed the side of her head near her ear. "Just go with it," I whispered.

"Do you know this guy?" he asked, through gritted teeth.

She gave me a weak smile. It wobbled and slipped out of place.

"You're late...uh, Sweetie," she said.

"Your directions weren't clear." My arm tightened around her as I gave her what I hoped was a reassuring hug and leveled a gaze at him. "Turn loose of her arm!"

"Leave while you can," he growled, "or you'll be picking teeth out of your tonsils."

I grinned. Who was this doofus?

She shot me a terrified glance.

I eyed him speculatively. He was probably a pilot. He'd spent a lot of time squinting into the sun. His hair, more silver than blond, was cut in a short military style. Deep lines around his eyes were made deeper by the fierce scowl he aimed at me. I guessed him to be fiftyish. He was shorter than I, but stockier. Fit, not fat. Which, now that I'm thinking clearly, made me glad Dad insisted on martial arts to improve my balance and agility. I could take this dude, but did I really want to show up at my tennis match with a black eye, and according to him, toothless?

He was sizing me up, too.

"Look," I said, "I didn't catch your name. I'm sure you're terribly important. But you aren't real smart or you wouldn't still be holding her arm. You're wearing a wedding band. I'm guessing your wife isn't going to be too happy about seeing your arrest on the 5:00 o'clock news. Come to think of it, an airport brawl isn't going to look good on your pilot's resume either. If I were you, I'd drop her arm. Now!"

My eyes narrowed. I took a step toward him. I was through playing around with this dip stick. I'm going to have to whip his ass.

He dropped her arm and stepped back.

She rubbed circulation back into her wrist. When I saw the red marks his fingers had left, my jaw tightened. I took another step forward. I wanted to knock his head off.

He saw the rage in my eyes and stepped back.

"I suggest—*Buddy*," I said, "you keep your hands off. My. Girl." With my arm still around her shoulders, I turned her, and we walked away.

"Where are we going?" I asked when we were out of earshot.

"I don't know about you. I'm going to the lady's room." Her voice shook. "I just got off a six-hour flight with no time for a potty break." She glanced behind us to make sure he was gone before shrugging out from under my arm. "You were going to fight him to protect someone you don't even know."

"Bullies like him are usually all talk," I said.

"I wouldn't count on that." She sneaked a nervous peek behind her. She stopped in front of the women's restroom. I moved her out of the path of a woman with a large red suitcase and toddler in tow. She bore down on us with the urgency of a frazzled mother.

I looked down into her huge brown eyes. Now that I had the chance to see her, I realized this girl was easily the most beautiful female on the planet. On any planet. She had a dimple near the corner of her mouth. I gulped air to make sure I could still breathe.

"Nobody ever stands up to him," she said as if talking to herself. She gazed into the distance. "He's some big-deal war hero. The airline thinks he walks on water. He gets by with stuff that nobody else would. " She looked back at me. "Thank you."

Her lips were perfect. I couldn't tear my eyes from them as she formed the words. I had no idea what she'd just said.

"I'll stick around in case he's not gone," I said, grateful I didn't have a connecting flight. "Do you have time to have a drink with me?"

She tilted her head as she thought. "Yes," she said, finally. "But right now," she motioned toward the restroom, "I gotta go."

"Do you want to leave that with me?" I asked, reaching for the small carryon she'd been towing.

She shook her head. "Be out in a minute. By the way, if you ever call me "Sibbypoo" again, you really will be picking teeth out of your tonsils." She backed toward the restroom. "I can't believe you weren't scared of him."

I lifted my hands in surrender. "I'm more scared of you."

She laughed.

Elated that I might have an opportunity to call her anything again, I walked across the concourse so I wouldn't be loitering outside the ladies' room and leaned against the wall. I've met the girl of my dreams. And she has spunk.

She went in looking like a super model and came out five minutes later looking like the gorgeous girl next door. She'd exchanged her uniform and heels for jeans, a plain T-shirt, and sandals. Her dark hair, free from the updo under her airline cap draped around her shoulders. Her face scrubbed free of makeup, looked fresh. Young. She scanned the crowd, smiling when she spotted me. She hadn't expected me to be here. That smile said she was glad I stayed.

We met in the middle of the concourse.

"Do you fly into BWI often?" she asked.

"Relatively," I said. "My dad is a senator. But today I'm here for a tennis match."

"That explains the racquet sticking out of your backpack. I thought maybe you carried it to pick up chicks."

I grinned. "Well, that hasn't worked."

"It's blue. Is it a Yonex?"

"Yeah. You know something about tennis."

"I know Yonex racquets are expensive," she said. "Are you wealthy or something?"

"They're my sponsor."

She looked up at me, blinked, and stopped walking. "Oh! You're Ridge Frazier."

"Yeah." I adjusted my backpack.

"I've seen you play on TV. Are you as good as everyone says?"

"Probably not. I'm working on it." We continued walking.

"You're not stuck up," she tilted her head as she looked up at me. "I think it would be hard not to be cocky with all the hype you're getting."

I thought about it. "I pretty much ignore everything. You can't ride high on good press or you'll crash and burn when they turn on you. And they will. Are you into tennis?"

"I'm into photography. I go to a lot of matches. Tennis is good for action shots."

"Have you been to any of mine?" I asked.

"Not yet." She smiled. For a moment I couldn't breathe. Little girls are born knowing that smile will wrap guys around their pinky finger

"Where are we going?" she asked, allowing me to lead the way.

"Phillips," I said, angling toward the escalator. "They have a killer Bloody Mary. Right now, I could use one,"

She nodded. “Good choice. The garnish is practically a salad.”

I nodded. “My mom will be proud I had veggies. Olives are a veggie, right?”

Her nose wrinkled as she thought. “They might be a fruit.”

“Phillips’ crab cakes are the best anywhere,” I said.

“You’re a crab cake connoisseur?” She peered up at me with those big eyes again.

My stomach did another somersault. Nobody has ever had this effect on me.

“Actually, I am. I’ve rated crab cakes in five countries and most states.”

She smiled. “We can discuss what makes a crab cake perfect while we eat them.”

We’ll be discussing more than that. I want to know why that bozo had his hands on her.

“Let’s order calamari, too. And maybe a shrimp cocktail,” I said.

I waited for her to step onto the escalator and stepped on behind her. Her hair smelled like strawberries and coconut.

“I am so relieved.” She turned and flashed that dimple.

“Why?” I asked.

“I’d never have a fake boyfriend who didn’t like seafood.

By the way, I’m Sable Amhurst.”

Chapter Twenty

Ridge

I sobbed, gasping for breath. Tears poured down my face. I leaned back in the seat and closed my eyes to block the pain. It didn't work. Sable had screamed my name when Dad had been shot. But she hadn't screamed all the way down. I'd been too traumatized to wonder why. Until now. The day I met her, I'd rescued her from Brett Nelson, but in the end he won. I couldn't save her or Dad. Not sure I can save myself.

I opened my eyes and checked the time. I'd been sitting here for three hours. Messages from Rye. No words. Praying hands, hearts, crying emojis. Her emojis touched me more than words.

I found half a sack of peanuts on the console, poured them into my hand, got out of the Forester, and tossed the peanuts to the chipmunk. We've become old friends. I'd named him Mortimer. I have no idea why.

I walked down the road along the guardrail. The sun had climbed higher and was shining from a different angle. The rays bounced off something shiny wedged in between some rocks on a ledge below. Not really a ledge, an overhang of rocks. I moved closer. The something was bright red. Sable's phone! That phone had a treasure of pictures. Nelson's threats were recorded on that phone. Along with the frantic 9-1-1 calls Sable had made that night. I had to reach that phone.

Dad made sure I always had blankets, a rope, a flashlight, extra batteries, jumper cables, bungee cords, a knife, water, and cat litter in case I got stuck in snow. And a hammer in case I went off the road into water and the electric system failed. Hopefully, those things wouldn't happen at the same time.

There was an aspen sturdy enough to hold my weight directly behind me. I went to the Forester for the rope. I'm going to be doing a bit of rappelling.

Chapter Twenty-One

April

"Why did we land in Dumas instead of Denver?" I demanded.

"Durango. You'd be in the wrong state. Riley Grace does that, too," Ron said.

"Does what?"

"Rattles off names of places whose only connection is they start with the same letter. Stand there and keep your mouth shut while I get the car," Ron ordered. He moved toward the rental window.

I seethed but didn't argue. As I watched him sign the rental contract, I wondered how he knows my daughter well enough to know she does that.

"Come on," he said, pocketing the keys and slinging his backpack over his shoulder.

With his other hand he picked up my carryon and started walking. He didn't look back.

"Where are we going?" I asked, hurrying to catch up.

"To the hotel. Lane said to get checked in before we do anything else."

My head throbbed with each step. I will never touch another glass of wine. "I don't need a babysitter. Especially, you!"

"Every time you open your mouth you prove you do."

"You didn't used to be so mean," I grumbled.

"You used to have some sense. Well, sometimes."

I bit back a reply. He had the rental car and hotel reservations. I didn't even know what state we were in. Apparently.

"There was no emergency. Lane just wanted to give you info on the car and reservations." I hurried to catch up. "Right?"

"Partially. There's more. This must be the Tahoe," he said, stopping beside a red SUV. He clicked open the back and slung our bags inside.

"Why did we need something this big?" I asked.

"Lane said it's all he could get with four-wheel drive."

"Why do we need four-wheel drive?"

Ron shrugged. "Lane leaves nothing to chance. I'm not questioning him."

I walked around to the passenger side and got in. "Tell me the rest of what he said."

"When we get on the road."

Ron adjusted the seat and mirrors while I found the controls for air. As provoked as I was by Ron and Lane's scheme, I was relieved. I don't do well when I don't know where I'm going, much less react quickly in traffic. Especially now. I probably shouldn't be driving. Or be alone. Even if that means I have to be with Ron.

"We'll go by the hotel, get registered, drop off the luggage, then head out to the accident site." He checked the rearview, then glanced at me for an indication I'd heard and wasn't going to argue.

I nodded.

"Lane said the road is dangerous if you're not familiar with it. Not safe in the daytime and worse in the dark," Ron explained as though reading my mind. "You can act like a spoiled brat if you have too, but things will go much easier if you don't. You need help right now, April."

"I don't need a keeper," I huffed. Although obviously, I do.

"I'm thinking about the safety of everyone else on this road," Ron glanced at me and winked. "I'm amazed that you can form a lucid thought. Although, you haven't shown much evidence of that lately."

"Funny," I grumbled. "Tell me what Lane said."

"I didn't get to the part about you being lucky people are willing to help."

"You're right. I promise to be more appreciative. What emergency?"

"It wasn't an emergency. Lane wanted us to know the authorities have Sable's phone with threatening voice messages and texts from Nelson. Now that they have proof he intended to kill Ridge and Sable, they've issued a warrant for his arrest. He's armed and dangerous. Lane warned us to be careful." Ron shook his head. "You wouldn't think someone in Nelson's position would be stupid enough to leave threats on a voicemail or text. He's lost it."

I was thinking about the armed and dangerous and looking-for-my-son part. He shot into a moving car from a moving car to kill Grant. He knew how to use a gun. "How did they get Sable's phone?" I asked.

"I don't know," Ron said.

"Yes, you do. If we're doing this, I need to know you're being honest."

Ron exhaled a long-drawn-out breath. Probably buying time while he considered.

"Okay," he said finally. "Ridge found it and brought it in."

"Ridge? My Ridge?"

He gave me an exasperated look. "How many Ridges do you know?"

"When?"

"Lane knew the CHP had it before we left Oklahoma City. So, before then."

"At least he was still alive this morning," I said. "So, there's that. I need one of those apps that tracks your kids. I'll be tracking Ridge when he's forty. Where do you suppose he is now?"

"If we don't know, hopefully Brett Nelson doesn't either."

"This is crazy. He shouldn't be a threat to Ridge now that the authorities know whatever it is that Ridge knows."

"April, Nelson had nothing against Grant. He thought Ridge was driving. He was after Sable and Ridge. Sable had filed harassment charges against Nelson," Ron said, readjusting the rearview mirror. "The airlines did nothing. The day before she died Sable had gone to the police. She filed rape charges. Ridge had been raising hell with the airlines over not protecting Sable. The other motive is revenge. Nelson and Ridge butted heads more than once over Sable."

"Sable had been raped? No! This man is a beast."

Ron nodded. "Now you know what Ridge is dealing with."

I thought about the pregnancy test I found in Ridge's bathroom. I'd originally been concerned that the baby was Grant's. But maybe it had been the result of rape. At any rate three people died in that wreck. If Nelson knew Sable was pregnant, it would be another motive for murder. Maybe.

"But why was Grant with Sable?" I wondered out loud. "Charges had already been filed. Wouldn't Nelson's wife know by now?"

“Maybe. Maybe not. Nelson’s way past thinking straight. We won’t know until we find Ridge. He was supposed to be with his team in Florida, right?”

“Right.”

“Was the tournament important?” Ron asked.

“Yes. They are all important. This one even more. Yonex was sending a photographer to get shots of Ridge playing with their new racquet. They were coming out with a big ad campaign and needed a big name to go with it. Yeah, it was important.”

“So, Grant would have insisted Ridge be in Florida, right?” Ron asked.

“Yes.”

“Did Grant know Sable had been raped?” Ron asked.

I thought about it before I answered. “Probably. Grant’s favorite beer was in Ridge’s refrigerator. Ridge doesn’t drink it. I think Sable had been there, too.”

“I’m guessing Grant told Ridge to go to Florida and he would help Sable.”

I nodded. “That’s exactly what would have happened. But help Sable do what?”

Ron changed lanes and slowed for the turn. “I don’t know. Here’s the hotel. I’ll get you settled in your room. You’ll want to freshen up before we head back out.”

“No. Let’s drop this stuff off and go,” I said. “I want to get this over with.”

Chapter Twenty-Two

April

Ron clutched the wheel as though an evil force tried to wrestle it from his grip. He's an experienced driver, but there are no roads like this in Oklahoma. Route 550, dubbed the widow-maker for good reason, wasn't the only source of his stress. He had no idea of what he would have to deal with at the wreck site. Namely me. He doesn't do well in situations when he doesn't know what to expect. Strange how I remember that now.

Sitting in the passenger seat clutching the wreath I'd picked up at a flower shop, I glanced out my window, grateful I wasn't driving. I stopped hating Ron long enough to be glad he was here.

Grant had been driving on this road. Late. The darkness would have made it more treacherous, but maybe less terrifying. At night he wouldn't have seen the depth of the gorge. Where had Grant and Sable been going?

"There aren't many guardrails," I observed. "There should be more guardrails."

"Snowplows couldn't clear the road. Snow would pile up. The hotel clerk said several snowplow drivers have died through the years. Evidently there are avalanches."

"Who," I asked, "would drive on this road in snow?"

"The people who need 'Remove baby before laundering' warning labels in baby clothes," Ron said as he slowed to the speed of the enormous travel trailer ahead.

"What happens when two RV's meet?" I asked.

Ron didn't answer and thankfully didn't try to pass.

"We should be getting close. I think it's right around the next curve. You sure you're up to this?" He shot me a worried glance.

"I have to see," I said. But even as I uttered the words, my stomach lurched. I'm an idiot for thinking I could have made this trip alone. I should tell him. But I won't.

"It's right here," Ron said. He eased the Tahoe off the road as far as possible. Tires crunched on gravel as we rolled to a stop. We were halfway off the road.

"Are you sure this is the right place?"

Ron nodded toward the jagged guardrail, set the parking brake and turned on the flashers. "You can't get out on your side. We're too close to the guard rail." He was right.

"Why is there one here," I asked, staring in horror where the car went through it.

"This is a particularly dangerous curve. Can you crawl over the console?"

I assessed the obstacle. Climbing over it wouldn't be something I'd even consider on any other occasion. I handed him the wreath. "Get out and turn around." I ordered.

I was wearing jeans. Still, crawling over the console would not be something I wished to turn into a spectator sport. It had been years since I took gymnastics. I gave it my best shot.

His back turned, Ron waited by the open door holding the wreath. The road was narrow. Traffic was sparse, but on a curve visibility was poor until cars, driving too fast, were on top of us.

I finally dominated the console and slid across the driver's seat. Ron handed me the wreath.

I followed him around the Tahoe in silence, inspecting the road for skid marks. There were none. No indication brakes had been applied. No sign that anything had happened at this peaceful scene at all. Except for the mangled guard rail.

The scent of pine filled the air. A chipmunk darted from beneath a root, stopping a couple of feet away. He regarded us with shoe-button eyes. Deciding we hadn't brought lunch, he returned to whatever important task our arrival had interrupted.

I stared at the wreath in my hands as though I'd never seen it. I'd had no trouble selecting the flowers. Grant loved sunflowers. I added yellow mums and wheat stalks. A masculine wreath. The wording on the burlap ribbon had been a different matter. I'd considered and rejected 'my darling', 'my forever love', or 'my heart'. Too over-the-top soppy. Grant would've laughed. It felt false. In contrast 'senator', 'husband', 'father', seemed too austere. In the end, because the flower shop lady expected a decision today, the ribbon said 'Grant'.

I spotted a teddy bear leaning against a shattered post beside two crosses. I remembered Sable had been pregnant. Who had brought the crosses and bear? Ridge? Sable's mother?

The thought of Sable's mother broke my heart. Tears dripped down my face. Her beautiful daughter, a life so full of promise, gone.

And Ridge. For the first time I considered what the loss of Sable would mean to my son. And the baby? If the baby was his, he would also be mourning the loss of his child, my grandchild. I lost my husband in the wreck. Ridge lost three people. His heart must be pulverized. No wonder he wasn't thinking straight. I cried for Sable's mother, my son, and myself. Ron stood by, giving me time to cry.

I wiped my eyes, blew my nose, stepped forward and leaned over the guardrail. I looked into the gorge in shock. I couldn't see the bottom. The ground dropped away at least four hundred feet. I had envisioned perpendicular rock walls going straight down. They didn't. Boulders the size of Dallas jutted out from both sides. The car would not have fallen straight down. It would have careened from boulder to boulder before coming to rest somewhere among the walls that lined the Animas river. My mind froze. I couldn't think.

The car was a convertible. Grant's phone could have flown out anywhere on the way down. Wherever it is, it had unanswered calls from me. Even after it sank into my brain that Grant was really dead, I had kept calling his phone. I pictured it ringing somewhere near his body. His wallpaper was a picture of Ridge holding a Wimbledon trophy. I imagined it lighting up when I called. The phone would be smashed into a million pieces as it bounced to the bottom of the gorge.

I glanced back at Ron, wondering if my horror was as visible in my eyes as the compassion I saw in his. He watched me, ready to take whatever action was required.

There is no way they could have survived. "How do you suppose they got them—out of there?" I wondered out loud.

"I have no idea." Ron shook his head.

"How—did—how on earth did—they remove the wreckage?"

Ron hesitated. "I don't know," he said. "It wasn't easy."

"Ridge was here that night?" I already knew the answer. But verbalizing it made it real. He must have stood where I was standing. There wasn't room to be anywhere else.

Ron nodded.

“How long was he here?”

“Most of the night.”

“Do you think he saw it happen?” I asked.

Ron’s face wore the pain I felt. “Probably.”

Ron had evidently seen a report I hadn’t. I wanted to ask but couldn’t form the question. I pictured my son standing here, knowing his father and Sable were down there with no way to save them—experiencing what I’m experiencing now. Times ten.

When I got the call from Riley Grace notifying me of Grant’s death, I’d been too shocked to cry. A few tears had leaked from my eyes at the funeral when Grant’s mom and brothers had arrived. But I’d had so much to do—announcements, a memorial service to plan, the trip to DC for the national memorial service. The avalanche of things needing to be done after a death. The things nobody gives a second thought to until it happens to them. I’d been too shocked to think or feel. The horror of that night had been shoved into a corner of my mind and held at bay. Now, those images broke through. A groan began somewhere deep inside, growing louder as it escaped. I howled. Like a wounded animal. I demanded to know why.

I sank to the ground barely feeling the gravel biting into knees. I couldn’t stop the torrent once it began. Ron knelt in front of me, wrapped his arms around me and held me. He murmured ”Moony”, an old nickname that only he had ever called me, in my ear. He soothed and rocked me as one would comfort a small child. Realizing he was sobbing with me, sharing my pain, I let him hold me. I have no idea what he said or how long we were there. I couldn’t breathe. Gasping for air, I kept sobbing, but eventually became aware of passing traffic, horns honking, and the danger the Tahoe presented parked halfway in the road.

Ron stood and pulled me up with him. My knees refused to hold me. He picked me up, carried me to the Tahoe, and eased me into the back seat.

“Can you breathe?” he asked.

I shook my head. I couldn’t catch my breath.

“We’ve got to get off this road,” he said, fastening my seat belt. “I’ll pull over when I can and move you up. You’re in no condition to crawl over that console. Can you talk?”

“I got snot. On your shirt,” I said.

“Okay,” he said, as he got into the front seat. “You can breathe.”

On the way to the hotel I wondered where I‘d left the wreath.

Chapter Twenty-Three

April

Concerned about leaving me alone, Ron walked me to my hotel room. I convinced him I'd be okay. And after a nap and a shower I felt better and gave him a call. He wanted to grab something to eat. I wasn't hungry but getting out for a while sounded better than sitting alone in this room. I dabbed makeup around my swollen eyes and tagged along looking like a tsunami survivor. Lane had suggested the Ore House and recommended the ribs. It was within walking distance of our hotel.

The restaurant's rustic interior was as inviting as it was interesting. It featured an elaborate Spanish antique bar which, I learned from the lady who seated us, required two flat railcars to deliver it to Durango. A stag with an enormous rack looked down on me from the wood-paneled wall with disdain in his glass eye. He had no right to judge me. My head wasn't the one hanging on a wall.

We chose a booth near the front. Despite not being hungry, I became ravenous as soon as I smelled the food. The waiter appeared with glasses of water and informed us that his name was Griffin. In case we couldn't read his name tag. He looked to be about Ridge's age.

Ron tore his attention away from the menu. "What kind of beer do you have?" he asked. "Anything local?"

"Several," Griffin said. "Would you like samples?"

"Yes. But we'd like to order first. The ribs?" Ron looked at me for confirmation.

I nodded.

"With baked potatoes," he continued. "What's your vegetable today?"

"Asparagus with a thyme aioli sauce," the waiter said.

"We'll have that. Does your salad have tomatoes?"

Griffin nodded as he jotted down our order.

"Hold the tomatoes on hers," Ron said. He raised a questioning brow.

I nodded.

I'd forgotten how he used to order for me. After all this time, he remembered I can't eat tomatoes. I should have been touched. Instead, anger burned in the pit of my stomach. For years that anger had flared at every mention of his name—which happened regularly. Ron has been our family attorney since the paint dried on his shingle. He and my dad stayed close after our breakup. Another thorn in my relationship with my dad.

"Did you ever love me?" I asked.

He blinked. "What? How can you even ask that?"

"I need to know if I've lived in the memory of a love that never was."

"April, you were my everything. You still..."

I cut him off and ignored the 'you still...' part intending to circle back around to that later. "Nobody ever just dumps their 'everything' with no explanation."

"April, that was twenty-six years ago. You really want to talk about it now? With all that's going on?"

“Twenty-seven years and three months. Damn straight I want to talk about it now. Why did you ghost me?”

I resisted the urge to throw my water glass at him. I realized I was yelling and lowered my voice. Too late. People at nearby tables stared, but their eyes slid away when I glared at them.

“I’m beginning to pick up on that.” Ron inhaled deeply and released the breath slowly. “Okay, here goes. There was this frat party. Natalie was there with some bozo. They were both hitting the bottle pretty hard.” Ron paused to think, rubbing circles on his temple with forefingers.

“It wasn’t yesterday. Some aspects are hazy.” He looked at me, hoping for leniency.

He got none.

“You remember Brandon?”

“The jerk. He was always playing jokes on you.”

“Ah, you remember Brandon.”

“Of course I remember Brandon. I’m the one who gargled the Windex he poured into your mouthwash bottle.”

“I’d forgotten that.” Ron smiled remembering the incident but had the good sense not to laugh. “I was in such a rotten mood that night it would have been dangerous for me to drink. I didn’t want to be there. I’d been carrying around the same rum and coke all evening. Brandon must have slipped something into it. One minute I was fine, the next I was out like a light. The next morning I woke up—in bed with Natalie Hodgins.”

“And her boyfriend?”

“He left early with somebody else.”

“At least one of you had some sense. And you don’t know how that happened?

“No. We were both confused. Brandon was all too happy to fill us in. To hear him tell it, Natalie and I made an acrobatic porn movie.”

A young lady brought beer samples in time to hear the end of that. She glanced at him in surprise. She arranged the samples in front of Ron, explained what they were, and hurried away, obviously not comfortable around aging porn stars.

"Did Brandon make a video?"

"A video. No...."

"You knew him! If it had actually happened, he would have made a video. You idiot!"

Ron grimaced. "I didn't think of that. I was in shock trying to figure out how to tell you. Knowing how upset you'd be."

I stared at him, wordless. Wondering how such a smart man could be so stupid.

Ron sighed. "I ran into Chuck Briggs a few years later at a conference. He was laughing about how Brandon pulled one over on me. He asked whatever happened to "ole Nympho Nat." Chuck had no idea I'd married her. Brandon's stunt derailed my life."

I stared at him. "Why didn't you talk to me?"

"I wanted to. I was ashamed. I couldn't face you. I was afraid of you."

His fear wasn't unfounded. "I knew you, Ron. You wouldn't have done that."

Ron rubbed his hands over his face. "You would have believed me?"

"We'll never know now, will we? Since you just ghosted me."

"You were mad at me all the time back then." He massaged the tension from the back of his neck. "Not unlike now. You would have killed me."

"I might have killed you for being stupid. But I'd hire a hitman."

"Big mistake. Hitmen aren't known for their exemplary character. They can't be trusted. Thousands of people are in prison because their hitman turned state's evidence."

"Thousands? Who did the fact check on that? How would someone find a hitman?

Angi's list? Craig's List?"

Griffin brought hot rolls and cold crispy salads, gave me a strange look, and hurried away.

Evidently he didn't know where to find a hit man either. While we were busy adding dressing to the salads, I thought about what Ron had said. I don't know what I would have done.

"My heart was shattered," I said quietly, "when I heard you were married."

"Natalie showed up, said she was pregnant and claimed it was mine."

I stared at him. "How did you even pass the bar exam? You had a one-night stand with Nympho Nat, which you don't remember, and assumed her baby was yours? Ron, she had a different guy every night."

Ron's fingers drummed on his water glass. "I didn't know that. Then. I was spending all my time with you. Can you imagine discovering your bride was known as Nympho Nat and Boardinghouse?"

"Boardinghouse?"

"Everyone slept there."

"So, you married her," I said facetiously, "as, of course, you would. Wait! Are you saying Ronnie Junior might not be yours?"

"No. She lost that baby. RJ came later."

"Was she even pregnant?"

"Hell, I don't know!" Ron shoved his fingers through his hair.

"Did you see an ultrasound?"

"No."

I snorted with so much force the candle flame flickered. "This just gets worse."

"You're mad again. It's been twenty-six years. And you're mad again."

"Twenty-seven years and three months. I'm mad still, Ron! She ruined my life."

"You aren't the only victim here, April! I married Boardinghouse. I not only didn't love her, I didn't like her. *And* I was in love with you. Your life wasn't ruined. You have an incredible career. Two beautiful kids. You married the guy everyone idolized, a senator on the road to the White House. You've gone places and done things the rest of us only dream of."

"I'm angry that you're stupid," I snapped. I probably shouldn't have used present tense.

"Well, welcome to the club. When I found out what Brandon had done, I'd been married four years."

"And had two kids. Do you remember making those babies?"

"Cheap shot." He frowned.

The salt and pepper shakers were each half of a bear. Salt was the back half. He handed it to me butt first.

"If you'd at least talked to me, maybe I wouldn't have hated you for twenty-seven years."

"And evidently three months." He frowned across his glass. "I tried."

"When?" I set the shaker down with a thump.

"I went to your dorm. Just as I got there you came out with Grant. People were waiting in a flashy convertible. You were laughing when you and Grant got in. I didn't want to mess up what you had going with him."

Could he have messed up what I had going with Grant by then? I don't know. "I would like to have had the choice," I said. But would I really? Grant's magnetism was compelling.

"Did you know Grant?" I asked.

"Everyone knew who Grant Frazier was. I didn't run in his circles." Ron propped his elbows on the table, rested his chin in his hands, and just looked at me. "I could never have given you what he gave you. What a ride you've been on."

He meant it and I was touched. I glanced down at the huge diamond on my finger, but knew he wasn't just talking about money. "You're right and I'm especially grateful for my kids. "

We ate in silence for a few minutes.

"When did Natalie die?" I asked.

"Eight years ago."

"I heard she had cancer. I'm sorry." I sipped my drink. "Was she a good wife?"

He shrugged. "By whose standards? And I wasn't the best husband.

"Was she a good mother?"

"I guess. You should ask our daughter." Ron's fingers drummed on his water glass.

"Dorinda left home as soon as she could. Natalie and I had different ideas about how to raise a family. But the kids turned out okay."

"Mother-daughter relationships are difficult." I said over my water glass, although he might have picked up on that last night when Riley Gracee stomped off to bed. I felt my face get hot. Not my finest hour.

"I assumed you would've remarried. You're handsome." I smiled. "Sort of."

"Getting married doesn't work when you're in love with someone else," he said. "I know. I tried. When you know where

'The One' is, you don't go looking for 'The One' somewhere else, April."

I dropped my fork. My mouth opened. Nothing came out. My anger had become a weapon I'd used against him to protect myself. Disarmed, I was speechless.

It didn't matter. He gave me no time to answer.

"Don't say anything. You asked. I told you. I have no expectations. It would be enough if you'd stop hating me."

"Telling me wasn't easy. Thank you. We were good friends. Once."

Ron sighed. "I know we can't go back, April."

"Nope. You buying? I need coffee." I reached for the desert menu. "And gooey chocolate."

Chapter Twenty-Four

April

I'm not some stupid woman who was dumped by a guy and never got over it. Yeah, right! I have no credibility whatsoever.

Since I was fourteen I'd assumed I'd love Ron the rest of my life. Maybe I have. Why else, for twenty-seven years and three months, would I have clung to the memory of his love like the last life preserver on the Titanic?

I was a train wreck when I met Grant six months after Ron's sudden disappearance. I have no idea why Grant gave me a second look.

I'd sworn off men. Forever. Still, there I was, without a snorkel, swept away in the current of Grant's persona. Grant was larger than life. He was the reason the term *joie de vie* existed. He exploded into my life and I was wearing this diamond before I realized what was happening.

My infatuation with Ronnie, on the other hand, had been different. In the seventh grade a boy grabbed my notebook and held it out of my reach. Ronnie walked by, took it from him, handed it to me, and kept walking. He didn't look at either of us. Awe struck, I worshipped him from afar. Not all that far—it was a small school. The summer between the eighth and ninth grade my braces came off, my bra filled out, the sun bronzed my skin and highlighted my long blond hair. Ron noticed.

The drama department began auditions for *Oklahoma* on September the tenth. A calendar hung on my wall for years with that date circled in red. Ron had no trouble landing the part of Curly. Even at fourteen, he had a strong rich voice. Mine wasn't great but I sight read quite well. I'm an alto. I didn't get the part of Laurie, but I snagged the part of Ado Annie. There weren't enough books to go around so Ronnie and I shared mine. By the end of the day, he was mine, too. Maybe it was after he heard me sing, 'I'm just a girl who can't say no'. By the time the play ran its course, we were inseparable. Our world revolved around music. And each other.

I knew Ronnie better than I'd ever known anyone. We were riding his motor scooter when he acquired the scar on his knee. He dodged a squirrel and we ended up in a ditch. The scar on his left thumb was from a barbed wire fence. There's another one on his right shoulder that required stitches. We took a shortcut through Dale Northcutt's pasture and his bull wasn't happy to see us. We'd rolled under the fence, laughing like we had good sense.

He fractured his collar bone in a football game. I was a cheerleader. When I realized he was injured, I broke from our pyramid and ran out on the field.

Ronnie hated beets and radishes. He didn't like sweet pickles but loved dills. He liked apricot and pineapple pies, but only if his mother made them. He hated apple. He wore size 32 x 34 Wranglers, which were almost impossible to find.

He had a small tattoo on the inside of his left wrist. Exactly like mine. We were sixteen when we skipped school to get tattoos. I let him talk me into it because I was mad at my father.

Ron said identical tattoos were more binding than a wedding ring. A tattoo doesn't just slip off.

Our life's mission had been getting our band grooving and becoming world-famous vocalists. Our tat symbolized music with a treble clef in turquoise ink. We always opened our act with my solo of "I'll Be Seeing You." Ron and Mark referred to it as "April's song". Slanted across the treble clef was a lowercase lime green 'h' for the name of our band. A capital 'H' didn't look right. The tattoo person helped with the design. She was an artistic genius but not smart enough to realize she could be in deep kimchee because we were underage. The 'h' had lots of swirls that intertwined with the treble clef. We thought the result was not only brilliant, but beautiful. Nobody who has ever seen the small tattoo on my inner wrist has understood it. Grant knew the 'h' stood for "Hitchhiker". My children have never asked. It was just one of their mother's idiosyncrasies. Like her shoe size or eye color. It's been a constant reminder of the man who broke my heart.

We couldn't agree on a name for a trio. Peter, Paul, and Mary was already taken. Ron and Mark looked nothing like Peter and Paul. Ron, with his dark curly hair and black horn-rimmed glasses, resembled a better-looking Buddy Holly. Mark looked like Danny Divito. Ron, Mark, and April didn't have the same ring. While Crosby Stills and Nash sounded great, Dale, Lang, and Horstholtzer did not. We considered ditching Mark for someone with a catchier last name, but he was a strong tenor, a gifted bass player and his parents let us practice in their garage.

Plus he had a car.

The search for our band name ended when Mark's '72 Plymouth broke down on the way to our first gig and we hitched a ride in a farm truck. We arrived smelling like chicken poop with feathers in our hair and we became the "Hitchhikers".

By our sophomore year of college, we were performing at coffee houses, campus events, weddings, and one funeral. Don't ask. We weren't a rock band. We did mostly bluesey ballads and the torch songs my mother had treasured. People would slow dance and fall in love. Something happens when you're sharing a mic, gazing into someone's eyes as voices blend in harmony so perfect it makes you want to cry. Every time we sang together, I fell more in love with Ronnie. He was my whole world all through high school, then our freshman year and half of our sophomore year of college.

And then he was gone. And I despised him as fiercely as I had loved him. There is a thin line between all-out passion-filled love and gut-wrenching hate. Ron's sudden desertion destroyed me. But he was only the most recent in a line of catastrophic losses.

I was ten when my mother died. Mom, Dad, Aunt Abby, and Grammy had all downplayed her illness. Now I know they were trying to protect me. But at the time their deception caused me to doubt everything and everyone I believed in. Unaware that Mom had been battling cancer, I'd been ambushed by her death. I thought she couldn't do things other mothers did because she "was not feeling well". I came home from school to learn she had died. They had told me she was "in the hospital again". I have major trust issues.

My love of music came from my Mom. My strongest childhood memories are watching her dance around the room to the music of the LP's she kept stacked near the old record player. Her favorite was a scratchy version of Billie Holliday's *I'll Be Seeing You*. She never tired of it. She had been a piano teacher. I can't remember a time that I couldn't play the piano. As a toddler, I sat on her lap picking out notes. After her death,

I pounded out *You'll Never Walk Alone*, another of her favorites, for hours at a time.

During Mom's illness, Grammy had moved in with us to care for me and my mom. She stayed on after Mom's death. Aunt Abby, who lived next door, took on most of the responsibility of mothering me even though she was hugely pregnant. My father had been so distraught over Mom's loss, he forgot he had a daughter.

Ali had been born almost immediately after my mom died and I loved her with my whole heart. For the next two years, my world revolved around her. But then, along with Grammy, she was gone. Abby had been driving Grammy to a doctor's appointment in Oklahoma City when a drunk driver ran a red light and broad-sided them. Grammy died at the scene. Abby was critically injured. While emergency crews fought to save them, someone lifted two-year-old Ali from her child seat and disappeared into the crowd.

I was inconsolable. And terrified. Abby was badly injured and distraught over Ali's loss and her mother's death. She had no capacity to care for me. Every horrible thing that happened in my life had happened without warning. I couldn't sleep. I imagined the unimaginable. Then Ron came along and swore he would never leave me. When he realized how much I loved *I'll Be Seeing You*, he made me a CD that repeatedly played the song. Finally I could sleep. Every night I dozed off with the haunting melody and the yearning strains of Billie Holliday's voice in my headphones. I loved the line, "I'll be looking at the moon but I'll be seeing you". I desperately needed something solid I could count on.

My conversation with Ron tonight revived memories that had been tucked away in a safe place for years. They swirled around in my head as Ron and I carefully picked our way over the uneven sidewalk from the Ore House back to the General Palmer Hotel.

Large even by today's standards, the hotel must have been majestic when it was built in 1898 by General Jackson Palmer, a Civil War general. He also built the narrow gage railroad to Silverton.

This area of Durango could be a scene from a hundred years ago. Some of these buildings would have existed back then, shouting their newness with the odor of freshly cut wood. The honkytonk piano from a distant saloon would be the same. And so would the San Juan mountains, now a deep purple. The air had turned chilly as soon as the sun slipped behind them.

I looked into the Indigo sky searching for the moon and began singing softly *I'll Be Seeing You*. Then I sang *Four Strong Winds*, a staple of our trio. Ron joined in on the chorus. Our harmony was as effortless as it had been almost thirty years ago. We sang our way back to the hotel and up the stairs.

The shock of Grant's death had left me numb. Then came a wave of fear. My handsome, dynamic, strong husband who had been my rock of Gibraltar was gone. I still couldn't imagine a future without Grant. But the familiar ease of singing with Ron brought a glimmer of hope. My heart could sing again—someday. The thought was a distant star. A pinpoint of light in a pitch-black sky of despair.

Chapter Twenty-Five

Riley Grace

I peered through the branches of the cottonwood looking for the moon. I do that anytime I'm out at night. I used to do it with Mom. She had a thing about the moon. It might have started with the book she often read to me, "Goodnight Moon". There was a song about a moon she sang, too. I don't remember much, but the last line was *I'll be looking at the moon but I'll be seeing you*. As she sang, she smiled at me in a way that let me know she was looking for my face in the moon. She sang a lot back then. I had forgotten.

The moon was full last week when I was up here in my tree house after Daddy died. Mom was gone. Like she is now. Ali was here, though. Like she is now, putzing around in the kitchen prepping stuff, chopping, sauteing and dicing. Through our big kitchen window I can see her dancing to some country song she's listening to on the radio. When Alise gets here we can throw stuff together for pizzas and get down to some serious movie watching. It was going to be a girl's night. Ali, Alise, and me. But Bronc wanted to come. Ali said of course he should come. Alise, not so much.

No moon tonight. I lowered my eyes. Bronc, who was sitting cross-legged across from me, had been watching my face, grinning. Our eyes locked and I smiled. When Bronc smiles, it's impossible not to smile, too.

"No moon tonight," he said.

"How did you know...?" It amazes me how many times he's picked up on my thoughts in the short time we've been together.

He just grinned.

"Daddy always made me smile, too. He filled up the whole room. If he was smiling, and he was always smiling, everyone around him smiled, too. I wanted to be wherever he was because that's where the fun was."

Bronc nodded. "He's going to leave a big hole in your life."

I tried to blink away tears before he saw them, but one escaped and rolled down my cheek. He leaned in and wiped it away with his thumb.

Embarrassed, I pulled back. "It's one of the reasons I went to Ridge's matches when I was little. I wanted to be with Daddy. I resented Mom for not being with us. Now, I feel kind of sorry for her. She missed out on some great memories."

"Sad," Bronc said.

"Sometimes I'm in the room with her for hours. I don't think she knows I'm even there. When Dad was with me, he was *with* me. I never wondered, not once, if he knew I was there. He might be on the phone but when I looked up from my book he'd be smiling at me. You kind of remind me of him. That's a compliment."

Bronc nodded, listening.

"Nobody said that at his funeral," I grumbled. "I would have told them my daddy always made me feel like seeing me was the best part of his day. That's huge. How you make people feel is important. That's what the old guy should have said at his funeral. Know what I wish?"

"What?"

"I wish Mom, Ridge, and I could have a funeral service by ourselves."

"You should do that." Bronc looked around at my tree house, checking out the levels behind and above us. "Did your dad build this for Ridge?"

"He built it for me. I used to spend a lot of time up here reading."

"Do you like horses?" Bronc asked, shifting his weight to get more comfortable.

"I love horses. I've had a pony since I was five. That was random."

"Not at all. I'd have to rethink loving you if you didn't like horses."

"You don't know me yet." I leaned back against a limb. "You can't love me."

Bronc grinned that intoxicating slow-motion grin. I don't drink so I don't really know how being buzzed feels, but when he smiles that way, something happens in the pit of my stomach. That probably has nothing to do with alcohol.

"*Au contraire*. I've loved you since the first time I saw you," he said.

"Some cowboy you are," I objected. "Cowboys don't say *au contraire*."

"You're an expert on cowboy lingo? What do cowboys say?"

"Get along dogies. Eee-haw. Yipee Ky-yay. Stuff like that."

Bronc laughed. "French cowboys don't. They say *au contraire*."

"Whatever. Get back to the first time you saw me."

"Stop interrupting."

"Okay. So, you were at school and..."

"No."

"I was at school and..."

"No."

"Wouldn't we both have to be at the same place?" I asked.

Bronc laughed again. "Yeah. But neither of us was at school."

"Where, then?"

"At the Love's Travel Stop on SW 89th."

"Huh uh."

"Was, too. Last August before school started. My family had just moved to town. I was taking hay out to my sister's horse and stopped for gas."

"You have a sister?" I scratched my nose.

"Yeah."

"She has a horse?"

"Yes. Stop interrupting. So, I'm just getting ready to pump gas when the door of the car next to me flew open and the most beautiful girl I've ever seen jumped out. She was barefooted. She ran right out into the street. I'm thinking just my luck. I find the girl of my dreams and she's crazy." He broke off and looked at me. "Is crazy okay here or is there a more cowboyish word you'd rather I use?"

"Like what?"

"Oh, I don't know. Addled. Plumb loco."

I tilted my head. And thought about it. "No. Crazy probably works."

"She was with some guy and he was yelling at her. He finally turned off the pump and ran after her. I thought he kidnapped her and she was trying to escape."

"How exciting," I said. "What's your sister's name?"

"Noelle. Stop interrupting. I moved closer so that I could see. In case I needed to go knock him down and save her."

"Very chivalrous." I grinned.

" I am. It's in my blood. An old man in a wheelchair was trying to cross the street and the light changed before he got across. Traffic was streaming around him."

"How old is your sister?"

"Twelve. So, she's out in the street trying to get the traffic stopped and..."

"Your sister?"

"No, the crazy barefooted girl. She got some of the cars stopped and the guy she was with was yelling at her." Bronc stopped talking and looked at me all serious. "I thought if she was my girl, I wouldn't be yelling at her like that."

"What's your sister's horse's name."

"Tonto. Stop interrupting."

"This is getting exciting. What happened?"

"It was chaos. Horns where honking, people were yelling....she got the old dude to the edge of the street without either of them getting squished, but she couldn't get the chair up over the curb."

"Did the idiot she was with help her?"

"Yeah. They got the old guy to safety. She ran back to their Forester and got him a bottle of water and some candy bars. I got a good look at her. That's when I fell in love. She was beautiful. But maybe it was because she ran out into the street to save a homeless guy."

"Did you ever see her again?"

He nodded. "The first day of school. I was walking down the hall and there she was. I looked at her and she looked at me and ran into her locker."

I was laughing so hard I could barely talk. "I was so embarrassed. Get back to your story. What happened?"

"The guy she was with was yelling at her again. I figured out he must be her brother. I wanted to know who she was. But he called her different stuff. Archie. Rye."

"He can't remember my name."

"He gave her some money and she went into Love's and got the old guy a sack of burgers and candy bars."

"Was she still barefooted?"

"Yeah. In fact, the rumor is she wasn't wearing shoes at her father's funeral."

"Oh, that is so not true! I didn't take them off until I came outside."

"She gave the old man the hamburgers and candy bars, took back the candy she'd given him earlier and put it back in the car."

I laughed. "Ridge buys these protein bars by the truck load. He special orders them from Switzerland, Savanah, South Dakota or somewhere. According to him they cost a fortune. He risked his life to help me get the old guy out of the street but wouldn't let him have his protein bars. Isn't that a hoot?"

Bronc shook his head. "Well, he bought burgers. As Clint Eastwood said, "A man's gotta know his priorities. So what was he actually calling you?"

Clint Eastwood didn't say that. I laughed. "Ridge calls me R.G. The Rye was right. He usually calls me Brat or Squirt."

I hear men say, "She doesn't know how pretty she is," about some woman. That's dumb. Of course she does. She has eyes, She looks in the mirror when she brushes her teeth. She just doesn't care. She has more important things going on. I know I'm pretty. People tell me all the time. I've just never really cared. I've been too busy perfecting my backhand. I want to be more than Ridge Frazier's little sister someday. But when Bronc looks at me the way he's looking at me right now, I'm happy he likes the way I look.

Bronc leaned in. "You are so stinkin' cute."

A beam of light from the security lamp outside our back door broke through the branches and cast swaying shadows across his face. His eyes were dark and shiny. I couldn't read the expression in them. His face was close to mine, I'm not sure who leaned the rest of the way. It might have been me. Our lips touched, but just barely.

"Was that a kiss?" I asked. "I'm not sure."

"I want you to be sure that our first kiss was a kiss." Bronc slid his fingers into my hair and positioned my head, then moved in.

Now that was a kiss. His lips were soft and warm. And tasted like the cinnamon gum he'd stolen from my purse. That thing in the pit of my stomach that happens when he smiles did cartwheels.

When I'm a hundred, I will still remember that kiss. I'm glad my very first kiss was with Bronc. In the tree house my daddy built.

Chapter Twenty-Six

April

Ron walked me to my room and reminded me he'd be picking up Lane at the airport in the morning. He asked if I'd like to ride along or sleep in. I opted for sleeping in. He warned me not to get in any trouble while he was gone. He was joking, I think. But maybe not. He remembered the days I'd been capable of getting into trouble.

After I showered and got into my jammies, I tried to call Ridge. As usual, his phone went straight to voice mail which left me wondering if he still had that phone.

Then I called home. We're one of the few families that still have a land line. It only rings when someone is overly concerned about my car's warranty, or thinks my house needs siding or a new roof. But I won't be getting rid of this phone line anytime soon—if ever. Grant's voice informs the caller of the number they reached, but not which residence—in case the caller is irate over the way Grant voted on a bill. Although our number is unlisted, we still get those calls. His message is short and upbeat wishing the caller a good day and advising them to make the world a better place for those around them. Pretty much the motto Grant lived by. His smile when he recorded it was evident in his voice. He smiled when he talked on the phone—except for the time Ridge fractured his wrist when he fell trying to get Riley Grace off the neighbor's roof. Grant blamed me for that. Also for the time she nearly drowned. Unfortunately, Riley Grace wasn't a child who enjoyed staying home to play with dolls.

I hoped nobody would answer our home phone so I could hear Grant's voice but Ali picked up on the fourth ring.

"I hear '*Dancing Queen*'", I said. "Is that the radio?"

"No, it's the kiddos."

"What kiddos?"

"Alise, Bronc, and Rye."

"Bronc is there?" I asked, although obviously he was. "I thought this was going to be girl's night."

"So did Alise. At first her nose was out of joint, but now she seems glad he came."

"He looks a bit like James Dean, doesn't he?"

Ali laughed. "The resemblance is rather startling."

"How was the pizza?"

"Good. Glad I made a lot."

"Who's playing the piano?"

"Bronc."

"Bronc? He's good!"

"Yeah," Ali said. "His mom is a piano teacher. But nobody can teach you how to play like that. You either can or you can't. The drama department is doing *Mama Mia*. Alise brought her playbook with her. Bronc's playing the songs."

"Sounds like fun," I said. It really did.

"But before that he was just noodling around playing some jazzy-bluesy stuff. You should have heard that. Your mom was a piano teacher, too, wasn't she?"

"Yes. We have that in common," I said. "I hear the girls singing. They harmonize well."

"They do. Gracie has a beautiful voice. Obviously inherited from you."

"Oh," I said, surprised that Ali had heard her sing. I couldn't remember the last time I had.

"We sing with the car radio."

"We used to do that, too," I said. I also couldn't remember the last time we had gone somewhere together.

I heard Riley Grace laugh and longed to be a part of what they were doing. But, if I'd been there, the dynamic would have changed. Alise wouldn't have come over expecting to have fun. Bronc wouldn't have been there. Ali had gone out of her way to create this. Something I don't do. That is going to change.

"I need to talk to Riley Grace for a minute," I said. "I hate to interrupt. Do you think she'll talk to me?"

"Of course." Ali yelled into the den, " Gracie, your mom's on the phone."

I'd noticed Riley Grace's friends called her Gracie. Grant called her Bino. Am I the only one who calls her Riley Grace?

She came to the phone laughing and breathless. "Hi, Mom, what's up?"

"Hi, Honey. You and Alise sound good. I thought it was the radio."

"Chorus is one of my electives. I didn't want to take French or Spanish, but I really like it. Sometimes a bunch of us hang out after school to sing. Alise's drama department is doing *Mama Mia*. You guys had some fun music back then."

"We did. Did you try out for the play?"

"Don't have the time."

"You do have a lot on your plate. Would you like to drop the math tutor?"

"Yeah!"

"She's not making a difference. I was terrible in math, too. I've done ok."

"Awesome! You better not be lyin'!" The excitement in her voice lifted my spirits. I've finally done something right.

"Tomorrow is your first day back in school. Are you ready?"

"I'll be okay," She sounded surprised I'd remembered. "I don't know..."

"Your friends came to the funeral," I pointed out. "They'll be glad to see you."

"Anyone who came to the funeral got an excused absence from school. I didn't know half of them."

There was a pause. I waited for her to fill it. "So, how are things?" she asked. "Did you find Ridge?"

"Not yet. I don't know where to look."

"Have you tried Sable's apartment? He has a key."

I hadn't known he had Sable, much less a key to her apartment. I realized with a jolt that Riley and Ridge are closer to each other than they are to me. Riley Grace was quiet while I collected my thoughts.

"I'll go by there. Thanks. I went to the wreck site." As I uttered the words, I knew Riley Grace is the only person who would understand how gut-wrenching that trip had been.

She didn't react for a minute, but then she asked, "Are you okay?"

"The drive up there was terrifying. I felt sorry for Ron. He had a white-knuckled grip on the wheel. I can't imagine why Grant and Sable were on that road."

"You're sure you found where it happened?"

"Yeah. It's one of the few places with a guard rail, and it was broken."

"You're okay?" The concern I heard in her voice touched me.

"I am now. I didn't handle it well then."

"Mr. Lang went with you?"

"Not *with* me. I didn't know he was coming. That was Lane's idea."

"It sounds like a good thing. You didn't kill him, did you? Tell me you didn't do anything embarrassing."

I laughed remembering the plane fiasco. "I've embarrassed you worse."

"I've Googled that road," Riley Grace paused. "It's called the Million Dollar Highway. It looks terrifying!"

"It is. But, oh my gosh, the scenery is gorgeous! Would you come back here with me sometime?"

"To Durango? Me and you?" Her surprise was evident.

"Yeah. There's a train that runs through the mountains from Durango to Silverton. I think riding it together would be fun."

"Just me and you?"

"Yeah. We haven't done anything together in a long time...."

"Sure." She cut me off. "Sounds like fun. When?"

"This fall when the aspens are turning. October maybe?"

"Let's do it," she said.

"Good! I'll let you go for now. I'll call tomorrow."

"Love you, Mom. Be careful."

"Love you, too, Sweetie. Bye."

She's never cautioned me to be careful. Was it because I'm her only parent now? Not the one she would have preferred, but the one she's stuck with.

I crawled into bed and whispered a prayer for the safety of both of my children. Especially Ridge. Wherever he is. I got back out of bed and down on my knees and prayed fervently for Ridge. He needs more than a casual prayer. I can feel it.

Chapter Twenty-Seven

Ridge

I stood motionless at the edge of the gorge contemplating life without love.

I once asked my mother how to know if you're in love. She'd been baking, filling the kitchen with that intoxicating scent of cookies. I sat at the bar with a glass of milk waiting for her to fill my plate with snickerdoodles. If they ever came out of the oven.

She'd laughed at the question. She laughed more back then. "You just know," she said, swiping at the flour dusting her nose. She got more on than she got off. She looked at me and realized I wasn't joking. She stopped laughing and got pretend serious, as though I wasn't eleven. "Oh. Are you in love?"

I hesitated. "I've never been in love. So, I dunno."

"Well," she said, wiping her hands on her apron, "that's a problem." She didn't ask who I was in love with, and I was relieved. She knew Rhianne Edwards' mother. I sure didn't want our mothers in the middle of whatever this is. It was already too crowded with me and Rhianne.

"I don't think God put enough thought into making girls. What they want changes every five minutes."

Mom took cookies out of the oven and pushed a few on my saucer before plating the rest. She slid another sheet of cookies into the oven, poured herself a glass of milk, picked up a cookie, bit into it and chewed. She considered what I'd said. Mom was always baking new stuff back then, trying out recipes for the restaurant.

"You put their happiness ahead of your own."

"How do you do that?" I reached for a cookie.

"Well, for example, if she really is hungry, you give her your lunch because helping her is more important to you than eating."

"Are you sure?" I was beginning to suspect Mom knew nothing about love. I wondered why I had even asked her.

"I'm sure," she said. "Suppose you both have ice cream. If hers fell off her cone into the dirt, you would give her yours."

I was pretty sure I wouldn't. "Why?"

"You wouldn't want her to be sad."

I wouldn't want her to be sad. But not more than I wanted my ice cream. Especially if it was chocolate.

"What flavor ice cream?"

Mom's head tilted as she thought. "Strawberry."

"Good." Strawberry is her favorite flavor, but not mine. I might give her my ice cream if it was strawberry. There's more to this than I thought.

"So, like if she wanted my chocolate pudding at lunch, I'd have to give it to her, right?" I really needed to know because it happened yesterday.

She nodded. "If you love her."

"Do I have to?" I reached for another cookie. "Just because she wanted it?"

"If you don't want to, you're probably not in love."

I chewed my cookie. Maybe Rhianne wasn't as important to me as I'd thought.

"Would you like to take some of these cookies to her tomorrow?" Mom asked.

"Sure," I said, knowing I'd eat 'em all on the way to school.

"How long has she been your girlfriend?" Mom leaned against the cabinet and bit into a cookie.

I scratched a mosquito bite on my shin as I thought. "I don't know for sure. I didn't know she was my girlfriend until she told me."

"Well, that can be a problem." Mom slid more cookies into the oven, turned around and looked at me all serious like.

"Yeah, see!" I was glad she understood. "It's already a problem! She wants me to kiss her. That scares me."

Mom was trying not to laugh. "Why does that scare you?"

"Our braces could get caught. That's a real thing. What if we couldn't get loose and had to walk down to the principal's office stuck together?"

Mom was drinking her milk. She laughed and choked.

I left. But I wasn't too mad to grab a few cookies on my way out. Mom was still laughing.

I stared down into the pit Sable had disappeared into. We had recently had a similar discussion. I was playing badly in a tournament. Dad felt Sable was a distraction. I couldn't argue. I have trouble thinking about anything else when she's around. But without her, I can't think at all.

Sable sensed the problem. She broke up with me over pizza.

"Look, Ridge, tennis is your family business," Sable had said, as she picked pepperoni off her slice and put it on my mine.

"It's what you're expected to do with your life. You're on track to become one of the best tennis players in the country, possibly the world. I'm in your way."

She'd looked at me through misery-clouded doe eyes.

"I love you too much to let you throw that away."

Her words reminded me of my mother's advice when I was eleven. Now I understood what Mom meant. Sable loved me the way I loved her—more than my next tennis match—my next breath. Without Sable, everything I had worked for, any status I'd achieved, turned to dust, and sifted through my fingers.

I should have been driving that car that night, not my father. I should have been the one to die with her. Without her, there's no reason to live. I looked down into the inky abyss. It seemed bottomless at night. I could end this unbearable agony. It would be so simple—jump into the nothingness.

A massive boulder jutted up from somewhere right below me. I eased down to it and peered up into the night sky. The stars were cold. Distant. I took a deep breath and prepared to jump.

Chapter Twenty-Eight

Ridge

"What are you doing, Ridge?"

Startled, I dropped the flashlight. It clanked all the way to the bottom of the gorge. I lost my balance, grabbed at anything I could find. My fingers closed around a tree root. Shaking violently, I grasped it and hung on. Night pulled in around me, suffocating, close. Then a voice. I couldn't tell where the voice had come from. Nothing. There was no shimmering form. No light.

I recognized the voice. My father's voice. It was dripping with disappointment. I'd heard that tone too many times when he was alive.

"Dad?"

"You're no quitter, Ridge. What are you doing?" The voice was breathy. Labored. But the inflection was my father's.

I inhaled in deep ragged gasps. "Dad? Dad! Where are you?"

"Not really sure..."

I pictured him looking around trying to locate a landmark. I looked around also for some indication that he was here. Nothing. Just a voice.

"I'm so sorry this happened to you, Dad. It was supposed to be me."

"Says who? Before I was even born, the days of my life were numbered. If you ever read your Bible, you'd know that. Nothing you do or don't do changes what God wills. This didn't catch God by surprise. You didn't cause my death. Not Nelson, either. It was my time. Mine. Tonight isn't your time. Get your ass off that cliff and get out of here."

"Yeah. Not as easy as it sounds." I couldn't see. With a foot I searched the edge of the ledge.

"Everything looks different from here," Dad went on as though I hadn't said anything. I was beginning to remember he did that often when he was alive.

"Ridge, you have to tell people this: life doesn't end when your body dies. It's like just walking into another room. People need to know that. There is nothing to fear Well. If you know God."

Dad doesn't blame me. Relief washed over me. I'd been holding my breath. I exhaled guilt, and shame. It left me exhausted. The weight was gone. I was so relieved I lost track of what he was saying. The root I clutched felt solid and rough in my hand. It provided more than a sense of safety. It was reality in an impossible situation. It had grown out of solid rock. Now, there's a Ted Talk on raw determined grit.

"Listen, Ridge. This is important. God loves you. More than you can imagine. Get to know him."

"I'm listening."

"God has a plan for your life. If f you jump off that boulder, you'll steal it. God doesn't take kindly to people stealing from him."

I'd flesh that one out later.

"You have to trust God the way you trusted me. No matter how things look."

"I don't know how."

"Spend time with Him. Read your Bible."

"I don't even know where it is."

"There's your problem. Your mom knows. Ask her." The voice was distant. He'd drifted.

"Dad?" I was afraid he was gone. "Dad?!!"

"Suicide is selfish. You're only thinking of yourself. What would this do to your mom? And Bino? They're already trying to deal with my loss. They're frantic over not knowing where you are."

I wondered how he knew that. I'd think about that one later, too. His words hung in the air and echoed in my brain.

"Your mom is young. She loved someone before me. I don't know who he was. I need you to help her find him."

"What? You what?"

"Watch your six, Son. Nelson is still gunning for you."

"I know."

"Stop coming out here. You're making it too easy for him to find you."

I hadn't thought of that.

"I'm proud of you, Ridge. I should have told you more often."

I wish he had, too. "Hey, Dad can I talk to Sable?"

"Sable? I haven't seen her since the wreck."

"Where is she?"

"I don't know. I don't know where I am. Now, get out of here. And remember...."

As he spoke, the voice drifted. Like the pine branches whispering above me. Moving. Faint. Distant.

"Remember? Remember what? Dad? Dad!" I was a little kid again watching my father drive away. I listened but only heard the echo of my voice. A rustle of air — he was gone. My suicidal thoughts were gone, too. They'd flown away with his first words.

How am I going to get off this ledge? Below me was nothingness. I was at least ten feet below the road. No flashlight, no rope, no phone. Left it in the Forester. I explored the cliff behind me. I'd been right. The root had grown out of solid rock. No protrusions or chinks in the rock to give me a foothold. Nothing to grab. I was stuck.

I shook uncontrollably. My knees refused to hold me. I sat cross-legged on the boulder. The encounter with Dad changed everything I'd believed about death.

My thoughts were jumbled. But I was certain of one thing. God had allowed this visit. I had to know what Dad said was important. He'd said to build a relationship with God. Considering my predicament, and the fact I can do little else, this seemed like a reasonable time to start. None of the prayers I'd learned in children's church seemed to work here.

Overwhelmed by the beauty of something that had looked cold and distant only a few minutes ago, I looked up into a black velvet sky studded with diamonds.

I could barely breathe. Couldn't think. When I could, I took a deep breath and said, "Hi, God, it's me—Ridge—Ridge Frazier..."

I finally added, "I've always admired your work...."

Chapter Twenty-Nine
Ridge

A car door slammed on the road. Nelson had found me. I stopped breathing. My car was parked halfway in the road. He knew I had to be here. Somewhere. It was only a matter of time until he found me.

"Frazier," he yelled, "Where are you?"

I froze. Did he really think I'm stupid enough to say, 'Here I am. Come shoot me'?

"Ridge!"

Nelson wouldn't have called me Ridge. I recognized the voice. Clay. Clayton Morley, the Colorado state trooper. He worked the wreck the night Dad and Sable died. He stayed with me long after everyone else left.

"Clay?"

"Yeah, where are you, Ridge?"

"Down here."

"Down where?"

"Here. Do you have a flashlight? I dropped mine."

"Ridge! You scared the crap out of me. What are you doing down there?"

"I—uh, tripped."

He stopped on the other side of the guard rail and aimed his flashlight in the direction of my voice. "Can you get out?"

"Would I be here if I could get out?"

"You're in a bit of a bind, aren't you?" He laughed. "Well, see you around."

"I'm glad you think it's funny," I grumbled.

He swept the light beam across the rock wall below him. "Not much to grab."

"Yeah, I noticed."

"Make yourself comfortable. I'll go find something and get you out. Be right back."

"Clay, wait! There's a rope in the back of my Subaru."

Without comment or questions, Clay went to get the rope. He came back, tied it to the tree, and tossed me the end. He lit my way with his flashlight being careful to keep the beam out of my eyes. I reached the canyon rim and Clay leaned down, stuck out his hand. I grabbed it and he pulled me up over the edge.

"What are you doing out here?" I panted. Out of shape for mountain climbing.

"Looking for you. And, by the way, so is Nelson. Did that ever occur to you?"

"Why did you think I'd be out here?" I asked.

"I sensed it."

"Get serious." I struggled to untie the rope. Clay had made sure the knot held.

"Ridge, I've been following your career for months. You're phenomenal on the tennis court. When you're on your game, no one can beat you. I thought you must be the smartest man alive. Imagine my surprise when I realized you're an idiot."

"What?"

Before I could say anything, he raised a hand to cut me off.

"I've been putting the pieces of this puzzle together. If I've got it right, that bullet was meant for you. How am I doing?"

"Yeah, go on."

Clay aimed his flashlight at the knot so I could see. "You're an idiot."

Embarrassed, I swiped a hand across my face. "So you said."

"How would you like to help me set a trap for him?"

Mortimer darted from his hole beneath a root to watch, his chipmunk eyes blinking up into the light.

"Yeah?" The knot came loose. I rolled up the rope. "I'm listening."

"I have a plan. Involving you could get me fired, but I need you for bait."

I stared at him.

"You need this. For closure. We've got to put this guy away before he destroys more lives. For Sable and all the other girls he's used and abused."

"I'm in."

"There's a bottle of Scotch at my house," Clay said as we walked to the road. "Follow me to my place. It's not far."

I don't often drink, but tonight is different. "What's the plan?" I tossed the rope into the back of the Forester.

"Somehow Nelson has stayed one step ahead of us. He must have hacked into our system, your phone, or both. We can use that to smoke him out. Feed him fake info."

"Hmmmmm. That idea isn't totally insane." I said.

"Thank you." He turned toward his Outlander, stopped, and said over his shoulder. "Hey, Ridge, do you know how many suicides change their mind after they've jumped?"

"Of course not," I said. "You can't know that."

"Nope. Neither can you."

Chapter Thirty
Ridge

True to his word, Clay had a fifth of Scotch at his house. I rarely drink. Not because my father has drummed into my head the thing about my body being a temple of the Lord. I don't drink because I am a fanatic about what I put into my body. I can't stay on top of my game unless my mind is sharp and I'm fit. The whole point here is because I hardly ever drink, it doesn't take much to wipe me out. Wish I had remembered that sooner.

Clay and I talked late into the night. Actually, he talked while I guzzled Scotch like a dying camel at an oasis. What he said made sense. As much as I can remember.

After we argued about where I should spend the night—Clay wanted me to stay at his place—he finally agreed to drop me off at Sable's duplex. He believed Nelson would be looking for my Forester. He insisted on hiding it in his garage. I'd stayed at Sable's a couple of nights without incident and thought Clay was being overly cautious, but I agreed.

As the night swallowed his taillights, I felt vulnerable. I'd left my gun under the front seat of my Forester, locked in Clay's garage. I wouldn't have forgotten it but I was smashed. Clay had to pour me into his SUV.

My head began to clear. Only slightly. Somewhere I had read that dark wouldn't be a thing without light. Dark is the absence of light—and the opposite of light—like evil is the opposite of good. I'm still too buzzed to think about anything that deep.

I unlocked Sable's door. I remembered another night I'd stood outside this door ringing the bell. I'd had the key that night, too. But I no longer had the right to use it. Dad believed my tennis suffered because of Sable. He had taken it upon himself to talk to her. She broke up with me. Again. I was really pissed at Dad. Back then Sable hadn't responded to my calls or texts. I hadn't heard her voice in a week. I couldn't stand it another minute and headed to Durango. Without a change of clothes. Without my shaving kit and toothbrush. Without a plan. I'd arrived outside this door at 4:00 AM. I hadn't eaten or slept for days and looked as bad as I do now. Something Sable pointed out when she finally opened the door.

"Good grief, Ridge, you look like hell."

"Can I come in?" I asked.

Once inside I didn't know what to do. I just stared at her. I'd hoped she would look as bad as I did. I'd imagined her looking gaunt, with smudged mascara, hair that hadn't been combed for a week. But no. She looked sleepy, but stunning. She wore one of my Yonex T-shirts which hit her mid-thigh. She looked at me and yawned.

I couldn't stand it another minute. I closed the distance between us and pulled her into a tight embrace. She didn't resist, but she didn't respond. I envisioned me driving back to Norman without this being resolved and had a moment of panic. But then she began to cry. Which gave me a little hope. I laid my cheek against the top of her head. Her hair smelled like coconut. Her hands were between us on my chest. She sniffed and pushed me away.

Fear tightened my chest. I desperately wanted to hang onto her. *Needed* to keep her close, but I let her disengage.

"Do you want some coffee?" she asked. "You look like you could use some." I shook my head. She turned away from me, shuffled into the living room in her big fuzzy house shoes, and sat on the sofa.

I followed and sat on the chair across from her. My desperation to see her was stronger than my need to be near her. I searched her eyes for the love I wanted to be there. She turned her head, keeping her emotions hidden—maybe from both of us. I knew this was killing her, too. She has a huge heart. Hurting me would be hurting her.

"The ball's in your court, Frazier," she said, and waited.

I was unable to articulate, even form a thought. She broke the silence.

"Your father is right. We both know it, Ridge. Tennis is your life. You don't have time for tennis, college, *and* me. Maybe later when..."

"You screwed up the order," I said, finding my voice. "You come first, Sable. You always have. Without you, there's no reason for tennis. Or college. My father wanted to be a tennis pro. He gave it up for something he wanted more. Politics. He lived his tennis dream through me." I pressed my fingers against my forehead rubbing in small circles to erase the tension headache. Sable watched me. Silently.

I continued. "My tennis lessons began at four, but he'd planned my career from the time the ultrasound confirmed I was a boy. I grew up knowing tennis was expected. Everyone gets swept along in the wake of Dad's enthusiasm. We're convinced his ideas are ours. Until I met you, I'd been too focused on making Grant Frazier proud to consider what I wanted."

I stood up and began to pace. Sable's dark eyes followed me. I turned around, walked back, and sat beside her on the sofa.

"Sable, this week has been hell, but it's forced me to examine my life. See it through my eyes. And yours. Instead of my father's. I existed before I met you, but I wasn't living. I can live without tennis, but not without you."

Sable looked down. A curtain of dark hair fell over her face, shutting me out. She finally turned toward me and looked up. She didn't raise her head, just her eyes. I fall more deeply in love with her every time those big brown eyes look up at me that way. It's like a secret weapon little girls are born with.

Her eyes melted my heart, but her words stomped all over it.

"Ridge, before your father asked me to back out of your life, I was planning to break up with you." She drew a deep shuddering breath and continued. "I love you. But I won't be with a man whose life is controlled by someone else. Even the illustrious Grant Frazier."

Stunned, I stood up and began pacing again. Unshed tears burned my eyes. She was right. My father ruled my life. And I had let him.

"When you took on Brett Nelson in the airport, Ridge, you completely blew me away," she said, "You were ready to fight to protect someone you didn't know. You had no fear. I fell in love with that Ridge. The man who is sure of himself and needs no one's approval. You have a great mind. The split-second decisions you make on the court are uncanny. No wonder you're ranked with the elite. But off the court, your father makes your decisions. Maybe in a couple of years..."

"No!"

Sable stood up and walked to the kitchen. "I need coffee."

She turned on the Keurig, came back out and stood in front of me to stop my pacing. She wrapped her arms around my neck and pressed her face against my chest.

"Do you?" I asked into her hair, my lips pressed against the top of her head. "Do you love me?"

She nodded. She was crying again. "You know I do. That's what makes this so hard. I need a man, Ridge. I'm three years older than you. That's always bothered me, even before I realized how willing you were to let your father make your decisions."

"But if you love me, we can make this work."

She shook her head. "People get married thinking love is enough. But it isn't. Which is why divorce attorneys are so wealthy. And breakup songs sell millions of records.

She looked up at me with those eyes. "Girls think they can change someone if they just love them more. It never works."

She was so close I couldn't help it. I lowered my head and kissed her. Her lips tasted salty. I wasn't sure if the tears were hers or mine. Loss tastes like salt.

She unwound her arms from my neck and went back into the kitchen. I followed and waited as she made two cups of coffee.

Sable had painted her kitchen a sunny yellow and hung white gauzy curtains over the window. The fact that her kitchen is big enough to have a window might be one of the reasons I found it charming. A sign hanging behind her Keurig said, "I like a little coffee with my cream and sugar." It's funny because although she's so into fitness, it's true.

She stirred cream and sugar into her coffee, carried both cups to the table and sat down. I pulled out a chair and sat beside her. With my elbow on the table, I rested my chin in my palm and exhaled deeply through splayed fingers.

Her white teapot-shaped clock on the wall behind her head ticked away seconds of our lives. Seconds when Sable still wasn't mine. In the pre-dawn silence it sounded inordinately loud. I wasn't getting anywhere. My stomach tied itself in a knot. Desperation crept in, like a cat with a laser beam on a mouse.

She pushed her chair back. "I have an early morning flight, Ridge."

"Wait! Give me a couple more minutes..."

She sighed. "If you'd never met me and your father hadn't been in your life, who would you want to be?"

"I've actually thought about that a lot this week," I said. I wanted to say I didn't give a damn about my life if she wasn't in it. But that wasn't what she wanted to hear.

From habit, she'd given me my favorite mug, it was heavy with a shaggy bison on it. A masculine cup. It always looked out of place among her China. I'd wondered where it came from but never asked. The bison stared at me as I thought.

"I'm majoring in business," I said finally, "with a minor in marketing. "But I can't see me sitting behind a desk every day. That would be a special kind of hell."

Sable nodded. "For you it would be."

"I might want to be a tennis coach. I love tennis. I'm just not willing to let it run my life anymore. I might want to be a sports agent. There's a lot of money in that."

"There's also a lot of stress," Sable spooned more sugar into her coffee. "It might be worse than sitting behind a desk. You're constantly on call. You have to drop what you're doing and hop on a plane at a moment's notice. But you could use your degrees with that."

I nodded, surprised. I wanted to ask how she knew that much about it, but I didn't want to get off the path our conversation was taking.

"I hope you'll do something that makes your heart happy," she continued. "No matter how much money is in it. Or not. You'd be a great tennis coach. What you can't teach is your instinct. You have something huge, Ridge, that can't be taught. Don't throw that away." Sable sipped her coffee, gazing at me across the cup.

I turned my cup, so the bison wasn't staring at me. "Sable, let's cut the crap. What I do or don't do isn't important. I don't care if I'm digging ditches as long as you're with me."

She gave me a long searching look. "Does your father know you're here?"

"I called him on the way."

"And told him what?" She added more sugar and cream to her coffee.

"I told him I'd walk ninety miles on my knees over ground glass if that's what it took to get you back. I told him I wanted to marry you. I told him I'm quitting tennis."

Sable raised an eyebrow. "What did he say?"

"He said, 'Well, Son, go get your girl'. Dad was stunned. He hadn't realized how deeply I love you. He's very fond of you. You know that.

Sable turned her cup in her hands. "Shouldn't you have talked to me about that?"

I shrugged. "If you remember, you weren't talking to me. But that's beside the point. With or without you, Dad will no longer be calling the shots." I exhaled slowly and scratched at something imaginary on the table. "I told him tennis was his dream, not mine. You are."

She stared at me for so long I was getting nervous.

"Do you?" she asked.

"Do I what?"

She rolled her eyes. "Want to marry me, Dipstick."

"Oh. Well, yeah."

"Well, shouldn't you get down on one knee or something?"

"What?" For a minute I was too stunned to think. My brain doesn't switch gears that fast. Except on the tennis court "Oh. Oh! We need a ring."

"I don't care about a ring," she said. "Here, this will work."

She went to a drawer and pulled out a rubber band. She sat back down and wrapped it around her finger.

"There," she said. "Now I have a ring."

"I can do better than that." I pulled the ring box from my pocket and got down on both knees. "Sable Amhurst, will you marry me?" I handed her the box.

She opened the box. Her eyes widened. Her lips formed my name.

I waited.

"Ohmygosh, Ridge, this is gorgeous!" She looked back at me. "When did you get this?" Unshed tears glazed her eyes.

"Two weeks before my father talked to you. You haven't said yes."

"Yes. Yes! Get up."

I got off my knees and back in my chair.

She took the ring from the box and handed it to me. "Here, put it on me," she said.

"Uh...there's a rubber band on your finger."

"Oh. Yeah," she said, removing the rubber band.

I slipped the ring on her finger. Perfect fit. I'd stolen one of her rings to get the size.

"What did you intend to do with this if I said no?" she asked.

"Rent a German tank. Call in the Blue Angels. Camp in your front yard until you changed your mind. "

She nodded.

"I'm not kidding. I have a tent in the Forester."

A fat tear slid down her cheek. This time her tears had a different meaning. My heart was doing something between a mambo and a salsa.

"Pretty sure of yourself." She turned her hand. The ring flashed colors in the light.

"I hear that's what you like about me. I am my father's son," I said. "Guess I got more from him than tennis."

She reached over and laid her hand over mine. She squeezed three times. Three of anything had been our secret signal since my first run in with Nelson. Three hand squeezes, three pats on a shoulder, three headlight flashes on a car backing out of a driveway on a dark morning, three quick kisses on the way out the door. Because if a situation, like the airport incident with Nelson ever came up, I wanted to be able to tell her without words, "I love you. I have your back. We've got this. Together." Three squeezes.

Sable looked into my eyes and leaned toward me. "I don't want you to quit tennis, Ridge. Tennis is who you are. You walk out on that court like you own it. I'm proud of how good you are. You're the best. Everyone says so. Let's see where your talent takes you. Where it takes us."

* * *

Unwilling to let that memory fade, I sat at Sable's table in the same chair I'd been sitting in that night, reliving that conversation into the early morning. But that memory drained me. And then there was the weird thing with my dad tonight in the canyon—too real to have been my imagination. I ran through what he'd said. He hadn't even mentioned tennis. What had been important to him was family. He didn't say, "Be a tennis star and make me proud." He said he was already proud.

This place, so familiar, tormented me. I had to get some sleep. Exhausted, I stumbled into Sable's room and crawled into her bed. Her pillow smelled like her. The clock on the nightstand blinked 4:00 AM. But tired as I was, sleep eluded me. So, I lay there wondering why I thought sleeping in this bed was a good idea.

Finally, I dozed.

"Ridge, wake up!" Dad's voice jerked me awake.

"Dad, I gotta get some sleep. You said..."

A car door slammed right outside the window. Reflex kicked in. I rolled across the bed and hit the floor a few seconds before a flashlight beam swept across the wall above my head. Nelson! Had he seen me? The shade had been pulled down, but I hadn't noticed the three-inch gap along the bottom.

The beam panned across the bed again. Slowly this time. Careful. Deliberate. As though he knew I was here.

I won't make the mistake of being without my gun again.

There was nothing to alert Nelson that I was here. The bed had been unmade when I crawled into it. Hopefully, it wouldn't look any different now than it would have if Nelson had been here before. Under my breath I cursed my stupidity for not making sure the shade had been pulled all the way down.

A baseball bat leaned against the wall in a corner. I retrieved it and waited.

Nelson moved to the door and turned the knob. He must know it would be locked. I held my breath. Would he try to break in? There was nothing in here that he wanted. Except me. No lights were on. No indication anyone was here. No Forester outside.

Gravel crunched as Nelson walked back to his car. The Pathfinder door slammed again. I waited until I heard him drive away before I got up and went to the window. The gray light of dawn stretched across the eastern sky. Morning had returned and I was still awake. I pulled down the shade, too tired to care if Nelson came back and noticed.

I was sleeping soundly when my phone rang. I checked the time before answering. 11:45 AM. Nearly noon. I rolled over.

"Hello," I croaked.

"Wake up Dude." Clay sounded way too cheerful. "Let's go catch a killer."

Chapter Thirty-One
April

Since Grant's death, the few nights I've slept—left me feeling like a Peterbilt was parked on my chest. My circumstances haven't changed. I still dread a future without my husband. I still have no idea where my son is. But this morning I woke with the weight lifted, as if a crisis had just been averted.

The air, fresh and clean, was cool on my face. Outside the open window a Ponderosa pine branch swayed gently and I remembered where I was. Durango, Colorado. That realization brought with it the memory of my conversation with Ron. For the first time in years the thought of him didn't trigger an avalanche of pain and resentment.

I got up, made coffee, and snuggled into an over-sized chair beneath a throw. I needed to think. But that option disappeared with the ringing of my phone. My aunt's face appeared on the screen.

I smiled as I answered. "Abby, you're the person I most need to talk to."

"Uh oh. Do you need bail money?" She laughed. "I heard Lane sent Ron with you.

In Lane's defense, he didn't know your history with Ron. You haven't killed him, have you?"

"Lane or Ron? I've been tempted to kill them both. But maybe I won't. Ron is picking up your son-in-law at the airport this morning."

"Good. I feel better with Lane being there. To referee."

"Ron and I had a long talk last night."

"He had a plausible explanation for what he did?" The banter left Abby's voice. "I want to hear that!"

"You will. After I have time to sort through it. If I'd swallowed my pride and demanded an explanation..." I sighed. "But then I wouldn't have met Grant and had my kids. I wouldn't change any of that. Still, I wish I hadn't wasted so many years being angry."

"Anger is always a waste of time. It only hurts the one who's angry."

I gazed out the window, watching squirrels chase each other around the pine. "It was more than anger," I said finally. "Ron dumping me proved I shouldn't get attached. To anyone. Except for you and Dad, everyone I ever loved disappeared. But then you were badly injured, and Dad was—unavailable."

"Ali's abduction overwhelmed me. I had no idea how much it affected you." Abby sighed. "I wish I had known how badly Ron hurt you. I wasn't there for you.

"I felt worthless. Ron knew me better than anyone, yet he abandoned me."

"Hold on!" Abby interrupted. "That's two different things. There was a six-year span of time there. When you were fourteen, you needed validation. We all do at that age. You were looking for someone to say, 'I see you. You are worthy. Worthy of my love.' Thank goodness that person was Ron. Most fourteen-year-old boys don't have a clue about love. Somebody else could have really messed you up. Ron didn't. He filled the places where you were empty. When he left, you had grown into a fine accomplished woman. You were older and stronger."

"I was still a screwup."

"Not true. You excelled at everything you did. Good grief! You were Miss Oklahoma."

"I got nowhere in the Miss America pageant."

"You were disqualified because you got into a fight with Miss Nevada." Abby laughed. "You can't count that."

"Where are you?" I asked.

"Your house. Russ is in Barcelona. Business. trip. I thought being here with the girls sounded better than staying home by myself or going to Spain again with him. Glad I came. The three of us had a nice chat last night."

"Riley Grace spent some time with you?"

"She came back downstairs after Bronc and Alise left."

"I wish I understood her."

"You haven't made much of an effort."

I felt like I had been slapped, but Abby was right. "I've been busy," I said, my voice sounding whiney even to me. "With three restaurants, the speaking circuit..."

"And Grant's campaigns," Abby interrupted, "You've been totally out of touch with your children. You didn't know Ridge was engaged, you'd never heard of Sable. April, you brought those children into the world. Your most important job is raising them. Not all this other stuff you're doing to prove your worth."

Her words stung. If anyone else had said that I would have been furious. But Abby practically raised me—even before Mom died. If this is the way she sees me, I'd better pay attention.

"Someone else could do most of the things you do, admittedly not as well," Abby continued. "But nobody else can be a mother to your children."

"Is it too late?" I asked. "Riley Grace doesn't like me."

"She thinks you don't like her. She gets so little of your attention."

"I've been home more," I said defensively.

"April, loneliness isn't being alone. You can feel lonely in a crowd. When you're home, you don't give that girl the time of day."

"She's always upstairs in her room. "

"Do you even know what she does up there?"

"Well, uh, homework, I guess." My voice sounded whiney and defensive to my own ears.

"You have a wonderful daughter. You should get to know her"

"She has no interest in being with me now. How do I change that?"

"Be vulnerable. Talk to her about the mistakes you've made. Let her see who you are. Be her mother."

"I don't know where to start."

"Where you are. You can't change the past."

"You're right." I exhaled slowly. "Ron said the same thing last night."

"You got a bit of help last night," Abby said.

"How so?"

"Gracie went up to the attic to look for Ridge's old yearbooks," Abby said. "Bronc and Ridge went to the same elementary school. Riley wanted to see pictures of him when he was a little kid."

"Did she find any?"

"No. But she found some of your old journals. She came downstairs crying with a lot of questions."

"Oh, no!"

"It's a good thing. She knew your mother died when you were young. She read how lost and confused you were. Her eyes were opened when she realized you also lost your Grammy and Ali right after that. It's difficult for children to see a parent as a person. She discovered her mother was once a little girl with a broken heart."

I sniffed and swiped at a tear.

"People hide pain with sex, drugs, booze—you tried to hide yours, even from yourself, with success."

Abby knew me so well.

"You've lost credibility with yourself, April."

"I'm smarter now than I was back then."

"I certainly hope so," Abby laughed. "What have you learned?"

"Don't get in a fight with Miss Nevada in front of the of judges."

Abby laughed. "You and your sweet child will be fine."

I checked the time. "I need to get myself together. Don't want to hold things up when Ron and Lane get here."

"Let us know as soon as you find out anything."

"I will. Glad you called. Talking to you is not always fun. But it's always exactly what I need. You are the one person I know will always tell me the truth. No matter how much it hurts."

"You know I love you."

"I know. Sometimes you were the only one who did."

I hit 'end' on my phone but stayed where I was. Tears streamed down my face. Not for the husband I lost, nor the son I couldn't find, not for the ten-year-old me who lost her mother. I cried for my daughter. Being discounted by the person who should love you most hurts more than having no mother at all. I have to fix this.

Chapter Thirty-Two
April

The Highway Patrol office was a small concrete block nondescript building five minutes west of town. As the three of us trooped in a patrolman sitting at the front desk looked up, and scowled. They obviously didn't get a lot of walk-ins.

"May I help you?" He asked. But his tone said, 'I'm overworked, we're under-staffed. Go away.'

Lane stepped up, and showed his ID. "We'd like to speak to the trooper who worked the Senator Frazier accident."

The patrolman looked at Ron and me. "And you are?"

"Mrs. Grant Frazier," Lane answered, "the Senator's wife and Ron Lang, the family attorney."

The patrolman's gaze swept over me. I wore jeans and an OU Tee shirt. Maybe I should have used a bit more discretion when I tossed clothes into a bag. I handed him my drivers' license and passport. He glanced at them and squinted up at me. I understood. The put-together me in the pictures looked nothing like the me in front of him.

"Trooper Clayton Morley is off today."

"I'd like his phone number," Lane said.

"That's against policy."

"I can get it," Lane spoke slowly as though explaining to a slow third grader. "It will save time if you just give it to me."

The trooper nodded and scribbled down the number.

"Thank you." Lane pocketed the number. "Trooper Morley didn't work that accident alone. Who else do we need to talk to?"

The patrolman's scowl deepened. Lane was falling from favor fast. "Trooper Howard."

Lane stared at him. "Well, is he here?"

"I think so." The trooper's chair scraped the concrete floor as he pushed back. He stood up and left the room. In a building this small how could there be a question of someone being there?

We looked at each other. I was wondering if Howard was a first or last name, when the trooper reappeared with an older man who looked no happier to see us.

Lane stepped forward. "I'm Lane Lanigan. This is Mrs. Grant Frazier and Ron Lang."

Trooper Howard gave me a curt nod. He shook hands with Lane and Ron.

"Mrs. Frazier has a few questions about the Senator's death," Lane continued.

"Lanigan? Lanigan—you wouldn't happen to be Stoney Lanigan's son would you?" the older man asked. "Of course, you would. You resemble your dad."

"You knew my father?" Lane's eyebrows raised in surprise.

"I did. Not well, but he was a fine man. A great sheriff. Boy, we could use him back here now. Damn shame what happened to him." Trooper Howard was warming up. "His kid was in the truck. They didn't find them for days. I forget how many."

"Three," Lane said.

Trooper Howard blinked. "Oh! Right. You're the son?"

"Yeah," Lane said. "That was me."

"Terrible. Just terrible." Trooper Howard scratched his head. "You were a little shaver."

"Dad's funeral was on my fourth birthday."

"You know who you should talk to?" Trooper Howard asked. He gave Lane no chance to answer. "Nate Johnston. Yes, sir. Ole Nate was a good friend of your dad's. He might have been your dad's deputy back then."

"He was. I remember him," Lane said. "Is he still around? Where can I find him?" "Last I heard he was in a nursing home up in Montrose. Give me a few minutes, I can probably find the address for you. He might not remember you. I hear he has his good days, but most of the time he's pretty out of it."

Trooper's Howard's attitude had changed. I gave Lane a smile, grateful he took the time to be here.

"I'd appreciate that," Lane said. "But right now, Mrs. Frazier has questions about her husband's death."

"Tell you what, you folks come on back to my office. I'll see if I can find another chair. Sylvie can make copies of the accident report for you. There isn't a lot I can add."

Trooper Howard talked over his shoulder on his way down the hall. As he passed an office, he grabbed a folding chair which at some point in time had possibly been caught in a combine. He dragged it along with him.

His office, painted a repulsive shade of pea green, was already crowded with his metal desk, chair, and file cabinet. With four people it was claustrophobic. I eyed the door wondering how fast I could climb over Ron in case of fire. I gingerly seated myself on a chair with a bent leg.

The now-friendly trooper squeezed past us to get behind his desk. He shimmied down into his chair, looked at me, and asked, "Now, what can I tell you?"

"You were the investigating officer at the scene?" I asked.

"Yes."

"You spoke to my son?"

"Yes, ma'am."

"How was he?"

"He was in shock, as of course he would be. But he was holding it together."

"Did he see the accident happen?"

Trooper Howard shook his head. "No. He arrived right after it happened, He was the first one at the scene. Wait a minute—have you not talked to him?"

Embarrassed, I avoided his penetrating gaze. "No."

"Not at all? Well, that's strange."

"It is strange. Very strange. It's why I'm here," I said. "I have to find my son." Trooper Howard gave me a look I couldn't read.

A lady, supposedly Sylvie, came to the door. She was stuffed into her undersized uniform as tightly as we were crammed in the office. She couldn't get into the room, so she leaned across Ron and handed me a manilla folder.

I would never have gotten it without Lane. I will be forever grateful that he came to help me. Ron, too. But Ron wouldn't be here without Lane's insistence.

I mouthed 'thank you'.

Lane nodded and winked.

I opened the folder and glanced at the report. There were several sheets of paper filled out by the two investigating troopers as well as photos taken at the scene, and reports from witnesses. Although I knew Ridge had been there, a chill snaked down my spine when I saw his signature.

I looked up at Trooper Howard. "The details are pretty sketchy. What I'm wanting to know is why can't I take my husband home."

"Well, you'll have to take that up with the coroner because..."

Lane cut him off. "When a body hasn't been released in this amount of time, it's because it either hasn't been properly identified, or the case is being treated as a homicide. Senator Frazier has been identified. So, is this case a homicide?"

Trooper Howard shifted uncomfortably in his chair.

"Yes," he said, finally. "We are investigating it as a homicide."

"Why?" Lane asked.

"The car had two bullet holes in it."

"That isn't mentioned in this report," I pointed out.

"The car was brought up four days after the report was filed. The bullet holes weren't discovered until then."

"Did either of the bodies have bullet wounds?" Lane asked. His tone had changed.

His eyes narrowed.

"Jorge, up front, said you're some kind of federal agent. Is that right?"

"DEA," Lane said.

"Your daddy would be right proud." Trooper Howard nodded. He leaned back in his chair, tented his fingers, and gazed up at the ceiling fan as he thought. "Yes," he said finally. "The Senator had a bullet in his skull. He would have died instantly. Before the car went through the guard rail." He looked at me, seemed to remember he was talking to the widow and added, "Which would be a blessing."

My stomach leaped into my throat. I couldn't breathe.

"What caliber?" Lane asked.

".45 I believe. The guy must have been a heck of a shot to plug a bullet into a guy's skull from a moving vehicle." He shook his head, then realized what he'd just said. I must have turned white.

"Sorry Ma'am," he added.

I nodded to acknowledge his apology. I'd been thinking the same thing. "Why isn't that in this report?" I asked.

"Well now, the coroner didn't examine the body for three days. It took a while to recover and bring up the body. I believe the coroner was out of town when his office received the body. This report had already been filed."

When I heard Grant referred to as "the body" I went cold. I would have been screaming if I hadn't had been concentrating on staying seated on a chair intent on throwing me off. I looked up at the unfinished picture of George Washington, the only decoration in the room, and wondered why there were so many prints made of that picture. He was elected president in the late 1700's. Surely someone would have had time to finish it by now.

"What about Miss Amhurst?" Lane asked. "Had she also been shot?" He reached over and squeezed my knee. I stopped shaking.

"Don't know," Trooper Howard said.

Lane's eyes narrowed again. He leaned forward. "Why would you not know?"

"Her body hasn't been recovered."

"What?" Lane and I asked at the same time. I almost fell off my chair.

"Have you been to the wreck site?" Howard asked.

Ron and I nodded. To my surprise, Lane nodded, too. He flew in this morning. When had he been there? He hadn't mentioned it. Which meant nothing. Of course.

"Then you know what we are up against. The gorge is deep. Four hundred feet at that point. How they recovered the car, I'll never know. Glad that's not my job. Besides being deep, the bottom is rocky and rugged. Boulders the size of a house in places. A few pines grow in that area, quite a few, actually. The search dogs are good but haven't found the other body."

Stunned, the three of us stared at each other. "But she was in the car, right?"

"9-1-1 calls indicate she was. Your son said she was, He had been talking to her."

I stared.

"Ridge?" Trooper Howard asked, as though trying to either establish that my son's name is Ridge or that I'm capable of remembering it.

I nodded again. I pictured my son staring into the ravine I'd stared into yesterday knowing his father and Sable were down there. My mother's heart had to find him—wrap my arms around him.

"Do you have Sable's parent's address?" I asked to keep from bursting into tears. "I'd like to send her family flowers."

"I'm not sure," Trooper Howard said.

"Okay," Lane said. "How do I find out who you notified?"

"Victim's Advocacy notified her next of kin."

"You've been very helpful." Lane smiled and handed him his card. "If you think of anything else, please call me."

"Trooper Howard stood up. "I'll let you know where you can find Nate."

Lane smiled a real smile. "I'd appreciate that. It was nice meeting you, Trooper Howard. Not many people remember my dad."

I handed trooper Howard a business card. "If you happen to see my son, please tell him to call his mother. And could you please let me know?"

Trooper Howard nodded but didn't make eye contact. He'd already moved on to the first item on his to-do list.

Chapter Thirty-Three

Ridge

I parked in the shade of the giant cottonwood in front of the General Palmer Hotel.

"Well," I said out loud, "let's see how this goes."

I took my phone from the handy holder on my console where it stays when I'm driving. I dialed Clay's number and waited. It rang four times before he answered.

"Officer Morley."

"Officer Morley, this is Ridge Frazier." I didn't have to fake nervousness. I could hear it in my voice.

"Who?"

"Ridge Frazier. Grant Frazier's son."

"Oh. Right. The Senator. Yes, Ridge, how can I help you?"

"I found it!"

"You found what?"

"Sable's phone. It has the messages and threatening texts Nelson sent her. It's the proof you need to arrest him."

"Nice. It was at the wreck site?"

"Nearby."

"Good work. Bring it in."

"Well, I don't have it yet. It's still out there. It's on a ledge about twenty feet below the road. I spotted it but couldn't get to it. I tried, but my rope wasn't long enough."

"So, where are you now?" Clay asked.

"In town. I came in to get more equipment. Pretty sure I can get to it now."

"Ridge, wait! That's too dangerous. Nobody in their right mind rappels alone. Professionals don't even do it. Don't go out there by yourself. I'll send out a team."

"Thanks for assuming I'm in my right mind. Your crew won't know where to look. What if Nelson goes out there and finds it before they get there? I can't take that chance."

"He won't. Use your head. Nobody would even suspect that it's not at the bottom of the ravine. Wait for help. I mean it. Don't go back out there."

"Your team won't find it. It's a miracle that I did. It's hidden behind a pile of rocks."

"I tell you what," Clay said, sounding very thoughtful. "Here's what we'll do. I'll call the team. When they are on the way, I'll call you. You can meet them out there and show them where it is."

"You can call them. I'm going back out to wait for them."

"I probably can't talk you out of that," Clay said. "Where are you now?"

"The Lone Spur having some breakfast," I lied.

"Wait there for me. I have a break coming up. I'll stop by and have a cup of coffee with you. I'm hungry. Order me the Grand Slam breakfast."

"Okay," I said. "But hurry. I want to get back out there."

"Copy that. See you in a bit."

I disconnected and watched through the windshield as a flock of birds, spooked off a highline wire, took flight. I looked over at Clay who sat in my passenger seat. He turned off his phone and wrapped it in foil.

“Do you actually think Nelson has hacked into the Highway Patrol phone system?” I asked.

“He stays one step ahead of us. He must be hearing our communication.”

“Isn’t that a felony?”

“Nelson doesn’t seem to have an issue with that.” Clay shook his head. “With the charges he’s stacked up, what’s one more?”

“Think this will work?” I asked.

“Don’t know.” Clay grinned. “Let’s go see.”

Chapter Thirty-Four

Riley Grace

My first morning back to school after the funeral would have been a nightmare if it hadn't been for Alise and Bronc. Nobody else talked to me. I'd catch people looking at me, but when I tried to make eye-contact their eyes slid away. Alise says it's because they don't know what to say. That's probably true but being treated like I have gonorrhea hurts.

Not that I know what gonorrhea is. For sure. I saw a gross video which convinced me I don't want it, but it's probably something someone came up to with to scare kids out of having sex. They're a little late. Almost everyone I know is already having sex. Except me. And well, Alise isn't either. Ridge is the only one in my family who gives me the third degree about it. Dad assumes his little angel wouldn't do that. I don't think it's even occurred to mom to wonder.

Until Bronc, I've been too busy with tennis and my math tutor to even have a boyfriend. I'm flunking math. The Senator's daughter can't flunk math. Apparently. My tutor has bad breath, dresses like a bag lady, and my grades are no better. Half of a cup and a half is three fourths of a cup. I can cut my brownies recipe in half. What more do I need to know? Numbers give me a headache. It's a good thing I'm into tennis and not basketball. I'd never keep the score straight.

Alise has never had a real boyfriend either. She blames it on her father being a cop. She says he would kill any guy he'd even suspected she had sex with. He makes a point of cleaning his gun anytime a guy walks into their house. Alise assumes it's the reason she rarely has second dates. But it might be due to her Farrah Fawcett fascination.

Three months ago, Alise decided if she cut her hair in layers, she'd look just like Farrah. Alise has dark hair and an olive complexion, but whatever. I wouldn't cut her hair so she did it herself. It's growing out but looks like she's been attacked by Mark Burnham with his chainsaw.

Alise is into something I call "exclusive dating". If she wouldn't consider marrying a guy, she won't go out with him. She says it saves time, energy, and razor blades. Because, and I quote, "Why shave your legs for someone who doesn't matter?"

While I see her point, how does she know he doesn't matter until she gets to know him?

She's also worrying about the whole soulmate thing. If there is only one guy out there who is right for each girl, Alise is afraid she might accidentally marry some poor girl's soulmate thereby robbing her of a life of wedded bliss. Also, if Alise married some guy who turned out not to be her soulmate, she would go through life just nominally happy instead of ecstatic. I asked if she knew many ecstatic couples. She couldn't think of one. There must be a lot of mismatched soulmates out there.

Alise and Bronc stayed beside me all day, something I'll appreciate until I'm old and can't remember who I am. Or who they are. I have to say their names in that order. Alise and Bronc. Alise says her name should always come before his in my mind because he hasn't been my boyfriend long and she's been my best friend since fifth grade. Also, it's in proper alphabetical order, something I hadn't realized was all that important to Alise until now.

The three of us sat together at lunch. It felt kind of weird in a good way. BB, (Before Bronc), the first thing I did when I walked into the lunchroom was look for him. Today I knew where he was. Beside me. Holding my hand. Which made it difficult to eat. Tomorrow I have to make sure he sits on my left.

Bronc's friend sat with us, too. I'm kind of hoping Alise will like him so the four of us can hang out. His name is spelled S-t-a-n-l-e-i-g-h which is cool. I guess. Because Alise is acting kind of interested. She's been doing flirty head tosses, which might be sexy except most of her hair is too short. It looks like she has a crick in her neck or tourette syndrome.

I couldn't get past his name. I can't imagine saying, "Oooohh, Stanleigh!" when you're making out. It's an uncool name. Like Herschel. Or Bartholomew which sounds like a noise a sick cat makes.

I'm not sure Stanleigh's cool spelling makes up for him being shorter than she is or his coke-bottle glasses that keep sliding down his nose. We'll see how it goes.

I crammed my backpack into my locker, slammed the door, turned around, and leaned against it while trying to psyche myself up to walk into my next class, alone. It's the one class Alise and I don't have together.

Bronc appeared out of nowhere. He placed his hands against the lockers on either of my head, looked down the hall both ways, and leaned in for a kiss.

Alise says that Bronc and I are still in the 'honeymoon phase". When I reminded her that we aren't married, she explained it was an obsolete term now because most couples have lived together for two or three years before getting married.

Then she added that it used to be the period of time after a couple returned from the honeymoon but the wife hadn't figured out that her husband wore a toupee or had false teeth.

"Why aren't you in class?" I asked.

"Had to make sure my girl was okay," Bronc said. "You looked worried when I passed you in the hall. What's up?"

"I got a note to go to Mrs. Hutchison's office after school. I can't be in trouble. I haven't even been back a whole day yet."

Bronc faked a look of terror, which made me laugh because it looked more like he had gas. But I appreciated the effort.

"I'm trying not to worry but Mom is in Durango. And Ridge is—who knows."

"If it was serious," Bronc pointed out, "someone would've come to get you."

"You're right." I sighed. "Before Dad died, I never worried about stuff. Bad things only happened to other people. Now, I expect it."

Bronc nodded. "You'll get over that. Come on. Let's get you to class."

I pushed away from the locker, and he walked me to the science room.

After school, I shoved through the sea of people rushing toward the front door like they were escaping the Titanic. When that last bell rang, even merging into the flow takes practice and timing. But when you're going against traffic, it's like a spawning salmon trying to swim upstream—dangerous, but without grizzlies. Usually.

I made it to the principal's office, but it was terrifying. And exhausting. Mrs. Hutchison sat at her desk frowning at her computer screen.

When I came in, she looked up and smiled. "Riley Grace Frazier, there you are, Dear."

I didn't know what to say to that.

Her hair looked like Alise had cut it. Grayish with hot pink and purple streaks. It stuck out. In weird places. Without gel. Not sure that's a good look for a high school principal, but I'm not here to judge. She sort of resembled Billy Idol if he had been run over by the Good Humor truck. At least she didn't have piercings. That I could see. I didn't want to think about that for very long. People call her 'guppy' because she often opens and closes her mouth without saying anything. You could be talking about something important like maybe the trade war in Nigeria and stop because you thought she had something to say. But then she doesn't. Although it isn't cool to like your principal, I kind of like her. She's always been nice to me. And she called me Dear, so I must not be in trouble.

"Your parents were here last month," she said. She hit several keys on her computer and looked up.

"My parents? My dad was here?"

"Yes, it was nice to meet him," she gave me a sympathetic smile. "Such a nice man. As you can imagine, though, he wasn't happy about our tennis program."

"I know. My mom came, too?"

"Yes. Sit down, Dear."

I perched on the edge of the chair and tried not to look at her hair.

"It was a shame we lost Coach Hardesty." Mrs. Hutchison twirled a pencil through her fingers as she talked. "Coach Garrison is a good basketball coach, but tennis just isn't her thing. She's not up to working with someone of your caliber." She smiled. "That leaves only me."

"You?" I blinked.

She laughed. "That was a joke. I was on the tennis team in college, but I've packed on a few pounds since then."

She'd packed on more than a few, but I'm too polite to say so.

"Why were my parents here?"

"They were hoping I could help them find a suitable personal trainer for you."

I was stunned. Neither of them had mentioned this to me.

"I tried to call your mother after your father died to tell her how sorry I am. And that I found you a coach."

"You did?"

"Yes. Have you heard of Eve Anna Evans? She was..."

"Wait! What?"

"Eve Anna Evans..."

"Ohmygosh! Eve Anna Evans? She's coached some of the biggest names in tennis!"

"Yes. Before that she was quite the phenom herself."

"She is coming here? Ohmygosh!"

"You already said that, Dear."

"How did you do that?"

"I'd love to take credit, but her parents live in town. They've been quite ill, which is probably why she agreed to come to Oklahoma. Although she's looking forward to working with Ridge Frazier's sister."

Too excited to sit still, I bounced in my chair like a little kid in Wal Mart who has had way too much sugar. "She is? Eve Anna Evans! I can't believe it!"

Mrs. Hutchinson tapped a couple of keys on her computer and looked back up at me. "When you talk to your mom, Dear, tell her I had to work hard to get someone of Miss Evans caliber," she winked. "But you are worth it. Please have your mother contact me as soon as possible. There will be papers to sign."

"Eve Anna Evans! Mom won't know who she is, but I can't wait to tell Ridge. Thank you!" I wanted to hug her but thought that might be a bit much. I went around her desk and hugged her anyway.

She looked embarrassed and laughed. Pleased, but embarrassed. High school principals probably don't get many hugs.

Alise and Bronc would be waiting by my car, but only one person would truly understand how huge this was. I stopped by the door and texted Ridge.

Me: *Ridge, guess what!!! You'll never guess! Eve Anna Evans is coming to Oklahoma. To coach me!!!!*

I added more exclamation points and several shocked emoji faces and hit send. My text tone beeped immediately. It was Ridge.

Ridge: *Eve Anna Evans??? Rye, that is huge! Way to go, Brat!*

I smiled. At least I know he's alive.

Chapter Thirty-Five
April

Outside the Colorado Highway Patrol office Ron flipped on the turn signal, waited for a green Forester to pass, turned left, and headed back toward Durango. He glanced at me in the rear view-mirror. "Where to, Boss?"

My eyes followed the Forester. It looked like Ridge's, but the driver was not Ridge. "I want to find Ridge. I have no idea where to look," I said.

"Sable's apartment isn't far from here. Let's check it out," Lane said. "I doubt he's there, but it won't hurt to look. Ron, turn left up here at the stoplight."

"Riley Grace said Ridge has a key. Staying at her place would be cheaper than a motel. Not that Ridge has ever tried to conserve money. But I have a feeling he'd want to be there," I said.

"I don't know," Lane said. "It's the first place Nelson would look for him."

"You're right. Hopefully Ridge is smart enough to stay ahead of Nelson," I said.

Wondering why Lane had asked Trooper Howard for Sable's address if he already had it, I leaned back in the seat and looked out the window.

The neighborhoods began to change as they slipped past. Trees were larger and older and so were houses. We were nearing the college. Groups of young people strolled down the street with, evidently, no thought of moving out of the way.

Ron pulled over in front of a duplex and stopped. "Here we are."

"Sable's apartment is the door on the left," Lane added.

Sable's door, flanked on each side by large pots of ferns, had been painted a bright turquoise. Three hanging baskets overflowing with vibrant color lined the porch. A large elm shaded the postage-stamp front yard and most of the street. An enormous well-tended flower bed filled most of her front yard. A gravel parking area stretched between the street and the sidewalk. I pictured how Sable's red convertible, now a mangled mess wherever it is, would have looked sitting in front of this house.

I imagined Sable walking up the path to the door, unlocking it, and going inside. And just like that, Sable became a real person to me. Someone who had lived, breathed, planted flowers, and painted her door—a girl who loved color and my son. The loss of Sable rolled over me like an avalanche, sucking the air from my lungs. The beautiful girl my son adored and I will never meet. Before tears gushed and while I could still see, I noticed Ridge's green Forester wasn't parked there either. But he had been in and out of that house often. And evidently, my husband at least once. Even Riley Grace knew Ridge had a key. How did I get so out of touch with my family?

Lane walked up to the front door, knocked, peering around the blinds. He shrugged and waited, giving me time to collect my thoughts and decide what to do.

Ron heard me sniffing and tossed a box of tissues back to me.

"Let's go grab something to eat and regroup," Lane suggested, as he slid back into the front seat. "I'm starving."

"Now, that you mention it, I could eat, too," Ron nodded. He looked in the rear-view mirror and caught my eye. "Okay with you? Are we through here?"

I nodded and blew my nose.

"We're only a couple of blocks from the hotel," Lane said. "We can park there and walk down the street to the Rusty Spur. A Joe's Special has been calling my name."

We parked under the giant cottonwood in front of the General Palmer Hotel, got out and jaywalked across the street.

"Okay, so tell me about this Joe's Special you've been talking about," I said. The life-sized bronze statues of three foals stared at us curiously as we passed. The talented sculptor, Joyce Parkerson, had caught their expressions in amazing detail. That lady knew horses. I stopped to take pictures to send Riley Grace.

"Almost every restaurant out west has their own version," Lane said. "But the Rusty Spur does it right."

"So, what is Joe's Special, exactly?" Ron's attention shifted from the train depot to look back at Lane. "What's the big deal?"

"The part of the story everyone agrees on is how it started in San Francisco in the 1920's," Lane said. "Supposedly, a bunch of hungry miners came into Joe's Original Café. He was low on supplies and didn't have much to feed them. To make matters worse, more miners showed up. Back then a piano player could get shot for playing the wrong song. Joe was a bit concerned. The miners were hungry and disgruntled."

Lane paused, looked around to see if his audience was paying attention. They were.

He continued, "There wasn't enough ground meat for hamburgers, so Joe threw what he had in a skillet and began browning it. He chopped some onions and threw them in. More men came in. The situation was sliding downhill fast. Joe was getting desperate."

Lane was obviously enjoying his narration.

We walked into the Rusty Spur past the bearskin hanging on the wall and a sign that advised customers not to squat with their spurs on. Ron slid into a booth beside a huge painting of cowboys driving a herd of white-faced Herefords. Lane sat beside him.

"Finish your story," I said. I sat across from them and gazed up at the huge lodge pole pines used as exposed beams across the high ceiling. "I won't be able to sleep tonight without knowing if Joe survived."

"He did, but just barely." Lane grinned. "Fortunately, a lady had come in that day with a crate of eggs. He scrambled a few dozen and threw them in. Then, in a stroke of genius, he remembered he had a bag of spinach. It didn't look too good. But he tossed it in the skillet, wilted it, and nobody noticed. Then he crumbled blue cheese over it. The miners were ravenous, so maybe that's why they thought it was so good. Anyway, the story of that meal spread like wildfire. Some places add mushroom, some drown it in Tabasco. So Joe's Special became a regular item."

"I see," I said. "We better order it." But I reached for a menu to see what else was on it. As a restaurant owner, I study menus like some people pore over sports scores.

The waitress brought us water and scurried away with a promise to be right back.

Ron and Lane were deep in conversation about the Dallas Cowboys blowing a game they should have won when Lane got a text. He glanced at his phone, then looked up at me.

"What?" I asked. "Who was that?"

"Nothing," Lane said.

"Liar, what's going on?"

Ignoring my question, Lane got up and headed for the door. "Order me the Joe's Special," he said on his way out.

"What do you suppose that was about." I asked, trying to convince myself it was nothing. But Lane's expression had said otherwise.

Ron shook his head. "Who knows?"

The waitress reappeared. Ron ordered two Joe's Specials. I ordered toast and poached eggs. I was pretty sure I couldn't eat the Joe's Special.

"Chicken," Ron chided.

Lane was suddenly back. He didn't sit down. "Can you two walk back to the hotel or find something to do around town?" Lane asked Ron. He held out his hand.

"Sure," Ron said. "Where are you going? We ordered your food." He dropped the Tahoe keys in Lane's hand.

"I gotta run an errand," Lane said. "Get a to-go box for my Special. I'll be hungry when I get back. April, I know this is a difficult time for you. But you're not alone. Ron is here to help you through this. I'll be back a soon as I can. Enjoy your meal. And try not to kill each other."

Before I could reply, he was gone.

Chapter Thirty-Six

Ridge

If I had jumped into the canyon last night, I would have bounced from ledge to ledge on my way down. More painful than a straight shot down. I wouldn't have died instantly. Too many scrub pines and rocky outcroppings. Like the one on I was standing on, between me and the boulder-strewn canyon floor. I won't be trying that again.

The shriek of a hawk pulled me away from my thoughts and back to the present. Shading my eyes with my hand, I watched him circle above my head riding an updraft in a cloudless sky. The sun reminded me I'd lost my Oakleys when I rappelled down to get Sable's phone yesterday.

"Hey, what's rustling in the brush?" I yelled. "Can you see?"

"It's probably your stupid chipmunk," Clay said, changing his position in the tree to get a better view.

"Mortimer would have to be wearing combat boots. It sounds like an armadillo. Or an elephant."

"Not many of those in Colorado."

"Armadillos or elephants?" I asked, watching a giant red ant crawl out of a crevice and make his way across a boulder totally unaware of my presence.

"Neither. Why? Does Oklahoma have armadillos?" Clay asked.

"Not as many as there used to be. Mostly roadkill," I said. "We call them possum on the half shell." I massaged a cramped calf muscle. "Hey, Clay, why did the chicken cross the road?"

"I don't know—or care. By the way. But you'll probably tell me anyway. I pray for the day a chicken can cross a road without its motives being questioned."

"To show the stupid armadillos it can be done," I said.

Clay snorted. "I can't believe I've wasted thirty seconds of my life listening to you."

"Like you would've done something profound with those thirty seconds. You aren't much fun on a stakeout," I grumbled. "I'm glad I don't do this for living. This looks way better in the movies. What time is it?"

"I'm Highway Patrol. We don't do stakeouts. This is a favor for a close personal friend," Clay said. "It's twenty minutes from the last time you asked. I don't think Nelson is coming. Your armadillo is a groundhog. I can see it now."

"Shoot it. I'm starving."

"You going to skin and clean it?" Clay asked.

"I don't know how. But I bet you do."

"I can't feel my feet and my heel is jammed into my crotch," Clay groaned. "I'm not skinning a groundhog."

I tried not to picture that, then wished I hadn't. He was right. About two things. He needed to get down. His position in that tree had to be brutal. Nelson wasn't going to show.

We had the rappelling equipment set up forty feet from where I hid. If Nelson arrived to do me in, Clay would come out of the tree and make the arrest. That should have worked.

Clay jumped down from the lowest limb, landing in front of me. He did a couple of deep knee bends.

"So, what now, Honcho?"

"Dunno." Clay stomped circulation back into his legs. "I only have one good idea a week."

"Well, you should have a couple left. This wasn't it."

"Wish we'd brought grub. I'm having second thoughts about that groundhog."

A car door slammed, startling us both. My eyes were probably as wide as Clay's. He pushed me behind him and peered around the pine. "It's not Nelson," he reported. "It's a red Tahoe."

"Hey, Ridge!" Someone yelled. "Where are you? Your Forester is halfway in the road. Did you flunk parking?"

I walked out from behind the tree, followed closely by Clay.

"Hey, Lane. Talk to Clay. He parked."

"Why was he driving your Forester?" Lane asked, as he navigated his way across tree roots and rocks toward us.

"I hid in the back seat. If Nelson saw us, he'd think Clay was me alone."

"Nelson was unexpectedly detained. He sends his regrets." Lane handed me a greasy brown-paper bag and grinned, taking in Clay's camouflage sweatshirt and cargo pants. "You must be Officer Morley. Nice Uniform."

"Day off," Clay explained.

"So I heard. Heck of a way to spend it. Nelson was supposed to think you're Ridge because you're wearing camo?" Lane looked at me. "That's how the well-dressed stud struts around the OU campus these days?"

I laughed. "Not exactly."

"The red OU cap is a nice touch," Lane grinned. "It covers some of that red hair."

Clay's face reddened to match his hair. "I, uh, don't have a lot of civvies. I wear mostly sweats and camo."

"Clay, I've got to take you shopping," I said. "You're not impressing that cute little waitress you're crushing on with your extensive wardrobe."

"Maybe not," Lane said. "But working on his day off is impressive."

"I was afraid Ridge would mess around and get himself killed," Clay mumbled.

"You weren't wrong. Thought you guys might be hungry," Lane said. "I stopped in town at the drive thru to grab some grub."

"Thanks! We were on the verge of eating a groundhog." I pulled two of the four burgers out of the sack and handed them to Clay. The wax paper wrapper was dripping grease.

"It was the only drive thru in Durango where there wasn't a long line." Lane said.

"All their customers died of heart attacks," I said, around a mouthful of burger. It was delicious. I offered Lane a burger. He shook his head. I dug into the other equally greasy bag for fries.

"Let's sit over here," Lane suggested. "I need to talk to you guys while you eat."

We followed him to a flat shady spot and sat down.

"I didn't bring drinks. Figured you wouldn't be out here without something to drink." Lane raised a questioning brow.

Clay nodded. "He has a thermos, and I have a Yeti."

Above our heads a blue jay squawked its displeasure over our uninvited appearance. I removed a rock I wished I hadn't sat on.

"Your mom thinks," Lane said, "I'm here to keep her out of trouble..."

"Mom is here?" I choked on my burger. "Why?"

Mortimer, smelling food, scurried out from under his tree root. He looked up at me, his chipmunk nose twitching. I tossed him a fry.

"Looking for you. She's worried sick." Lane's eyes narrowed. "Never scare her like this again, Cupcake. Got it?"

His tone ticked me off.

Lanigan is some hot shot federal agent who married Mom's cousin. Everyone thinks he walks on water. As far as I'm concerned, the jury's still out.

"Well, wait a minute! Nelson was in OKC. He followed me to Dad's funeral. The only way to keep Mom and Rye safe was to come back here. This hasn't been a picnic."

"Well, as self-sacrificial as that sounds, you could have called to let her know you're alive."

"Okay. You're right," I grumbled. I didn't say if I heard Mom's voice I'd lose it, which wouldn't have been good for either of us.

"Would you guys like to know what's going on?" Lane asked.

I nodded, my mouth too full of burger to speak.

"DEA has been tracking Nelson for months. You thought he was a perv. That's the tip of the iceberg. He's a pawn in an international cartel. As a pilot, he smuggled drugs and money past TSA. Flight staff isn't checked carefully. He used flight attendants when he felt TSA was getting suspicious. The attendants were terrified of him. Sable was his downfall." Lane looked at me. "As you know, Nelson was obsessed with her. Then you got in his way, Ridge."

"I wanted to kill him," I said. Rage had become a part of me as soon as I learned that Nelson had raped Sable.

Lane's eyes bored into me. "I had to get to him before you did to keep you out of prison. Clay's plan had a good chance of working. But this morning Nelson decided to cut bait and run. Something you guys couldn't have known."

I grabbed a paper napkin and mopped grease from my chin. "Why now?"

"He knew the feds were breathing down his neck." Lane handed me another napkin. "That would be me. The cartel not only wouldn't protect him from us, but he'd also become a liability. In a rare lucid moment, he realized my men, the cartel, and local law were closing in. Not to mention you and Rambo, here. He panicked and scurried for cover like the rat he is. My men were waiting for him at the airport. He strutted in wearing his flight uniform with the flight crew. He was carrying enough money, drugs, and diamonds to put him away for a long time."

"What happens now?" I retrieved a runaway pickle and tossed Mortimer another fry.

"I'm counting on him to turn state's evidence. We've been after the big guns for over a year. Snagging him should help. If I can keep him alive long enough to testify. At some point in time, he'll have to face what he did to Sable. And the murder charges. But he has a mountain of federal offenses he's going to have to wade through first."

"Lane is with the DEA," I explained to Clay. "I don't get it. Why would Nelson get involved with a cartel?"

"Money. His wife kept a tight rein on hers," Lane said. "Nelson wanted out of his marriage. But he'd grown accustomed to his lifestyle. He had signed a prenup."

Lane shook his head. "He thought smuggling was a way to make big money fast, but he sold his soul to the devil. The cartel. You don't get out alive. When he raped Sable in Germany, he had gone too far. He'd raped other flight attendants, always out of the country. They didn't speak German, had no idea how to notify authorities or ask for help. They desperately needed their jobs and were afraid of Nelson. He counted on that. But Sable speaks German. She had no trouble notifying the authorities and getting to a hospital." Lane checked something on his phone and pocketed it.

"Thanks for the burgers," Clay said, digging into the bag for napkins. "Best burgers I ever had."

"You're welcome," Lane said. "A man can work up an appetite on a stakeout. Clay, I need you to meet me at your office."

"Clay blinked. "Why?"

"You've helped your government collar Nelson. We value you. Your boss needs to know how much."

Clay shook his head. "He's not going to be happy that I've been communicating with the Feds. You guys' nabbing Nelson when we couldn't find him doesn't look good."

"Your unit doesn't have the bells and whistles that we do. It has nothing to do with being better. We have more toys," Lane pointed out. "You're out here on your day off. Your plan might have worked if I hadn't ambushed it. You've aided in the arrest of a federal fugitive. That's going to look good on your resume."

"Thanks." Clay's brows puckered in confusion. "But why do I need a resume?"

"You never know when a better offer might come along." As Lane handed his card to Clay, he looked at me. "Ridge, I'm having dinner with your mom tonight at 7:00. You're invited."

"Where?" I knew by his tone the invitation wasn't optional.

"I'll text the details when I know. We'll surprise April."

"Does she hate me for killing my father?"

"What? You of all people should know that once your dad made up his mind, it was set in stone. You couldn't have changed the outcome."

I nodded. That's what Dad said last night. Basically.

"Give me a half hour." Clay told Lane. "I have to run by the hospital."

"What?" I asked. "Why?"

Clay ignored me.

Lane nodded. "Oh! Right. You don't look so good, Ridge."

Clay peered into my eyes. "My grandma would say you're looking a little peeked, Son. You could use a checkup."

"What? I'm fine. I..."

"He's right, Ridge," Lane agreed. "You're green around the gills."

"I'm fine!"

"No, you're not," Clay said. As he walked to the passenger door of my Forester, he tossed me the keys across the hood. "You drive, Ridge."

"Lane's right," I grumbled getting in. "You can't park worth a damn."

Clay grinned. "Shut up and drive."

Chapter Thirty-Seven

Ridge

"Is this some kind of joke?" I asked as we got out and walked across the hospital parking lot. "Seriously, What are we doing here?"

"I need a blood test. Needles make me nervous. You're here to hold my hand."

"Yeah, right," I grumbled. Curiosity outweighed irritation and we walked toward the Taj Mahal of hospitals. With its towering glass walls reflecting a cloudless sky, Durango's Mercy Hospital was stunning. We went inside.

The door of room 28 was slightly ajar. Clay stopped, knocked gently. Without waiting for a response, he pushed it open.

I looked into the room.

An older woman sat in a chair, her dark hair haloed by sunlight streaming through the immense window behind her. She laid her book aside and stood up.

Luna Amhurst. Sable's mom.

I stepped into the room and stared at her. "Luna? What's going on? Are you okay?" I looked back at Clay for answers. He was gone.

"Luna?"

"Ridge, thank God you're here," she said. "I was afraid you'd gone back to Oklahoma."

Stress had tightened the skin around her eyes and mouth and robbed her usually jovial face of its youth.

"I went back for my father's funeral. But I couldn't stay away. Why are you here?"

Luna motioned to the bed. Someone was lying there, surrounded by whooshing beeping machines. Half of the face was swathed in bandages. The other half was purple and swollen.

"Jocelyn?" I asked. "Ohmygosh, Luna! What happened to Jocelyn?" I couldn't fathom the heartache of Luna losing one daughter and something terrible happening to the other.

Luna shook her head. "Go look."

I took a step forward. At first she was unrecognizable. But my heart knew. "Sable!" I gulped, scared that saying her name would make her disappear. "Sable?"

Luna nodded.

I couldn't believe—was afraid to believe!

The night of the wreck, my brain hadn't been able to process the horror I'd witnessed. I couldn't feel. Or think. My brain wasn't working any better now.

I inched toward the bed. Fearful of setting off an alarm on the machines wired to her, I touched her leg. Lights didn't flash, sirens didn't blare, and most importantly, her leg didn't vanish. It felt solid. Familiar. Warm. Sable's leg. Here. In this hospital. Not the morgue. Not the bottom of the gorge. Here. Beneath my hand. Her other leg was elevated in a giant cast.

Tears streamed down my face.

Luna's long skirt swished as she moved around the bed and wrapped me in her arms. Luna always wore long skirts. In the summer she wore them with sandals. In the winter she paired them with boots. She held me as if I were her son and let me cry.

I pulled myself together and pushed back far enough to look into her red-rimmed eyes. I had questions but my thoughts were too jumbled to form them. I couldn't articulate them.

Luna watched me with the same big brown eyes she'd given her daughter. When I first met her, I'd been surprised by her beauty. Luna was an older version of Sable.

"How?" I cleared my throat and tried again. "How?"

"A man picking up trash along highway 550 found her. Last Tuesday."

I quickly calculated. A week and a half ago.

"She wasn't visible from the road," Luna continued. "He heard a moan. Looked for where the sound was coming from. That's when he saw her, tangled in the branches of a tree. He tried to get down to her but couldn't. He called for Rescue. They came, got her out of the tree. She had no ID so they labeled her 'Jane Doe.'"

"Sable was here in the hospital three days. That's when a Highway Patrol officer connected her to the missing body at the wreck site. They called me and I identified her." Luna choked.

I waited.

"I thought I was coming to identify a 'body.'"

I wrapped my arms around this woman. Luna had become my second mother.

Sable groaned softly. Our eyes flew to her face. I moved back to the bed, close enough to touch her. I needed to feel her warmth beneath my hand to convince myself she was actually here.

"The authorities posted a guard outside her room until Nelson was arrested," Luna said. "I assume he has been captured, or they wouldn't have let you in."

"The Feds found him this morning. He should be in DC by now."

"What a nightmare. I can't believe it's over." Luna gazed through the window at the distant mountains and absently ran fingers through her hair. "I guess I can tell Jocelyn she still has a sister. She's been through hell, thinking Sable was gone. I had to swear not to tell anyone until it was safe. Ridge, I so wanted to call you, but I couldn't. I'm sorry."

"I'm glad you didn't. Nelson would have followed me here. I couldn't have stayed away." I shook my head trying to clear it. "She's been here about ten days?"

Luna nodded. "The authorities said she must have jumped from the car."

"She would have been near the ledge where I found her phone yesterday," I said.

"How did they get her out?"

I jabbed my fingers through my hair while I thought. "Three days? She was out there three days? How did she survive?"

A doctor swept imperiously into the room exuding importance. He was a tall thin man who wore blue scrubs and wire-framed glasses. His hair was cropped short and infused with grey. We stopped talking.

The doctor was followed by two nurses whose wariness, weariness, or maybe both registered in their faces. The doctor nodded to me, then went straight to Sable.

Luna and I backed out of his way. My eyes never left his face, searching for a sign to hang my hope on.

After a brief examination, and consulting with the nurses in hushed tones, he turned to us.

"Dr. Tisdale," Luna said, "this is Ridge Frazier, Sable's fiancé. Ridge, Dr. Tisdale is Sable's neurosurgeon."

He nodded curtly, wasting no time on pleasantries. "Sable was concussed. Her brain was thrown around in her skull rather like a shaken baby."

Luna had obviously heard all this.

"We'll know more when the swelling diminishes. We X-rayed her immediately. She had a blood clot near her brain and some internal bleeding. We performed emergency surgery to stop remove the clot and stop the bleeding. She sustained a broken clavicle. A compound fracture to her left femur. Minor scrapes and contusions. The ER doctors can tell you more about that." He paused. "I imagine you have questions?" He raised an eyebrow.

"I don't know where to start," I said. "I just want to know if she'll survive."

The doctor nodded. He glanced at his watch, then looked out the open door into the hall. "She isn't out of the woods. But she's young, healthy, and her heart is strong."

"She's a runner," I said. "Except for pizza and the stuff she puts in her coffee, she's a fanatic about her diet."

Dr. Tisdale nodded again. "That works in her favor. It's too soon to predict the long-lasting effects of her head injury, but the surgery was successful. The brain is amazing in its capacity to heal. The rest is up to her. Your name is Ridge?"

I nodded.

"She said your name several times when they brought her in. Nobody could understand what she was saying. Makes sense now. She should do better now that you're here."

"When will we know?" I asked.

"She's in a medically induced coma. She was hysterical. We need to keep her quiet until her brain has time to heal. Fortunately the cool nights kept her temperature down. The EMSA workers said she'd been thrown into a tree instead of falling into the gorge. The foliage protected her from the sun but made it impossible to see her from the road."

"It was a miracle that she was found," Luna breathed.

"If you believe in such things." The doctor nodded. "In her case, you almost have to. She wouldn't have survived much longer."

"What about her leg?" I asked.

"Ask her orthopedic surgeon," Dr. Tisdale said. "He's scheduled here tomorrow. It will be some time before she runs any races." With that the doctor walked out the door.

Still shaken, I looked at the bed. Sable was lying so still. She had been calling my name. Had she known I was close by? I hadn't been able to stay away from the wreck site. She kept pulling me back.

The enormity of it hit me. I cried harder than I had when I believed she was dead. The thought of her alone, her body broken, ripped through my heart. Had she been conscious? Scared? I sank into the chair beside Sable's bed. Luna pulled up another chair and quietly sat beside me. Noises from the nurses' station drifted through the open door. I barely heard them.

"She's a fighter," I said, remembering the first time I ever saw her at BWI Airport with Nelson grabbing her raised fist. She was scared, but defiant. That spirit is one of the things I love most about her.

"She takes care of herself," I said, thinking out loud.

Luna attempted a smile.

I took a deep breath. "The baby?"

Luna shook her head. "Gone. She lost it."

My tears blinded me. They dripped from my nose and chin. I couldn't catch my breath. I gulped air in ragged snatches. We hadn't had time to focus on the baby. We had only learned she was pregnant a short time before the wreck. We'd never discussed children—when, or how many. We certainly hadn't planned on having a child this early. The timing was terrible. She'd been certain the pregnancy was the result of rape, but abortion had never been an option. I had noticed the way she instinctively protected her stomach. She wanted this baby. Because she did, I wanted it, too. I hadn't realized how much until now.

I pulled myself together and reached for Sable's beautiful hand. I leaned over and kissed the small scar on her thumb. She'd cut her hand last fall washing a wine glass.

Holding Sable's hand beside her mother, I thought about the women in their family. Strong women. They all had dark hair and huge dark eyes. Sable's grandmother, Rainbow, still lived on the land beside Luna. Rainbow worked like a man in her garden. She had grown up in a commune. Her mother, Hope, and Hope's mother, Indigo, had all been free spirits.

Indigo's Kiowa mother, Moon Flower, had married a white prospector passing through her Oklahoma reservation on his way to California. He sweet talked her into going with him. She and her husband landed in Silverton, Colorado, when their horses and money gave out. He went to work in the mines. Moon Flower designed beautiful jewelry to sell. She became well known for remedies and healing potions made from herbs she found growing in the woods. That knowledge had been passed down through the women of the family, along with an intense desire to leave the world better than they found it. They fought for pristine water, pure air, and tree preservation.

I can recite Sable's heritage for five generations, but don't know the name of my great grandmother on either side of my family. There's something weird about that.

I'd thought about it before. I want daughters with those qualities. And dark unfathomable eyes that penetrate deep into your soul. Their mother's eyes.

"Don't give up, baby," I whispered. "I'm here. Always."

Her fingers, ever so faintly, squeezed around mine. One...Two... Three.

My eyes widened. "Did you see that?"

"The doctor said not to get excited if she moves. It's reflex," Luna said.

"No! Threes of anything is our signal. Three hearts on a Valentine or on a note. It means 'I love you,'I've got your back'. She knows I'm here."

Luna smiled. She wasn't convinced but she was happy that I was happy. I squeezed her hand back three times. Just in case.

I persuaded Luna to go down the hall to the cafeteria. She looked like she hadn't eaten or slept for days. I could relate.

Alone with Sable, I willed her to get stronger. To heal. I talked to her. Even with her hand in mine, I pinched myself to be convinced that this was real. I talked to her about everything. Except Nelson. Mostly, I rambled. I reminded her of all our firsts: first meeting, first date, first kiss, first time she came to my tournament. Boy, had that been a challenge.

I'd spent hours on the phone with Sable the night before, trying to talk her into coming. The match had been particularly tough. I'd won, but it had been a struggle. I'd emerged from the locker room exhausted, hungry, and not excited to find a cluster of screaming blondes waiting for me outside. I have nothing against blondes. All the females in my family are blondes. They just wanted selfies and autographs. Sable is okay with my fans now, but back then she hadn't been prepared. It almost destroyed us before we started.

"Ridge, I'm not interested in being president of your fan club," she'd said.

"Who says you'd be president?"

She glared at me.

"Come on Sable, I don't have a fan club."

"You will."

I was at a loss for words. This was all new to me, too. I wanted to tell her that she had my heart from the moment I first saw her, but that sounded hokey, and she wouldn't believe it. I didn't know what to say, but figured if all else failed, go with food.

"I'm starving. I never eat before a match. Let's grab a pizza."

She stared at me for so long, I was sure she'd say no. She must have seen my desperation. Her expression softened. "I'm older than you."

"So you keep saying. Old people have to eat, don't they? We're just having lunch. No big deal."

She looked as though she didn't know whether to laugh or hit me. She smiled and came.

The day I met her at BWI we had totally agreed on seafood. We just rode the escalator up to Phillips and ordered almost everything on the menu.

But pizza at Luigi's Pizzeria and Tanning Parlor, was a different matter. We talked about the merits of some toppings, the glitches with others, and argued about why pineapple doesn't go on pizza. Ever. So, her half was Hawaiian. Mine was 'meat lovers'.

"Sable," I'd said around a mouthful of pizza, "I'm not asking you to marry me. Today. Although, I would if I thought you'd say yes. So, between then and now, can we be friends?"

Wordlessly, she looked at me with those eyes.

"You can't have too many friends—in case you need a transfusion or something."

She chose another pizza slice. "Long-distance relationships don't work." She strung cheese across her chin when she took a bite.

"Let's just see how this goes" I said. "You can call me anytime day or night. If I'm in the middle of a tennis match, or like saving the Titanic, I'll call you back."

"You're a little late on the saving the Titanic thing."

"Story of my life," I said. She allowed me to wipe the pizza from her chin.

After that conversation, I began calling Sable twice a week, but it soon slid into texting a good morning as soon as I woke up and talking every night before we went to sleep. I ended those calls with, "Good night, Sable, come find me. I'll be waiting in your dreams."

Luna slipped back into the chair beside me. We kept a bedside vigil until my text tone beeped.

Lane: *Muleshoe Bar and Grill. 19:00. See you there. At the back table.*

It broke my heart to leave, but there was another woman I needed to wrap my arms around. It was way past time to face my mom. I was familiar with the Muleshoe. It was one of Sable's favorite places. I had been there with Clay.

I leaned over and whispered, "Love you, Angel. Find me. I'll be in your dreams." I kissed her cheek and smoothed back her hair.

Chapter Thirty-Eight

Ridge

I paused inside the door of the Muleshoe Bar and Grille, scanning the dim interior. Lane said they would be sitting near the rear. He spotted me as I came in, stood, and waved. Their table was located between the kitchen and the restrooms. Near the karaoke stage for our entertainment pleasure. Great. Just great.

Mom sat between Lane and Ron Lang. Her back was to me, but as I threaded my way through the tables, she turned to see who they were waving at.

Lane said he'd keep my arrival a surprise. If Mom's expression was any indication, he was successful. She stood up and took a step forward. Her mouth opened. Her lips formed my name. Shock and joy raced across her face in that order. She burst into tears, closing the distance between us. I opened my arms and she fell into them. She felt fragile and unfamiliar as she buried her face in my shoulder and sobbed.

We cried together, both of our hearts breaking with the shared loss of my father. I pulled it together, looked around at the upturned faces of people who'd stopped eating to stare at us and wished someone had planned this better.

Mom sniffed and blinked up at me. "I thought I'd lost you, too."

"I'm sorry, Mom." That sounded inadequate.

"I've been so worried. Are you all right?"

"I'm better now." I looked at Lane. He gave me a thumbs up. It was true. Sable is alive, Nelson is in jail, and nobody is blaming me for Dad's death. I took a deep breath. It felt good.

Mom stepped back, placed her hands on both sides of my face, and looked into my eyes the way mothers do when they don't believe you.

"Can we sit down, Mom? We're causing a scene." With my hand in the small of her back, I ushered her back to the table.

She eyed Lane and Ron. "You knew, didn't you?" she demanded.

"Hey, Mr. Lang," I said, "I'm surprised to see you." Huge understatement.

He stood to shake my hand. "You're a man, Ridge. It's time you called me Ron."

Mom watched us, managing to look confused and surprised at the same time—her face an open book. "How do you know each other?"

Ron laughed and winked at me.

"Good grief, Mom, he's RJ's dad."

"Your best friend, RJ?"

"Yeah."

"The RJ in Cheyenne Falls?"

"Yeah."

"They were joined at the hip," Ron explained.

"When RJ wasn't at the farm, I was at his house. Mr. Lang took us to the circus. He taught me to hunt and fish. You knew that."

She shook her head. "Ron is RJ's dad?"

"Yeah. That's what I meant when I said, 'he's RJ's dad'."

Lane folded his arms across his chest and leaned back in his chair, laughing.

Mom looked at Ron for clarification. "Ronnie Junior, is Ridge's friend RJ?"

"Right," he said. "R.J. Ronnie Junior."

"You're RJ's dad who used to take Ridge hunting!"

"Good Grief, Mom, you're usually not this slow on the uptake." I shook my head.

"Ridge could hit a target that RJ and I could barely see. Especially after he bought that Sig Sauer target pistol," Ron said. "I'm guessing by the way he can gauge the speed of a tennis ball he can still hit a moving target."

"You've seen Ridge play?" Mom asked.

"He and RJ have been to several of my tournaments," I told her. "I haven't been hunting or camping since RJ and I were in high school. Coffee in a tin cup sure tasted good on a cold morning."

Ron laughed. "Even full of coffee grounds?"

"Yep. What did RJ decide about the Corvette?" I asked.

"He decided it had too many unknowns for the money."

"That's what I told him. Like Stephanie," I grinned. "Good looking but overpriced and problematic. High maintenance. I'm glad he dumped her and passed on the 'vette."

"He stayed with her way too long," Ron agreed.

Mom shook her head. "I can't believe this. Where did you go camping?"

"A place not far from here, actually," Ron said.

"You brought my son to Colorado without my knowledge?"

"Didn't think I needed your approval. He was living with Jackson. He came with us."

"Yeah," I grumbled, "It was supposed to be a guy thing. Gramps brought Rye."

Mom shook her head as though trying to clear it. "Oh!" She pulled out her phone and handed it to Lane. "Take a picture of us," she demanded, pulling me in close.

He took the picture. Mom looked at it and smiled, but tears glistened in her eyes when she looked up.

"I can't believe you're here."

"Mom, sit down." Afraid she was going to make another scene, I took the empty seat across from her.

Mom was busy with her phone but explained. "I'm sending this picture to Riley Grace, so she'll know I found you." She set the picture as her wallpaper and slipped the phone in her purse.

My text tone chimed. It was Riley Grace. She sent me a thumbs-up emoji.

Riley Grace: *Way to make Mom cry, Doofus*

She added four hearts, a kangaroo, and if the kangaroo wasn't weird enough, she threw in something that looked like a sheep with no head, and a pomegranate, because let's face it, you can't have enough pomegranates.

I sent her an okay emoji. And a heart.

Clay's favorite waitress, Marcy, came to take our drink order. She's cute, perky, and I think she likes Clay. I've got to do something about the way he dresses.

She studied my ID like she'd never seen it before, then grinned. "You having the prickly pear beer?"

"Yeah," I said, pocketing my ID. I looked at Lane and Ron. "It's their specialty brew. You guys should try it."

They followed my advice. Mom ordered her usual Arnold Palmer. The drinks came while we were studying the limited but extensive menu. Although it featured only burgers and sandwiches, there were twenty-five burgers and almost as many sandwich choices. I ordered my favorite, the Toxic: two quarter pound patties, bacon, American, Swiss, and bleu cheeses, fried onions, green chilies, lettuce, tomatoes, and avocados. It came with or without a fried egg. I ordered it with. I need the protein. I also ordered fried green beans in lieu of fries. I'm on a diet.

Lane grinned. "You gonna eat all that by yourself, Hossfly?"

"I haven't eaten much lately. Tonight, I could eat a cow."

"You forget I just watched you snarf down two burgers and a bag of fries."

I grinned. I couldn't argue.

"Well," Lane prompted, "are you going to tell your mom the news? A couple of interesting things happened today."

"You guys haven't told her?" I asked.

"Do you think she'd be sitting here this calmly if she knew?" Ron asked.

Mom looked at Lane. "What? You have more secrets?" Mom accused, looking back and forth between Ron and Lane. "Tell me what?"

"First," I began, "Brett Nelson has been arrested and is in custody. Lane can give you the skinny on that but more importantly, Sable was found. Alive!"

"Whaaaatt?" Mom's eyes widened. "Ohmygosh! That is wonderful news! When? How?"

"She isn't out of the woods yet. She's in a coma., but she's breathing on her own and she knew I was there. It's a miracle she's alive. I'm celebrating." I filled Mom in on what I knew.

"You've seen her? Of course!" Mom teared up again. "Oh, Ridge, how wonderful!"

"I've spent most of the afternoon with her and her mother. She's a fighter. We'll get through this."

"Ridge, I'm so happy for you!" Mom's eyes were shining through tears.

"Now, maybe he'll stop hanging out at the wreck site."

Mom looked at Lane. "Nelson's been arrested? Seriously?"

Lane nodded. Then our food arrived. Conversations paused. Marcy lingered to ensure everyone had what they ordered.

"You thought Lane was in Durango to ride herd on you," I said when Marcy left. "He had other reasons for being here."

"We've been watching Nelson for a while," Lane said, reaching for the salt. He recapped what he'd told Clay and me earlier, then added, "Nelson's a small cog in a big crime wheel. Sable knew too much. She wouldn't play his game. When Ridge and Sable got engaged, he knew Ridge would know everything Sable knew. Nelson had to eliminate both of them," Lane said. "The night of the of the wreck, he thought Ridge was driving."

Mom gasped. She wanted to interrupt and ask questions, but she leaned back and let Lane finish, something new for her.

"The cartel regarded Nelson as a liability. A loose cannon." Lane continued, "He was making stupid choices. It was just a matter of time before he made major mistakes. The cartel put out a contract on him. My department has been trying to bring them down for over a year. Nelson is my chink in their armor. I not only had to find him before he found Ridge, but I also had to find him before the cartel got to him." Lane's eyes narrowed. "My job now is keeping him alive long enough to testify."

Mom and Ron listened intently.

I leaned back, drank my beer, and bit into my burger.

"He's that important to them?" Mom asked.

"He's that important to me," Lane clarified. "He knows enough to bring who he knows down. They know enough to bring the whole thing down. The cartel will do whatever it takes to shut him up. For good."

"But if he's in custody, surely they can't get to him."

"I wish that were true, but you have no idea the lengths they will go to." Lane moved his beer glass in circles on the table, leaving wet rings. "Members of the cartel in prison can take care of Nelson. But they have to find him first." Lane laughed. "And that won't be easy."

"I'm glad we don't have to worry about him anymore," Mom said. "Lane when you get back to DC, will you contact the *Post* and get Grant's name cleared? That kind of info needs to come from a reliable source."

"Top of my list," Lane said, reaching for the catsup.

"Grant's reputation was important to him." Mom removed a tomato from her salad.

"People need to know the truth," Lane agreed. "Grant died like he lived. A hero."

Mom smiled. "Clearing Grant's name and finding Ridge were my top priorities. Now I can move on to lesser things like establishing world peace and reducing the national debt."

"And knitting sweaters for the homeless," I added. "When you learn to knit."

"Ridge," she asked, "did you know all this?"

"It's been coming together like a puzzle. A piece at a time. Sable knew Nelson was smuggling but she had no proof. The other flight attendants knew but were afraid to talk. Nelson was trying to intimidate Sable when I met her at BWI." I scowled.

"She'd overheard conversations and had been asking questions. It got back to Nelson. He wasn't happy. Sable couldn't be bought or frightened. He had to get rid of her." Reaching for the pepper, I added, "And me, too."

Lane saw Clay come through the door before I did and motioned him over. Clay reached our table in time to hear the end of the conversation.

"More flight attendants have filed charges against Nelson since they heard what happened to Sable," Clay added.

He stole a chair from a nearby table and sat down next to me. "They were terrified, but angry enough to want to put him away."

I introduced Clay to Mom and Ron.

"Clayton Morley," Mom said. "Why does that name sound familiar?"

"If he'd said Officer Clayton Morley, you'd know," Lane said.

"Oh, the other trooper that investigated Grant's death," Mom said.

"Yeah. But he's a lot more than that. He stayed at the scene with me long after everyone left. He's become a good friend. Pretty much family now."

As the words left my mouth, I remembered what Dad had said about making friends. I hoped he knew. Now I understand why he didn't know where Sable was.

Clay flashed an 'aw shucks' grin.

Mom reached across the table to squeeze his hand. "Thank you."

"You're welcome, Ma'am."

Lane grinned. "These two had a plan to nab Nelson, which was dangerous as hell, but it might have worked. Another reason I had to get Nelson in custody. Save him from these two cowboys."

"Wait a minute, there," I objected. "What do you mean 'might have worked'? It was brilliant."

Lane laughed. "You were out there waiting for a guy who was halfway to DC."

"Well, except for that..."

"Seriously, it would have worked," Lane admitted. "If Nelson hadn't decided to run."

"How did you know about our plan?" I asked.

"My friend, Larry. He learned that Nelson had hacked your phone. It didn't help him much because you weren't calling anyone, so he never knew where you were going." Lane finished his beer and lifted his empty glass, signaling our waitress.

"So, some of your men are here?" Mom asked.

Lane nodded. "Were here. They came with me to get Nelson. They're on their way back to DC with him. I've been getting paid to be here and ride herd on you." He winked at Mom. "That's how good I am."

"I've been following Ridge," Clay told Mom, "He's one of the tennis all-time greats."

I picked at a thumb nail and grinned. "What's this 'one of' stuff?"

"Ridge has the fastest serve ever clocked," Clay went on, ignoring me. "166 MPH. That's a weapon! You don't defend against a serve like that. You look for a place to hide."

"How do you know that?" I demanded. "That's not on record anywhere."

Marcy appeared at our table with Lane's refill. "Hey, Clay," she said with a big smile. "What can I get you?"

"I'll have one of those," Clay said, motioning to Lane's beer. "And a Toxic." He winked.

"With no pickles," she said, and was gone.

"Must be recorded somewhere, or I wouldn't know it, would I?" Clay said, as he watched Marcy walk away. He shook his head. "Dang, she's cute!"

"Clay, we've got to get you some new threads. How do you expect to attract women in the stuff you wear?"

He ignored my comment and reached for my saltshaker. "Who's your fiercest opponent?"

"My sister," I said, without having to think. "Probably because I always underestimate her, but that girl has an arm. She's smart and tough. She grew up watching me play. She knows my weak spots. She knows where I'm going to put the ball before I do. In a couple of years, she'll be untouchable." I swallowed the lump in my throat realizing that Dad wouldn't be here to see it.

"You really think she's that good?" Mom asked.

"Damn straight," I said. "She's smarter than I am. She loves the game more."

"I told you she's good," Lane said to Mom.

"I hope Eve Anna Evans gets her on strength training," I said, "She's got to build muscle in her hips and shoulders to protect those joints. Being good on the court's not enough if you're injury prone."

Mom gave me a surprised glance. "Who is Eve Anna Evans?"

"Rye's new tennis coach. She texted me as soon as she found out."

A couple of karaoke singers began butchering songs. I'd been right. We were way too close to the stage. As the evening wore on more people were buzzed enough to believe they could sing.

After we finished eating, Ron pushed away from the table and walked to the stage. He whispered something to the emcee, then took the mic and said to the crowd, "Ladies and gentlemen, you're in for a treat tonight. The former lead singer of the Hitchhikers is in the house."

"What is he up to?" I yawned

"Miss April Dale." Ron led in a round of polite applause.

Mom's eyes widened.

"What?" I'd been leaning back in my chair. It came crashing down.

"Come on up here, April," Ron insisted.

Mom shook her head and glared at him. If looks could kill, he'd be dead.

I leaned back and crossed my arms. Oh, this is going to be good.

Chapter Thirty-Nine

Ridge

The applause was polite. Except for the guy wearing a Stetson hat and cowboy boots in the corner. He was whooping. He stood up and waved like he was flagging a taxi. He'd either heard of her or was seriously buzzed. Maybe both.

He was stomping and chanting, "April, April!"

"Get a life," I grumbled.

"Come on up here, April," Ron said. "This is April's song," he announced.

What? My Mom? On stage? Singing? What was Ron thinking?

She didn't get up. Ron walked back to the table and took her hand. Mom looked shell shocked. But, she allowed him to pull her to her feet. She followed him to the small stage. I was embarrassed for her. She took the mic, looked over the crowd, smiled, and began singing. Her voice, rich and smokey, grew in strength and confidence as she sang.

The guy in the corner went wild. The room quieted. I was shocked. She could have had a career singing jazz. She was as good as Norah Jones or Adele. Who knew? Evidently, Ron. And the cowboy in the corner.

Ron sang backup. Even to my untrained ear their harmony was good. Really good. Mom used to sing to me when I was little, but in hushed tones to get me to sleep. It might have been this song. It sounded familiar. She had sung a ballad that went on forever about a woman whose lover left on a train and never returned, so she wandered alone over the moors. No, that was two different songs. She used to sing. A lot. I had forgotten. But when did she stop singing?

Everyone had stopped talking. They weren't looking around, eating or drinking. Even the eyes at the bar were focused on the woman on the stage. My mom is a beautiful woman. Most of the time I don't notice. Even now, ravaged by grief, she is stunning.

When the song ended, there was wild applause. Ron sang the next song. *Scotch and Soda*. Mom backed him up. Then the music switched to a hard driving beat. Ron came back to the table, smiled, and sat down.

"She needed this," he said, in an aside to me. "She's forgotten who she is. Watch."

Mom had only warmed up on the previous songs. She slipped out of her denim jacket, swung it around her head and tossed it to me. When the guitar kicked in she began moving to the seductive rhythm. Stage lights turned her pale hair and white shirt blue. I pulled out my phone and began videoing. Rye would never believe this.

She began singing Melissa Etheridge's *I'm the Only One*. She danced a few steps as she looked out over the audience, making everyone feel that she was singing to just them. She owned the stage, cradling the mic like it was an old friend. Who was this woman?

There was a line in the song about my demons being gone. Maybe some of them. Nelson was no longer a threat to Sable or my family. Still, I'm pretty sure my demons won't be going away any time soon. I'll be seeing taillights disappearing into that gorge whenever I close my eyes. But they can't destroy me now. Knowing Dad was gone before the car left the road and Sable wasn't in it makes it more bearable.

The song ended and Mom came back to the table, laughing and breathless. She sat down to a thunderous applause. I sent Riley the video.

She texted me back immediately.

Riley: *ten shocked -wide -eyed emojis. WTF???*

Me: *laughing emojis. Watch your language, Missy!*

As Mom settled back into her chair, a man walked to our table. He stopped beside Mom. The cowboy in the corner. His wife hovered beside him.

"Ms. Dale, we don't want to bother you. We lived in Oklahoma during our college days. OSU. Go Pokes! We remember the Hitchhikers. You sound as good tonight as you did back then. I'm so glad we came," he said.

He slipped an arm around his wife, drawing her forward. "We're celebrating our anniversary. Your being here tonight singing *I'll Be Seeing You* is a miracle. We fell in love listening to you sing that song, and here you are."

Mom's smile widened, erasing stress line around her eyes. Years disappeared from her face. Something happened on that stage. The shell of a 47-year-old woman cracked and a young lady stepped out. Mom thanked the man graciously, engaging his wife in the conversation. The three of them chatted like gossipy old women at a quilting bee. Ron had been right. She had needed that. But how would he have known?

It's not like I grew up thinking Mom didn't have a life before I was born. Well, actually, I guess I did. She was my mom. Who she'd been before that momentous occasion couldn't have been all that important to her after she had me.

"I have to admit I had a huge crush on you back then," the guy was saying. "But it was obvious you were in love with him." He nodded at Mr. Lang. "It did my heart good to see you two still together tonight."

"What?" Mom shook her head. "No! We aren't..."

"Thank you," his wife added. "You just made our anniversary." With a smile and small wave to acknowledge the rest of us they turned and walked away.

I was stunned. "What was that about?" I demanded. " You and Mr. Lang? In love?" He was back to being Mr. Lang.

"Ridge, that was long ago in a far-away land," Ron said, placing a hand on my arm.

I shook it off. But not before I saw the small tattoo on his wrist. Exactly like Mom's.

Mom stared through me as though unaware of my existence. Anyone's existence.

"Mom?" I exhaled forcefully.

She waved her hand dismissively. "Ron was my first boyfriend."

"But that guy just said..." I stared at her. Questions stampeded through my mind, stomping all over each other before I could articulate any of them. Starting with that tattoo.

"Ridge," Mom rubbed her hands across her face, and sighed. "Ron and I were together through high school and two years of college. Something happened and we broke up. Before this trip, I hadn't seen him in years."

Anger, hot and heavy, burned deep inside me. Reason told me I was mistaken. There was nothing to this. But why were they here in Durango? Together. In front of my eyes. Not even two weeks after my father's death. With matching tattoos.

"But that guy said..." I didn't know where to go with that. I stood up.

"He was wrong. Ronnie and I haven't sung together since college."

"Ronnie?" I stared at her. "Ronnie?" My voice rose three octaves.

"He was Ronnie back then." She looked at Mr. Lang for help with a deer-in-the-headlights expression.

But it was Lane who rescued her. "Sit down, Ridge," he ordered in a no-nonsense tone.

Grudgingly, I sat.

"This is my fault," he said. "Hell or high water couldn't have stopped April from coming. She was worried about you, and Grant's reputation." He aimed a sarcastic smile in her direction and added, "Which is so unlike her."

Lane's good. He says it's his fault but immediately points out that it's mine and Dad's.

"I sent Ron because I couldn't go. I didn't know their past. Imagine the trouble your mother could have gotten herself into out here alone. Ron understood what a disaster that would be." Lane ignored the scowl he got from Mom. And me.

"He didn't want to come." Lane continued. "He was able to reschedule his appointments. I'm grateful. You should be, too, Ridge." Lane paused and leveled a look at me.

"Would you have wanted your mom driving out to the wreck site alone?"

"No way," I conceded. I remembered that Dad had told me to help her find some man from her past. And here he is.

"April had no idea Ron was coming." Lane stopped talking but his eyes still bored into me. I'd hate to be interrogated by this guy.

"She was furious when she saw me on that plane," Ron added. "She's hated me for twenty-six years. I knew there was no way this would end well."

"Twenty-seven years," Mom corrected. "I've hated him for twenty-seven years."

"And three months," Ron added.

"It looks like it ended pretty well to me," I scoffed. But Lane was right. I would never have wanted Mom driving anywhere on 550 alone. My anger fizzled, but I was too stubborn to give it up completely. And there was that tattoo.

I've known Mr. Lang since I was nine. He's never lied to me. The more I get to know him, the more I respect him. I believed them both but needed some place to dump my anger.

I've had some weeks from hell. Enraged every time I think of Nelson murdering my father. And what he's done to Sable. Angry at God for allowing this to happen. But most of all angry at myself because my father is dead instead of me. Last night Dad said something about not blaming Mom for things I don't understand. I think. But he didn't know all this stuff about Ron. No, *I* didn't know all this stuff about Mr. Lang. Dad did. That's what he was talking about.

Mom didn't know Mr. Lang is RJ's dad. She isn't a good actor—she hasn't stayed in touch with him. Trying to figure it out gave me a headache. I needed time and space to sort things out. Somewhere else. Someplace quiet. Someplace where my mother wasn't looking at me through tears. And drunks weren't trying to sing without falling off the stage.

I stood up again.

This time the restraining hand on my arm was Mom's. "Where are you going?"

"Back to the hospital." I nodded at Clay. "Catch you later, Bro."

"Ridge, wait." Lane stood and handed me his card. "We need to talk. You can reach me at this number any time. We have way more in common than you realize."

Before I bolted for the door, Mom stood and blocked my path. "I'm going with you."

"No, Mom..."

She cut me off. "It's past time I met Sable." Her eyes pleaded.

I sighed. I am such a sucker. I can't say no to Rye either. Well, I can but...

She heard the capitulation in my sigh and smiled. How do Mothers do that? I hesitated. She was the one I needed to get away from.

"Come on," I shrugged. "Let's go."

She grabbed her jean jacket. Without saying anything, she walked out ahead of me. I am so going to regret this.

Chapter Forty
Ridge

In freshman chemistry class, I heard about an old man who cut off his dead wife's hand and kept it in a jar of formaldehyde. He said he'd been holding that hand for sixty-seven years and couldn't bear to part with it. At the time, I'd thought it was stupid, besides being against the law and totally gross. He couldn't hold that hand. It was in a jar in his basement. Now, although I think it was gross and stupid, I can understand the love behind it. This afternoon I watched Sable breathe, grateful every time she inhaled.

I'd been uneasy about my super-sophisticated mom meeting Luna. My anxiety increased as we drew closer to the hospital. I was aware of my need to protect Luna from my sometimes over-bearing mother. Mom picked up on my mood, but not knowing the reason, she kept quiet.

I found a parking space near the visitor's entrance, and we went in. Mom followed me down the hall. An older lady shuffled toward us, pushing her walker. Her oversized blue robe matched her hair. Despite obvious pain, a smile lit up her face. The reason for the big smile was the young lady carrying her grandmother's IV. She wore gym shorts and a T-shirt that proclaimed, "I run like a girl. Try to keep up." Seeing them together was further proof love is the world's best medicine. I looked at Mom. We smiled, sharing the moment.

Mom looked far from urbane tonight. She wore one of my Oklahoma University T-shirts. It was oversized and loose on her small frame, quite the contrast with her skinny jeans and sandals. Mom speaks to hundreds of women at conferences looking as though she just stepped out of Vogue. She's flown across the country to speak to huge crowds campaigning for my dad. She's been perfectly comfortable behind a mic addressing rapt audiences. What could she possibly have in common with Luna who spends most of her time in her garden, seldom leaving her five acres. She can get more out of a plot of ground the size of a scatter rug than anyone I know. Luna's also inherited the knowledge of herbal therapy. Both Moms are amazing, but in different ways.

Sable's door was slightly ajar. I pushed it open and stood there a moment. Luna motioned me in. I stepped back to let Mom enter first. She hesitated just inside the door. Her eyes adjusted to the dimness, then darted to Sable's bed.

Luna saw Mom and stood up.

"Mom, this is Sable's mother, Luna."

Luna rushed forward. Mom hurried to meet her. They met halfway and embraced like two old friends, both in tears.

"Luna?" Mom asked. "What a lovely name."

"I've been praying for you," they both said.

"I am so sorry about your husband," Luna said.

"Thank you," Mom sniffed, and looked around for a tissue.

"He died saving my daughter. I will never forget that," Luna choked on the words.

I brought them the tissue box from Sable's nightstand.

"Luna, this is my mom, April," I said, needlessly.

Holding Mom's hand, Luna led her to the chairs by the window. They sat down, their heads close, conversing quietly. They needed no help from me. Two women sharing a tragedy. They'd both spent a lifetime loving and praying for their children. This common ground overshadowed differences and bound them into a sisterhood I couldn't fathom. I know nothing about women. Something Sable often points out.

I went to sit by Sable's bed. "Hey, Beautiful, I'm back. Did you miss me?"

Sable's hand moved restlessly on the bed. I wrapped my fingers around her hand. Her fingers curled ever so slightly around mine. It was such a small thing, but I wanted to break into a dance of joy. She was aware of me. Unlike the two women across the room.

We'd been there about fifteen minutes when I felt Mom's presence behind me. I glanced back. She was looking at Sable.

"Ridge, can I sit there for a few minutes?" She asked.

Reluctantly, I turned loose of Sable's hand and moved. Mom sat in the seat I'd vacated, reached for the hand I'd been holding, and raised it to her lips. For a few minutes she held it there. She sighed and leaned down.

"Sable," she said, so softly I could barely hear, "I'm April. Ridge's mom. Thank you for making my son so happy."

I heard the tears in her voice. They dripped onto Sable's cheek. If I live to be a hundred, I will never forget this picture. She stopped and sighed again.

"When you're stronger, we're going to spend some time together. You are beautiful, brave, and strong. You are a remarkable young lady. Ridge has good taste. We will all get through this together." She stopped, glanced at me, and smiled. She turned back to Sable. "I love you already."

Mom released Sable's hand, patted it, and turned to me. "Ridge, I think I've talked Luna into going to my hotel room to get some sleep. If you don't mind, I'll stay here with you and Sable tonight."

She must have seen my expression. She hurried to say, "I won't get in your way, I promise. I need to spend some time with you. I'm going home tomorrow. I'm guessing you won't be coming home for a while."

"You're leaving?" I hadn't given any thought to how long she planned to be in Durango. I flashed back to being a kid who needed his mom. I could still lose Sable. "Luna is going to your room?"

"Luna lives 45 minutes from here, but she doesn't want to be that far away. She hasn't left since Sable was admitted. She can freshen up and get some rest at my room."

I nodded. "Right. Good idea." I looked at my watch. We had been at Muleshoe longer than I realized. "There's not much night left. You need sleep too, Mom."

"I can sleep on the plane," she said.

Luna hovered behind me. I got up and gave her my chair. She leaned over to brush hair from Sable's face. She kissed her cheek and whispered in her ear. I could identify. It's hell saying goodbye to Sable. Even when she's not in a coma.

Alone with my mother, I felt uneasy. There was much to be said, but I was not inclined to say it. She didn't seem to know where to start either, so we sat quietly.

She broke the silence. "Ridge, I have so many questions. Why were Grant and Sable on that road?"

"They were going to Luna's."

"Why was Grant driving Sable's car?"

"Let me back up," I said. "Nelson wasn't going to stop until Sable and I were dead."

Mom gasped, “I had no idea all this was going on.”

“Right. We knew you would worry. We agreed to wait until it was over to tell you. Dad, Sable, and I met and decided to move Sable to Norman until something was done about Nelson. Dad rented her a furnished apartment under a fictitious name in case Nelson found my place.”

Mom nodded. “He did.”

“Sable needed her car. I didn’t want her driving alone with Nelson circling the field. I intended to blow off my tournament, fly here, and drive her to Norman. Dad said no.”

Mom opened her mouth to say something but changed her mind.

“Dad talked me out of coming. He said he’d drive Sable to Norman. He flew to Durango. Sable was packed and ready, but records and transcripts for her OU transfer were at Luna’s, along with some of her clothes and her Shih Tzu. Sable takes Izzy everywhere she goes. Izzy has logged more air miles than most people.”

Mom could relate. Our Rottweiler, Chester, is definitely her dog.

“Sable wanted to get Izzy and say goodbye to her mom. But Nelson ambushed them. Dad had his gun, but no opportunity to use it. I was on the phone with Sable when Dad was shot. I blamed myself for Dad’s death,” I said, realizing I had used past tense.

“I hate to introduce sanity into your pity party,” Mom said, “but what do you think you could have done? I would have lost you.” She exhaled a long heavy sigh and looked off into the distance. “Lane gave you his card, right?”

“Yeah. But why?”

"His father was murdered, too. Ambushed on a mountain road. Not far from here. Somewhere in Southwest Colorado. Lane was with his father."

I tried to wrap my mind around that. "When?"

"Lane was about four, so a good while ago. He was the only witness. I'd forgotten about that but a trooper at the CHP office this morning recognized the name Lanigan." Mom shifted her weight, trying to find comfort in a chair that made it impossible. "Lane's dad was a sheriff. In a small town near here."

"So, Lane's been interested in our case for several reasons," I said.

"This just came up this morning. I think the trooper at the highway patrol office might have known Lane's dad."

"Okay. I'll call him," I said. We have things to talk about.

"Good. I'm glad I came," Mom said. "I had to see where it happened." She tried to smile. It slid away. "But I found you. And met Luna and saw Sable."

"I'm glad you're here," I said. I really meant it. It felt good having my mom beside me. We sat in an easy silence, Sable's machines providing background noise.

"I didn't know you and Mr. Lang had been—uh, had been... Uh, had a band. Heck, you guys could go on the road now," I said, examining a scratch on my arm and wondering where it came from.

She smiled a real smile. "I don't need another career. I'm trying to figure out how to get out of some of what I do now. But music was a big part of my life."

"Tell me about your early life," I said.

"You want to know about my early life?" She blinked. "Well, okay, I'll tell you some day, There isn't much to...."

"We aren't doing much right now. Will you tell me?"

"Oh." Long pause. "I guess. Where do I start?"

"The stuff I don't know. Your mom died when you were young, right? Start there."

She gazed up at the ceiling, sighed, and began. She told me about feeling betrayed by her mother's illness and subsequent death. She told me about the car wreck, Ali's kidnapping, Abby's serious injury, and the death of her grandmother in the wreck.

I had heard bits and pieces as a child but had never put it all together.

She told me about Gramps remarrying and moving to the country, and why she moved in with Abby. She told me about dating Ron and how his presence helped her to heal. She told me about the song, *I'll Be Seeing You*, and its meaning for her.

She allowed me to turn over her wrist and rub a finger over her tattoo. "Tell me about this," I said. "Tonight I noticed Mr. Lang has one, too."

She nodded. "Ronnie and I skipped school when I was fourteen and hitched a ride to Oklahoma City to get the tattoos. The 'treble clef' symbolizes my love for music. The 'h' is for Hitchhikers, the name of our band." She had a far-away look in her eye. As if she had forgotten I was there.

"Wow. You were fourteen? You hitched to Oklahoma City? Are you crazy? You would have killed me if I had done something like that."

She did a half shrug. "You've probably done worse."

"You must have really been into him."

"He was my whole world. I assumed we'd be together forever." She sighed. "But a stupid prank his roommate pulled broke us up. I didn't think I could survive without him."

"I know how that feels."

"Yes, you do." She nodded. "Everyone I ever loved had left me— my mother, Grammy, and Ali. Ron swore he'd never leave. I believed him. But then he was gone. Without a word of explanation. I didn't know what happened. So, he became another check in my loss column."

She paused for so long I thought she was through.

She sighed and continued. "I transferred to OU and moved to Norman where I met Grant."

Hearing her story in her voice did a number on me. The bits and pieces all pulled together. She had been through hell. How was she even sane? I would have felt bad for anyone with a story like that. But my mom—I wanted to say something but I couldn't find the words—or get past the lump in my throat.

She gave me time to digest all that. Or maybe she needed she time. She seemed unaware of me again.

"You weren't having an affair after you married dad?" I hated to ask. I had to know.

"No! Ridge, until this trip, I hadn't spoken to Ron for 27 years. I would never do that to Grant!"

"Did you love Dad?"

"Yes! Of course! Have you met your father? Nobody could know Grant and not love him."

I'm not sure that's true. Dad had some major political enemies. But I let that go.

"How could you marry Dad so soon after breaking up with Mr. Lang?" I asked.

She gave me a wistful smile. "You know how persuasive your dad can be. Could be," she amended. "Grant was a force of nature. He made up his mind and I got swept along."

Even though she smiled, her eyes glistened with pent up tears. "By then Ron was married."

I nodded. She was right about Dad. I never liked RJ's mother. I often wondered why Mr. Lang had married her.

We sat in silence for a few minutes. She watched me sort through my thoughts. She smiled when she saw that I understood. We were on the same page again. How do mothers do that?

"If you'd married Ron," I said, "I'd be someone else. RJ and I would be brothers. Or maybe I'd be part RJ and part me."

"That sounds like something Riley Grace would say. You're overthinking this. Grant was an amazing man. Besides your uncanny resemblance, you're like him in so many good ways, Ridge. You're the man you are because of your dad. Grant lives through you and Riley Grace. She may look like me, but she has his walk and smile. I look at you and see him. You have his drive, wit, sense of humor, strong jaw, and chin. Both you and Riley Grace have inherited his fierce determination."

"I'll never be the man he was," I said.

"You don't have to be," Mom said. "You're your own person. You'll do different things. You'll be great in your own way. Grant's genes aren't the only ones you have. You have some of Jackson's expressions and some of the things that come out of your mouth sound just like my father. You're blessed to have grown up under the influence of good men—including, evidently, Ron."

"When Rye and I stayed in Cheyenne Falls with Gramps and Penny, I hung out a lot at his house. Mr. Lang treated me just like he treated RJ—like a son. He taught me to make fishing lures. When we played board games, if I made a bad move, he showed me what it would cost me down the line. What I could have done differently. Where I could have moved instead. He taught me to think ahead. I learned to anticipate problems before they occur. Dad taught me tennis, but I've used what I learned from Mr. Lang to play smarter. He taught me how to shoot a gun, hit a moving target, and gauge the speed of a bird in flight. I can do it with a tennis ball, too. That ability has been invaluable. He invested time in me. He didn't have to, and I'm grateful."

Mom stared. "I had no idea."

"Will you and Mr. Lang get together again?"

"I doubt it." Mom tented her fingers in front of her face and blew through them.

"When I was little, I used to listen to my mother's 45's," she said finally. "There was an old song about trying to put love back together but not being able to find all the pieces. So much time has passed. Ron and I are different people."

I chose my words carefully. "People do change. Circumstances change them. I'm who I am today because of choices I've made and things I've experienced. But who we are here," I placed the hand that wasn't holding Sable's over my heart, "doesn't change."

"Maybe we can be friends again. He's been a good friend to you. I appreciate that. But I need time. I still feel married. I have children to reunite with. My first order of business is getting you both back. The three of you," she said, nodding to include Sable, "will be the center of my universe for a while. I need to fix what I've broken."

"Not much was actually broken, Mom. I moved away, too. Rye and I will work on it with you." I squeezed her hand.

"I've missed you," I said. But until tonight, I had no idea how much.

Chapter Forty-One

April

"Ridge, tell me about your childhood."

Confusion wrinkled his brow. "You were there."

"I'd like to see it through your eyes."

The look he gave me was exactly like his father. "What do you want to know?"

I considered that. "What kind of mother was I?"

"Good grief, Mom!" Ridge grabbed the back of his neck.

He's done that in stressful situations his whole life. Why had his childhood been stressful? Ridge had been a sensitive child. If he was in trouble, it broke his heart. Riley Grace, on the other hand, couldn't care less. As soon as she'd been scolded, it was on to the next big adventure. Ridge had been an easy baby. Riley Grace fought being born with a vengeance. I was certain the length of my labor should have been written up in medical journals. She was practically born with colic. She's seventeen and hasn't grown out of the terrible twos. If she'd been born first, she would have been an only child.

"You were good," he said. He paused, then added, "When you were home."

Well, I asked him to be honest. He was unaware he'd stabbed me in the heart. But I needed to hear how he saw things.

"On a scale of one to ten I'd give my childhood a seven," Ridge began, his voice tentative. "Plus," he added when he saw my expression. "Yeah, I'd say maybe even an eight." He nodded for emphasis. "On the whole, it was good. I've heard horror stories at college. I have friends who were raised by the Munsters."

"Would you have rated your childhood higher if you and Riley Grace hadn't spent so much time in Cheyenne Falls?"

"No! We loved the farm. Rye had Picasso, I had RJ. We both loved Gramps and Penny. I could be a kid there." The force of his answer surprised me.

Ridge has been places and had learning opportunities few children are afforded and his favorite part of childhood was living at the farm?

"I don't understand. Why couldn't you 'be a kid' at home?" I asked.

"At the farm Gramps and Penny didn't expect me to watch Rye. I could do my own thing. At home, I was always in trouble because my sister didn't think like other people. She believed she was Wonder Woman. When she was five!"

Ridge kneaded the back of his neck again. On the brink of refuting that statement, I shut my mouth. One of my go-to phrases as a motivational speaker is a quote from Stephen Covey: "Seek first to understand, then to be understood." I needed to follow my own advice.

Conversation was interrupted by a nurse who bustled in to check Sable's IV. While Ridge watched the nurse's every move, I digested what he'd just said and studied his chiseled profile. My son had grown into a very handsome man.

"Help me understand what you mean," I said when the nurse was gone.

Ridge sighed. "Remember when Riley was two and almost drowned in the Rankin's pool? Dad yelled at me. Why should I be watching her? You were there. I didn't see her jump in. I'd been having fun playing with friends."

"She was three. Almost four. I'm sorry Grant yelled at you. He was scared. We almost lost her. He was mad at me. You're right, I should have been watching her. Thank goodness Grant arrived when he did. That was a nightmare."

"Then there was the time she climbed up in the neighbor's tree and couldn't get down," Ridge continued. "She was so high we couldn't get to her. The limbs wouldn't hold the weight of an adult. The neighbor called the fire department. She had to be rescued with a hook and ladder truck."

I remembered. Grant hadn't been too happy about that one either. It happened during the first gubernatorial race. Pictures of a fireman high on a ladder rescuing his daughter appeared on the front page of both newspapers. Two-inch headlines proclaimed:

LOCAL FIRE DEPARTMENT RESCUES SUPERMAN'S DAUGHTER.

It's funny now, though it certainly hadn't been then. The whole neighborhood had gathered around that tree. Riley had been screaming, "Daddy," at the top of her lungs. The other times she'd needed her father played through my mind. It was Grant she called when she had nightmares. She's going to be lost.

"...and that wasn't the only time," Ridge was saying. "The next year she crawled out one of the third story windows of the Governor's Mansion and got on the roof and couldn't find her way back in. The fire department had to come get her down then, too. They probably had our phone number on speed dial."

I laughed, remembering. Although, it hadn't been funny at the time.

"And that doesn't even include all the times she ran down the sidewalk chasing a ball or her dog and got lost," Ridge grumbled. "I had to find her before you guys knew she was gone."

"Aren't you exaggerating?"

"Mom, have you met my sister?"

"I'm beginning to wonder if I've ever known anyone," I said.

"And then there was the time she played hide and seek with her friends. She hid in a pile of clothes in the laundry room and went to sleep. Nobody could find her and thought she'd been kidnapped. Someone called the police. The search and rescue team went through the whole house. They couldn't find her either.

I laughed. "I'd forgotten about that one, too."

"I couldn't relax when she was around. I had to watch her every minute. Everything she did was somehow my fault."

"Well, she's older now, and..."

"She's worse," Ridge interrupted. "Last fall Dad asked me to take some tax papers out to the farm for Gramps to sign. Rye wanted to go. I kind of missed her when I was at college, so I thought it would be cool."

Sable made a slight noise. Her head turned toward us. She quieted and Ridge's attention moved back to his story.

"On the way home, I stopped to get gas. I heard brakes squealing. Riley had run out into traffic to help an old homeless guy in a wheelchair. I swear my first thought was how I was going to explain to Dad why his precious angel had to be extracted from the grill of a Peterbilt. Rye got traffic stopped, but couldn't get the wheelchair over the curb, so I ran out to help her. She created a big traffic jam. It's a miracle there weren't wrecks. I imagined more newspaper headlines—*Senator's Son and Daughter Cause Nine-Car Pileup*."

I laughed. "Okay, I get it. You're right. I'm sorry."

"No, I rated my childhood a seven plus. For the most part, it was good. Parts were even great."

Sable grew restless and Ridge's attention returned to her. He stood by her bedside whispering to her as he patted her swollen face with a cool damp cloth. As far as he was concerned they were the only two people in the world.

Through tears I watched my son care for the girl he loved. My mind replayed what he'd just told me, certain the parts of his childhood he classified as "even great" were the parts he'd spent out at the farm. I'd hated that farm. Dad had built that house because Penny had wanted to live in the country. He'd married her after Mom died and pretty much forgot he had a daughter. I resented Penny, although it's impossible to dislike her. And I tried. I barely spoke to Dad and stayed in town with Abby. He'd been too immersed in his own grief to consider mine. Tonight when Ron said Jackson had gone with them on their Colorado hunting trip, I realized that Dad might not have been there for me, but he has practically raised my kids.

My text tone chirped. Lane sent me the info I needed for catching a later flight out of Durango. It gave me four more hours with Ridge. Lane asked if Ridge could take me to the airport. Ridge had already offered.

The morning nurses bustled in and busied themselves around Sable's bedside. They seemed to be pleased with her progress. Although it hadn't been record-breaking overnight, her vitals were good, her heart was strong, her breathing had improved and she was moving more. Ridge was elated that Sable was trying to come out of the coma.

Luna returned looking refreshed. She'd slept and washed her hair. Her smile momentarily smoothed the stress from her face. I gave her my seat beside Sable's bed and went to find a restroom. My text tone chirped again while I brushed my teeth. The text was from Ron.

April, I'm going back to Oklahoma on our scheduled flight.

Hope your flight is uneventful. I'm grateful for memories made on this trip. I've pretty much worn out our old ones. I never dreamed we would ever be together on stage again. Thanks for the chance to explain what happened years ago. I feel better knowing you've heard the truth. I'll call you in a few days. There's a matter I'd like you to consider.

Relieved he wouldn't be on my flight, I read the text again. I need time to process the events of the past few days and work through my tangled emotions. Being up all night with Ridge had been eye-opening to say the least. Our conversation had left me with a lot to think about, something I couldn't do sitting next to Ron. Hopefully I can sleep through the flight. I'm exhausted.

Chapter Forty-Two

April

The mountain air was crisp, perfect weather for a flight home. I couldn't wait to board the plane and get home to Riley Grace. The beauty of the morning almost obliterated the exhaustion of being up all night. I had achieved even more than expected on this trip. I'd discovered the truth of what had happened to Grant. Now his name could be cleared. The world would know he'd died the way he'd lived. A hero. I found Ridge. Actually, Lane found him, but whatever. Above and beyond all that, Sable was alive! And I had begun to reconnect with Ridge. Nelson was behind bars where he was no longer a threat to my family. Last, but not least—oh, maybe it was least—I had reconnected with Ron. At least I no longer hated him. I had stumbled under the load of resentment far too long. That weight had lifted.

Passengers were called for boarding. I turned to wave at Ridge one last time before hurrying toward the plane. He didn't see me. He sat in his Forester near the gate looking down—probably scrolling through messages. After finding him, it was hard to leave. Like Lot's wife, I kept looking back.

Ridge had promised to come home for a few days when Sable was out of the woods. Together we would try to salvage his school semester. He promised to attempt to save the Yonex sponsorship. Both of these are good signs. He was facing a future without his father.

I was halfway to the boarding ramp when I felt more than heard someone behind me. Startled, I made a half turn and recognized the man I'd seen lounging against the chain-link fence when I came through the gate.

"Mrs. Frazier?" he asked.

"No! Go away." I was much too tired to be fake polite.

He hovered in my body space, entirely too close.

He leaned in. "I have a gun," he said into my right ear. "Come with me."

Hard metal jammed into my side. My first impulse was to scream. Terror snaked down my spine. I was in total disbelief. I've seen enough news to know things like this happen—to other people. Not me. I thought fast. If he was going to kill me, it would not be in some secluded spot after he'd done unimaginable things to me—which I actually imagined all too well. No! It would have to be in this crowd. In front of witnesses. Lots of witnesses. I was not going with him. I stopped abruptly causing him to run into me. If I'd taken time to think, I might not have whirled around and jabbed a finger in his chest.

"I'm not going anywhere with you. If you plan to kill me, do it here." I spat the words in his face which was way too close. I could see enlarged pores on his nose and whiskers he'd missed when he shaved this morning. Nose hairs curled from one nostril. He was middle aged, medium height—not much taller than I am and medium weight. His reddish hair had been buzzed. In other circumstance, he would not look intimidating, but I had a feeling I'd be seeing his pockmarked face in my nightmares for a long time. If, of course, I have a long time.

He looked uncomfortable in his ill-fitting wrinkled suit. He wore dark sunglasses. I couldn't read his eyes, but I had surprised him. A jaw muscle twitched, he was tense. He took a step backwards.

"Mrs. Frazier, I advise you to come with us," he said through clenched teeth.

"Us?" I asked.

I took a step back. He couldn't shoot me here. Too many witnesses. My fear lessened. Still unaware of the unfolding drama, people moved around us bumping into us, boarding the plane. Glancing at them I wondered if he would follow me on the plane if I joined them. If so, more people might die than just me.

"I wouldn't do that," he said reading my mind. "Riley Grace needs her mother."

"What?" I said, stupidly.

"Such a sweet young thing," he said, sarcasm dripped from his words. "I have a fondness for sweet young things."

I froze. "Riley Grace?" I stammered. "My daughter? Where— Where is she?" I looked around as though expecting her to materialize in the crowd. I gasped for air. How would this guy know my daughter's name? Desperate, I looked for Ridge. I couldn't see his car. People swarmed between me and the gate.

"There." The guy jerked his chin in the direction of a smaller jet on the tarmac.

"You have my daughter? On that plane? No, you don't! She's home..." I started to say in Oklahoma but realized he may be bluffing and had no idea where she was. "I don't believe you! I'm not stupid. I pay to be this blonde."

"I assure you most of her is on that plane," he sneered.

That sent an icy chill down my spine. "Most of her?"

I looked over my shoulder for Ridge. The Forester was still there, but I couldn't see him. I had no idea if he could see what was happening.

"What do you mean?" I gasped.

"All of her except for this." He pulled a small cylinder, a plastic pill bottle, from his pocket. It contained a pinky finger—a small pinky finger.

Light-headed, I felt like I might faint. "You son of a bitch!" I yelled. "What have you done? I'll kill you!" Bile rose into my throat. Choking and gagging, I lunged for his neck.

In one quick move, he grabbed my wrist, spun me around, twisting my arm behind me. He growled into my ear. "If you want to see your daughter alive, I suggest you come quietly."

I screamed and couldn't stop. The polish on the fingernail had been blue. The same shade of blue on Riley Grace's toes three days ago.

Chapter Forty-Three

Riley Grace

Country music blared from the CD player. Bronc, a huge fan, sang along with Merle Haggard, slapping the steering wheel like a bongo drum as he drove. Listening to his music reminded me of being with my grandpa. It was a good feeling. Like I was home.

Bronc liked the old stuff. Really old. CDs by Dwight Yoakum and Buck Owens slid from under the seat whenever the truck rounded a corner, along with a rusty screwdriver and a lone work glove. It had never occurred to me that I'd fall in love with a cowboy who would turn me on to country music. Bronc thinks some of Larry Gatlin's lines are pure poetry. He's not wrong.

We'd taken a load of hay out to the horses and were on our way back to town. Everyone in Bronc's family has a horse. When Bronc and I go riding, which is often, I ride his mother's horse, a pretty little bay gelding named Ringo.

The windows were cranked down. Wind whipped my hair into tangles. I don't even care that Bronc's pickup has no air conditioner.

Bronc loves this truck so much because it belonged to his grandpa, but that's not the only reason. Bronc's father found the pickup in a shed on the family farm and he and Bronc began restoring it. Supposedly, Bronc's father had been conceived in this truck. I found that hard to believe when I met his grandma. She's dinky short and quite wide. I couldn't picture her climbing up into this truck.

When Bronc's father didn't come back from Afghanistan, Bronc was determined to finish what they'd started. That single-minded determination is one of the things I love about him. He never gives up. I'm glad he didn't give up on meeting me. Being in a relationship with Bronc has been even better than my dreams.

Don't think the irony of Bronc and me getting together at my father's funeral went unnoticed. Dad, the most important person in my life, was suddenly stolen from me. But then Bronc appeared when I needed him the most—like God giving me a consolation prize, only Bronc is so much more than that.

Most of Bronc's paycheck goes to restoring his truck. He's been looking for a better radiator to go with the new belts and hoses he bought last month. Parts for a pickup this old aren't easy to find. When I'm not working with my new tennis trainer, Eve Anna, I'm in salvage yards with a ratchet wrench following Bronc through crippled cars. Last month I didn't know a ratchet wrench from a hoof rasp.

Salvage yards, I've discovered, are a real business. Wrecked cars are hauled to a place where people harvest parts they need. It's like panning for gold but more like a treasure hunt. It's exciting when someone stumbles across a part that has eluded them.

Alise says it sounds boring, but she isn't aware of the danger. Rattlesnakes and wasps make nests in discarded cars. I once saw a picture in an old *National Geographic* of a wasp nest that totally filled an old Plymouth.

My feet propped on the dash, I'd been painting my toenails blue which wasn't easy because the road was rough. Shocks for a '60 Ford pickup are hard to find.

"I need gas," Bronc announced as he turned into an On Cue station and circled the pumps. He pulled in behind the Volvo leaving a pump. "That's weird," he muttered, looking in the rearview.

"What's weird?" I asked. I screwed the lid back on the nail polish and dropped it into my purse.

"That black sedan has followed us since we got on I-44," he said.

"That is weird," I teased. "A snail moves faster than you drive. You'd have thought they would've passed us."

Bronc wasn't listening. His eyes were still glued to the rearview mirror. "They followed us in here but parked on the other end of the building. They're going inside."

He sounded relieved. I hadn't realized he'd been concerned.

"Give me your card," I said. "I'll pump gas while you go to the restroom."

"I can wait. I don't think you can remove the gas cap." He checked the rearview again. "And I don't feel good about leaving you out here alone."

"You've been talking about how bad you have to pee for fifteen miles. Go. I'll be fine. I don't want to be responsible for causing your bladder to burst or something. Can you even imagine the scorn and derision I'd receive for letting that happen? Everywhere I went people would be pointing and and..."

"All right!" Bronc looked down at my feet. "I'm going. Put your shoes on."

"Can't. My toenails are still wet." I hopped out barefooted. "Go!" I ordered.

Bronc sighed, but he got out and pocketed the keys.

He hadn't lied about how difficult the gas cap was to remove. He couldn't unscrew it either. He got a wrench from behind the seat and whacked the side of it. When it finally came loose, he tossed the wrench behind the seat, handed me his card, and jogged off to the restroom.

I inserted the hose. Nothing happened. "If Bronc isn't peeing any faster than this, we're going to be here all night," I muttered. I jiggled the hose and gas began flowing.

A woman filling her white Lexus at the next pump practically sneered at me. I don't have anything against a Lexus. My mom drives one. But Barbie Doll rolled her eyes when she saw me hop out of Bronc's ancient pickup, barefooted, wearing cutoffs and a T-shirt covered in horse snot. Not meeting her high standards might have ouched a bit if I had no self-confidence or cared about what she thought. I grinned as I watched her fill her tank in a pink Armani suit, careful not to break her manicured nails.

"Hey, little Mama, you will come with me. I have a knife," a Hispanic voice whispered in my ear. At the same time, a tattooed forearm came across my throat pulling me roughly against him.

"Do not make a sound. I will cut your throat." His cold calculated tone scared me more than if he'd yelled.

I looked down. He held a machete close to his side. The blade had something on it like rust or—dried blood. This didn't look good at all. Ridge would have said, "Well, Rye, this is another fine mess you got yourself into."

Dad made us all take self-defense classes. But that was a few years ago. I kind of wish I'd paid more attention. I'd learned how to escape a hold like this. It was coming back. Sort of. I think I'm supposed to stomp on his instep as hard as I can. If I was wearing spike heels, I could turn them into a weapon. So to speak. I've never worn spike heels in my life. I'm also not wearing shoes of any kind. Guess that's out.

In a carjacking, I should throw the car keys as far as I can. He would have to turn loose of me to go after them. Dragging me with him would attract attention. Good idea.

Only Bronc has the keys. And this guy doesn't seem to want them.

"There's a blonde over there in Prada shoes with a Lexus and you're carjacking me in an old Ford pickup?" I croaked. "Do you have no standards?"

He chuckled. "I don't want this piece of junk."

"What do you want?" Talking while being choked is not as easy as one might think.

"Your little finger," he said.

"What? My little finger?" I gulped. "What does that even mean?"

"Lay your hand on the truck and spread your fingers," he ordered. "Now!"

Oh! He meant it. The brown stains on that machete took on a whole new significance. This day was not going well. At all.

"You can't have it," I said. "I'm using it." Which was true. My fingers were curled around the gas hose nozzle. I thought fast. The self-defense guy had said to weaponize anything you can get your hands on. My hand was already on the gas hose. Alrighty then.

I yanked the hose from the tank and slung the nozzle over my shoulder aiming it where his voice had been. Hopefully, pumping gas into his face. If his screams were any indication, I was doing fine. He released me and clawed at his eyes. Wailing like a banshee, he spouted words I was glad I couldn't understand.

He backed away. I followed, spraying gas into his ear. He turned and ran blindly into the street—directly into the path of a black F-150. The pickup was probably doing 60 when it hit him. The thud was sickening.

I screamed. It didn't help. So, I screamed again. He flew into the air and landed in the opposite lane. The cars that hit him couldn't stop. Tires screeched. A car rear-ended the pickup. Horns honked as traffic came to a standstill. Everything was instant chaos.

Sirens wailed in the distance. In the street, cars still skidded to a halt and crashed into each other. It was like a scene from *The Fast and the Furious*. I totally expected Vin Diesel to appear.

Shards of glass shattered on the street. A black sedan squealed to a stop between me and the street. The driver jumped out. I had no time to react. His arms clamped around mine pinning them to my side. He dragged me toward the car. I still held the gasoline gas hose but couldn't use it as a weapon. My hand slid off the trigger and it stopped spewing gas. I bit, kicked, and screamed. My bare feet slid in the puddled gas.

This guy was bigger. He tried to shove me into the car. The gas hose reached the end of its length and jerked from my hand, leaving me weaponless. He lifted me, kicking, biting and screaming. I braced my feet against the car seat and stiffened my legs.

Bronc came out of nowhere. In a flying tackle he hit the guy's knees, driving all three of us into a puddle of gas. They both landed on top of me. I gasped for air but only inhaled fumes. The guy pulled his arms out from under me and tried to push Bronc off. They were squishing me. In a super-human effort I wriggled free, jumped up, reached into the car, grabbed the keys , and threw them as far as I could. A bit of overkill there, but it felt good.

Bronc was still grappling with the guy when a patrol car drove up. Bronc was younger, stronger, and in better shape. He had landed on top and had momentum.

An officer jumped out of a squad car and pulled Bronc off. "What's going on here?"

"He was trying to kidnap me!" I yelled. I pointed to the dude with the broken nose who was screaming obscenities at me. I couldn't say more. I bent over, gagging, choking, throwing up. Not my best look. I couldn't escape the fumes. My clothes were saturated.

But Lexus Barbie, my new BFF, didn't have a problem with taking over the narrative. She had called 9-1-1 when the man with the machete grabbed me. She had videoed the whole thing.

"Where is he now?" the officer asked.

I wiped my mouth and pointed to the street where traffic had come to a standstill.

The officer, slightly older than my father, looked me over carefully. "Are you okay young lady?"

"I don't know. Maybe." I bent over and barfed again. My knee was skinned and burning bad. My shoulder hurt. My mouth tasted like gasoline. I was pretty sure some had gone up my nose when my face was in the gas puddle.

His eyes widened. "You're Senator Frazier's daughter, aren't you?"

I nodded again.

Well. That got Lexus Barbie's attention. She'd been showing another policeman her video along with a blow-by-blow account. She overheard our conversation, looked at me and blinked.

"I have the whole thing on video," she trilled. She realized this story was big and might have imagined being up for a starring role on the evening news. She looked around for a film crew.

"Do you think this is connected to your father's death?" the officer asked, ignoring her. "Reportedly, his wreck was an accident."

"I don't know." My voice quavered. Shock was setting in. I shook violently. "But weird stuff has been happening." I said through chattering teeth.

"What did he want?" the officer asked.

"Her little finger," Lexus Barbie chimed in.

"Your little finger?" The officer stopped writing and looked up at me. His face registered disbelief or confusion. I couldn't tell which.

"He didn't get it," I said, showing him all ten of my fingers. I nodded toward the dropped machete lying near the pump and ran through a brief account of what happened. I told him what the first guy said. The part I understood.

"That beats all," the officer muttered, jotting down notes.

Bronc came up from behind and slipped an arm around me. I leaned into him. We both dripped gas. E10 at $3.79 a gallon.

"Good work, Son." The officer smiled. "You saved this young lady's life."

I hadn't had time to absorb the what ifs yet. But it was dawning on me now.

"Good thing she has those strong tennis legs, or she would have been gone before I got there," Bronc said. He gave me a little squeeze. "But when I saw what was happening..." He choked back a sob. His voice trailed off and he shook his head. "He would have got her in that car over my dead body."

"You picked yourself one tough little cookie, here." The officer smiled and winked at me. "You might want to keep that in mind."

“I certainly will, Sir,” Bronc said.

A guy from EMSA interrupted the officer. “I’ve got to get this gasoline off their exposed skin. And check that bump on her head.” He ushered us to an ambulance. He and his partner began cleaning us up.

Vans from all of the local TV stations began arriving. As I watched news crews pouring from vehicles and setting up equipment, I wondered how they all heard about it at the same time. They must all have police scanners. Of course they did.

Lexus Barbie, pranced over to the nearest camera crew who had taped the last part of our conversation with the police.

“Are you alright?” Bronc asked when we were both a bit calmer. And cleaner.

“Yes, thanks to you. If you hadn’t shown up, I would have been toast. I’m never going anywhere without you. Ever again.”

Bronc smiled. “That’s kind of the plan.”

In front of On Cue, traffic was at a standstill. Police were directing vehicles around the accident scene. An EMSA crew had covered the machete guy’s body with a sheet but left him in the street. Bronc pulled me close. “This will be on the ten o’clock news.”

“Not a first for me,” I said.

“Man, before I met you, nothing like this ever happened. Tell me you aren’t going to need to be rescued every day.”

I thought about the big red fire truck getting me out of the Foster’s tree and a year later when I crawled out of a third-floor window onto the roof of the Governor’s Mansion and couldn’t find my way back in.

“Not every day,” I said.

Chapter Forty-Four

Ridge

Mom squeezed along the tight space between the Forester's hood and the airport's chain link fence. I'd parked a little too close. At the gate she smiled and waved before going through. Sleep deprived, I could hardly keep my eyes open, but I felt closer to my mom than I had in years. In the daylight she looked thinner than she had at the restaurant last night. Diminished. Dad had been right. She needed me. I resolved to stay close.

My phone vibrated. Clay's number lit up the screen.

"Hey," I said, keeping an eye on Mom, "What's up?"

"I need your statement. I can run it by the hospital for your signature. Just look it over to make sure I got it right, sign it, and drop it back by the office."

"I'm at the airport. Mom is on her way to OKC. I could swing by your office on the way to the hospital. Save you a trip."

I looked up. A rough-looking guy had been lounging by the fence near the gate. He'd fallen in step with Mom. I got the feeling he'd been watching for her. He was entirely too close. She turned toward him. Shock registered on her face. I saw the man's gun the same time she did.

"Gotta go Clay! A dude just shoved a gun in my mom's back!"

"Ridge! Wait! Stand down! I'm close. Be there in a sec. I'll call airport security and the sheriff on my way. Stay in your car."

"Not going to happen," I said, opening my door.

"Ridge, Stay in your car! Ridge."

I was already out. I ended the call and patted my pocket to make sure my gun was there. The phone rang again before I reached the gate. I figured it was Clay and almost didn't answer, but I checked the screen. I didn't recognize the number but picked up anyway.

Airport security wanted details. Clay hadn't wasted time. I filled them in, describing what Mom and the gunman were wearing. Keeping an eye on the situation, I wondered how a day that started out well could turn to crap so fast.

"It looks like they're passing the Boeing now boarding on the tarmac. He's dragging her toward the Lear on the far runway," I told security.

"Gotcha," the security guy said. "I'm sending that information on. My name is Joe, by the way. Who are you?"

"My name is Ridge Frazier. I'm the victim's son. Who owns that Lear jet?"

"Let me check real quick." A moment later he said, "We don't know."

"How did it get here?" I asked. "Even a Lear jet can't land without being seen."

"We got a partial flight plan last night. Don't really know anything about this plane."

Things went south while we talked. Mom stopped and faced the gunman. He pulled something from his pocket. She screamed. My blood ran cold. There were too many people between us to see exactly what was happening. A guy, obviously a Pittsburgh Steelers lineman, stopped in front of me to adjust his backpack. I couldn't get around him. I lost Mom in the crowd. My frustration morphed into panic. Where had all these people come from? I could barely move.

Mom's scream had attracted attention. When people saw the gun all hell broke loose. They stampeded over each other trying to escape. Nobody knew which way to run. Two men stumbled and fell, then others tripped over them.

"Mom!" I tried to shove through the panicked crowd but couldn't move. It was like a dream sequence.

The crowd thinned out and I could see them. The guy's right hand held a gun to Mom's head. He dragged her by a fistful of hair. I had been right. They were moving toward the Lear. Its engines revved, ready to take off.

My heart pounded against my ribs. I had no hope of reaching them before he got her on that plane. Sweat trickled down my spine. My gun was in my pocket. In this crowd I couldn't risk a shot. My mind wrapped around one thought. I can't lose my mom, too.

A deuce-and-a-half security vehicle roared past the plane and wedged itself under the Lear's nose, grounding it. That plane is going nowhere. I sighed in relief.

"Great move," I said to Joe who was still on the phone. I'd been giving him a play-by-play of the action as it happened. Often yelling in his ear.

The Lear's engine droned to a stop. The perp showed no indication of giving up, continuing to drag Mom toward the plane. I moved my gun from the back pocket of my jeans to easy reach in my jacket pocket. My fingers curled around it.

Three men jumped from the truck, wearing shirts with SECURITY emblazoned across the front in large black block letters. They blocked the gunman's progress, but when they saw the gun at Mom's head, they stopped but held their ground.

The night Nelson showed up at Sable's house looking for me, I'd been defenseless. I could only hide behind the bed. I vowed never to make that mistake again. I'm keeping my gun close for a while. I can't assume this is over. The weight of it in my pocket felt good.

I was still connected to security guy Joe.

The crew inside the Lear slammed the door of the plane, locking themselves in. The three airport security men and everyone else were locked out. Gun Guy hadn't realized that yet. I felt a flash of relief knowing he couldn't get Mom on that plane.

Approaching sirens reminded me of the night of the wreck. Help was on the way.

This time, if I had anything to do with it, they wouldn't be too late.

"I told you to stay in the car." Clay glared at me as he passed. "Stay back! Frazier, I mean it! I'll arrest you for interference with a police officer." I'd been reduced to a bystander by the use of my last name. He might be my friend, but he was a cop first. And he was in charge.

Palms up, I stepped back, acknowledging his authority. I stayed behind but followed him. He quieted the spectators and addressed the nervous guy in the cheap suit who held a gun to my mother's head. I had stumbled into another nightmare.

The Sheriff's crew arrived, followed by local police and highway patrol. Since Clay had already engaged the gunman in conversation, they stayed back, keeping the crowd under control and at a distance. But they made a great show of force. The gun at my mother's head shook visibly.

I was close enough now to see and hear what was going on. I heard the gunman demand the freedom of Brett Nelson. My fear turned to fury. My jaw tightened. Hands clenched into fists.

I'll be damned if I lose both parents because of Nelson! I concentrated on my breathing. Inhale. Exhale. Inhale.

These guys were after Nelson. They were sent by the cartel to kill him. They were no amateurs who wandered in off the street. They were cold-blooded assassins. My nightmare ratcheted up a few more notches.

I could see Mom, but she hadn't seen me. I watched her closely. She seemed almost serene. She's good in a crisis. I thought back to the time she saved my life by remaining composed.

* * *

I had been three or four. Mom had been hugely pregnant. It had been July-hot at the dude ranch where we were vacationing and they were preparing for a rodeo. All day the air had been filled with the aroma of the pig turning on a spit behind the bunkhouse.

While I slept, a cattle truck unloaded Brahma bulls into a corral. When I woke up from my nap, I set out to find Mom and Dad. But when I saw the bulls, I made a detour to the pen. I'd never seen anything so huge! Mesmerized, I stood watching them huffing and snorting. A dark grey bull, standing next to the fence, lowered its head and watched me through the rails. He snuffled at my hand, his breath hot and moist. The bull drooled on my arm. I wiped it off on my shorts. His eyes tracked me as I climbed through the fence rails. I walked past him and made more friends. The other bulls noticed me and stopped milling around. Poised to stampede if I proved to be scary.

Mom came looking for me. When she saw me, she ran toward the pen. The ranch owner grabbed her arm. "Hold on there, little lady," he warned. "You can't run up there like that. If you spook 'em bulls, they'll stampede. Calm down, we'll get him out."

"How?" Mom asked.

"He got in there, he has to get himself out. Call him."

"Ridge, Sweetie, I made you a peanut butter sandwich. Come and eat."

"Okay, Mommy," I said, switching directions. I had to step carefully. There were big piles of poop everywhere. The bulls watched and huffed, but none of them moved. They wouldn't get out of my way. I finally got to the fence.

"Can you climb through the rails?" Mom asked.

Well, of course I can. I got in there, didn't I?

As soon as I was out, Mom swooped me up. She was shaking.

"Mommy, is something wrong?" I asked, looking into her tear-streaked face.

The ranch owner looked stunned. "That was a miracle," his voice quavered. "Tonight, in the arena, those bulls will try to destroy any cowboy they see."

* * *

During that incident, Mom had stayed calm when she needed to. She looked calm now. I'm guessing she isn't. Neither am I. But we'll play it cool until I get her out of this mess.

Gun Guy just figured out that he was locked out of the plane and in a bit of a bind. He grew visibly agitated. I might have felt sorry for him if his hostage hadn't been my mom. As I stood on the fringe of the crowd, I remembered standing on that boulder the other night with my Dad's voice telling me my mother was going to need me. I don't think he had this in mind. But if I had taken my life that night, I wouldn't be here today. My hand slipped back into my pocket. My fingers curled around my fully loaded gun. I was ready. I waited.

Chapter Forty-Five
April

Last night, laughing and joking at Muleshoe Bar and Grille, Officer Clayton Morely had looked like one of Ridge's college friends. Today along with a uniform he wore a calm confidence as though he negotiated hostage situations every day.

"Good morning, Mrs. Frazier," he said, with a curt nod.

I would have nodded back, but cold steel pressed against my temple. And so far, nothing about this morning had been good.

The gunman had moved around behind me. A sweaty forearm across my throat held me against him. The hand holding the gun against my head, trembled more than I did which did nothing to lower my blood pressure.

"Stay calm, April," Clay advised.

His smile was meant to still my rising panic. But his use of my first name eased my fear. My life was in the hands of someone who knew me. I'm not a nameless statistic.

Clay turned his attention to the gunman.

"What's your name, Sir?" he asked, taking a step forward. He stood apart from the crowd, about twenty feet from me. Close enough to communicate without having to yell.

"Gavin," the gunman growled. "Stop right there or this'll be the worse day of her life!"

"Wrong," I said. "My husband just died. This doesn't even come close."

"Gavin, do you have a last name?" Clay had stopped but raised a palm to show the gunman he was following instructions.

"Finkelstein," the gunman responded.

Finkelstein? His name was Finkelstein? Normal people like accountants, bank officials, and attorneys, especially attorneys, have names like Finkelstein—not gunmen. It should be etched in glass or painted in gold leaf on a door. *Finkelstein and Higginbotham, Attorneys at Law*.

I pictured the headlines of tomorrow's newspaper. **Senator's Wife Shot in the Head by Gavin Finkelstein in Hostage Situation Gone Wrong**. Too wordy.

I should be relieved his name wasn't Mac the Knife, Jack the Ripper, or Mad Dog Harry. I tried out the last one. Mad Dog Finkelstein. No. Gavin the Ripper? No!

Finkelstein perspired like a 400-pound opera singer under a spotlight. His beet-red face pressed against one side of my head. I felt heat and a nerve jerking in his jaw through my hair. What trickled between my boobs, being absorbed into my bra, came from the sweaty arm across my throat. Yuck!

"I'm Officer Morley," Clay sounded almost chatty. "Can I call you Gavin?"

"Sure. Mind if I call you pig?" The gunman sneered.

Unfazed, Clay asked, "So, what do you want to happen here, Gavin?"

"Brett Nelson," he said. Then he must have noticed the army of law enforcement. "And all of you to back off," he added.

"Brett Nelson?" Clay scratched the side of his face, his expression suggesting he'd never heard the name. "Friend of yours?"

"Don't play stupid with me," Finkelstein growled. "You get the lady when we get Nelson." He jammed the gun harder against my skull for emphasis.

According to Lane, Nelson had been flown to DC immediately after his arrest. Clay had nothing to bargain with. What was dripping from my jaw could have been tears, sweat, snot, or all of the above.

Clay didn't blink. "Well, now that might take a bit of time," he said as if chatting with a neighbor across the back fence. "But see, here's the thing, Gavin, I'm not at all sure Nelson would want to go with you."

Panic hit hard. On the verge of hyperventilating, I gasped for air. To keep from fainting, I scanned the gathering crowd and focused on the woman wearing frayed cutoffs and a faded tank top, both two sizes too big. She looked like a refugee from a prisoner of war camp. Except for the nose ring and a large safety pin in one eyebrow. Silly me, I didn't know eyebrows could fall off. It looked as though the book of Exodus had been tattooed on her neck and down one arm. Her mousey brown hair had escaped from the thing she'd tied it back with and hung in damp strings around her face. Her eyes were closed, her lips moved without ceasing, and her hands were raised. She was praying. Fervently. For me. Her freckled face suddenly became the most beautiful thing I'd ever seen.

"But just to be clear, you'd let Mrs. Frazier go if I bring you Nelson?" Clay asked, nodding as though trying to ascertain what the gunman had just said.

He sounded like a slow third grader. It was intentional. De-escalating the situation—slowing Finklestein down. If I hadn't been so scared, I'd have been impressed. Like a skilled fisherman Clay had been letting out the line then reeling Finklestein back in.

"That's right," Finkelstein said.

"Well, like I said, I think ole Brett would rather take his chances with us."

"I don't care," Finklestein growled. "Get him out here now!"

Radio and television news crews had arrived along with additional law enforcement. The sheriff's department did a good job of holding them all at bay. Facial expressions would have been interesting in any other circumstance, but with my life hanging in the balance, some of them made me furious. Like the two women laughing and talking as though exchanging recipes. They could be witnessing my death and didn't care one way or the other. I'll be remembering their insensitivity for a long time—if I have a long time.

I'd never given the death penalty much consideration. Mainly because my opinion made no difference to the powers that be. But in that moment, examining the faces of those two women, I felt public executions were cruel and unusual punishment. A person's final moments should be private. No matter what they've done.

Most of the faces around me registered shock or fear. Besides my tattooed angel, a few other people prayed. For that I was grateful. Every face glistened with perspiration. The sun had climbed higher into the sky, reminding everyone that it was, after all, a ball of fire. But unlike Oklahoma, where the wind blows most of the time, not even a slight breeze stirred in Durango.

From the corner of my eye, I noticed the narrow band of gold on Finkelstein's left hand. He was married. That jarred me. Who would marry this monster? Did his wife know his job description included kidnapping, murder, and hostage situations Did she ever wonder what a normal workday was for him? Did she say, "Darling, if you have time between murders, could you pick up the kids?" On wash day did she ever mutter, "Oh darn! He left a finger in his pocket again."

I realized I had totally lost it when I remembered the joke about a woman who'd heard on the news someone was driving the wrong way on the highway her husband would be taking to work. When she called to warn him, he said, "Just one? There's hundreds of them!"

What kind of woman marries a man who carries fingers around in his pocket like a roll of Tums? The thought of that finger set off a new wave of nausea. One of Riley Grace's beautiful hands was missing a finger. Which one? Had it come from her right hand or left hand? Was she in pain? What was happening to her on that plane? My body heaved with gut-wrenching sobs.

"Stop that!" Finkelstein ordered, tightening his grip.

"Clay, my daughter is on that plane!" I yelled. "Please! Give him what he wants!"

"He's lying," Clay said.

"She's there," Finkelstein insisted.

Clay turned his attention back to Finkelstein. "Prove it. If you have her, let's see her."

"Not happening until I get Nelson," Finkelstein said.

"We could probably arrange to get Nelson here," Clay scratched his head, as though considering. "But you have a bit of a problem, Gavin. Your compadre, there," Clay's chin jutted toward the plane, "He seems to have you locked out."

I looked into the crowd. My angel still prayed. A flood of love and gratitude washed over me. I was too shocked to pray for myself, but she had prayed nonstop. Had the situation been reversed, would I have prayed as passionately for her? I'm pretty sure I wouldn't. A lot of things are going to change if I survive.

The fly buzzing around my head had become more than an annoyance. It landed on my nose and crawled downward. It hesitated beneath my nostril. I was afraid to lift an arm to shoo it away, but what if it crawled into my nostril and got stuck? I held my breath. If I breathed, I'd suck it up my nose. It finally flew away. My attention returned to the conversation. What had Clay agreed to? 'We could probably do—what?'

"You're lying," Finkelstein growled. His breath smelled like roadkill. Which may be the reason the fly was now buzzing around him. And it brought friends. Finkelstein began jerking his head to dislodge the fly. But every time he did, the gun slammed into my ear.

"Finkelstein, you're in a mess here. But there's still a chance to get out of this alive." Clay said, ignoring my gasp.

"Clay," I begged, "do something. Please!" My voice cracked. I tried again. "My daughter..." I choked. Tears streamed down my face.

"I'm not the one claiming to possess a girl I don't have," Clay said. "I tell you what. Release Mrs. Frazier and we'll back off. See if your buddy will let you back inside the plane." Clay sounded as though he was holding all aces.

"I'm not stupid," the gunman said.

"You can't prove that by the mess you're in. You'd be smart to let Mrs. Frazier go."

Someone in the crowd began singing *I'll Be Seeing You*. Ron. Ron is here!

I closed my eyes, shutting out the world around me, and concentrating on his voice. The words a fourteen-year-old me had listened to in my bed every night. I'd felt so alone then. But, I hadn't been. And I'm not alone now.

Someone began singing with Ron. I was shocked to realize that it was me. If my life ends here, it will be with Ron and me harmonizing, which I would have thought beautifully fitting. When I was fourteen.

I felt Grant's presence beside me. I stopped singing. I knew it was impossible, but the feeling was so strong. Familiar. "Grant?"

"Nobody sings that song like you do, Babe."

"Grant?"

"Yeah. I'm here. You've got yourself in quite a pickle here, haven't you?"

"This is... Wait! Are you here to usher me into heaven?"

"What? No. You're not going to die. Well, you are. Just not today."

"Right now, I'm too tired to care."

"That guy you were singing with really loves you.."

"How would you know?"

"He still has a broken heart. He deserves another chance."

"You came here now to tell me that? Now?"

"You aren't doing much. Figured now was a good time. Listen, April, I was just a chapter in your life. I don't want you stumbling through the rest of it alone. Give this guy a chance. He'll put up with your crap and take good care of you."

"I can take care of myself!"

"You do know you have a gun in your ear. Right?"

"About that stunt you pulled at your funeral..."

Grant laughed. "Damn that was fun!"

"How did you do that? I didn't know that video existed."

"Listen, Babe. This is important. Skylar is going to ask you to join his campaign. Don't do it. Bino is going to need you."

"Okay. I love you," I said.

"What? You love me? Lady, who are you talking to?" Finklestein demanded. "Shut up! I can't think."

"You shut up!" I shouted, desperate to hear Grant's voice.

"Einstein here probably doesn't think much better on a good day," Grant muttered.

"Finklestein." I said.

"WHAT?" Finklestein demanded.

I sensed Grant was gone.

"Grant? Grant! Don't leave me. Please." I screamed.

Silence.

"Bino isn't on that plane," Grant finally said from a distance.

I looked around frantically. His voice had moved to the other side of Finklestein.

"Grant?"

"Stop that!" Finklestein demanded.

"I will always love you, April." Grant's voice was faint. "Always... always..."

"Grant, wait! Grant, I have so many questions." I was sobbing uncontrollably which shook my whole body and left me gasping for air.

"Be still!" Finklestein growled. "You are the worst hostage."

"Well, they don't teach courses on how to be a good hostage in Home Ec. Although they probably should."

"Mom!"

I looked into the crowd. "Ridge?"

Ridge stood slightly behind Clay. He held up his cell for me to see. "Rye's on the phone. She's home. She has all her fingers and toes."

"She's home?"

My knees went weak with relief, or maybe it was the shock of hearing Grant's voice.

The gun banged against my temple. The sudden turn of events had unnerved Finklestein. He'd lost control and he knew it.

"Lady, shut up!"

"No, you shut up!" I said. I no longer cared if he killed me. Riley Grace was safe and I was exhausted.

"Give it up, Gavin," Clay ordered. "You're out of options. Nelson is in DC. Even if I could grant your demands, it would take a good twelve hours to get him back here. You gonna stand out in this heat all day? That gun must be getting heavy. I tell you what, let her go and we'll talk about a deal."

A sniper was in place on the airport roof. Finkelstein looked up and saw him. Then he realized an army of uniforms had gathered behind Clay and Ridge.

Sweat from stressed people smells different. Gavin Finkelstein was stressed. Because of our proximity, a gun to my head and all, I realized how damp he'd become. The more he sweat, the worse he smelled.

"I'm through talking," the gunman snarled. He dropped the hand holding the gun to my head. He braced it on my shoulder and aimed the gun at Clay. "You're gonna die, pig." The arm across my throat loosened as he moved.

Everything happened at once.

"Avalanche!" Ridge shouted.

I dropped to the ground, landing on my butt with a teeth-jarring jolt. As I went down, I heard two gunshots, so close together they sounded like one.

Finklestein screamed. The gun flew out of his hand. I watched it slide across the tarmac. A deputy moved in and grabbed it.

Clay rushed Finkelstein. "You shot the gun without hitting his hand," he said to Ridge as he clicked handcuffs into place. "The way Finklestein is howling, I thought you shot off his arm."

The sheriff and three deputies rushed in and took the cussing, screaming prisoner away.

And then Ridge was on his knees beside me. "Mom, are you okay?" He wrapped me in his arms and pulled me close.

"Yeah, I think."

"I thought I had lost you, too," he gasped. "You fell hard. Can you stand?" He stood up, gently pulling me to my feet. "Thank God you remembered," he said, "if you hadn't, Clay would be dead."

Relief and anger gushed from my eyes and soaked Ridge's shirt.

"Avalanche?" Clay said. "Avalanche? What was that?" Beneath his freckles, his face had drained of color.

"Yeah," the sheriff echoed, "what was that?"

"Dad came up with that idea years ago—in case we were ever in a hostage situation. He said, 'With a gun to your head, just fall.' *Avalanche* was our secret code word for emergency. If someone came to pick us up from school, they had to know the word before we would go with them. I wasn't sure Mom would remember or put it together. Thank God, she did."

"That was risky," the sheriff said. "I should arrest you."

Ridge ignored the sheriff. "That guy was intent on separating your head from your shoulders," he said to Clay. "When the gunman turned that gun on you, his expression changed. I could see it in the set of his jaw and couldn't wait any longer."

"You cut that one pretty close." Ron nodded to the five-gallon paint can on the runway. White paint leaked through a bullet hole onto the concrete.

Clay went even more pale. "That bullet had my name on it."

"Good work, boys. You two are a team to be reckoned with," Ron said. "Lane underestimated you."

"I hoped Clay could talk him down," Ridge said. "I hated to put Mom through more stress than necessary, but if we could end this peacefully, we needed to try. When Finkelstein went after Clay, he took away my choice."

"Good shooting, Son." Ron turned his attention to me. "You okay?"

I couldn't speak. It was Ron who had taught Ridge to shoot. Ron had just called Ridge, Son. Ridge's words from last night raced through my head. "Mr. Lang treated me like he treated RJ...like a Son." While I'd thought of Ron as the most vile creature to ever walk the earth, he had been helping raise my son.

"I thought you were on a plane," Ridge said to Ron.

"The flight your mom and I were supposed to take was overbooked. I was bumped to the later flight. When April didn't board and I noticed something was going on outside, I decided I better see what it was."

Ridge's phone rang. He answered it and handed it to me. "Someone wants to talk to you." My hands were shaking too much to hold it so Ridge held it to my ear.

"Mom? Are you okay?" Riley Grace demanded.

"Yes, Sweetheart, are you?'

"Yeah. Now that you're okay. Ohmygosh, I've been so worried!"

"It's so good to hear your voice, I thought they had you, too."

An EMSA crew approached with a gurney.

"Ma'am, we need to get you checked out," the crew leader said.

"I have to go, Sweetie, I'm okay. I'll call you as soon as I can. I love you."

"Love you, too, Mom."

I searched the crowd for my inked angel. I wanted her to know how much her presence and prayers had calmed me. But she was gone.

Blood seeped across the left knee of my jeans. Hopefully, my tailbone wasn't fractured. I assured the EMSA guy I could walk. Not smart. My legs felt like rubber.

We made our way to the ambulance. The three of us. Ron's arm supported me on one side. My son, the hero, on the other. Ridge couldn't save his father. But he had just saved his mother—and Clay.

I looked up into the beautiful blue sky I'd noticed when I first arrived. My mind still couldn't formulate a prayer. So, I just whispered, "Thank You." God had sent Grant to me. So I added, "For everything."

Chapter Forty-Six

April

Believing Finkelstein had Riley Grace's finger in his pocket had been the worst part of my ordeal. Had I known she was safe, this morning would have gone much differently. While I waited in ER, I called her. Ali had kept her home today. She'd escaped her ordeal with minor injuries, but she was in no mental shape to be in school.

Her voice soothed my jangled nerves and convinced me she was okay. I'd had no idea what she had been through but she was eager to fill me in. And, of course, she had a million questions about what happened to me.

"So, Ridge pretty much saved your life?" she asked.

"Yes, thank goodness he was there," I said. "If he hadn't seen that guy jab a gun in my back and called for help, Finklestein might have got me on that plane."

She groaned dramatically. "Now he really is your favorite. How am I going to top that?"

I laughed. My first unforced laugh since Grant died. "You've already topped it. You survived. You saved the life of my only daughter."

"I can't even claim that. That would be Bronc."

"I am so grateful..." Nothing could get past my suddenly clogged throat.

"Come home, Mama," she pleaded.

"Just as soon as I can, I promise. I won't be able to rest until I see you. And count your fingers and toes."

Riley Grace laughed.

We're both going to need counseling to get through this. One of the assailants died in front of her. No seventeen-year-old should experience what she's been through.

The ER doctor, when he finally made an appearance, was most concerned about the bump on my head. Compliments of Finkelstein's gun. I was grateful it wasn't a hole in my head compliments of Finkelstein's gun. In fact, I had several bumps. But the doctor seemed to be concerned only about that one. I also had a nasty bruise on my arm where Finklestein had grabbed my wrist and a large bruise on my ribs. I have no idea how that one happened. The doctor wanted to admit me but I was adamant about that not fitting into my plans. I can be very convincing.

Since I didn't die this morning, I have a new obsession about living. I'm going to make every moment count.

After a shot for shock, a careful examination, a lecture, and a CT scan, the doctor treated my scraped knee and released me with a prescription for pain and orders to stay in Durango tonight. He wanted to see me before I got a flight out in the morning. Today's last flight left without us, anyway. Ron and I will be on the same flight home after all.

Ron and Ridge had followed the ambulance to the hospital in the Forester. Ridge had gone down the hall to check on Sable. Ron went to get my prescriptions filled, and to rebook rooms for another night at the hotel.

Ridge and I had been “invited” to come by the sheriff’s office after my release from ER. Ron and I rode with him since Lane had assumed we were on our way back to Oklahoma City and kept the Tahoe.

The Sheriff’s office was considerably more spacious than the Highway Patrol office we had all crammed into—was it only yesterday morning? So much had happened since then, it seemed like at least a week had passed. A large La Plata County map covered the wall behind the sheriff’s desk. Clay was already there when we arrived. We had each gone through our version of what happened this morning several times in case something important had been overlooked.

Probably in his mid-thirties, the sheriff stood well over six feet tall. If the nameplate on his desk was an indication, his name was Aaron Knightly. He was a nice-looking man with surprisingly long prematurely silver hair tied back into a low ponytail. The color looked good with his deep tan and piercing blue eyes, probably more piercing than usual today. Sheriff Knightly had not been happy about Clay and Ridge “overstepping” their boundaries. The airport was in the Sheriff’s jurisdiction. Clay is Highway Patrol. But because Clay had been on the phone with Ridge at the time of my abduction, he was first on the scene. Although Knightly could not argue with success, his nose was out of joint.

While we talked, deputies marched a man down the hall. As he passed our door, he looked in. His eyes locked on me. His recognition sent a cold chill down my spine. He was deeply tanned with lighter circles around his eyes which looked like a skier’s tan to me, but he’d be hard pressed to find snow this time of the year. Then it dawned on me. The pilot had finally been coaxed from his plane.

"The pilot," the sheriff affirmed, in answer to my unasked question.

"Were he and Finkelstein the only two people on the plane?" I asked, embarrassed by my quavering voice. At least my teeth had stopped chattering.

Knightly shook his head. "Another guy got off the plane and gave himself up after Finkelstein was in custody. The pilot held out a few hours longer."

The sheriff pulled a vape from an office desk drawer, took a couple of hits, and replaced it. He leaned back in his chair and grinned. "I'm guessing conditions were less than favorable in this heat—like sardines cooking in their tin can."

"Who did the finger belong to?" I asked. "Was it even real?"

"It was real, all right," Sheriff Knightly said. "But I have no idea where he got it. The M.E. has it now. He thinks it was taken from a dead body. There would have been blood otherwise. Finkelstein had it on him when they flew in. I'll know more when we find out where the flight originated. I haven't questioned the three of them yet. I doubt I'll get much out of them."

I wrapped my arms around myself and shivered. The finger wasn't from my child. But it had once been attached to somebody's child.

I was still thinking about that when Lane walked through the door.

"Hey, Fly, Howzit going?" Lane asked, grinning at the sheriff.

"Renegade? What the hell are you doing here?" The sheriff stood up and leaned across his desk to shake Lane's hand.

"Heard you had some excitement this morning," Lane said as he shook the sheriff's hand. "Sorry about that. I left my wife's cousin unsupervised. You can't take her anywhere."

He winked as he walked past Ridge and Ron to give me a hug. "Are you okay?" he asked. His direct gaze demanded a truthful answer.

"I'm pretty shook up and my tailbone hurts. But, thanks to Ridge and Clay, I'm alive."

"Good shooting, Ridge," Lane said. He gave Ridge's shoulder a squeeze as he walked back by him to look for an empty chair. He found one and edged it over to join the group.

"I could have arrested him for discharging a firearm in an airport."

"It wasn't *in* an airport," Clay pointed out.

"Technicality," Sheriff Knightly said, not amused. "And I'm not through with you, Trooper Morley. The airport is my jurisdiction. You had no business there."

"Well, now Fly," Lane dusted something from his knee as he crossed his legs, "Trooper Morely is the only officer in this county to have negotiation training at Quantico. He did a fine job. Have you talked to Finklestein yet?"

How would Lane know that, I wondered. He wasn't here.

The sheriff nodded a reluctant concession. "Not at length. I haven't had a chance to do an interrogation. I'm guessing when he realized things were going south, he planned to shoot Officer Morely knowing the SWAT team would take him out. He would rather die by cop here than face the consequences of a failed mission."

"Can't say that I blame him," Lane said.

"So, Renegade, you're responsible for this mess?"

"Not entirely," Lane said. "We try to keep April contained, but she keeps getting out."

"How many sheriffs do you know?" I asked.

Lane leaned back in his chair. "I don't think I've ever figured it up."

"The Cheyenne Falls Sheriff was in your wedding," I said, helping him out. "The Santa Fe Sheriff came with Stormy and Lyle."

"What? Wait! You got finally married?" Knightly asked with a grin that made me wish Lane had been here earlier when Knightly had not been so jovial.

"Smartest thing I ever did," Lane said.

"Chief was at your wedding, and I wasn't invited?" Sheriff Knightly demanded.

"Didn't know where you were, Fly, but I do know your aversion to weddings," Lane said. They both laughed at some private joke.

"We all played football together," Lane explained. "In Santa Fe."

"I'm sure there's a reason you call him Fly," I said. Lane grinned. "If Aaron ever snagged a pass, he couldn't be caught."

"When I could pick up a decent block," the sheriff said, looking pointedly at Lane.

There was something off about Sherrif Aaron Knightly. Something bothered me. I couldn't quite pin it down...

"I hate to break up your trip down memory lane here," Ridge interrupted, "but I need to know my mother and sister aren't still in danger."

"That hadn't occurred to me," I said. "Are we?"

"I doubt it," Lane leaned back in his chair. "They'd have to be really stupid to mess with Riley Grace again." He chuckled.

"I know that's right," Ridge said, pride evident in his voice. "That girl has some guns! Her two-handed backhand is a weapon."

"What do you think, Fly?" Lane asked.

"I agree. The cartel won't give up trying to get to Nelson, but my guess is they'll move on. They've learned not to mess with the Fraziers." He leaned back in his chair and clasped his hands behind his head. His edge had disappeared with Lane's arrival.

"Score: Fraziers 5, Cartel 0," Lane grinned. "From what I hear, the three at the airport are in better shape than the two that went after Riley Grace. One died when he ran into traffic, the other went down hard when her boyfriend tackled him. He's in the hospital with a cracked skull."

"Would you like to see the video?" the sheriff asked me.

"Wait! My little sister has a boyfriend?" Ridge demanded. His gaze rested on me. "You're letting her date? What are you thinking?"

"She's seventeen," I reminded him. "When you were seventeen, you'd dated everyone in the senior class."

"I can pull the video up on the news feed in the other room. Would you like to see it?"

"Where did you get a video of the attack?" Lane asked

"Channel nine news. Some lady at the next pump videoed the whole thing," the Sheriff said, standing up and heading for the door. "It made national news."

I thought about it, not sure I wanted to see it. But in the end, we all trooped into the next room and crowded around the small screen. As I watched the attack on my daughter, I realized I'd been holding my breath. I made myself exhale and breathe. Hearing about it was one thing. Seeing it was something else. When I saw the part where Riley Grace threw the keys, I cracked up.

"Ridge, did you see what she said?"

"Yeah, I read her lips too," he said, without taking his eyes from the screen. "She said 'take that, Doofus'."

"It's what she says to Ridge if she beats him at anything," I explained to the others. "That girl!" I added under by breath,

"She makes me crazy, but I love her so much." I nearly lost her before I realized how much.

"She says that when I miss her killer serve," Ridge added. We looked at each other and smiled, sharing the moment. Ridge was as proud as I was.

The video continued with a police officer telling Bronc that Riley Grace was "one tough little cookie".

"I had to grow up with her." Ridge announced. "I should've been drawing hazardous duty pay. Retroactive."

"Poor Baby," Clay jeered. "Dang! Your sister is good looking."

"Back off Son," Ridge said, with a grin. "You should see her when she's not fighting for her life. She cleans up pretty good. But I'm thinking you don't want to tangle with that boyfriend of hers."

Our attention shifted back to the video. Bronc was saying, "When I saw that guy trying to shove her into that car..." His voice trailed off and he shook his head, "Over my dead body," he said through clenched teeth.

After that there were pictures of feet, gas pumps, and the roof which changed at dizzying speed. Someone had forgotten the video was still on.

"I like that kid," Lane said.

"Who is he?" Ridge asked. "Why do I not know him?"

"Bronc. Thank God for him!" I gasped. Books should warn expectant Mothers that they'll never sleep through the night again. Once that child is in the world, a Mother can't stop worrying about it until she draws her last breath.

"How can my little sister have a boyfriend I don't know about?"

"Ridge, you have a fiancé your mother hadn't met," I pointed out. "And when were you around for anyone to tell you anything?" I'm not the only guilty party here.

"She's too young!" Ridge huffed. "What do we know about this guy?"

"He saved your sister's life." I added, "and he plays a mean piano."

"He has a mighty fine flying tackle," the sheriff pointed out. "In cowboy boots. We could have used that kid back in the day."

Lane nodded. "He got a full ride to OSU. Texas was after him, too. I met him after Grant's funeral. Good kid."

"His father was a war hero. He died in Afghanistan saving the lives of his squad, including Skylar Watkins' brother," I said. "The Vice President was impressed with him."

"Yeah, fine," Ridge waved the information away as though it were a pesky mosquito. "I'll have to check him out."

Ridge's text tone chirped. He pulled his phone from his pocket and scanned the message. He looked up at me, his eyes wide.

"It's Luna," he said, heading for the door. "Gotta go! Sable. She's waking up!" he threw back over his shoulder and was gone.

"Wait," the sheriff yelled, "We aren't through here."

"Well, Fly, looks to me like you are," Lane said.

Chapter Forty-Seven

Sable

A force drew me upward. I craved the warmth, peace. Light. But it was a trap. Evil lurked. A tsunami waited to crash over me, break and destroy me. With the light came fear. Terrifying. I slid back down into the deep, huddling in the safety. The dark welcomed me back. Only, the dark no longer felt safe either.

Am I dead? I hadn't thought being dead would hurt this much. I tried to remember—something. Anything. I listened for clues in the noises around me. Beeps. Distant voices. Closer, familiar voices. My mother—and Ridge.

Ridge? Have to get to Ridge. Fight to get to Ridge.

"She opened her eyes," my mother said. "Briefly."

"Did she recognize you?" Ridge asked.

"I don't know. She became agitated, hysterical. The nurses rushed in and gave her a shot. It knocked her out. I think she was remembering."

"Did she say anything?" Ridge asked.

"She called your name. Then began screaming. The doctor thinks she wants to wake up, but she's too traumatized. It's safer where she is."

Where? Safer where? Where am I? What was my mother talking about?

Grant! Where is Grant? Then I remembered.

* * *

The car sliced through the night. No streetlights this far from town. As US 550 began its climb north through the mountains, the welcoming lights from windows blinking through trees had become a thing of the past. Usually, the complete darkness of this road didn't bother me.

The moon had pulled itself above the Ponderosa pines thirty minutes ago. Through the car window, I'd charted its progress. Now, from its lofty height, it haloed lesser trees. A full moon turns ordinary landscapes into magic.

My attention turned to the driver. I tried to remember a time he was less than confident. I came up empty. I studied his handsome profile. The profile he'd passed to his son. There was no tension in the set of his jaw. I was tense enough for both of us. I huddled farther into my seat.

He saw the movement and smiled. "Try to unwind," he said, giving my arm a fatherly pat. "Do some breathing exercises."

"Have you ever been scared?" I asked.

Smooth jazz oozed from the radio. The gold chain he wore on his right wrist, a gift from his wife, gleamed in the light from the dash as he turned down the volume.

"Yeah, sure. When I was a kid."

"What about now?"

"If one of my children is in danger." His nod in my direction included me. I haven't had a father for years. He'll never know how much that meant.

"Probably other times," he continued. "They don't come to mind right now."

“What about when you pulled those people from the burning car?”

He laughed. “You heard about that?”

“The whole world heard about it.”

“It wasn’t that big a deal. And it wasn’t the whole world.”

“I’m guessing it was a big deal to the people whose lives you saved.”

“When the car started burning, it was a matter of time before it exploded. I didn’t have time to be scared,” he said. “I was busy. ”

“I think I’ve misjudged you,” I said.

“Oh?” He shot me a surprised glance.

“I’ve thought you pushed Ridge into something he might not have done otherwise.”

“Tennis?”

“Other things, too. You are very persuasive.”

He barked a laugh. “That’s not what they call it in DC.”

“Now that I know you, I realize how much you care. Tonight, you’re rescuing me. I thought you wanted Ridge to stay in Florida because the tournament was important to his career. But that wasn’t the only reason. You came to protect him.”

“I came to protect you,” he winked. “Maybe I thought Ridge couldn’t handle it.”

I knew he was kidding, still I felt the need to defend Ridge. “You’ haven’t been there when Ridge took Nelson on. He was amazing. Nelson isn’t used to being bested.” Ridge knew what Nelson was capable of. Grant seemed to be underestimating him. Which concerned me. Big mistake.

He pulled a pack of gum from his pocket and offered me a stick. I took one and handed it back. It was peppermint. I didn’t like peppermint but thought the act of chewing might calm my nerves.

"Thanks." As I unwrapped the gum, I reflected on what he'd said.

"Obviously, you love tennis. What do you like about it?"

"Few things are as satisfying as the sound of a ball hitting the sweet spot on your racquet. Or the way a good racquet fits in your hand. Team sports don't interest me. My brothers were way into football. Dad never missed a game. Football is good for teaching high school kids to strive for a common goal. Showing up and giving it their all in practice prepares them for the future. They learn good work ethics. But your team can let you down."

"How?" I shifted in my seat to face him.

"You have a good offense, but no defense?" he was saying. "You won't win many games. Or let's say you've got the world's best quarterback. If nobody can catch a pass or his line doesn't protect him, he can do nothing. There are great athletes who were never signed by a college or made it to the pros because the rest of their team didn't know a football from a pumpkin. No matter their record, any team can be beat if their key players are sick or their head isn't in the game. Success is often luck and circumstances."

He checked the rearview mirror again, although there was no traffic.

"If I play tennis badly, I have nobody to blame but myself."

"Is that where your confidence began? On the tennis court?"

"Heck, no," he joked. "I'm good at golf, too."

I laughed. He's always been amiable, but because of who he is, I'm intimidated by him. I realized I was enjoying our conversation and began to relax.

"No, seriously, teams are good. My team in DC is great. I handpicked each one of them. They're excellent at what they do. I'm fortunate to have them. But my real confidence comes from God," he said. "Whatever happens, I know He's in control."

Grant paused and ran a hand across his chin. "When I stay focused on God, the craziness around me doesn't seem insurmountable."

He began pushing buttons on the radio searching for another station. The selection isn't that great in the mountains, but he found a song he liked, leaned back, and smiled. Conversation stopped while he listened. He sang along haphazardly, not remembering all the words. There was something about smoke getting in your eyes. He was lost in the moment. I had noticed in the past that he totally engaged in everything he did. When he was with Ridge, he turned off his phone and gave his son his undivided attention.

"My mom loved that song," he said. "I can see her in the kitchen rolling out pie dough and humming."

The song ended and another began. "How appropriate, "April Love". Ever heard it?" Without waiting for my answer, he began singing along. He knew all the words.

"It's lovely," I said.

"It was written before April and I were born, but it's better than any song out today."

"Tell me about you wife," I said.

He glanced at me, light from the dash playing across his face. I saw his surprise.

"You don't know April?"

"I want to know how you see her." I didn't admit not knowing her, as though not meeting my fiancé's mother proved me lacking. I gestured toward the radio. "Maybe it's the love songs."

"Whoever named her got it right," Grant began. "She's a breath of fresh spring air. Or a sudden storm." He chuckled. "I'll never forget the first time I saw her. She was the most incredible creature I'd ever seen. She still is."

He scratched his nose. "I was at a friend's wedding. They'd hired a trio to play during dinner. She walked in and I forgot to breathe. I was in love with her before she even sang. But that voice! Her first song was about a moon. Haunting. I'll never forget it. She has a thing about moons."

He paused to listen to the next song on the radio, then resumed his story. "My date was sick and spent most of the evening in the restroom. She wanted me to take her home but I didn't want to leave. I couldn't take my eyes off April. When I got back, she was gone. I was told the band was from Stillwater, but nobody remembered the band name or who she was."

He smiled. "Then fate stepped in. Eight months later she showed up at a fundraiser in Norman near the OU campus. That time I didn't let her get away." He absently rubbed his chin and glanced out the window. "She's the only woman I have ever loved. I had a hard time convincing her. Some guy had broken her heart. She never quite believed that I wouldn't break it, too."

"But what's she like?"

"Fiercely independent, funny, smart, and wise," he said without taking time to consider.

"Smart and wise aren't the same, you know. She'll take on anything. She's fearless. There is nobody on earth like her." He thought for a minute. "Except maybe our daughter. She's fearless, too."

"The woman is a saint," I said, only half kidding.

"She loves with her whole heart. She's a great mother, but she's aways put me first. I don't deserve her." He shook his head. "We hardly ever get time alone anymore. I've booked a two-week European river cruise for the two of us. It's a surprise. I can't wait to get her away."

"A relationship like yours is so rare," I said.

He nodded, "I'll be loving her when I take my last breath. April will make a great first lady," he added almost as an afterthought and laughed. "She'd probably be a better president than I would."

A car that had been following us for several miles came up behind us fast but didn't pass. Its lights, on high beam, were blinding.

"Is that Nelson?" Grant asked.

He squinted as he adjusted the mirrors. No cause for alarm. Just another day at the office. He increased speed. The speed scared me, but not as much as Nelson being behind us.

"I think so." I couldn't see the car's color in the dark. But as it neared, I shuddered. It was white. "Yes!" I heard hysteria in my voice as I reached for my phone.

I hit 911 and was relieved when someone immediately answered. "Thank God! I wasn't sure I'd get a signal!"

I reported what was happening, having trouble explaining our exact location. Even if there were mile markers out here, we were flying too fast to matter.

Ridge was trying to call. I disconnected from 911 to answer him and quickly filled him in on what was happening.

"I'm calling 911 too," he said, "to give them a bit more background. I'll call you back."

"No, Ridge, don't hang up!" Desperate for that connection, I felt like a drowning victim desperately clutching at a lifeboat drifting from his grasp. "Ridge, no! Don't go!" He'd already disconnected.

A bullet plowed into my car's trunk. Then another.

I screamed. "Ohmygosh, Ohmygosh, he's shooting!"

Grant sped up, but Nelson stayed right behind us. I dialed 911 again. They picked up as soon as it rang. The guy who answered knew it was me. “Help is on the way,” he assured me. “Stay on the line with me.”

“He’s shooting,” I sobbed.

A bullet came through the back window. I screamed. The bullet passed between us and exited through the windshield. I watched in horror as thousands of tiny cracks formed around the hole.

“You know the shooter?” the 911 dispatcher asked.

“Yes,” I sobbed. “Brett Nelson. He’s trying to kill me!”

“Sable,” Grant instructed, “unbuckle your seatbelt. Get the gun under my seat.”

I left my phone on the console still connected to 911. I crawled closer to Grant. But just as I reached under the seat, Nelson bumped us with amazing force. The impact threw me into the dash. Hard. I fell to the floor. We shot forward but Grant didn’t lose control. I crawled back up on the seat and started to fasten my seatbelt.

“No,” Grant said. “Get back down on the floor. He’s going to shoot again.”

Terrified, I slid off the seat to the floor, clutching my phone. Ridge was calling again. I disconnected 911.

“Ridge, he’s shooting!” I screamed.

“I’m almost there,” he said. “I’m closing in. I see his taillights.”

Grant heard. “No! Ridge, go back. There’s nothing you can do!”

I reached under the seat for the gun. My hand closed over the cool hard metal. The car swerved and it slid out of my grasp. I stretched a little farther and had it. It was bigger and heavier than I expected. I had trouble getting it out from under the seat. “Got it!” I looked up. Nelson was beside us. His passenger-side window had been lowered. He raised the gun.

"Grant, look out," I screamed.

He didn't have time. I saw three flashes of light. A bullet shattered the driver-side window into tiny fragments, peppering my arms and legs. Another bullet went through the passenger window where I had been sitting. The third bullet slammed into Grant.

Grant didn't make a sound. His whole body jerked. Blood, flesh, and bone splattered over the dash, across my shirt, and ran down my face. I wiped it from my eyes.

Nelson's white Pathfinder zoomed past us and was gone.

"Ridge, your father has been shot!"

"Is Dad okay?" Ridge asked.

What was left of Grant's head bobbed on his chest.

"I don't think so." I heard myself screaming. I couldn't stop.

I was on a winding mountain road in a car driven by a dead man. Grant's foot fell off the gas. The car slowed, but we were flying toward a curve we would never make. Still clutching my phone, I opened the door. And jumped.

Chapter Forty-Eight

Riley Grace

I feel like I'm living in a sitcom gone horribly wrong. My father died—and not just normal died. His death caused a national scandal. Mom says it will be cleared up now, but for two weeks I've lived with the media in tents on my lawn. My brother is too busy dodging a killer to come home. Sable is in a coma, but at least she isn't dead like everyone thought. Some guy tried to lop off my finger and then died right in front of me. My mom was held hostage at an airport. Which would have me hysterical if all that other stuff hadn't happened. I'm too tired to be delirious. Seriously, who writes this stuff? What would the media do for news without my family?

Alise says she's having a T-shirt printed that says *Close personal friend of the Fraziers*. She thinks she could sell them for a lot of money. Nothing ever happens to her.

I found out yesterday the guy who killed Dad has been stalking Ridge. The killer was at my father's funeral looking for Ridge. No wonder Ridge looks like an escapee from *The Walking Dead*.

When Ridge called to tell me Mom was being held at gunpoint, he didn't know about my situation. Yet. We stayed on the phone discussing what was going on with Mom and how it was tied to the attack on me. He should appreciate my taking his mind off the fact some deranged weirdo held a gun to Mom's head. He'll say I did it by freaking out. But whatever.

When Ridge said, "Gotta go," he left me holding the phone, screeching his name. I thought Mom was dead. It was thirty minutes before he called me back to tell me it was over and she was okay. The worst two hours of my life.

During that time, I remembered Mom stuff. The songs she used to sing when I was sick or sad or scared. The time she stayed up all night making a costume I needed for a fifth-grade contest. I got throwing-up sick during our vacation in Cabo San Lucas. Mom stayed with me on the bathroom floor holding my hair back while I puked. She could have been on the cruise around the famous El Arco rock formation at Land's End with Dad and Ridge which was the reason we were even there. Who knew it was her last chance to see it up close? I miss that Mom. I didn't realize how much until I thought she was dead.

When I'm this wired, I go out back and hit tennis balls. But even that hasn't helped. Ali keeps trying to get me to talk. I know she's worried, but I don't want to *think* about what happened, much less talk about it. Not that it matters. I can't get it out of my mind.

When Machete Guy died, I was too relieved he'd dropped the machete and stopped trying to cut off my finger to care. But now I keep hearing the thud when the pickup hit him and I'm pretty sure I'll never get that sound out of my mind. Ever. Or the panic of the other driver that hit him. The pickup driver just sat staring through his windshield, but the other lady got out, saw him under her car, started screaming and didn't stop. She couldn't have missed him. After the pickup hit him, he flew up in the air and landed in front of her car.

He had a name. Bobby Ramos. I read that in the paper. Knowing his name made him a real person. Not just someone who carried a machete and smelled like a bull moose in mating season.

I left my room and went upstairs, my hand gliding over the familiar smoothness of the banister. Passing Ridge's room made me sad. I need him to be home. Safe. In that room. The sign on his door said BE NICE OR LEAVE. THANK YOU. He made it when he was a sophomore in high school. I don't think it especially meant me, since he never let me in his room. Although the one that used to be on his door did mean me. It said: KEEP OUT! THIS MEANS YOU!!! I was the "YOU!!!" It didn't keep me out.

Mom describes our house as "stately". It was built before I was even born—before anyone was born. It's in Nichols Hills. All the houses in Nichols Hills are ancient. Mom calls our yard "the grounds". It's expansive. So is the house. The columns across the front are three stories tall. Like the White House. That's probably why Dad bought it. There's a massive staircase that begins in the entry way, which Mom calls it "the foyer." It winds around two walls. My room is off the landing. It used to be a ballroom or something grand. I know that because it has a parquet floor and a crystal chandelier. When I had sleepovers with lots of friends, we danced and pretended we were at an exclusive club we were too young to get in. But they let us in anyway because we were beautiful movie stars. We pretended the chandelier was a strobe light. That was a hoot when we were younger. We're too old for that now—most of the time. Alise still holds a hairbrush and sings into it like a microphone. Someday she'll be singing like that for real. If Adele ever heard Alise sing "Rolling in the Deep" she'd probably retire or something.

The cool thing about our rooms being in the front of the house is Ridge and I could sneak out without waking up Mom and Dad. Their bedroom is in the back, which is like being in another country. Ridge used to sneak out all the time. He never got caught. He owes me big time. He also used to sneak his girlfriend in when he was dating that cute girl with the squeaky voice. Dad called her Miss May because Ridge had a different girlfriend every month. I think she's on a TV series now.

My father was murdered. Something you think will never happen to anyone you know. Alise watches *Dateline* and expects weird stuff to happen. She thinks about death a lot and calls it "the other side". That's rather macabre, if you ask me, like reading Poe with ravens quothing and stuff. But maybe she's right. I'm thinking about it more now. More to the point I'm thinking about how life can end so suddenly. Dad died because some guy I never heard of who lived someplace I barely heard of started smuggling stuff months ago—or maybe years. That had nothing to do with us. And then *boom*. Because of him, my father was gone.

Alise says when you listen through a stethoscope, a beating heart sounds like "ta dump, ta dump, ta dump". She says at any moment there could be a ta with no dump. And I should be grateful for every dump that I have. And, of course, I am. While I'm beginning to see her point, there has to be a better choice of words.

Bronc and I are like two survivors of the same armed robbery. Nobody can relate to what we've been through. Sharing the experience ties us together forever. He saved my life. If he hadn't stopped peeing when he did, I don't know what would have happened. My body might not ever have been found. So, my list of things to be grateful for has grown to include Bronc's small bladder. My boyfriend is a hero. We've been on every news cast. You can bet the next time he's concerned about a car following us, I won't blow it off.

I've never almost died before—that I know of. Alise says things happen every day that could kill us if we had been there just a few seconds sooner or a few minutes later. She says she wakes up every morning thinking this could be the last day of her life. That's sort of morbid. But maybe if everyone did that, we would treat each other better.

I caused a man's death. This wasn't just an accident. I didn't trip and drop a baby off the Grand Canyon or something. He couldn't see because I sprayed gasoline in his face. I'm a murderer.

Ridge was there when Daddy died. For the first time I wondered if he saw it happen. How horrible! He might feel guilty, too. Duh! Of course, he does! That's why he's been avoiding Mom. The more I thought about that, the more I wanted to talk to Ridge. He would get how I feel.

I pulled out my phone and texted him. He texted me back almost immediately.

Me: *Ridge, I killed a man.*

Ridge: *What?*

Me: *He ran into the street and was hit by a pickup because I sprayed gas in his face and he couldn't see. I'm a murderer. I need to talk to you.*

Ridge: *You are not a murderer.*

Me: *I need to talk to you.*

Ridge: *I'm coming home in a few days.*

Me: *I need to talk to you NOW!*

Ridge: *Come to Durango. You can ride back with me.*

Me: *You mean it? Cool! I'll ask Mom when she gets home.*

I cut him off cause Bronc was texting me about a movie he wants to see. Like a regular date. It feels like we have been together forever, I know him so well, but we have never had a date like ordinary people. Our only date was my father's funeral. Okay, that wasn't really a date. I hijacked his truck.

Since Dad died, there has been nothing normal about my life. Nothing! A person should be able to grieve for her father without having to think about his murder or someone trying to hack off her finger or worry about someone ambushing her mother. Or how long it's going to take her boyfriend to pee.

The movie he wants to see was filmed in the Tetons. He's kind of missing Wyoming. He says the scenery in the trailers is beautiful, a sort of a cross between *Yellowstone* and *Longmire*. If the horses are pretty and none of them die, I'm there. I thought Alise and Stanleigh might go with us, but Alise doesn't "do movies". She said not to sit in the back rows because the seats are covered in dried semen. Yuck! I don't know how she knows that. Now I wish I didn't. She has me rethinking the whole movie thing. Bronc says we'll sit up front.

When I got to the attic, I cleared the dust off a trunk, sat down, and dug around in an old chest until I found one of Mom's journals. I'm shocked by how much like me she was when she was my age. I've felt some of the same things she wrote about. Seeing them written out in her handwriting made me realize I don't know her at all.

Mr. Lang ghosted her in college. I had no idea they were a thing. He better have a darn good reason for breaking her heart. Now I understand why she acted the way she did the other night on the patio when she was guzzling wine like a dying camel at an oasis. But 26 years is kind of a long time to be steamed. Why didn't she go find him and say, "What in the heck is going on, Jerkface?" I would. If Bronc did that.

Mr. Lang wasn't even good-looking like my daddy. Or Bronc. He looked like Buddy Holly. After he got his teeth fixed.

If she had married Mr. Lang instead of Dad, I'd probably look like Popeye's Olive Oyl with teeth like Austin Powers.

If Daddy was here, I'd be talking to him about all this stuff. I miss the way he listened. The way he laughed, the way he could always make me laugh, the way he smelled. I miss the me I used to be when I was with him. The me that felt happy, and important. And safe.

I've figured out that grief is loving someone with your whole heart and not have a place to put all that love when they're gone.

I stared, mesmerized by dust particles dancing through a shaft of light.

Tears slid down my face and dripped on Mom's unopened journal in my lap. I was still sitting there when the sun went down.

Chapter Forty-Nine
April

After I left the sheriff's office, I went straight to my hotel room. As soon as the door locked behind me, I stripped and left my clothes in a pile on the floor. They smelled like three-day-old roadkill. Finkelstein's sweat. I never want to *see* those clothes again. Which is a shame because the bra and jeans are my favorites. They fit. The hotel probably has a policy against bonfires. I stepped over them and walked naked into the bathroom. It was symbolic.

After a shower I felt better. The shot the ER doctor gave me finally kicked in. I crawled into bed and slept.

I called Riley Grace as soon as I woke up. We talked for at least 45 minutes. Mostly, she talked, and I listened. But it was a real conversation about things that matter. Bronc. Death and life—how we don't give one enough consideration and aren't grateful for the other. And Bronc.

Young people don't understand mortality. Unfortunately, at seventeen, Riley Grace has learned the hard way that our grasp on life is tenuous at best.

I listened carefully, pondering each response before I spoke, so afraid she would remember that I'm her mom, not someone important, and yank away this precious gift she is offering me of herself. If my ordeal gestated this embryo of closeness, I'd gladly go through it all again.

She asked if she could fly out here and ride home with Ridge. Surprised that he'd offered, I considered it a sign that he intends to rejoin the family. I'll talk to him before I go home.

Ridge said Sable spoke a few words. She recognized Ridge and her mother. She aced a few questions the doctor asked. She knew the year and where she went to school. She asked for her dog, Izzy. The doctor had tried to put a lid on Ridge's over-the-moon excitement but admitted he was "optimistic". Ridge was on his way to pick up some things for Luna and get Izzy.

Ron didn't answer when I returned his call but texted me immediately saying he was on a conference call. This trip has probably cost him a lot in missed business. I felt guilty but grateful he'd made the sacrifice.

The only clothes I'd brought with me were what I'd worn on the flight here and subsequently to the wreck site, along with the clothes piled by the door. I bagged them, went shopping, and dumped them in the trash on my way out.

Fortunately, I found a darling little dress shop nestled between a saddle shop and a boot repair store and right down the street from the hotel. I bought a pair of capris with a matching top that looked comfy to wear home and a summery dress. When I tried them on, I realized I've been losing weight since Grant's death. The dress was a smidge too short for someone my age, but it was breezy and cute. I won't be home a week before it's hanging in Riley Grace's closet. But it's mine tonight. I felt pretty in it, something I desperately needed.

Back at the hotel, I fell asleep. A nightmare woke me up. A man held a gun to my head. Instead of Finkelstein, it was Rayford Ruefford. He kept shouting "This woman is a fraud! She isn't a Senator's wife. Her husband is dead!" It was very unsettling.

Ron's business calls finished, he'd noticed he was starving and called to see if I wanted to grab something to eat. I was surprised to discover I was hungry, too. I hadn't eaten today. He suggested we go back to the Ore House where we ate the first night we were here.

I applied makeup and took time to style my hair, trying to hide bruises and the couple of bumps on my head compliments of Finkelstein's gun. The big bump on my forehead had turned purple. Not much I could do about that one.

Ten minutes later Ron knocked on my door. When I opened it, his eyes widened.

His mouth dropped open.

"April, you are—simply stunning," he said.

"I have a knot on my forehead and a bruised jaw. My wrist is purple. My eye may be turning black. I can look better than this."

He seemed not only surprised but also embarrassed by what he'd said. "I, uh, haven't seen your hair down in years. You usually wear it up or pulled back."

"Not that you've seen me, much in the past," I said. "But you're right. I keep it out of the way when I'm working. It's a habit. It's down tonight to hide the bumps on my head. I had nothing to wear, so I went shopping."

"That dress was made for you," he said.

He watched me make sure my key was in my purse before I locked my room. It made me self-conscious. I gave him that look of disapproval that all men get.

He shifted gears. "I hope you aren't going to be bitchy tonight."

"I just need you to back off and give me some space." I snapped.

The elevator arrived and the doors opened. A father moved his small daughter back a few steps to make room for us. I swallowed what I was going to say.

The little girl looked up at me, eyes huge. "You have a bump on your head," she announced.

"Yes," I agreed. "I do, but I'm alive." Tonight I'm not taking that for granted.

The family got off at the next floor.

The elevator stopped, interrupting conversation as we stepped out into the crowded lobby. We navigated our way through the people checking in at the desk.

We walked through the hotel's massive front door into an evening still warm but cooling fast. We made our way down the steps and crossed the street. Ron suddenly stopped and turned to face me. "April. I am so sorry. After what you've been through, you have every right to be short tempered. I was an ass. Will you forgive me?"

I tilted my head as I thought about it.

"Please."

"It's impossible to erase something already said. It's like stopping a bullet once the trigger's been squeezed." That analogy flashed back to images of this morning, which I'd been trying to block. "Stupid choice of words. I'm too tired to be mad tonight. Yeah. Let's start over."

He looked relieved. We resumed walking. "Nice night," he said in a comical effort to appear blasé.

I laughed. The second time I've laughed since Grant died. I feel guilty every time I do. But Grant would want me to get on with my life. Grant wanted everyone to be happy. Always. But he died. He doesn't get a vote. I will grieve. He can't stop me.

"You are so full of it," I said. "But you're right about one thing."

"What?" He asked as he opened the restaurant door for me.

"You are an ass." I walked inside.

We were seated in a quiet corner. The crowd was light tonight, but this was a weeknight.

The last time we were here I had wanted to order the trout but had promised Lane I'd try the ribs. I glanced over the menu but knew I wanted grilled trout.

Griffin appeared at our table and recognized us. "Welcome back," he said. "Do you know what you want to drink?"

"Water," I said.

"Have a glass of wine tonight," Ron suggested. "You've had a rough day."

I nodded. "I still want the water, but do you have Moscato?"

"Glass or bottle?" Griffin asked.

I glanced at Ron.

He shook his head. "I'm going to try another of their local brews." He ordered one from the samples he'd had the other night.

"Glass," I said.

Griffin left with our order.

"When you texted me this morning, you said you had something for me to consider. It's kind of weird. I got a phone message today from Skylar Watkins. He has something for me to consider, too. This must be my day for considering and I'm too addled to string two thoughts together. But I'll try. What've you got?"

"You'll need time to think about it."

"Sounds serious," I said.

"It is. I want you to file a civil suit against Brett Nelson."

"What kind of suit?"

"Wrongful death."

"Why would I do that?"

"He robbed you of Grant's future earnings which I'm guessing would be sizeable. He deprived you of your husband and your children of their father. Think about it April, he denied the nation of a future president. He needs to be held accountable."

I stared at Ron without a clue of what to say. He sensed my hesitation.

"Think of Riley Grace. You'll want her to go to a good college. In the future she'll want a wedding and honeymoon. Her father won't be walking her down the aisle. Nelson should pay for that, too."

The thought that Riley Grace wouldn't have her father at her wedding hadn't crossed my mind. Yet. Ron had been thinking.

Griffin came back to the table with our drinks and took our food order. I decided, due to the weight I've lost, to order the trout fried instead of grilled. It came with a salad and baked potato.

"Nelson hasn't had a criminal trial yet," I said.

Griffin waited by our table for my reaction to the wine. I sipped it and smiled. It was good.

"Wouldn't it be easier to win my case after a jury finds him guilty of murder?" I asked after Griffin left. I watched him walk away thinking about the last time we were here. Then, Griffin had reminded me of Ridge. I had been so worried about him that night. Tonight I know where my son is. He's safe and Sable is alive. I have so much to be grateful for.

"That will be a slam dunk," Ron said. "There are eyewitnesses. Sable saw him do it. Ridge saw him drive away."

"I don't want to put Sable through that," I said, surprised by the maternal instinct I felt .

"She'll have to testify against him at his trial. This would prepare her."

"What if Lane is right? What if Nelson is knocked off before he's tried?"

"You sue his estate. He owes you, April. Sable's family doesn't have money. The hospital bills will be astronomical. If Sable and Ridge have a big wedding, you'll want to help with it."

I sipped my wine as I thought about it. Grant had a sizable life insurance policy. If I sell a couple of the restaurants and get a good price for them, we should be okay. The house is paid for, but taxes and utilities are sky high. We would have to tighten our belts and cut some corners for sure. Ron's points are good. I haven't had time to put pencil to paper and see where we are.

"I would feel better knowing you had a cushion." Ron raised his beer glass and leveled a gaze over it. "In case of emergencies. Only God can see around corners. You don't know what the future holds."

"Would you be representing me?"

Ron shook his head. "I don't practice that kind of law. But I know a guy." He did a goofy thing with his eyebrows as though suggesting something sinister.

I laughed. "Okay, I'll consider it. Is that all?"

He held up a hand. "No. But wait, there's more!"

I laughed again. "Good grief. What?"

"We should talk to Sable and Luna about a lawsuit against the airlines for failure to protect. Sable may not make a full recovery. We don't know yet if she will ever be able to work again and as I mentioned medical bills are already piling up. It sounds like there are other flight attendants filing charges against Nelson. The airlines shouldn't get by with ignoring the safety of those girls either. They put their whole staff in harm's way in spite of the myriad complaints they were getting about Nelson.

They should have been protected. Sable isn't the only one whose life has been destroyed. She will never fully recover from the shock of witnessing Grant's death."

"Do you do that kind of law?"

"No. But I have a friend who specializes in righting the wrongs of powerful corporations. He's quite good."

"Well, what *do* you do to earn your keep?" I asked, only half kidding.

"Taxes, estate planning, deeds and trusts. The boring stuff ..." Ron stopped talking when Griffin appeared at our table with another glass of Moscato that I hadn't ordered.

"This one is on me," he said, setting the glass down and picking up my empty. "I'm so sorry about what happened to you. Are you okay? I mean besides that bump on your forehead and bruised jaw?"

"Other than that, I'm okay. A bit stiff and sore, but alive." I forced a smile. "Thank you for the wine. And concern. That is so sweet."

"That was nice," Ron said, when Griffin left. "He's going to get a big tip."

"Speaking of nice, I appreciate your concern for Luna and Sable. You don't even know them."

"They're important to you," Ron said simply.

"I'll be sure to tell Ridge. Now that it looks like Sable is going to recover, Luna might be able to think about other things. I don't imagine she has given medical expenses a thought yet. Do you have a business card I can give Ridge? I'll have him call you."

Ron handed me two cards. "My friend is incensed that the airlines did nothing to protect those girls. We all are, but he knows what to do about it and he's chomping at the bit to get started."

True to his word, Ron left Griffin a generous tip.

* * *

The sun was sinking below the San Juan mountains when we left the Ore House. Our walk back to the hotel in the golden haze was much more subdued than the first time we'd made this walk. I looked up into the constantly changing sky. This sunset would have been just as spectacular without my eyes to see it. I was overwhelmed with the magnitude of being alive and vowed to never take the gift of life for granted again. But of course I will.

Back at the hotel, we exited the elevator and walked down the hall, stopping at my door. I leaned against the wall, closed my eyes, and exhaled one long shaky breath. Ron waited while I searched for words.

"I don't know who I am anymore."

"You probably don't." He smoothed a strand of hair away from my eye. "Find that fourteen-year-old girl I fell in love with. She was brave. Be her."

"She was a mess," I whispered. "And she knows too much now. I've depended on Grant's wisdom and strength for so long, I've forgotten where I lost mine. Probably in the Atlanta airport along with my luggage." Everyone who knows me knows how much I hate the Atlanta airport. After this morning, I'm not too crazy about the Durango airport either.

Ron waited while I searched for words.

"I've told thousands of women at seminars they were enough. But what if I'm not? Behind that microphone I'm invincible. I preached that they possessed the strength to move mountains if they would dig deep inside to find it."

"Sounds like a good message," Ron said.

"I believed it then. But I was a fraud. I have no idea what it's like to raise babies on my own or be deserted by some guy and have no skills to get a job with decent pay. I wasn't living in my own strength. I was living in Grant's. Without him, I hardly have the motivation to get out of bed in the morning. And he's only been gone a few weeks. When reality hits that he's never coming back, I'm...."

I shook my head. I didn't know how to complete that thought—didn't want to complete it. And didn't want to cry in front of Ron again.

"Grant hasn't been gone long enough for you to realize that yet. With time and experience, you'll gain confidence."

"Grant always knew what to do."

"Don't underestimate what God thinks you can do. God invites us to live in his strength. You can do this. And you aren't alone April. You have an army of people who love and support you. We aren't Grant, but we'll be here when you need us."

He looked down at me. I saw the compassion in his eyes. "Lean on your father for a while. Jackson would love that. He needs that. Ridge does, too. He'll step up. I know him well enough to know he's responsible and committed to his family. Probably something he inherited from his father."

I stared at him. "The fact that you know my son at all, is still a surprise."

"I have a whole new admiration for Ridge since this morning," Ron chose his words carefully. "Not because of what he did. Because of what he didn't do. He had that gun in his pocket but had the fortitude to wait. He's possessed that kind of strength since he was a child."

I felt a flash of irritation that he thought he could tell me something I don't know about my son. But he was right. Maybe I was irritated because he could.

"The depth of my rage shocked me when I saw that gun jammed into your temple," Ron continued. "I wanted to kill that guy when I realized how easily he could destroy my..."

He left the thought unfinished but his unspoken words echoed through my brain.

" Ron, I can't promise you—anything. I need time to figure out who I am. If you find someone else..."

Ron placed two fingers on my lips. "Stop. When you know where the someone who owns your heart is, you don't go looking someplace else. I told you that the other night. April, there are worse things than living alone."

I looked up at him. Waiting.

"Living with someone who is not you. I know. I tried for 12 years."

I stared at him, stunned.

Ron shoved his fingers through his hair. "Loneliness isn't being alone. Loneliness is living without love."

The truth of that washed over me. "I won't give you false hope, Ronnie. I have no idea what my future holds. Right now, I feel guilty if I smile or laugh."

"I know. I'll wait." He leaned down and kissed the last words into my forehead. "If it takes forever."

I watched him walk down the hall to his room.

"Goodnight," I whispered to his back.

Chapter Fifty

April

I managed to grab my phone before it stopped ringing without knocking it, or anything else, off the nightstand. I assumed the caller would be Ron. We have an early flight. I looked at the clock. It blinked 11:45. I'd barely been asleep an hour.

It was Riley Grace. She was crying. She didn't say anything. She just cried quietly into the phone.

Instantly awake, my heart leaped into my throat. "Sweetie," I gasped. "What's wrong?"

"I miss you," she said.

"You miss me?"

"Uh huh."

"But you're okay?"

"Will we ever be okay again?" she whispered.

"I don't know," I said trying to be honest. "Not for a while. Not the same okay..."

"Were you asleep, Mom?"

"Well, yeah, it's ..."

"Will you sing to me?"

"Sing to you?" Fully awake, I sat up in bed.

"Yeah. Ridge sent me a video of you singing. When I was little, you used to sing to me. I remembered."

"What do you want me to sing?"

"That song you used to sing." She sniffed. "About the moon."

I began singing "I'll be seeing you in all the old familiar places..."

"Uh huh," she said softly to let me know that was the right one.

When I finished, I waited.

"Sing the other one."

"What other one?"

"The one about the moon seeing me."

I began singing *Blue Moon*.

She joined in. Our harmony was surprisingly good. After we finished, there was silence. "When are you coming home?" She asked, her voice small.

"Well, if I can actually get on the plane tomorrow, we should land around noon."

"Okay. I'll meet you at the airport. With Ali."

"That will be nice," I said. "Maybe the three of us can have lunch at Zio's. It's near the airport."

"I would love that." She stopped talking, but she hadn't disconnected.

I could hear breathing.

"Bye. I love you," she said finally.

"Love you, too," I said.

I went to sleep still holding the phone. When it rang again, I glanced at the clock. It blinked 3:05. This time it was Ridge. Instant fear yanked me fully awake. I sat up.

"Ridge, what's wrong? What's going on?"

He heard the fear in my voice. "Everything is fine, Mom. Were you asleep?"

"Well, yeah. It's 3:00 AM."

"Sorry, I had no idea." He sounded confused.

"Ridge, you don't' wake someone up at 3:00 AM for no reason," I said. "Although. your father used to."

Grant! He had been there this morning! Or had he? Was it my imagination? I had been in shock. And so tired by then, I could hardly stand up. What had he said? I couldn't think.

"Mom? Mom!"

Oh! Ridge. I forgot he was on the phone.

"Mom. Sable wants to talk to you. I'm so sorry. Could you come talk to her."

"Now?"

"She's agitated. She's insisting that she has something that she has to tell you. I don't think she'll relax until she does."

"Me?"

Ridge exhaled into the phone. "Yes, Mom, you. Now."

"She's talking?" I sounded like a stupid third grader.

"She isn't reciting the Gettysburg address, but she makes her wishes known. I know you have an early flight. But, uh, can I come get you? She's quite adamant."

"I'll get dressed and wait for you outside."

"No! Good grief, Mom! Stay inside where it's safe until I get there. I don't want to have to shoot anyone."

I laughed.

"You're worse than Rye," he grumbled. "I'll be rescuing females the rest of my life."

"Yeah, probably." I disconnected and got dressed.

Twenty-five minutes later I followed my son into Sable's dimly lit room. She was awake. She watched as Luna rose to give me a hug, then moved aside to give me her seat. A small Shi Tzu, that I presumed to be Izzy, lay at the foot of the bed. She raised her head and watched me lower myself into the chair.

Sable reached toward me. “April,” she said.

“Yes, Love, I’m here.” I took her hand and smiled. “It’s about time I finally get to meet you.” She stared at me solemnly for so long I became uneasy. Just articulating my name had been an effort.

“Sable, you don’t have to talk.”

“Yes!” Her eyes flashed.

Well, she certainly made that clear. “Okay....”

“Grant...”

“Grant? What about him?”

“Grant said ....” She paused and I held my breath. She had my attention. Sable was the last person to see my husband alive, to hear his last words. I waited.

“He scheduled a cruise—he wanted to take you...”

“A cruise?”

“Yes.”

“He booked a cruise for the two of us?”

“Yes.”

“Where?”

“River cruise. Europe.”

I looked at Ridge.

He nodded.

“Thank you, Sable. I’ll look for it on his computer.”

“There’s more,” she said.

I waited.

“Grant said...”

I leaned forward as though my being closer could help her get the words out.

“...you would make a good First Lady.”

“What? Grant said that?”

“Yes.”

I smiled. So, he did have aspirations of moving into the White House.

"He said—you could be president. You're a better com...communicator than he is."

You certainly couldn't prove that by my kids. "Did he say anything else?"

"He—you are the only woman he ever loved. He said you loved someone else once, and that..."

"Wait! Grant told you that? I didn't think he knew." I glanced up at Ridge. He listened intently. Then I remembered Grant telling me that this morning. But I had a gun in my ear at the time. I thought I was delirious. What if I wasn't. What if he was really there? I added Grant to the list of people who think Ron should be in my life.

"Yes." Tears leaked from the corner of Sable's eye nearest me and puddled onto the sheet. "Grant said you sang with a guy at a wedding."

"Wedding? What wedding? Are you sure? I met Grant at a Republican..."

"No!" she said. "That was later. He saw you first at a wedding. Singing. You took his breath away. He loved you then and said he'd love you with his last breath...and he did...love you with his last breath. You should know..."

"Yes," I whispered. "I should." Tears streamed down my face. I reached for a tissue on the nightstand. Grant had seen me before I met him at the Young Republican membership drive. I never knew.

"Thank you, Sable, when you're well, we will talk about this again."

Her mission accomplished, Sable closed her eyes. Visibly relaxed, her hand loosened its grip on mine. I thought she was asleep, but her eyes flashed back open.

"He saved my life. Shooting. He pushed me on the floor. He..."

She was gone again. I leaned over and kissed her cheek.

"Think about something else, Sweetie."

"She's asleep," Ridge said. "She's been doing that. She talks. She tires. She sleeps. She wakes up, remembers something and wants to talk again."

I nodded.

"She's asked for you every time she woke up. I don't know how she knew you were in Durango."

"She must have heard us talking last night," I said, thinking out loud.

"She's been remembering.... She wakes up screaming. It's traumatic. For all of us. The doctor is giving her a combination of meds to allow her to wake up easily without reliving the terrifying details."

Ridge looked out the window into the night. The strain around his eyes tugged at my heart. I got up and hugged him.

The scent of flowers filled the room. I looked around. An enormous bouquet of peonies, dahlias, mums, roses, and a few exotic flowers I'd never seen in a large seahorse-shaped vase sat on a table by the window.

"Wow! Someone spent some bucks on those," I said. "Who sent them?"

"The airlines," Luna said. "They came yesterday."

"Too little, too late," I muttered. Realizing the time, I turned to Ridge. "I've got to get packed. My plane boards in an hour and a half."

I gave him a rueful smile. "I intend to catch this one."

"I know you have to go home," he said, massaging the back of his neck. "Rye needs you, but I don't want you to go. It's hard to admit I still need my mom."

I gave him another hug. He couldn't know how much I needed to hear that.

"I'm only a phone call away. I wish you had remembered weeks ago."

"I know. I'm sorry. I wasn't thinking straight."

"Tell me anything else Sable thinks I should know." As I said the words, I wondered if he would know how important hearing how much it would mean to me to know what Grant had said about me. But Sable knew.

"Yeah, I will."

I leaned down and kissed Sable's cheek. "I love you, Sable," I whispered in her ear. "Rest easy, angel, you're safe now."

Ridge and I walked out into the cool predawn air. The sun had not yet climbed above the mountains, but the sky had lightened in the east and a rosy glow hugged the horizon with promise of its arrival.

I buzzed down the Forester's window and looked up at the few remaining stars as Ridge drove me back to the hotel. Despite the terrible circumstances, I had fallen in love with this town. I would be back.

Chapter Fifty-One
Riley Grace

Bronc and I sat at the table on the patio outside Mom's bedroom. Yesterday had been crazy hot, but the surprise rainstorm that blew in last night cooled. At any rate, the koi were lively today, flashing gold and orange as they chased each other just below the pond's surface. Cricket chirps blended with the sounds of a day shuffling to a close.

Ali came outside carrying a plate of cookies and a pitcher of lemonade on a tray. I smiled my gratitude. When Ali makes the cookies, they're peanut butter, her favorite. Bronc's favorite, too. Mom makes snickerdoodles. I always thought it was because they're Ridge's favorite. As it turns out, she likes them, too. If I make cookies, its chocolate chip or brownies. Lately, Eve Anna has worked me so hard I haven't had energy for anything else, which has me worried. I haven't had much time to spend with Bronc and when I do, I've been too tired to be my super-entertaining funny self. What if he thinks I'm a boring drut and moves on to someone more exciting?

If Ridge were here, he'd say, "You're no more boring than usual, Rye, and you aren't all that funny." Ridge believes he was put on earth to keep me from being 'full of myself' and I should thank him for keeping me grounded and humble.

Mom's been back from Durango for three weeks and things have settled into a new routine. That's my way of saying things have really changed. For one thing, Mom's taking tennis lessons from Eve Anna. I'm guessing there are several reasons for her new interest in tennis. To make up for lost time with me, and she wants to better understand the game. It's one thing to have a basic knowledge, but unless you play, you don't appreciate the nuances. She's been getting up early to return my serves when I'm practicing. It's been good for her. She's working hard on her forehand. Her arms are getting toned and looking good.

She's moved out of the crying in her bed all day phase that she fell into when she came back from Durango. Things had slowed down and she finally had time to grieve for Dad. She's getting fresh air, sunshine, and exercise. I'm proud of her. Mom and Eve Anna finished up the lesson and followed the flagstone path which meandered through rose of Sharon bushes and beds of phlox and larkspurs to this patio.

Mom's Rottweiler, Chester, had been lying under the table. As Mom and Eve Anna approached, he raised his head from my foot. His eyes followed their progress, but he didn't get up and run to meet her. Chester had been another causality of Mom's long absences from home. Dad bought him to protect us when he first moved to DC. Chester had immediately become devoted to Mom, sleeping beside her bed every night. But lately, he's become more attached to me. Mom noticed. She's trying to win him back. But he's no pushover.

Mom and Eve Anna joined us at the table.

"April," Eve Anna said, in her low smooth voice, "I have something I hope you and Riley Grace will consider."

Mom looked up from sorting through cookies as though she expected to find a snickerdoodle hidden in there somewhere. "Sounds intriguing," she said.

"There's an event coming up in August outside of Paris. It's an International in-depth training camp. It's a four-week course. Almost impossible to get into. They only take ten applicants. They have invited Riley Grace to apply. It's quite an honor."

I almost choked on my cookie. "How do they even know about me?" I asked.

"I sent them videos of of your practice sessions. They were quite impressed."

A month? I would live in France? That must be terribly expensive...Mom?"

"We could make it work," she said. "If Eve Anna thinks..."

"Oh, I think." Eve Anna lifted a hand. We stopped talking and waited to see what she had to say.

"I've had a few weeks to evaluate you now, Riley Grace. I'm glad you're all here." She looked around the table. "I wish Ridge was here, too, but I've discussed this with him."

Eve Anna's gaze swept around the table again, resting on me.

"Riley, I believe you have more potential than anyone I've ever worked with." She smiled. "Maybe even myself."

"What?" I must've misunderstood her.

"You have incredible talent. But above and beyond that, your instinct for what your opponent will do is phenomenal. After the first few times I played with you, I called Ridge. He agrees. He knew what I was talking about. He had assumed you did it with him because you are so familiar with his game. But your instincts are that good with me as well. Quite amazing."

Her fingers drummed on the table as she thought. "On top of that, you have a good work ethic. You put in the time and effort it takes. And, as far as I can tell, with nobody pushing you. Most of our work needs to be on strength training. Ridge agreed. I had looked forward to the opportunity of working with you because you're Ridge Frazier's sister. I underestimated your raw talent. Someday people will say Ridge is Riley Grace Frazier's brother."

"Yes!" I did a fist pump.

Having said what she had to say, she poured a glass of lemonade. And waited.

Mom looked dazed. "I never took her tennis seriously. Ridge..."

"Ridge knows how good she is," Eve Anna said. "He's mentioned wanting to manage her someday. Getting her into the right tournaments, promoting her, getting her sponsors. All the things I won't have time do. The time I can give her in the future depends on my parent's health. We don't know how much time we have, so we have to work hard now."

Mom nodded. "Ridge said she was good."

"He did?" I'm blown away that he said that to both Eve Anna and Mom.

"She's highly motivated," Eve Anna said. "She's put herself through strenuous workouts. Many girls her age are too boy crazy to put in the time and effort it takes. If she doesn't get distracted ..." She looked pointedly at Bronc.

Bronc has this lopsided grin that he does when he's embarrassed or thinks something is funny but shouldn't laugh. Like when Mr. Schroeder sneezed in Lit class and almost lost his dentures. The corner of Bronc's mouth turns down. It's different from the smile that shows off his dimple.

He smiled. The half-smile. "Her grit is one of the things I love about her."

"That's what you like about me?" I demanded. "If I'd known that, I wouldn't have wasted money on mascara."

Ali laughed.

"I said one of the things," he clarified. "I love your big heart, too." He pulled a small box from his pocket. "I didn't intend to do this in front of a cast of thousands," he looked around at four pairs of curious eyes. "Riley, if you will wear this, I promise to give you space, and still be there for you when you need me." He handed me the box.

"What is it?" Mom asked, looking over my shoulder as I opened it.

It was a gold ring. A tiny diamond nestled in the center of a tiny heart.

"A promise ring," Ali said.

"What's a promise ring?" Mom asked.

"A ring that promises a later engagement ring," Ali explained. "Right, Bronc?"

"Right," he said. "But it's more. It's to remind Riley that I promise to protect and defend her." He looked at me. "And be your best friend. Forever."

"You'll have to fight Alise for that spot," Mom said. "But you've proven the protecting part."

I could barely see him through my tears. I slipped the ring out of the box and onto my finger. "I love you," my lips said, but no sound came out.

"I'm getting ready to be busy with football, too. We won't be able to be together as much. You have my heart. Now you'll be wearing it on your finger, too."

By the time he finished, I was crying for sure, and he was looking embarrassed that he had said all that in front of everybody.

I got up and walked around the table and kissed him. "Even if I'm in France?" I asked, as I sat on his lap and wrapped my arms around his neck.

"It's just a month. But even if you're in Outer Mongolia," he said.

Chapter Fifty-Two

April

Waking up without Grant this morning had been excruciating. Grief is a complex companion. When you think you've figured out what to expect, it blindsides you. Like yesterday. I'd gone to the hardware store. For some weird reason, sacks of quickset were stacked along the sidewalk. Soon after we were married Grant and I decided to tile our kitchen floor ourselves. Big mistake. We got into an argument over what kind of quickset to buy. Like either of us was an expert. That memory did me in. I stood on the sidewalk staring at those sacks blubbering like a baby.

I'm having trouble in social situations. I don't always follow the thread of conversation. Alise, the epitome of knowledge, says when you don't know what to say, just smile. And nod. I'm not sure that's enough.

People would think I'm crazy, so I'm careful who I tell about Grant being with me at the Durango airport shootout. By the time he showed up I was exhausted. But I am confident I didn't just imagine it. He was definitely there. Only Grant would have said what he did. And he also literally talked Ridge off a ledge a couple of nights before. Something I'm just now finding out about. I think it was a one-time thing in both instances. We were both in critical third down situations. But I'm keeping an open mind on how thin the veil is between heaven and earth. I've been digging through my Bible and reading what people I trust have to say on the matter. But after talking to Grant, I don't feel that he is as gone as I once did.

Today I need the kind of advice I would have gone to him for. I am so used to handing my problems to him. I need a man's viewpoint. So, I came to see my father..

I leaned against the cedar rail, running my fingers across its rough texture. My gaze followed the lane past the barn and into the meadow. Shimmery heat and Oklahoma wind had robbed the grass of the vibrant green it wore last spring. The scene's serenity should have eased the edginess I always feel around my father. It didn't.

I had been so angry when he built this house. Penny wanted to live in the country. Away from the house I grew up in. The home he'd shared with my mom. Away from me. I tried to resent Penny. I couldn't. She's just so sweet.

So, I took my anger out on Dad. I stopped calling him Daddy. From then on, he became Jackson. He didn't notice.

The door opened and Jackson walked out. He leaned against the rail beside me and sipped his coffee. "Not sleeping well, are you." It wasn't a question. "It's tough. But you'll survive. Some days don't feel like it, though."

The voice of experience. I nodded, unable to speak. His unexpected sympathy knotted my throat.

We watched Riley Grace race across the distant pasture on Picasso. She rode bareback, her long blond hair bouncing with the pony's stride. She grew up in the city, but she's a country girl. No wonder she's attracted to Bronc.

"Ain't she somethin'?" Jackson shook a cigarette from a pack of Camels and cupped his hands around his mouth as he lit it.

His eyes tracked the girl on the horse. "She sure enough has my heart," he said, shaking his head.

I tried to remember him ever saying that about his daughter. Me. I came up short.

"When you bought that pony," I said, "I thought he was too big for her. She was so little."

"He was too big for her back then. He's large for a Welsh. Might be part Arabian. He was gentle even though he was young,. He had some sense. I knew he wouldn't hurt her and she'd be riding that pony for a long time."

We watched together, along with a few curious Angus who lifted their heads from the love grass, as girl and pony sailed over a ditch. Butterflies startled from wildflowers in their wake.

"What brings you out here so early?" Jackson exhaled a slow steady stream of smoke above my head.

I've watched him do that for years.

"Get tired of the big city? Didn't know you were coming to Cheyenne Falls today." Jackson continued. "Does Ron know you're here?"

"Yeah. He's on his way out. I have some financial matters to discuss with both of you." I nodded toward his coffee. "You got any more of that?"

"Reckon I can rustle some up. Come on in." He held the door for me.

I walked in wondering where the resentment had gone, which usually followed me into this house. The kitchen was big and open. Homey. Although I've never felt at home here. Sunlight poured through the large east window over the sink and puddled on the floor around my feet.

Jackson took a mug from a shelf, poured the coffee, and handed it to me knowing I drank it black.

"Thanks," I said, watching steam curl from the mug. The coffee was too hot to drink, and I needed time to organize my thoughts.

"You said something about financial matters?" Jackson glanced over his shoulder before nosing around in the cabinet for plates. He carried them to the table and went back after a cake. Strawberry. I wasn't hungry but have never turned down Penny's strawberry cake. I went to the drawer and got four forks and a knife.

Jackson grimaced as he eased himself into a chair.

"You're moving kind of slow. Did Whiplash throw you?" I teased, knowing it would get a rise out of him. Even if his big buckskin gelding had tossed him, he wouldn't admit it.

"Course not! Just getting old and creaky."

I mentally calculated his age, jolted by the fact my strong father was finally showing age. I shouldn't be surprised, but while the rest of us changed through the years, Jackson had not. He was totally bald at 40. He looked exactly the same at 70, his piercing eyes clear, his face still unlined despite hours spent the sun. Thanks, I'm guessing, to the cowboy hat he never took off.

"I'm glad you can finally be around Ron without wanting to scratch his eyes out. I never did know what that was about." He looked up from cutting the cake.

"Yeah. I'm past that now."

"I've always liked that boy." He handed me the cake and cut himself a slice.

"I know. That's the problem. Ron broke my heart. You were supposed to hate him because I did." I cut into the cake. "Like a normal father," I added under my breath.

"Well, first, I didn't know your heart was broken. You weren't talking to me."

"I didn't think you'd noticed," I grumbled.

"And second, I knew him. I knew who he was. He couldn't do anything terrible."

Jackson was right. Ron would never deliberately do anything to hurt anyone. I should have known that, too.

"You were always on his side," I said. "Fathers are supposed to think nobody is good enough for their daughter. I think it's in a rule book somewhere."

"Liked him better than you," Jackson said with a twinkle in his eye.

"That's probably true."

Jackson sighed. "I hoped the two of you would work things out."

"I know you did."

"But I gave up on that idea when you brought Grant home." He took a long drag on his cigarette and ground out the butt in a horseshoe shaped ashtray.

"Ron was married by then," I reminded him.

"Well, yeah, there was that."

I got up to pour myself more coffee and glanced at his cup.

He shook his head. "I'm fine. But here's what I think. Grant Frazier was a whirlpool, Girl. The current had done pulled you under. I never met anyone with a personality so strong. There was no escaping that charm."

"I could have escaped. If I wanted to," I muttered. But as I said the words, I remembered how he'd bulldozed his way into my heart the night we met. Jackson was right. I hadn't known what hit me.

"Why didn't you escape?" he asked.

"I was afraid nobody would come find me," I said, surprised at what tumbled out of my mouth. I left the words hanging out there, waiting for a rebuttal that didn't come.

We sat in silence. Questions and accusations floated between us, bobbing and dancing like balloons losing their helium. Most of them weren't worth the effort to wade through.

"Everyone liked Grant. Why didn't you?"

"He liked classical music."

I laughed. It was no secret that my father hated classical music. If it wasn't Willie, Waylon or the boys—he didn't listen. But I saw the twinkle in those startling blue eyes and wanted to see where this went.

"You don't like classical music?"

"No, Sir!" He shook his head.

"Why not?"

"It's always in a big fidget about something. You can't rest with all those cymbals crashing. I tried to like it once. It expects something from you. I could never figure out what."

I almost understood that. "Why did you really not like Grant? You're the only person I know who didn't."

"He wasn't good enough for my daughter. Fathers always think that about guys their daughters marry." He winked. "Heard that somewhere." .

I laughed. "Be serious. Why didn't you like him?"

"Liked him fine. I didn't like who you were when you were with him—some hoity-toity gal I barely recognized."

I wanted to tell him he was wrong. But he wasn't.

The night before we left Durango, I told Ron I didn't know who I was without Grant. Ron said to find the fourteen-year-old me and start from there. I think that's what Jackson is saying, too. I'm not sure I remember who that girl was. My finger traced the rim of my coffee mug. I can't bring Grant back, but maybe I can find me.

It just dawned on me. My father and I were having a real conversation. My dad. Not Jackson. "Dad, before Ron and Riley Grace get here, I want to apologize."

He raised an eyebrow. "For what?"

"I was angry back then. About so many things when Mom died. Nobody told me how sick she was. I thought she was just in the hospital again. When she died, I felt betrayed. By everyone I loved. I took it out on you."

He wiped crumbs from his shirt. "I'd do a lot of things different now. Thought I was protecting you."

Tears, as unwelcome as the resentment had been, filled my eyes. "I lost my mom. Then I lost my dad. You had no time for me. You married Penny and moved out here."

"I'm sorry," he said, simply.

"I was too young to understand that you were grieving, too. You never cried. I thought you didn't miss Mom."

"I cried plenty. Not around you. Your mother was the love of my life. I married way over my head. Never could figure out what she saw in me."

He inhaled deeply and exhaled a long unsteady breath. "Always knew I couldn't keep her. Angels don't stay in one place very long."

I nodded, remembering him playing Willie's "Angel Flying Too Close to the Ground" on his pickup CD player.

"I've done the same thing." I blinked back a tear. "I haven't been there for Riley Grace. I've been so focused on clearing Grant's name and finding Ridge, I forgot I had a daughter."

"Started before then," he said, quietly.

"You never cut me any slack. But I can't argue when you're right," I said. "Riley Grace has always been a Daddy's girl. She didn't need me."

"Girl needs her mama. You of all people should know that," Jackson said. "You can't fix what-might-have-beens any more than I can. We'll do better going forward."

"I just wanted to tell you I'm sorry." I brushed away a renegade tear.

"Done," Dad said. "You needed advice. What about?"

"Skylar Watkins called."

Dad eyed me over his raised coffee mug, waiting for me to go on.

"He wants me to step into Grant's senatorial position and finish out his term."

"You could do that? I mean without an election? I don't know how that works."

"I don't either," I said.

"Do you have the qualifications?"

"Beats me. I don't know what they are."

"Well, I'll be danged. My daughter. From Hicksville, Oklahoma. It's an honor just to be asked." Dad's fingers drummed the table as he thought. "You gonna to do it?"

"I might have considered it a couple of months ago. There are things I'd like to fight for in DC. I wish I believed one person could make a difference."

"Would Riley move back out here?"

"If I've realized anything since Grant died, it's that my kids are the most important thing in the world to me. I have too much time to make up with her now."

Dad nodded. He gazed past me through the window.

I turned to see what had captured his interest. Riley Gace was back from her ride. She'd removed Picasso's bridle and slung it across one shoulder. The pony followed her into the barn.

"It was flattering to be asked and fun to think about," I continued, "but I'm not leaving that girl again. Ever."

"Well, she's always welcome. We sure like having her around."

"I know Dad, and that means more to me than you will ever know. But you and Penny have already done more than your share of raising my children."

"Looks like you've started thinking for yourself again."

"This will be Gracie's senior year. She won't have much time for me, but I want to be with her every minute that she will let me."

"Gracie, huh?" He grinned at my use of her name. Glad to hear you say that." He thumped another Camel from the pack. "You've just lost your husband and survived a hostage situation." He paused to light it. "As your father, I'd like you to stay home and rest. As an American citizen, I can't think of anyone I'd rather have in DC fighting for what's right."

"Thanks, Dad," I said, surprised by his words. We sat in a comfortable silence for a few minutes and drank our coffee.

"Are you still drinking too much coffee?" I asked.

"About four cups."

"That's kind of a lot."

"Need 'em," he said. "Couldn't get out of bed without the first one. The others are to keep me out of jail. I deal with a lot of idiots." He grinned. "Penny's not one of 'em."

I looked around. "Where is Penny?"

"She's at some women's lah-de-dah lady thing at the church. How's Bronc?"

"Good. I like him," I said. "You'll have to meet him."

"I have," he said. "He's a good kid."

"When? Did you meet him, I mean?"

"Well, to start with, he was at that whoop-de-do restaurant of yours after Grant's funeral. He's been out here. A couple of times. He treats Riley with respect. Like a man should treat a woman."

"They were here? Why?

"Looking for a U-joint."

"What! Why would Riley Grace think you had pot?"

Dad shook his head. "How are you even my child? They were looking for a part for Bronc's pickup. Riley remembered my old Ford out in the shed."

"Oh," I said. "Did you? Have parts he could use?"

"A few." Dad sipped his coffee, set down the mug, and grinned.

"He'll be in Stillwater soon. Football practice starts in a couple of weeks."

The door opened. Riley and Ron trooped in laughing and chatting like old friends.

She smelled like sunshine, fresh air, and horse.

"Oh, yay! Strawberry cake. Hi, Gramps." She washed her hands and stopped to hug him on her way to the cake.

Ron went to the coffee urn and poured himself a cup. I watched them, marveling at how comfortable they both were in this house.

"You didn't put that horse back in the barn, did you?" Dad asked.

"Nope. I turned him out in the pasture."

"Good. I'm going broke buying feed for that nag," Jackson grumped. "Gonna have to get a second job to feed him or auction him off—worthless thing. Can't plow. Won't herd buffalo."

His peevishness had always upset me.

Riley Grace snorted. “Why would you plow with a horse when you’ve got that monster John Deere out by the barn?” She pulled his sacred hat from his head and swatted him with it.

I gasped, certain his head would explode.

Ron looked up and winked at me, enjoying their repartee.

“Girl, you know better than that!” He huffed. He grabbed it out of her hand and repositioned it, getting the angle just right. “Set your butt down and eat your cake.”

Riley Grace hugged him again. “Yeah, I know. Don’t mess with a man’s hat.”

“That’s right,” he huffed. “I taught you better than that.”

Riley Grace laughed and nearly choked on her cake.

My mouth fell open. His gruff grumbling was his way of saying, “I love you.” Riley Grace got it. Why had I never understood? I watched my father and my daughter teasing, joking, and laughing, with Ron jumping in now and then. Even when the conversation moved on to more serious topics like finances, lawsuits and what I should or shouldn’t do, I felt strangely at ease. These two men, both concerned with my well-being, were putting their heads together making a plan for me. A plan that I could trust.

Riley Grace laughed at something Ron said.

This kitchen finally felt like home.

Chapter Fifty-Three

Riley Grace

Our kitchen smelled like freshly baked cookies, cinnamon, and sugar. Ridge's favorite. Snickerdoodles. I pulled a cookie sheet from the oven, replaced it with another and set the timer for eleven minutes.

Mom was making some kind of French pastry, testing for "menu worthiness" for one of her restaurants. Probably *Café des Amis*. I figured that out with my uncanny deduction skill. The French restaurant is the only one she has after selling *Mambo* and giving *Bamboo Cru* to her friend Mayra as a wedding gift. Mom and Mayra had owned it together. Mom gave her half to Mayra.

Café Des Amis is French for come eat with your friends. That's the only French I know. I'm probably not saying it right. Alise says you have to stand on a chair and hold your nose for correct French pronunciation. She never ate there. Alise believes French restaurants only serve snails and horse meat. I told her that's not true, but she's pretty sure it is.

The kitchen is my favorite room in our house. Ali decided the walls needed more color and selected an awesome desert hue that changes with the light. Hue is a word I never used before Ali. She says the paint has the slightest hint of green in it, but I don't see it. It just looks tan to me. She had it specially mixed to make a great backdrop for Mom's matador abstract. The painting is huge and looks even bigger because of the massive frame. Mom met the Spanish artist when we were in Los Cabos, Mexico. She fell in love with his work. Wicked expensive, but she convinced Dad her life would be barren without it. This piece depicts a matador about to be gored by a bull. The title is "Courage in the Face of Adversity". Mom liked the sound of that. I think it should be called "Too Buzzed to Know What I'm Doing", but I'm no art connoisseur.

Our kitchen is almost the size of the kitchen in the Governor's Mansion and the reason Mom wanted this house. I think the people who lived here before had a bunch of servants. We don't need a kitchen this big, but it comes in handy during the holidays when everyone is cooking—Penny, Aunt Abby, Ali, and Mom.

It has three ovens, two fridges and a freezer. That's why we always have Thanksgiving and Christmas dinners at our house. We have a bar, but we don't eat there. We have a kitchen nook shaped like a bay window that faces the east and is light and airy. There are two pantries bigger than the bathroom in Ridge's apartment. In fact, the "kitchen complex" as Mom calls it, could hold his whole apartment.

I'm learning to cook. Sandwiches are my specialty. I do a great Reuben, a killer BLT, and I've fried a million eggs for Ridge's sandwiches. I've been making my own PBJ's since I was four.

Mom has been humming a song. Some tune I've never heard. Even when she just hums you can tell she has a great voice. She used to sing a funny song about a frog who wanted to be a giraffe but ended up being a toad. The moral is he should have been happy with who he was. I just figured that out.

Mom poured herself a glass of milk. She slid some cookies, hot from the oven, onto a plate and carried them into the breakfast room.

"Gracie, can you come here for a few minutes? I need to talk to you."

Before Dad died, that would have scared me. Before Dad died, it wouldn't have happened. Since our counseling sessions, we've been talking more. A lot more. And before Dad died, she wouldn't have called me "Gracie" like my friends and Ali do. At first it felt kind of weird. Forced. I think it made her uncomfortable, too. She says she has been working on being vulnerable. I think maybe she's always been vulnerable. She just didn't know it. Still, her saying she "needed to talk" was weird. We'd been talking all morning.

"Sure Mom. Should I get me some cookies, too?" That's an example of my hilarious sense of humor. She had almost a dozen cookies on the plate.

She laughed.

I poured myself a glass of milk, checked the oven timer—nobody likes burned cookies—and followed her into the breakfast nook.

"What's up?" I slid into a chair across the table from her and snagged a cookie.

There's an antique buffet beside the table where Mom keeps Great Grandma Ida's silver and China. We never use them. But we "have" them. It's where Mom keeps the "formal" tablecloths that fit the dining room table. She has different colors for each season, red for Christmas and orange and gold for Thanksgiving. But I digress.

Mom opened a drawer and pulled out a jewelry store box and handed it to me.

I looked up at her. "What's this?"

"It's from your dad. Open it."

"Dad?" Curious, I crammed the rest of the cookie in my mouth and wiped my hands on my shorts. You don't open jewelry boxes with crumbly fingers. Inside the box was a note written in dark blue ink on the back of a jewelry store receipt. Dad always carried that pen with him.

Happy Birthday, Bino,
this will be late.
The jeweler designed it for you.
Like you, it's one of a kind.
You are my golden girl.
My shining tennis star.
You have more talent in your little finger
than I ever had.
You're my favorite, you know,
but don't tell Ridge.
Love you forever and always,
Dad

I had to read his note several times because I couldn't see through my tears. When he said this was late, he meant for my birthday. He had no idea that whenever I received anything from him would be the absolute best time. "Bino" is short for Bambino, which Daddy has called me from the time I was born. I have no idea why. He was Irish, not Italian. He'd drawn a winking smiley face after the "don't tell Ridge" and a heart after the "forever and always".

I blinked back tears.

A necklace lay on black velvet. The diamond-cut gold chain caught the light slanting through the window over my shoulder and winked it back at me. Suspended from the chain was a small gold tennis racquet. A tennis ball, a perfect pearl, sat on the sweet spot of the racquet.

I looked up at Mom. She was smiling. Tears filled her eyes, too.

"Can I help you put it on?" she asked.

I handed it to her and pulled my hair up so she could fasten the chain.

"The jewelry store called to say this was ready right before Grant's funeral. I wasn't here. Ali took the call. She told me, but I forgot. They called again yesterday," Mom said.

Ridge walked through the kitchen on his way out to the tennis court, his blue Yonex racquet in hand. Evidently, he found where I put it in his room the day of Dad's funeral.

"Hey, Brat, wanna play?" He grabbed some cookies on his way to the door, not waiting for my answer.

"Better not tell him Grant said you're his favorite." Mom said.

"Yeah, like that's going to happen!" I snatched a cookie and followed him out.

"Hey, Ridge, check this out!"

Chapter Fifty-Four

Riley Grace

I looked up into a sky so blue it made me want to cry. Scattering Dad's ashes from a hot-air balloon was my idea. This morning seemed the perfect time. Bright sun. Light breezes. I keep the memory of his arrival in a hot air balloon on my fifth birthday safely tucked away in my heart.

Far, far below us, tractors moved through fields like migrating elephants turning golden wheat stubble, remnants of this year's harvest, under the red earth to prepare the field for the wheat kernels, seeds of next year's crop, to be dropped into it. Life to death to life again. Rayford Ruefford said something about the cycle of life at Daddy's funeral.

Our pilot, Frank Greer, talked a lot as we ascended, telling us what to expect, and explaining what he was doing. But as the balloon rose through the morning mist, with Muskogee shrinking below, he realized we weren't apprehensive. Understanding our mission, he stopped talking, leaving us in our private reveries as the balloon drifted toward Lake Tenkiller.

It has taken Mom, Ridge, and me different roads and lengths of time to get here, but we're ready to turn loose of Daddy's ashes. After much discussion, we decided on Lake Tenkiller as a site because Daddy loved to fish there. Actually, he didn't care for fishing, he just enjoyed getting his *StarCraft* on the water and the lake is beautiful.

Alise says people are like candy bars. We have a chocolate-gooey-caramel center—the part of us which laughs, cries, thinks, believes, dreams, and loves. That part of us lives on with God forever. What's left behind is just the wrapper. I like that. Alise would say we are discarding Daddy's wrapper today.

It's been four months since Sable's car flew off into that ravine taking my daddy's wrapper with it. Sable said Dad died instantly. He didn't see the bullet coming. He was looking down at Sable and didn't feel anything. That doesn't do anything to fill the empty places in my heart but hearing how it happened took away some of the horror I had imagined. I hope I'm unaware when I die, too. Woody Allen said he wasn't afraid of dying. He just didn't want to be there when it happened. I used to think that was funny. Now I can relate.

Mom let me fly to Durango to be with Ridge and Sable a few weeks ago. Talking to Sable helped me almost as much as talking to Ridge. We had some great discussions about life and death, Ridge, and Dad. The more I get to know Sable, the more I see why Ridge loves her. When she looks at you with those big brown eyes, you want to tell her your deepest secrets. Most of them. I haven't told her about the time I ran out on the highway to save a kitten and caused a wreck. I've been too scared to tell anyone, even Ali, about that. Nobody was hurt. But three cars were involved.

I think if I had seen my father's body, I could accept his death. But I haven't and sometimes it doesn't feel real to me. While I was in Durango, the coroner finally released "the body", but it was immediately cremated. Ridge and I drove back to Oklahoma with the windows buzzed down because the Forester's air conditioner went out. The discussions we had on that trip home, with Dad's ashes on the console between us, helped me heal more than all my counseling sessions put together. I'll always have scars that nobody sees. Ridge will, too, but scars are the toughest part of the body. Once when I broke my wrist, the doctor told me that when a break heals, the bone becomes stronger at the break site. Alise says scars prove you've done something and should be worn proudly. But I think sometimes they just prove you were stupid.

Sable still can't travel. Coming to Oklahoma for Thanksgiving would be out. So, we are all going to Durango. Sable, her sister, mom and grandma, Mom, me, Ridge, Bronc and Bronc's mother and sister will be there—if Bronc's mom can get off work. I hope so. I really like her. We've been running together with the school cross-country team. She's training for a marathon and I'm building my stamina for tennis. Mom rented a huge mountain cabin big enough for all of us. Thanksgiving is still a few months away, but you gotta get your reservation in early or you end up with something that looks like an outhouse. I've never been in an outhouse, but I've seen pictures.

When I was in Durango, Ridge took me to the wreck site. We had a memorial service out there. Just the two of us and Mortimer. Ridge took peanuts for the chipmunk. I placed a wreath beside the one Mom had left and the one someone else placed there.

I'd looked down into the canyon where boulders the size of houses banked the Animas River. While Ridge fed Mortimer peanuts, I leaned against an old Ponderosa pine. Ridge told me about standing near there the night he planned to jump into the ravine and Dad stopped him. I'm a little jealous. I want to hear Dad's voice, too. How terrible it would have been if Ridge had jumped that night and Mom and I had lost him, too. But what a tragedy it would have been if Ridge had died because he didn't want to live without Sable and then Sable woke up and discovered Ridge died because he thought she was dead. I think there might be a country song there.

We've all changed since Dad's death, but of the three of us, Mom has changed the most. She cancelled her speaking tour and only has one restaurant now. She's home more. Like a normal person. She listens. Most of the time. She's trying. We've cried about a billion tears together. We went on the river cruise Dad had scheduled for the two of them through Europe. It wasn't easy for her. Dad should've been with her, but we had a good time.

Dad's death has pulled my family together in a way I could never have imagined. If he hadn't died, we would have just gone on expecting our days to spill into one another like a beautiful never-ending gift, unaware that at any moment It could end or change us forever. Anyone I love could be gone in an instant. I almost lost my mom and Ridge, too.

Ali once explained that contrast is what makes a painting dramatic. Dark makes the light stand out. Ali says without contrast, a painting would be boring. That applies to life, too. If all our days were sunny, we'd take their glory for granted. But too much sun creates deserts. So, there you have it. You gotta have some storms mixed in there. That's profound for someone as shallow as I am.

As I thought about that, a scary-dark storm blew in from the Southwest. It's making our ride a bit rough. A lot rough. The gondola is bucking like a bull just released from chute number three. I looked at Mom and Ridge. Like me, they were hanging on tight. But they were laughing. This day was supposed to be so perfect, and it's turned into this mess. It shouldn't be funny. We've just tossed Dad's ashes into a hurricane-force wind.

They're probably nowhere near the lake. If Dad was here, he would be laughing the hardest. I can't shake the feeling that somewhere he is watching this and cracking up.

"Dad's ashes are probably in Minnesota," Ridge said.

We don't know where we are. Neither does Frank Greer. He'd been scrolling through the news feed on his device looking for weather updates when he suddenly stopped. "Hey, you guys are going to want to hear this," he said. "Speaker Rayford Ruefford just released a statement. He said, 'Senator Frazier died a hero's death saving his future daughter-in-law from an assassin.'"

Greer stopped reading and looked up at us to make sure we could hear him above the wind. "This is what Ruefford said, and it's a direct quote. "Grant Frazier's life mission was to improve the lives of others. He lived an exemplary life. He was gone much too soon. One of the greats has been taken from us. Grant Frazier was truly..."

Before Greer could finish reading, the three of us at the same time looked at each other and quoted along with him, "...one of the chosen few." It was the one thing all three of us remembered in Ruefford's eulogy at Dad's funeral.

Frank Greer thinks we're delirious because we think this is amusing. We don't care.

The road ahead of us will be bumpy. There will be other storms. But we'll hang on tight and get through those, too.

Together.

The End

(And I mean it!)

Acknowledgments

For Nissi

A huge thank you to former Police Chief Dennis Baker who answered my law questions. A girl has to know what laws she's breaking. OKC Fire Chief Richard Kelley who tried to answer my questions about removing wreckage from a gorge. And the officer in front of the Durango Highway Patrol Office who actually wasn't much help but looked good in his uniform. I'm deeply indebted to my great friends and beta-readers: Donella Strawn, Marilyn Baker, Liz Kelley, Mick Benderoth, Lou Ann Myers, Joann Rogers, and Robert Williams. Especially Robert, who waded through my rough draft three times, and Donella, who pointed out the words and phrases that I am way too fond of using. She's had my heart since October 6, 1959. And Kaylee McCoy just because she exists. I am humbled by your love and support. A huge thank you to Trina Lee and other friends at Writer's Corner. A writer needs to hang out with great writers. And I did. Every Wednesday. Your talent inspired me to write better and kept me on track.

My everlasting gratitude to Woody Gimbel. My everything. My life coach, my writing coach, my editor and the reason I breathe.

About the Author

Carol Gimbel grew up in a small Oklahoma town, exploring the surrounding area on her buckskin gelding, Sanchez. It's only natural that her books are often set in small towns. She's extended her love of exploration to Ecuador, Guatemala, and Panama where she and her husband lived for a year.

Her weekly cooking column appeared in an Oklahoma City newspaper for eight years. She's been a frequent contributor to *Guideposts Magazine*. During her ten-year radio career, she interviewed celebrities, county music artists, and people with interesting lives. It was during an interview with a DEA agent on her talk show, *This That and the Other*, that ideas for two books were born, *Ghost Horse* and *And Then He Was Gone*.

She currently resides in the Pocono mountains in Pennsylvania with her husband, Woody, and schnauzer, Sage. When she isn't writing, she's reading, cooking, painting, or riding. She's still crazy about horses.

www.ingramcontent.com/pod-product-compliance
Lightning Source LLC
LaVergne TN
LVHW100508110826
845146LV00002B/559

* 9 7 9 8 9 8 8 6 7 4 5 1 1 *